Christmas by Candlelight

Karen Swan is the *Sunday Times* top three bestselling author of twenty-five books and her novels sell all over the world. She writes two books each year, which are published in the summer and at Christmas. Previous summer titles include *The Spanish Promise*, *The Hidden Beach* and *The Secret Path* and, for winter, *Together by Christmas*, *Midnight in the Snow* and *The Christmas Postcards*.

Her historical series, called 'The Wild Isle' and starting with *The Last Summer*, is based on the dramatic evacuation of Scottish island St Kilda in the summer of 1930.

Karen lives in Sussex with her husband, three children and two dogs.

Follow Karen on Instagram @swannywrites,
on her author page on Facebook,
and on Twitter @KarenSwan1.

Also by Karen Swan

The Wild Isle series
The Last Summer
The Stolen Hours

Other books
Players
Prima Donna
Christmas at Tiffany's
The Perfect Present
Christmas at Claridge's
The Summer Without You
Christmas in the Snow
Summer at Tiffany's
Christmas on Primrose Hill
The Paris Secret
Christmas Under the Stars
The Rome Affair
The Christmas Secret
The Greek Escape
The Christmas Lights
The Spanish Promise
The Christmas Party
The Hidden Beach
Together by Christmas
The Secret Path
Midnight in the Snow
The Christmas Postcards

Christmas by Candlelight

Karen Swan

PAN BOOKS

First published in paperback 2023 by Macmillan
This edition first published 2023 by Pan Books
an imprint of Pan Macmillan
The Smithson, 6 Briset Street, London EC1M 5NR
EU representative: Macmillan Publishers Ireland Ltd, 1st Floor,
The Liffey Trust Centre, 117–126 Sheriff Street Upper,
Dublin 1, D01 YC43
Associated companies throughout the world
www.panmacmillan.com

ISBN 978-1-5290-8429-0

135798642

A CIP catalogue record for this book is available from the British Library.

Typeset in Palatino by Palimpsest Book Production Ltd, Falkirk, Stirlingshire
Printed and bound by CPI Group (UK) Ltd, Croydon, CR0 4YY

Visit **www.panmacmillan.com** to read more about all our books
and to buy them. You will also find features, author interviews and
news of any author events, and you can sign up for e-newsletters
so that you're always first to hear about our new releases.

For Tina
Original Teabag and dearest friend

WHITEOUT

Chapter One

Durham University, April 2014

Libby lifted her head for a moment, the whispers carrying through the stacks, before she dropped back into her work again like a dreamer drifting in and out of consciousness. Time had long since ceased to mean anything. The streetlights outside had been shining for hours now and the chocolate bar wrapper on the desk was proof she'd had dinner, should her mother text and ask.

She felt hands upon her shoulders suddenly, faces pressed to her cheeks.

'There you are!' someone stage-whispered excitedly, the words carrying halfway down Billy B hall.

'Hey! What are you guys doing in here?' she hissed, turning to find Zannah, Coco and Ems standing in a huddle behind her.

'We saw you from the street!' Coco whispered excitedly. 'We were standing out there like lunatics, calling you, but you didn't even look up!'

'Well, no, she did look up,' Ems corrected. 'But you didn't look *out*. Libs! How can you still be here at this time of night?'

'What time is it?'

'Quarter to midnight!'

'Oh.' Libby glanced around the library; it had been full all day but now only a few people were still at the study cubicles. It was always the same faces, as well. 'I'm just finishing a paper.'

'Naturally,' Zannah nodded. 'When's it due?'

'Tuesday.'

Zannah's eyebrow flexed up. 'Tuesday. And you're working in here till midnight five days before, because . . . ?' She twirled her hand around, waiting for Libby's good explanation.

'I don't like getting behind?'

Zannah tutted and sighed, looking at the others with rolled eyes. Her beautiful auburn hair spread over her shoulders like a fur cape, piercing blue eyes highlighted with a green powder on her lids.

'Libs, I've got an essay due tomorrow at twelve. It's worth twenty per cent of my final grade and I've done, like . . . ten per cent of it,' Coco said, pressing her hand to her heart earnestly. 'But I work better under pressure.'

'*Really?*' Libby stared at her in amazement. Perhaps the demands of a Psychology degree were different to Law, but she just couldn't imagine how it could be feasible to leave something like that until the very last moment. Didn't her friend see that their entire futures relied on their performance here? Or was Coco's future assured anyway? Rich parents, the right schools, contacts . . . ?

'Don't look so worried! I've got all morning to get it done.'

'*Tomorrow?* You mean you've not come here to start it now?'

Libby watched as her three housemates folded with laughter, as if she were the one acting crazy.

'Oh Libs, you're a riot!' Zannah cackled. 'Fancy arriving here at ten minutes to midnight to start working – on your housemate's birthday!'

'Huh?' Libby looked at them blankly.

'It's Charlie's twenty-first, dummy!' Ems grinned.

4

'Oh shit, is it?'

'Yeah. Didn't you get any of our messages? We've been snapping you all day.'

'Oh. No, I . . .' She glanced down at her bag. 'Notifications are on silent. I was trying not to get distracted . . . it's been a shit day.'

'Oh no hon, no, no, no,' Zannah said with a shake of her head. 'I had a dental appointment *and* a smear test this morning. That's what we call a shit day! But I'm still out.' She gave a 'beat that' shrug.

'We're meeting the boys at Klute now and you've got to come,' Ems said.

'Oh, no, I really can't,' Libby said, pulling back.

'Yes, we insist!' Coco said. 'All for one and one for all, remember?'

It was the girl housemates' mantra and usually invoked when one or more was hellbent on making a bad decision. If one went down, they'd all go down together.

'We're not leaving without you,' Zannah said, squatting down in front of Libby and making direct eye contact. This was her shorthand for showing she wouldn't take no for an answer. 'You've been in here for hours – yet again – and it'll be pretty crap if you don't show for his birthday.'

'But I really don't think my presence will be missed.'

'Says who? Charlie adores you!' Zannah said loudly, prompting someone further down the stacks to clear their throat disapprovingly, as Libby shot her a disbelieving look. 'He's much nicer to you than he ever is to me.'

'That's because you keep finishing his bread.'

'Nonsense. He eats my granola,' she shrugged. 'No, he thinks you're better than the rest of us animals – he says you're the only person in the house with a moral compass.'

'That's code for virgin!'

They all laughed.

'Which I am not!' Libby added, even though she had yet to have an overnight guest at their house; the very few fumbles she had experienced over her three years here had been profoundly disappointing and scarcely worth the bother.

'Yeah, yeah, yeah. Whatever. You're coming with us,' Zannah said bossily, reaching over and closing her reference book. 'We are staging an intervention. You said yourself that paper's not due for another five days. Look at Coco's predicament! She's the one in the shit and she's not freaking out. If she's got the time, you've got the time. Come on!'

'But I'm not . . . I'm not dressed for Klute!' Libby protested as Ems began putting her books into her bag and Zannah pulled her up by the arm. They scanned her jeans, thrift-shop Adidas sweatshirt and Vans. Light frowns creased their pretty brows.

'Well, what's under that top?' Zannah asked, yanking it up and having a look.

'Just a cami—'

'Yeah great, that'll do.'

'But I can't . . . I can't wear that! It's basically a vest!' she hissed, mortified. She looked around them to make sure no one was listening. 'And . . . and I'm not wearing a bra.'

'*Really?*' Ems looked surprised. As a fellow D-cup, it was a bold call.

'Well, I knew I'd just be sitting here all day. It wasn't like anyone was going to see me.'

'No bra, even better,' Zannah declared loudly, prompting many more heads to turn their way. Libby crossed her arms over her chest; it had always been bigger than she liked and she deliberately dressed to conceal it. As her older brother Rick

6

liked to tease, she had woken up one morning to find puberty had chosen violence.

'Absolutely not. There's no way,' she said firmly. 'Besides the boob situation, just look at my hair—'

'There's nothing wrong with your hair,' Zannah frowned.

'And I've got no make-up—'

'Oh, I've got a load,' Coco smiled reassuringly. 'Don't worry about that. We can do you up in the loos.'

Libby became aware that her friends had gathered up her books and, encircling her, were gently herding her towards the stairs. 'No, guys, seriously, I can't . . .' she protested, a feeble laugh escaping her as they escorted her down between them like bailiffs. People were staring from the cubicles, puzzlement on their faces to see *her* – always so quiet, so disciplined, so docile – being manhandled by *them*. Her housemates enjoyed something of a reputation as party girls.

'Mm?' Zannah asked, looping her arm through so that they were linked and escape was impossible. 'What's that?'

'I can't hear anything,' Ems shrugged, her arms swinging jauntily.

Coco produced some miniature vodka bottles from her pockets and held them out to her. 'Down the hatch, then, Libs.'

Libby looked at them, knowing full well she had a nine a.m. tutorial the next day. Knowing full well they didn't give a damn. She gave a groan of defeat and took the bottles as the girls cheered, shepherding her through the glass doors and into the night.

'Charlie!' she shouted, having to call over the crowd. He was still three people away but she couldn't seem to get any closer. The club was tiny and cramped, with low ceilings and sticky floors.

'Liiiiibs!' He waved at her, lunging through the bodies and somehow pulling her towards him. His face was flushed and his dark blonde hair damp with sweat, and she quickly realized he would be swaying a lot more dramatically without the crowd holding him up. He and the others had been drinking all day, of course. She had turned up for the closing minutes.

'Happy birthday, Charlie,' she said, reaching up to give him a hug.

'Here, have this,' he said, glassy-eyed and handing her a shot glass.

'I can't, I've got—'

'Drink it. On the birthday boy's orders.'

'Fine.' She drained it and gave a shiver – bubble-gum vodka. The girls had made her down four minis on the way over here.

'And now this one.' He held up another.

'Charlie!' she protested. Where was he getting them from? She looked across and saw Rollo at the bar, one elbow on the counter like a country pub regular, passing them back.

'Please drink it!' he implored. 'You're saving me here! I can see three of you.'

'Oh.'

'Everyone keeps forcing them on me,' he said sadly, swaying again. 'I'm so pissed, I can't feel my own face.'

'So say no!' Loyally, she drained the glass for him.

'In here? With all of them? I'm their prisoner.' A hiccup escaped him.

'Well then, that makes two of us,' she grinned. 'I was just kidnapped from the library. The girls staged an intervention.'

'Yes, quite right too!' He hiccupped again. 'Arch said he saw you there at lunch and laid a bet you'd be there till midnight.'

'In that case, he just lost it. The girls got me out at ten to.'

'Good. So then I'm ten quid up,' he said, proudly thumbing

his chest and looking down as he did so, as if to make sure he wouldn't miss. 'Whoa!' he exclaimed, eyes widening as he noticed her in her cami. 'Libs! You look . . . you look amazing!' He looked back at her, open-mouthed. 'Like, who fucking knew!'

'Knew what?'

'That you're so . . . sexy!'

He sounded so surprised that Libby wasn't sure whether to be offended, but she'd had enough vodka now to not especially care. '. . . Thanks, I guess?' she said, pulling the cami up at the front a little. Coco had 'done' her face as they stood in the long queue, dotting, dabbing and blending on her skin, while Zannah had styled her long dark brown hair into a high pony, 'but with vibes'.

'You should . . . you should definitely dress like that more often. You're a *speshal* person. Don't hide your light under a bushel, Libs,' he slurred.

'Thanks, but no. My boobs are not my so-called light . . . Where are the others, anyway?' she asked, quickly changing the subject as the crowd jostled and squeezed around them like a boa constrictor's coils.

'Over there somewhere . . . oh,' he said, pointing towards the corner, where Coco and Zannah were talking to some of the rugby lads. Both tall, with bright, glossy manes shining under the lights, they were easy to spot in the crowd, throwing their heads back in laughter and talking excitedly. They always looked so interesting; such fun. Libby wished she could have some of their social ease, but she forever had too much to do.

She watched Charlie watch Coco for a few moments, seeing how he clenched his jaw and released it, a nervous tic, as if he was trying to gather momentum within himself.

'Why don't you just tell her?' she asked him, feeling drunk enough to finally broach the topic.

He looked back at her, surprised to find her watching him. He closed his eyes and sighed, far too drunk to even attempt a denial. 'Can't,' he sighed.

'Why not? You're mad about her,' she said, seeing how his head lolled, already defeated.

'Because, in case you hadn't noticed, I've been firmly friendzoned.'

'She thinks you're really cute. She told me once when we were having a girl chat. She likes your eyes and she thinks your mouth is really kissable.'

'Yeah?' He brightened briefly, his fingers moving automatically to his lips as if to check them for himself. He swayed again as he looked down. 'No, I can't. It would be awkward now. She doesn't see me that way. She told me once I'm like the big brother she never had!'

'But you're a month younger than her.' Coco's birthday had been celebrated in the Easter holidays – a dinner for fifty at the 'proper' Ivy in London. Libby hadn't been able to make it; she worked at the bakery back in her Herefordshire village during the holidays, and the train fare alone would have wiped out a day's earnings.

'I know. Go figure,' he shrugged, hiccupping at the same time. 'Besides, house rules.'

Libby bit her lip. At the beginning of their tenancy – just before she had moved in – the others had drawn up various commandments for living together: no leaving the washing-up in the sink (routinely ignored), no hogging the washing machine (the boys had yet to use it), no pinching each other's food (a pointless directive) and no hooking up with housemates.

'Come on. You know those are flexible to say the least.'

'She's a believer, though. She says it would ruin the atmosphere in the house if everyone was hooking up.'

'But she hooked up with Archie!'

'Everyone's hooked up with Archie!' he groaned. 'And besides, that was in first year. It doesn't count.'

'Last year too.' According to Zannah.

'Agh, *really*?' He winced as she nodded. 'Fuck.' He ran a hand through his hair, looking pained.

'But you know it doesn't mean anything.'

'That only makes it worse,' he groaned. 'Arch had her and didn't even *care*. Whereas I . . . I . . .' He looked over to where Coco was standing again, open longing in his eyes.

Libby put a hand on his arm. 'Look, she's friendzoned you, yes. So you need to make her see you in a different way. You're so lovely and respectful. You listen to everyone's problems. You never make any drama. But perhaps you should.'

'Me? Be dramatic?' he scoffed.

'Yes. Be more forceful. Stop putting everyone else first. Go over there and make it clear what you want. Coco likes a confident guy.'

'I'm confident.'

'Only in your calculus lectures,' she tutted, knowing that was the real reason why he liked her; nothing to do with moral compasses, they were both introverts trying to survive in an extroverted world. 'Go on, be brave and take a chance – you've got some Dutch courage in you. Make your move before one of those rugger buggers does it for you.'

'. . . You think?' he mumbled. 'What would I say?'

'Tell her she's the most beautiful girl here.'

'Yeah. Okay, I will,' he said after a moment. 'Because she is,' he added, swaying dramatically again.

'Exactly.'

He looked back at her, staring openly at her chest in a way that would make him cringe when he woke up tomorrow. 'But Libs, you're the sexiest.'

She slapped her arm over her chest, mortified. 'Oh my god, shut up! Just go and talk to her right now,' she cried, rolling her eyes and pushing him away. She could only hope, for both their sakes, that he wouldn't remember this conversation in the morning. 'Go tell her that you like her.'

'—kay.'

She watched him stagger back through the bodies, hoping she'd done him – and Coco – a favour, but not entirely sure. The vodka had well and truly hit now, and her own judgement was impaired. She closed her eyes for a moment, feeling the bass of the music reverberate in her chest. She looked around for Ems, but she was snogging Prock against a pillar; Rollo was leaning in now and talking into a girl's ear, telling a joke; from the way the girl pulled back, honking with laughter, it looked like he might be getting lucky too. There was no sign of Archie, although he ran with a more glamorous crowd and was no doubt carousing in a nearby castle, or up at a black-tie dinner in Edinburgh for the night.

Charlie was making slow progress through the bodies and she could see Coco and Zannah were still occupied with the number eight and the flanker. She had been separated from them when she saw a couple of girls from her course on the way in and they got chatting – always a bad move; there was safety in being pinned to her flatmates' sides. Distinction by association. Of course, she knew she could go over to them at any time, but they had been ahead of her, drinks-wise, from the start tonight, and although fairly drunk, she wasn't anywhere near drunk enough to try for her own random hook-up. She just wasn't like them – she needed more than a cute face and muscles to get turned on, and every encounter she'd had where she'd forced herself to 'go through with it' had left her feeling empty.

She watched everyone flirting and dancing and drinking around her and felt a sudden, pulsing loneliness, a sharp sense of dislocation. She was here and yet still, somehow, not. It was painful to admit that she wasn't a part of this; that no one really cared if she was here or not. She had seen Charlie now, chatted with the birthday boy for a few minutes, and her presence beyond that was an irrelevance. She turned away and headed for the exit.

The queue that had snaked up the narrow street earlier had disappeared now, and the cold night air immediately made her shiver and stop. Too late, she remembered her sweatshirt – and books – were still with Coco's bags. She hesitated for a moment, debating whether to brave the crowd to get them, but that would risk being pulled into another conversation; Coco would bring them back with her, she was certain, and she turned up the road instead, walking briskly and grateful that so few people were about. Everyone was either in bed or in the club.

She headed home, keeping to the shadows where she could, and trying to look less drunk than anyone she passed. She walked with her arms crossed over her chest, her chin tucked in, wishing she could teleport, or be invisible, or afford a cab.

She was turning onto their street twelve minutes later when the sound of drunken voices startled her and she looked ahead to find a couple arguing in the middle of the road. The guy was so far gone, he was staggering about like a comedy drunk, waving his arms ineffectually as the girl shouted at him. She was wearing pegged black leather trousers and a man's white shirt, the tails wrapped and tied around her slender waist, chunky gold rings flashing on her fingers; the effect was a delicious clash of delicate femininity and androgyny and Libby studied her, hoping she could remember it for . . . well, one day. She had to hope there would be a point in her future when her life was more glamorous than this and she would get to be *that* girl, even if only for a moment.

Libby reached for her keys in her jeans pocket, crossing the road and keeping her head down as she approached. She knew exactly who the angry fashionista was, jabbing her finger now, her clipped vowels becoming ever sharper. Her name was Arabella Tait and according to *Durfess*, the Durham gossip site, she had already appeared twice in *Tatler*'s Little Black Book and had been scouted for *Made in Chelsea*. Archie had been seeing her for a few weeks and although Libby had never actually seen her in the flesh before, there had been enough talk in the house about her recently for Libby to feel – ridiculously – excited to see her here now. The hype, it appeared, was fully justified.

Arabella must have seen Libby cross between the parked cars, because she faltered, interrupting her furious stream of invective and regaining a modicum of self-control. She tipped her head back and ran a hand through her blonde mane, exhaling like a yogi.

'Belly,' Archie slurred, taking advantage of the brief pause and reaching for her with an outstretched arm, his head lolling from the effort. 'Just come in and . . . we can talk . . . I'll make it up to you.'

'Fuck you, Archie!'

'But Belly . . .'

'—Don't *Belly* me! You're a mess! You've got fucking issues, you know that?'

Briefly, the two women made eye contact as Libby approached, and Arabella swept a passing glance over her vintage Levi's and bottle-green Brandy Melville cotton camisole. Libby turned onto the short front path outside the house and Arabella – seeing which house – began to turn and walk away down the middle of the road. 'Don't call me, Archie. Ever!' she warned him. 'I'm blocking you on everything!'

'Belly!' he wailed, lunging after her again and tripping over his own feet. 'Baby!'

But Arabella didn't turn back as she stalked away, her phone already out and calling someone to apprise them of this status update in her life. Libby stood at the front door, unseen by Archie, who was still flat out in the middle of the road, and waited for him to get up. This lovers' spat was none of her business and absolutely par for the course for him; Archie was wild – 'a degenerate' was how he chose to describe himself – everyone knew that. This was just his typical Thursday night. He'd have someone new by the weekend.

And yet . . .

She turned back. He was lying on his side, groaning, largely hidden in a dark spot where the light pools between the lamp posts didn't quite meet. She sighed, just able to imagine the headlines: *Aristocratic scion crushed by Uber*.

'Archie,' she said, going over and crouching beside him, but she was drunk too and she almost ended up on her bottom as she tried to balance on her toes. Just because she wasn't as drunk as him didn't make her sober. '. . . Archie, you need to get up. You can't stay here.'

'Wha . . . ?' he groaned, rolling onto his back and looking up at her. She could tell that, like Charlie, he was seeing three of her. 'Who . . . ?'

'It's me. Libby. Your housemate, remember?'

'Libby?' he queried, as if he'd never heard the name before.

She looked away, feeling that desolation wash through her again. Here, but not here . . . God, was she really so forgettable that even her own housemate couldn't remember her? 'Look, let's just get you off the road and into the house, okay?'

She stepped back, trying to pull him up by his arm. There was a rip in his shirt and a thick streak of mud all down his jeans. What had he been doing? Bush jumping? For reasons she couldn't fathom, jumping or being thrown into bushes was one of the male undergraduates' favourite pastimes. That and stealing traffic cones; there was still one in the boys' bathroom on the first floor, upon which a single roll of toilet paper was balanced.

'Come on, you have to try to help yourself,' she said as he dangled on the ground like a limp noodle. 'I can't lift you by myself.'

'No,' he frowned, looking at her and still trying to focus. 'You're very . . . little,' he said, chuckling as though her petiteness was funny. She was five foot three if she really straightened her spine.

'Archie, get up.'

Somehow he folded his legs and she was able to pull him up; but verticality was not his friend and he staggered about again, reaching for the nearest support. She caught him before he could topple over once more. 'Whoa,' he laughed, his eyes wide as she grabbed his shirt at the waist and stood as a counterbalance to him.

'Put your arm over my shoulders and lean on me,' she commanded, her knees almost buckling as she took some of his weight and they began to stumble back to the house. It was like walking with someone who had their shoelaces tied together – small, faltering steps; balance erratic, and not helped by the fact that with almost a foot's difference in height between them, he was having to stoop just to find her shoulder.

'Right, stand there,' she said, propping him up against the pebbledashed wall of the narrow porch with one hand on his chest to keep him upright as she fished in her jeans pocket for the key. Unfortunately, she had slipped it into the small coin pocket at the front and it was now firmly wedged sideways. 'Ugh,' she muttered, trying to wrest it free with one hand and hold him up with the other. 'Come on.'

'Libby,' he mumbled from his supported position, watching her struggle, his eyes half slitted as oblivion beckoned. 'Libby! I know herrrr . . . !'

'I should hope so.'

'But . . .' He gave a confused frown as she felt his eyes drag over her like a rake, settling heavily on her chest. 'She's not you.'

'No? Who am I, then?' she asked, bored already of baby-sitting him. For a man with such natural charisma, he made for a tiresome drunk.

'. . . Banging . . . body,' he whispered, looking back up at her with something approaching focus. She felt his gaze catch her, though she hadn't been aware she was falling, and for a second it felt like she glimpsed his soul and he glimpsed hers, as if they were shadows passing behind their eyes.

He lunged – or was it fell? – towards her, his mouth upon hers with an expert aim that not even a bottle of whisky (or whatever it was he'd emptied) could deter. For all his drunken clumsiness, his lips somehow still worked, pulling an instinctive response from her. He smelled of smoke and Miss Dior; he tasted of a doubtless-expensive single malt. It was exactly as she might have imagined, yet she still couldn't believe Archie Templeton was kissing her.

She felt his hand move unhesitatingly up her waist to her breast, caressing her lightly with a practised touch and prompting a blush of goosepimples to rush over the surface of her skin. She froze, a groan escaping him as he discovered her braless state.

'Fuck,' he whispered as he pulled back and looked at her like she was something wondrous. For a moment, neither of them stirred, his hand still upon her as if in reverence.

Then instinct kicked in.

She gasped and slapped him hard, once, across the cheek. '*Don't* do that. Don't ever touch me without my permission,' she hissed.

'Ssss—' His hand and head fell back as he sagged against the wall, his eyes closing as a pink handprint began to glow on his cheek. 'Sssorry . . . sssorry . . . Libby.'

She felt her own cheeks burning too as she released the key at last and, getting it into the lock, pushed open the door. She stood back to let him in first. With his hands on the walls, he wove a jagged path straight towards the sofa, toppling over the back of it and falling slightly askew on the cushions.

Libby shut the door behind her and walked over to him. He was lying face down, one leg hanging off the front, already almost unconscious. She stared at him – beautiful and wretched all at once – and wondered what he had done to get Arabella Tait to dump him tonight. No doubt they would be back together again by this time tomorrow. They made a dazzling couple – her looks, his heritage . . . People like them should be together. They just *fit*.

She retrieved the yellow bucket reserved for emergencies such as this and positioned it in the appropriate spot beside him, then climbed the stairs to her room and sank onto her bed. She stared at the wall, trying to calm herself and make sense of what had happened in those few moments; her heart was still pounding fast, her mind a riotous confusion. The orderly calm of the library felt very distant now, and that girl who had spent all evening working in the window already seemed so different from the one on this bed. She had thought she knew herself – what she wanted, what she stood for – but now the world seemed to have inverted somehow, becoming as wobbly on its axis as Archie had been on his legs; because she wasn't upset by what had happened downstairs. She didn't hate him for it.

But she *ought* to, and that was where her confusion lay. He was paralytically drunk, yes; he hadn't known what he was doing – she knew that. Just like she knew he still couldn't touch her without consent, no matter how drunk he was. What she couldn't wrap her head around was that it hadn't been instinct that made her slap him, but conditioning.

Her instinct hadn't been to stop him, but to let him.

To her surprise, she had liked it. And to her shame, she had wanted it.

That one, unexpected touch had woken her up, just as he passed out.

He would never remember it, she knew; he had been there, but not there. And she had been alone in the moment, once again.

Chapter Two

Just off the A1M near Thirsk, North Yorkshire,
22 December 2023

They rounded the bend, the headlights of an oncoming car blinding them both so that they reached, in unison, for the sun visors.

'Wanker,' Max muttered below his breath. Libby caught sight of her own reflection in the overhead mirror and checked her make-up; her smoky eye was holding up well, considering she'd applied it eight hours ago. A little blush though, perhaps? she mused, reaching behind her for the handbag wedged into the eight-inch cavity behind her seat. Coupés were all well and good until you actually had to travel anywhere in them.

She dabbed cream blush lightly onto the apples of her cheeks; the temperature was plummeting outside, snowflakes smudging the windscreen, but she still wanted to look like she'd been skipping in a summery field of daisies.

'What did you think of the dress?' she asked him.

He arched one eyebrow up ever so slightly, his gaze lifting off the road for a fraction of a second. 'Yes.'

It was his usual sardonic reply when he didn't want to give an answer. He was far too clever – and too well trained as a corporate lawyer – to incriminate himself.

Libby chuckled. 'The ruffles were ill-advised, I felt.'

'Hmm.'

He reached forward and changed the radio station. They were heading deeper into the moors now and reception was becoming patchy, static crackling as the horizon dropped down and peeled back, further and further away. Traffic was changing with the landscape too, the small city hatchbacks and articulated lorries on the motorway now swapped for tractors, Landies and Mitsubishi Shoguns. Max was beginning to wince every time they passed one as the roads grew into narrow lanes. The Mercedes was low-slung and wide-hipped, and he was forced to slow almost to a crawl against the hedgerows, to be sure of avoiding scratches in the glossy paintwork.

Still, it had been great fun travelling to the wedding in it, sunlight glinting off the windscreen and his hand on her thigh, the two of them drawing curious stares as they stopped – vastly overdressed in morning suit and navy Me & Em silk – at service stations.

Libby looked out across the moorland, the lights of far-off houses glinting in the encroaching dusk. It had been a long time since she'd been up in this neck of the woods, although she had never really known the moors at all, only ever passing through them on the train to Durham. She swallowed, feeling a small flutter of nerves in the pit of her stomach, as she always did when she allowed her mind to travel back there. She had spent the past nine years keeping her sights focused on the path ahead of her, not the one at her back, and yet she had a sense of it always there, like a shadow stitched to her.

'So remind me again – the one who sent the email, practically begging you to come to this dinner, is—'

She brought herself back into the moment. 'Ems. Emma Proctor. Married to Jack, but he's only ever known as Prock.'

'Right,' he murmured, his finger tapping lightly on the wheel. 'And they're pregnant.'

'Exactly. The reason for doing this, tonight's a sort of Last Hurrah. I guess things will be different once the baby comes.'

'Really?' he asked. '. . . Yeah, I heard something similar about babies too. So self-centred. It's all about them.'

She grinned, liking his sarcasm. 'Ha ha.'

He winked at her. 'And then there's a . . . Susannah, right?'

'Yep. Known as Zannah. Or Zany Zannah – which pretty much tells you all you need to know about her.'

He glanced across at her, as if picking up on the slight tone change, but she was looking out of the window. 'And what does she do, this Zany Zannah?'

'Last I heard, she heads up the tennis division at IMG, sports event management.'

'Oh yeah.' He gave a semi-impressed nod.

'She moved to New York straight after graduation. Apparently she's on first-name terms with Serena, Rafa, Roger . . . you name them, she knows them.'

'Sounds like she'll have some stories to tell, then. Hopefully I'll be sitting beside her at dinner.'

'Well, if it's stories you're after, then you want to be sitting next to Roly. There is no situation that man can't tally back to a *Blackadder* quote and some escapade from boarding school.'

'Ah. I feel I know him already,' Max said dryly.

'It's true, he is a type,' she conceded. 'But you'll love him. Everyone loves Roly. He's a teddy bear.'

'Which is exactly what I look for in new acquaintances. Anyone I won't "love"?' He said the word with a frisson of distaste. He wasn't a man given to extremes of emotion.

'No. They're all great.' She was still looking out of the

window. A thin ribbon of sunset stretched like a banner above the horizon, peeping through the thick clouds.

'Uh-huh.'

She looked back at him, knowing scepticism when she heard it. 'What does that mean?'

He shrugged. 'Nothing.'

'Tell me,' she said, shifting position slightly so that her legs were angled towards him. 'You don't believe my friends are all nice people?'

'On the contrary, to hear you talk about them, they sound wonderful. Which is why I don't understand why you had pretty much lost contact with them.'

She missed a beat. 'That's not true. Charlie and I email.'

'But you don't meet up.'

'Well, no—'

'Not once in nine years.'

'Excuse me, he's busy too. Charlie's no slouch when it comes to his career either. He gets how it is,' she shrugged, feeling defensive. 'Email just works for us. He keeps in touch with the others and briefs me on what they're all up to.'

'*Briefs* you?' Max laughed. 'Jesus, Elizabeth, and I thought I was bad at switching off.'

She didn't reply, but she was stung by the comment. He knew better than anyone the demands of this career; having a personal life was like gravy on roast beef: one was vital, the other a luxury. Just look at *them* – they were five months into an office affair, because who else was she ever going to meet outside of a nineteen-hour working day? Keeping the relationship hidden from their colleagues only seemed to add to the sexual tension, and neither one of them had brought up introducing each other to their friends or families; 'they' existed only in her flat or his, and sometimes this car in the underground car park. They had only attended this wedding together because the groom was an Associate Partner at the firm and they had been able to pass off travelling together as convenient.

A silence lengthened and he glanced across at her again. He placed his hand on her knee and squeezed it, seeming to sense he'd upset her. He looked straight at her, holding her stare for a moment, before having to look back at the road, but she saw in his eyes that he recognized currents below the surface. Max Prince was reputedly soon to become the youngest partner in their company, and he hadn't achieved that by failing to observe what went unsaid. 'And how would they describe you, if I were to ask them?'

'Oh.' The word was drawn from her like a sigh as she stared out at the sleet smashing itself against the windscreen. 'In disappointing terms, I'm sure. I was very much the odd one out back then. I only lived with them for two-and-a-bit terms.'

'Really? How so?'

'I was in another house with some lawyers to begin with. Until there was a prolonged rainy spell in the October and we woke up one morning to several huge structural cracks in the walls and the beginnings of a sinkhole. We had to move out that same day. The house was condemned and there was no time to get anything sorted all together; we just had to find new digs asap.' She shrugged. 'I was friendly with Zannah through Debating Society so she sweetly offered me the top room in their house. It was actually a pretty great room. I couldn't believe my luck.'

'They had a bedroom going free?' Max puzzled. 'Why weren't they using it?'

'Because it had a single bed,' Libby said with a look. 'And let's just say my new housemates were not the type to put up with that sort of nonsense!'

He laughed. 'I see. It was like that, was it?'

'Oh yes. I went from a house that was almost monastically silent, with five lawyers beavering away in it, to a full-on party house.'

'Frat house.'

'Exactly.'

'Huh. You did well to graduate against the odds, then.'

'You have no idea,' she agreed.

'I'm amazed they let a room go spare though, single bed or not. I had a single bed at Emmanuel and I managed just fine.'

'I'm sure you did,' she said, seeing the smile flicker at the corners of his mouth as some memories zipped through his mind; she could well imagine how popular he had been at Cambridge. 'But everyone in that house was rich enough that they didn't need to slum it, so they just split the difference between them.'

'Lucky them,' he said, not in the least bit envious. 'And have they all gone on to be the massive success story that you are?'

'I wouldn't call myself that.'

'No? Big career; fancy pad in Chelsea; Birkin bag . . . killer body,' he winked.

She smiled, but noticed he didn't include himself in her list of so-called wins. *Lover, partner, boyfriend.*

'They're all very successful in their own ways,' she replied loyally. 'Charlie set up his own AI company and recently sold it. Roly went straight to Sandhurst and did a few tours before coming back to Yorkshire to help his brother with the family farm.'

''Twas ever thus. Is he the oldest brother?'

'No, Roly's younger.'

'So he didn't inherit, then?'

'Hmm. I'd never thought about it, but no, probably not.'

'Big farm?'

'Yes, I think so. Not the same scale as Archie's estate, of course, but still pretty impressive. Why?'

'No reason. Just trying to get the lie of the land.'

'Oh. Well, Prock's a surveyor and has his own company too, and Ems is an accountant; they live in Harrogate. And Coco is a very influential influencer. She's TikTok famous apparently.'

'Indeed,' Max replied, a vibration of scepticism in his voice again. 'And our host?'

She sighed again. 'Well, Archie proves the exception to the rule when it comes to personal achievement, but his inertia is deeply inbred.' It was her turn to deliver the sarcasm.

'Part of the aristocratic condition, you mean?'

'Exactly.'

Max chuckled. 'Does he work at all?'

'Well, I think he has a lot of chummy lunches at the Pall Mall clubs that he passes off in the name of asset management, but I think he's primarily been killing time, waiting to come into his inheritance.'

'Which he now has.' His finger tapped the wheel again.

'Which he now has,' she muttered. Archie's father, the 11th Viscount Templeton, had passed away the previous year. She had read the full-page obituary in *The Times* while eating her lunch at her desk, her gaze constantly drawn to the black-and-white photograph of a pre-pubescent, cherubic-looking Archie standing with his father outside what looked like Westminster Abbey. He bore no relation to the lanky, hell-chasing libertine she had lived with for seven months.

'Well, I'll be interested to see the place. I looked it up to get directions. Grade One, apparently. Capability Brown park.'

'I wouldn't get too excited. Charlie says that apparently the heating is indifferent and the dry rot's so bad, someone recently went through a floorboard up to their knee.'

Max gave a snort of amusement. 'Can't wait to get there.' He leaned forward to turn off the radio once and for all. Reception was almost wholly gone now, the lanes so narrow they had to rely on passing places to squeeze by the locals. The sky had deepened to a deep purple bruise, and the moon was beginning to glow behind the clouds. The silence outside the car was gathering strength as the landscape muscled into a wilderness and snowflakes were dashed against the glass with growing violence.

Libby smoothed her silk dress over her thighs – the wrap style meant it kept falling open, to Max's preference – and sank a little lower into her seat, settling into her thoughts. In spite of her equable comments about her former housemates, she felt trepidatious about seeing everyone again. Had her friends all remained the same, or was she not the only one who had moved on? As ever, Max had cut straight to the chase; she hadn't seen them in over nine years and most of what she knew of their lives, she knew from Instagram and the sporadic emails from Charlie. She had politely declined every one of their annual house reunions and made her excuses of work or travel whenever anyone was 'in town'. It was only Ems's utter determination not to accept a 'no' before the baby came that had forced Libby into accepting this dinner invitation. Ems had sold it as a 'small detour' on their way back from the wedding, assuring them that they could be on the road again in 'three hours, tops'. If they left by eleven, they could be at Max's place come four. It was far from ideal, but they had both pulled enough all-nighters at work not to be unduly bothered by a late bedtime.

Still, as the road led them ever closer to where her past lay assembled, she felt her nerves pitch and swoop like a flock of starlings. Three hours, she told herself as she stared out into the darkness, her own ghostly reflection blinking back at her. She could do that. Then she would be free again.

Chapter Three

April 2014

The bathroom door opened just as Libby went to pass, plumes of steam billowing out and releasing a strong scent of coconut and mango.

'Hey.' Muscles and teeth were what she saw first.

'Hey,' Libby murmured, offering a friendly nod back to the man-mountain walking out in a three-sizes-too-small pink dressing gown with lilac dots, and stepping back into Zannah's room. She recognized him as the First XV number eight from Klute.

She continued on down the stairs, past the boys' floor and down to the sitting room. There was no sign of Archie on the sofa, no impression of his collapsed body on the cushions; only the warmth still in her skin of where his hand had touched her.

'Oh my god, who finished all the fucking bread?' Coco was wailing as Libby descended to the basement. Her housemate was standing by the food cupboard in a rugby shirt and sheepskin Birkenstocks. Charlie was sitting at the tiny table, reading a day-old copy of *The Times* and trying not to look at Coco's legs.

'Morning.'

29

Coco spun round, her mouth dropping open as Libby stepped into the kitchen. '. . . Libs?'

'How is the birthday boy feeling this morning?' Libby asked.

'Broken, as you might expect,' he said in a croaky voice, pale-faced and with bags beneath his eyes. 'But what are you doing here? Did the moon fall from the sky? Don't you know the library will fall down without you in it?'

'Ha ha. I overslept.'

His eyes narrowed. 'You never oversleep. In fact, I'm not convinced you do sleep.'

Libby stuck her tongue out at him. 'I just couldn't drop off. And then when I did, I just couldn't wake up.' Her dreams had been feverish, chaotic and disordered; she'd had no desire to step back into this reality.

'. . . *And* we're out of jam!' Coco complained, throwing a hand in the air in despair. She had gone back to staring at the barely stocked larder.

'Well, it's not like you had anything to eat the jam on anyway, so . . . ' Charlie gave a hapless shrug.

'I've got cereal if you want some.' Libby reached past Coco for the small box of Frosties on her shelf and sifted some into a bowl.

'I . . . Ooh,' Coco said, spying a stack of waffles on Ems's shelf instead.

Libby caught Charlie's eye while her back was turned and threw a questioning look in Coco's direction; as feared, he shook his head sadly. She offered him a consoling smile and he shrugged. Bad news shared in silence.

'When did you leave last night, Libs?' Coco asked, popping the waffle in the toaster and turning back to face her, her usual good mood restored now that she was going to be able to fill her stomach. She was as lithe as a gazelle and yet could match the boys for appetite; keeping her sufficiently well fed was a constant struggle, and the 'hanger' was real. 'I didn't see you once we got in.'

'Um, I'm not really sure, to be honest . . . One-ish?'

'Ah, a French exit, was it? Did you get lucky then?' Coco smiled, peering over her coffee cup.

'What do you think?'

Coco gave a despairing sigh again. 'I don't get it. There's twenty thousand students here – that's roughly ten thousand men! There must be someone you like!'

'I'm sure there would be, if I looked.' Libby took the milk from the fridge and poured it onto her cereal. 'But my focus is on work. I can't afford not to get a first.'

'But there is a halfway house. You can study *and* still get laid . . . Same goes for you too, by the way, Charlie. Don't think I haven't noticed you playing the celibacy card as well.'

Libby and Charlie swapped looks.

'I take it you had a successful night then?' Libby asked.

'Hmm, define successful. It certainly wasn't as successful as he thought,' Coco muttered, missing Charlie's wince.

'Is he still here?'

'Ugh, worse luck. I'm not going back up there till he's gone. I think I'm going to swerve the rugger buggers for a while.'

'Probably wise,' Charlie murmured, staring at the newspaper.

'Oof! Did you hear about Archie and Arabella?' Coco gave a scandalized smile as her waffle popped up and she began to butter it. 'She's dumped him. Again.'

'No, not the golden couple?' Charlie asked with mock horror, sitting forward suddenly and having to rest his face in his hands as another wave of nausea hit . . . What did he do this time?'

'Suggested a threesome – *with her best friend*!' Coco cackled as she took a huge bite of waffle.

'Yeah, because she's fit,' Archie himself mumbled, coming down the stairs. They all looked over as he walked in, barefoot and pale with his dark floppy hair sticking up at odd angles. He was wearing only jeans, which hung low on his hips, an Anderson & Sheppard label sticking out of the waistband of pale blue cotton boxers. He paused as he saw Libby leaning against the counter, eating cereal. 'You.'

Libby stopped chewing even though her heart sped up. 'Yeah?'

'You're here.'

'Yeah . . . So?'

'That's what I said,' Charlie muttered.

'She overslept,' Coco provided, taking another bite of waffle, butter running down her chin. 'Couldn't get to sleep.'

'Not like you, Arch, hey?' Charlie asked him. 'You were passed out on the sofa when we got back.'

'Right,' he murmured, staring at her with a look that was both blank and searching, as if the memories of last night were floating within him, just out of reach. If he remembered his argument with Arabella, did he remember what he'd done to Libby too? And her delay in pushing him off?

He turned away suddenly and stood for a moment in the middle of the floor, looking at a loss.

'You okay, Arch? Need to throw up?' Coco asked him. 'I saw the yellow bucket . . .'

'No.' He looked at her, seeing the butter drool down her chin; catching it with his finger, he licked it carelessly. Libby's gaze travelled between her three housemates, all of them wearing their beauty and privilege lightly; even pallid with hangovers, they were still somehow burnished. 'I need to eat. I'm starving,' he grumbled, going over to the fridge and staring in, his arms looped over the door, his head right in.

Libby stole a look at his bare back; it wasn't hugely muscled like the rugby boys', but lightly sculpted from a lifetime spent hunting and skiing. She caught Charlie watching her and he gave her a small, sympathetic smile, seeming to understand they were both in the same boat.

Coco jumped up onto the counter, long legs dangling down and kicking the cabinets as she ate. 'So you've remembered that you're single again, have you, Arch?' she asked him, talking with her mouth full.

'I wasn't aware I ever wasn't.'

'Arabella?'

'That wasn't official,' he muttered, rubbing his face in his hands.

'But official enough that you asked to have a threesome with her and her best friend!'

He shrugged. 'Like I said, she's fit.'

'Archie!' Coco laughed. 'You take it too far! You've got to stop.'

'Stop what? I just ran into *your* latest conquest on the stairs.'

She shrugged. 'It's not the same. You take hook-ups to a whole other level. You're chasing all these dopamine highs but it's empty and meaningless. It'll never make you happy, you know.'

'You're right,' he drawled with his signature sarcasm. 'I felt really unhappy when Belly and I were—'

'Don't!' Coco cried, holding up a hand. 'Spare us the details, please. It's too early and we're all hung to hell.'

He shrugged. 'I don't see what the issue is if it's consensual.' He finally pulled his head out of the fridge. 'Have we got any bread?'

'Nope,' Charlie muttered.

He sighed and put it back in again. '. . . Where's Roly?'

'Not back yet.'

'Prock?'

'Shagging Ems,' Coco replied, leaning over and reaching for the waffle stack again. 'I'll buy her some more,' she mouthed to Libby, who merely shrugged. 'See, that's my point, Arch. If you fall in love, you'll get even more sex. But it'll be better sex, see?'

'Not really.'

'Your problem is you're permanently chasing your next fix—'

'Have I got a problem?'

'Yes! You're all about the next girl, threesomes, bondage, whatever. But what you're missing is *connection*. You just target girls and then discard them.'

He looked back at her as he pulled the milk carton out. 'How do you know they're not discarding me?'

'Because for reasons none of us can understand, women can't seem to get enough of your bad boy routine. But why don't you try actually dating someone properly?'

'Why don't you?'

'Stop deflecting.'

'Fine. Well, seeing as you're guilty of everything you're accusing me of, maybe *we* should date.'

Coco spluttered crumbs everywhere, Charlie's head jerking up in alarm. 'Absolutely not! I've seen way too much living with you. I wouldn't trust you as far as I could throw you.'

Archie looked at her skinny arms with a tut. 'Rude.' He sighed and drank the milk straight from the carton, glugging it down until only a finger-width remained. Everyone watched in appalled silence as he returned it to the fridge again.

'You know mate, there might be something in that,' Charlie said slowly. 'Coco's right, you are on a dopamine spiral. You

34

keep wanting more and more, but each time you get it you feel less. So there's only really one solution to that.'

'Oh yeah, and what's that?'

'Go cold turkey and reset your system. You've got to starve yourself of what you want, get past the cravings.'

There was a silence as Archie looked back at Charlie. '. . . Are you proposing *celibacy*?'

Charlie shrugged.

This time it was Archie's turn to splutter. 'And how'd you figure *that* as an answer?'

'Well, you know what they say – abstinence makes the heart grow fonder.'

Libby had to chuckle, the sound prompting Archie to glance over at her, as if he'd forgotten she was there. His gaze felt threaded with tiny needles that dragged over her skin and she looked down into her bowl again.

'Yeah,' Charlie said more enthusiastically, beginning to warm to his theme. 'Perhaps a little time off the field *would* do you good. Give you a new perspective again. You could focus on cultivating a relationship that isn't based solely on sex. Connection, like Coco said.'

Archie shook his head with a baffled expression. 'Words are coming out of your mouth, Earnshaw, but they're making no sense.'

'Don't sleep with someone till you've caught feelings,' Charlie clarified. '*Force* yourself to wait.'

'I think we all know I'm not capable of that.'

'We also all know you've never yet seen a bet you didn't like.'

Archie's eyebrows shot up as he gave an astonished laugh at the B word – but Charlie was regarding him with a look of utmost seriousness. There was another disbelieving pause.

'. . . You actually want to *bet* I can't swear off sex till I fall for someone?'

'Yeah. Why not?'

Coco gave a delighted laugh, drumming the cabinets with her feet. 'Oh my god, that is the best thing I've ever heard!'

'No it isn't, because it's completely unworkable. You couldn't possibly quantify it, for one thing. I could fake feelings just to get a girl in bed . . . I already do! That is what I do!'

Libby stared at the floor.

Charlie made a sceptical sound. 'I know, but I reckon *we* know you well enough to recognize the famous Templeton tricks. We'd know if you were faking.'

'Uh-huh. Uh-huh.' Archie had his hands on his hips and was nodding ferociously, a slightly wild look in his eyes. 'And if, in this fictional world of yours, I did catch feelings for someone, I've got to – what? Tell you before I seal the deal? Afterwards?'

'Either. It wouldn't matter.'

'Defo,' Coco agreed. 'Like Charlie-boy said, we could tell if you were faking feelings.'

'I think you're all vastly overestimating your interpersonal abilities,' Archie replied, looking between the both of them. 'Plus, you realize I could hook up with anyone, anywhere – in the library, her place, pub loos, car . . . and you'd never know?'

'That's true. No one's denying you're a rakehell,' Charlie said. 'But you are also a man of honour and I don't believe you'd renege on a gentleman's agreement.'

Archie stared at him. They all knew the code word for his factory settings had been pushed: *honour*. '. . . How much are we talking?'

'A grand.'

'A grand!' Archie spluttered.

'Well, it's got to be worth your while to keep you going with it,' Charlie shrugged. 'And as I recall, you said you were in hock after that poker game the other week.'

'How the hell have you got a spare grand?'

'I've been doing a little crypto investing,' Charlie shrugged. 'Had a few good returns.'

'Jesus.' Archie raked a hand through his hair, holding it there for a moment and allowing Libby a good view of his bare back. Was she being paranoid, or was he deliberately turned away from her? At the very least it was rude. Or perhaps he really did keep forgetting she was standing there. 'How long would I have to do it for?'

'How long's a piece of string?' Charlie shrugged. 'Until graduation or until you catch feelings.'

'And if I break, you get a grand?'

Charlie shrugged. 'It's all within your control. I'm the one exposed here.'

Archie began to pace. 'Fucking hell! That's so . . . that's just so . . .' He shook his head, his hands on his hips. 'That is no bloody way to end my uni career.'

'The women of Durham will be devastated, granted; they might even announce a local day of mourning. But the many's loss will be one woman's gain – we hope . . . And you could be a grand out of hock *and* in love.'

'You're a slippery bastard.'

Charlie only smiled. 'So are we on?' He held his hand out for a handshake. Archie stared at it like it was venomous.

'Fine. But only because I need the money,' he muttered finally, shaking it before sauntering off back upstairs.

'Hey, where are you going?' Coco called after him.

'To toss off in the shower!' he called back. 'I may as well start as I have to go on!'

He disappeared back upstairs again as they all laughed. His exits were as dramatic as his entrances.

'I can't believe you just came up with that,' Coco chuckled. 'This is going to be so much fun! He'll never make it.'

'I don't know – he really does need the money,' Charlie smiled.

'But he's loaded!'

'Only in principle; it's all tied up in assets. His father's a miserly bastard and we all know Archie's fondness for a little flutter.'

'Dopamine chasing, like I said,' Coco sighed with the weariness of the Psychology undergrad.

'. . . Uh, Coco,' Libby said, frowning slightly as she looked up suddenly at the wall clock. Eleven forty. Her own tutorial may have long come and gone, but . . . 'Didn't you say you had an essay due in at midday?'

Coco's eyes widened as her smile faded and a small pause bloomed. 'I was going to do it this morning,' she whispered.

'. . . And did you?'

She shook her head slowly. 'Fuck. What am I going to do?'

Libby held a hand up. 'Okay, don't panic. Just ask for an extension. Say you've woken up with norovirus. Everyone's entitled to one extension.'

But Coco winced. 'This would be my . . . ' She counted in her head. 'Third.'

This time it was Libby's eyes that widened. 'Coco!'

'I know. But he's always really cool about it.'

'But didn't you say this one's worth twenty per cent of your final mark?'

Coco didn't move for a moment. 'It'll be okay. It'll be okay, right?' She looked to Charlie for support as he shot Libby an alarmed look.

'I'm sure,' he replied, sounding anything but. 'But contact him now. Don't leave it any later.'

'My phone's on charge upstairs,' she whispered, eyes wide.

'Okay, so then . . . ' He thumbed towards upstairs.

They watched as she ran out of the room like a startled fawn. Libby waited for Charlie to look back at her once Coco was out of sight.

'Shit,' he muttered.

'Tell me truthfully, did you concoct that whole charade just to keep Arch away from Coco?'

He shrugged, a small smile tipping his mouth sideways again. 'Let's say it's an insurance policy. I didn't want him giving himself any ideas. We all know he could have anyone he chose.'

And Libby knew he would never choose her. It was a simple truth that even yesterday wouldn't have hurt. But now . . .

'What happened last night with Coco? I thought you were going to seize the day and tell her how you feel,' she asked, dragging her thoughts forward.

He shrugged. 'Her night was already a done deal by the time I got over there. She asked me to hold her drink while she went outside for a smoke.'

'Oh, Charlie,' Libby sighed.

'You can talk,' he said pointedly.

Libby met his eyes but made no reply.

'Does he know?'

'Oh god, can you imagine?' she asked, mortified. 'No. No one does. But it's just a crush so don't deep it,' she said quickly.

'Fine,' he shrugged, going back to his paper. 'But maybe this will do you a favour too. We might both get what we want.'

She rolled her eyes and went back to her cereal. 'Yeah. Meanwhile, back in the real world . . .'

Chapter Four

22 December 2023

Max gave a low whistle as he turned off the engine and stared out over the steering wheel, snowflakes dashing past the windscreen like speeding bullets. 'One, two, three . . .'

'What are you doing?' Libby asked him.

It was another second before he answered. 'Counting the windows.' He looked back at her. 'Fifteen upstairs.'

'The heating is indifferent. Remember that,' she said with a slight shake of her head. 'You'll be glad to get back to your two windows on Elystan Place tonight, trust me.'

Still, they were quiet for a few moments, taking in the sight of the vast pale stone country house. The slightly domed windows were tall on the principal floors, intended to drink in light, but at this hour they were throwing it out, discreet dormers peeping from behind a baluster parapet that skirted the slate roof. There were quoins at the corners and the facade was bluff, with a small flight of steps leading to the double door.

'And eight chimneys,' Max murmured, still counting.

'That is a lot of chimneys.'

'The parties this place must have seen. Have you been here before?'

'No. But I've heard plenty of stories from people who have,' she replied, remembering all the talk of Drewatts Park among their friends and everyone's unabashed awe, the rarefied aura it had given Archie as he caroused through his three years at university. She had imagined something grand – a nice manor house, she supposed, something that would feature on the pages of *Country Life* stacked in her dentist's waiting room – but this . . . this was a level she hadn't imagined. Was a house of this scale suitable for actually living in? Or was it a museum?

'Well, there aren't many places you can walk into straight from a wedding and not feel overdressed,' he said, unbuckling his seatbelt. 'But I suspect this is one of them.'

She opened the car door, climbing out as elegantly as she could manage from the low seat, but it was difficult against the gusting wind. The snow eddied around her in dizzying airborne torrents. 'God, it's absolutely wild up here!' she gasped, immediately shivering in her thin dress and heels as her long hair began to fly.

'I'll get your coat,' Max said, reaching into the boot.

'No, no need, we'll be indoors in ten seconds,' she said, wrapping her arms around her body.

'Okay.' He grabbed the bottle of Puligny-Montrachet wedged between their bags and put a hand to the small of her back as they began crunching over the gravel. Libby noticed the fountain in the central island wasn't running. Frozen? Or just broken?

'At least it's not settling,' Max said, still looking up at the imposing house.

'No, thank god,' she muttered, her own gaze fixed on the ground as she navigated the gravel in three-inch heels. Other cars were parked in the drive – a mud-spattered silver Shogun with a large dent on the back wheel arch; a black Porsche

Carrera; a bronze-green Mark II Land Rover and a Bentley Continental R sitting on bricks, which drew a small snort from her.

Plus ça change . . . She was fairly certain she could guess which car belonged to whom and she made a mental note: the Shogun was the Procks'; the Porsche, Coco's (it was too flashy for Charlie); the Landy would be Rollo's and the shored-up Bentley could only be Archie's late father's. Which left Zannah and Charlie . . . How had they got here?

They climbed the steps, which were guarded by a pair of giant Portland stone lions, their heavy heads resting on their paws. Max stood in front of the double front door, looking at a loss for a moment – it was big enough to drive a horse and carriage through – before pulling on a metal rod that set a bell ringing through the ancient reception hall.

He tugged on his morning-suit jacket and straightened his tie. She knew he was probably aware how handsome he looked and what an imposing figure he cut – Max wasn't one for false modesty – but it had been sobering to watch his effect on women at the wedding. Through the crowd at the drinks reception and across the tables at the wedding breakfast, she had seen women's eyes linger on him; he wasn't an outright flirt but he liked the attention, appearing to always say just the right thing because they laughed, as if on cue, every few moments.

But jealousy wasn't her style. Other women might be more beautiful, or more elegant, or better bred than her, but they couldn't relate to him in the way she did; there was something about working together, understanding the nuances and the stresses of the job and being his intellectual equal, that connected them. They were a good match, she could see that even from the outside looking in.

The door opened and a tall woman stared back at them with keen eyes. There was something kestrel-like in her movements – a watchful patience interrupted by sudden, brisk movement. Libby knew immediately who she was: the housekeeper, known affectionately as Teabag by those in Archie's inner circle.

'Good evening. Miss Pugh and Mr Prince?' She spoke with received pronunciation, a stickler for etiquette, no doubt; in which case she would be pleased by their formal attire.

'Yes, hello,' Max said, his tails flying heroically in the wind.

'Hi,' Libby smiled, trying not to shiver in her scrap of navy silk, and wishing she'd taken up the offer of the coat after all.

'We've been expecting you. I'm Mrs Timmock, the housekeeper. You'd better come in before you're blown away.' She stepped back, allowing them into the hall.

Libby saw the housekeeper measuring up Max – formal, polite, professional, removed – as he waited for her to step in first, his gaze greedily falling through to the impressive space beyond. The reception hall was double-height and cavernous, the walls and ceiling dressed with all-white intricate plasterwork tattoos and the marble floor worn down from centuries of foot traffic. Two huge fireplaces, topped with pedimented friezes, were set opposite each other and festooned with bright-green foliage across the mantel; beside them sat lopsided log baskets the size of a hot-air balloon's gondola.

Libby had to remember to close her mouth. This was a grand space on a scale that could host formal balls, and if they had come in wearing cravats and crinolines, they still wouldn't have been overdressed. Finally she understood the hype that had surrounded Archie back then, for he was no pretender to the realm. This was the real deal, and it felt almost comically perverse to think of him living in that small terraced house in their final year, the basement kitchen permanently damp and blooms of mould in the bathrooms. It was a wonder, looking back, that none of them had grown sick from the living conditions there, and yet she had never once heard him moan or complain. He had never hidden who he was and yet, she saw now, he had worn his heritage lightly. Very lightly indeed.

It must have been heavy, though. At second glance, she could see faded outlines on the wall from where portraits and paintings had formerly hung. Had they been sold off at auction, perhaps? Archie had always been outspoken on the topics of his father's drink and gambling issues. And a vast rug, at least five metres long, was so threadbare as to be almost colourless. How could such a thing be replaced or repaired? What would the running costs be of a place like this?

She stared up at the fat-bellied twenty-five-foot Christmas tree standing in the middle of the room. She was as much a fan of Christmas as the next person but there was something incongruous about seeing something of that scale, so totemic of the natural world, inside a house. It was laden with ornaments that seemed to hail from the 1960s, but she noticed there were no presents underneath. It was probably all exactly as it had been fifty years ago – a hundred, even. Only the people moving through this space would ever change – Archie's parents were no longer here. He and Mrs Timmock were the last ones standing on this watch.

'Have you no bags?' the housekeeper asked, seeing their lack of luggage.

'I'm afraid we're not staying,' Libby said. 'We're only here for dinner. We have to get back down to London tonight.'

'London? Tonight?'

Libby bit her lip, knowing perfectly well their plan was madness – it was a five-hour journey through the dead of night, but Max had been insistent it was the only way. It was Christmas in three days and he had almost all of his gift shopping yet to do. 'We were at a wedding in Durham, you see, and as we were sort of passing, we said we'd just stop in for a bite to eat and see everyone.'

'Indeed. Well, they're gathered in the drawing room. The other guests arrived a few hours ago, so the festivities have begun. Follow me.'

Libby glanced at Max as the two of them trailed after the dour housekeeper. He winked at her, their footsteps echoing in unison, but didn't reach for her hand. He never did in public. They passed through into another hall where a grand carved-oak cantilevered staircase twisted to the upper floors, a monumental window on the half-landing giving onto the gardens. A carefully arranged collection of military paraphernalia bore down from the walls: countless swords and spears, some shields and a few breastplates, studded with stag heads.

'How old is the house, Mrs Timmock?' Max asked.

'It was built in the 1770s by the third viscount, with a couple of additions bolted on in the early nineteenth century.'

'I read that Capability Brown did some work here, too?'

'Indeed. In fact, this was one of his final projects. He planted the oak copse on the eastern flank and installed the lake. But the pavilion is just ruins now; the eighth viscount was sadly frivolous with money and let it fall into disrepair.'

The sound of voices began to drift through to them as they walked along a wide corridor, past twisted *os de mouton* walnut chairs and verdure tapestries on the walls. Did anyone ever sit in those chairs, or stop to admire the craftwork in those stitches? Or did they just rush past in an unseeing blur? A grandfather clock ticked loudly, giving the space a pulse, and at the far end, in a shallow niche, stood a suit of armour – with a cigar poking through the helmet and a purple feather boa wrapped around the neck.

Libby felt another frisson of excitement – and nerves – at the sight of it, recognizing her old housemates' signature sense of humour. *Had* anything changed in nine years? Had they? Had he?

Mrs Timmock opened a set of solid double doors and a babble of voices escaped. Libby took a breath, bracing herself as she looked up, but there wasn't even a moment to register—

'Libs!' someone shrieked, rushing over to her with outstretched arms and a paper crown on her head.

'Ems!' Libby mumbled into her friend's curly hair as she was enveloped in a bear hug and the smell of eucalyptus shampoo. It was several seconds before she could breathe freely again.

'You made it! You actually made it!' Ems breathed, pulling back to get a better look at her. 'I said I wouldn't believe it till I saw you with my own eyes, but here you are! I can't believe it! And oh my god, just look at you! So glamorous!'

Libby gave an embarrassed laugh as Ems looked her up and down with wide-eyed admiration. 'It's so good to see you too. I—' She was taken aback as she caught her first glimpse of her friend's baby bump. She bit her lip as she was hit with an unexpected wave of emotion. 'Oh my. It really is real. You really are having a baby.'

'I really bloody am,' Ems laughed, cupping it delightedly and showing it off in her stretch emerald dress. 'Less than three weeks till the big reveal.'

Libby bit her lip, daunted. 'How have you been? Has it been okay?'

Ems clasped her arm and shot her a serious look. 'Hon,

46

when I tell you the nausea has been a whole other level . . . Anything triggers it: the sight of a cereal box. Rolled-up socks—'

'Rolled-up socks?' Libby laughed.

'Anything!' Ems shrugged. 'It's so embarrassing! And once I start retching, I just can't stop.'

'She even retched because of the way I made her sandwich the other day,' Prock said, coming over and casually looping an arm over his wife's shoulder.

'Yes, because you didn't skin the cucumber!' Ems protested.

Prock arched an eyebrow, as if to say 'see?'

'Prock, I'm so happy for you both,' Libby said, reaching up to give him a kiss on the cheek. 'You'll be incredible parents.' She turned slightly to bring Max into the group, aware she had just fallen straight into conversation without making any introductions. 'Guys, this is Max Prince. We work together,' she said, stepping back and bringing him into the loop. 'Max, this is Jack and Emma Proctor. We all lived together in our third year.'

'Call me Prock,' Jack said, offering his hand.

'Hey,' Max said, shaking their hands. 'Good to meet you. And congratulations both.'

'Thanks, it's good to meet you, Max,' Ems replied, taking in his morning suit. 'So you really weren't making it up when you said you two were on your way back from a wedding?'

'Why would we have made it up?' Libby laughed, but she knew the point her friend was making. Her excuses for not attending the various group events had been varied over the years, and only her apology for being in Asia at the time of their wedding had had the ring of truth to it.

'Whose wedding?' Prock asked. The past decade had been kind to him, his boy-next-door looks weathering softly, although Libby suspected that had something to do with having been blissfully in love for all that time.

'It was a work colleague's,' Max replied. 'In Durham Cathedral.'

'Ah, site of the grand old *alma mater*. What's your line of work?' Prock asked him.

'Corporate law.'

'Yes of course, had to be.' He motioned between them as if their union was inevitable. 'Our Libs was always the star among us, getting her starred first. Headed up DebSoc, edited the *Law Review* . . . And you work for the same firm, do you?'

'Yes. Woodford May and Wessing.'

'Oh yeah, I've heard of them. What's your area?'

'I'm in media, entertainment and mining. Elizabeth covers tech, comms and energy.' Max's voice relaxed as they moved into work matters. 'How about you? What field are you in?'

'Me? Oh, I'm just a chartered surveyor.'

'Why do you say "just" like that?' Ems asked crossly, jogging him with her elbow so that some champagne splashed from his glass. 'You've got the biggest practice in Harrogate.'

Prock gave her an affectionate smile. 'That is true.' He looked back at them with shining eyes. 'I do indeed have the biggest chartered surveying practice in Harrogate. I'm a god. A living legend.'

Max and Libby laughed as he kissed his wife's temple affectionately.

'And Ems is an accountant,' Libby said to Max. 'What are you going to do after the baby's born? Will you go back?'

Ems shrugged. 'Probably, although—'

'Excuse me, are you intending to hold her hostage all night, or are the rest of us going to get a few words in?' a voice asked over Ems's shoulder.

'Charlie!' Libby smiled, reaching over to hug him. 'Charlie, this is Max Prince. Max, Charlie Earnshaw.'

'Earnshaw,' Max murmured as the men shook hands. 'Why do I feel I know that name?'

Charlie gave a perplexed shrug. 'No drinks?' he asked, seeing their empty hands. 'Christ, the world really is in a state of irreversible decline. Where the hell is Arch?' He looked around the room for their host, Libby taking the opportunity to scout for him too, but there was no sign of him. There was, however, a taxidermy peacock perched on a mahogany torchère in the far corner.

'Come on Max, we'll get you a drink and I can introduce you to Roly, he's a character . . . Do you shoot, by any chance?' Prock said, leading the way to the drinks cabinet on the other side of the room.

'I'm just popping to the loo,' Ems whispered to Libby. 'My poor bladder's never going to recover from this bowling ball of a baby bouncing on it.'

'That's a lot of Bs,' Libby said under her breath as she found herself alone with Charlie suddenly. She gave him a sheepish look. 'So . . .'

'So,' he echoed. 'We did it. We finally snaffled you.'

'Looks that way.'

'It only took almost a decade.'

'Yeah, but what's a decade among friends?' she shrugged. For much of that time, he'd been living in California, and he now had the sun-kissed hair and light tan to prove it; he was looking lean in his dinner suit and seemed to radiate health, as if there actually was some basis to the protein smoothies and wellness culture of the Golden State.

'. . . Have you seen him yet?'

'Who?'

49

He gave her a look.

'Oh jeez, don't . . . please don't think . . .' She sighed. 'I moved on from all that a very long time ago.'

'Really?'

She gestured towards Max as if he was proof. Admissible evidence in a court of law of her Moving On. But Charlie didn't look fooled.

'And yet you've kept your distance.'

'I've been busy.'

'Mm-hmm.'

'Well, how about you?' she asked, determined to shift the focus off herself. 'Have you moved on?'

He knew perfectly well to whom she was referring. 'I've been living five thousand miles away. Of course I've moved on.'

'And yet, you haven't brought a significant other here . . . ?' she murmured, scanning the room for unfamiliar faces and finding none.

'. . . No, I haven't,' he conceded, his usual half-smile on his lips, but that guarded look in his eyes telling her she had her thumb on a bruise. Out of all the guys in the house, he had always been the one she felt closest too. They were birds of a feather – 'geeks surrounded by lunatics', was how he'd put it once.

'So how is our Coco? I haven't seen her yet either.'

'She's the same.'

'Chaotic? Beautiful? Lovable?'

'Something like that.'

'And does she know?'

'Know?'

'About your success?'

'Ah.' His eyes narrowed at the pointed look she gave him,

and he slid his jaw slowly to the side, looking around the room quickly before looking back at her. 'So *you* know then?'

'Of course I know, Charlie, it's my area,' she shrugged. 'And for the record, I'm officially – uppercase O – pissed off that you didn't hire me as your lawyer.'

He gave an apologetic grimace. 'Never mix business and pleasure, Libs.'

'That deal would have made me partner.'

'You're still a little young for that, aren't you?'

She gave a small scoff. 'But you're not too young to make a hundred mill before you're thirty?'

'Shhh.' He looked genuinely panicked.

She arched an eyebrow. 'What?' She saw how he scanned the room nervously, as if checking no one was eavesdropping on their conversation. A laugh escaped her. '. . . *They* don't know? How can they not know?' His £100 million sale of his AI business to Alphabet hadn't exactly flown underneath the radar. Coco only read *Tatler* but it had been all over the business pages. Then again, Roly only read *The Field* and *Racing Post*; Prock, though? Archie?

'That's all a different world, and I'd rather not make a big thing about it. These guys know I'm doing well, they don't need to know the details. Everyone's got their own stuff going on.'

'But—'

'I don't want to come off as the Big I Am.'

She looked back at him, modest to the point of effacement. 'You could never. That's not who you are. But this is a big thing to keep from them.'

He gave a shrug, dismissing the topic. 'Well, then it looks like we're bonded together over *another* secret, doesn't it? Come on, let's get you a drink. Everyone always needs a stiffener after watching someone else sign their life away.'

They walked over to the drinks cabinet where Max, Prock and Ems were standing talking with Rollo Walwyn. To add to the allsorts ensemble of this evening's dress code, he was still wearing his shooting breeks and claret wool knee-length socks, brogues and a tattersall shirt; but as Archie's best friend from prep school, Ampleforth and then Durham, he was almost part of the furniture here and could wear what he liked. Libby suspected Mrs Timmock actually smiled at him and gave him seconds of her apple pie.

'Another hard day in the field, Roly?' Libby asked as if she'd seen him only that morning. She reached over to kiss his cheek but he closed his free arm around her and lifted her easily so that her feet left the floor. At six foot three, there was quite a way to drop.

'Pugh Bear! Where the fuck have you been hiding?'

'Not you too,' she groaned, rolling her eyes as he set her back down again and Charlie placed a flute of champagne into her hand.

'I was convinced you were dead. I demanded proof of life tonight or I was going straight to the cop shop!'

She took a sip. 'A likely story. You've got far too much to hide to risk anything as crazy as that.'

He winced as if wounded, sucking the air in through his cheeks. 'Ooh, you've polished some sharp edges in your absence, I see.'

'She's a corporate lawyer these days,' Ems said, giving her a sisterly wink. 'So you better put your big boy pants on, Roly. Libs swims in the shark tank now.'

'She *is* the shark,' Max quipped, drawing admiring looks from the others and holding her gaze.

'Says you,' she replied. 'Max is up for partner in the next round. If he gets it, he'll be the youngest in the company's history.'

She was aware of looks being swapped as she and Max stared at one another.

'So you work together?' Roly clarified.

'Yep.'

'But you're also . . . ?' He looked between them expectantly. '. . . Boffing?'

Libby spluttered on her drink. 'Roly! What are you, twelve?'

'What? I'm just trying to get a handle on things.'

'Are *you* seeing anyone?' she asked him instead.

'Actually, no. Just got dumped the other week, in fact.'

'Oh, I'm sorry.'

'Don't be. It was doomed from the off. She's allergic to horses and Bessie never took to her, which is always a red flag.'

'Oh dear.'

'But that wasn't the worst of it. She was – brace yourself – a vegan.'

Libby spluttered on her drink again. Roly was a committed carnivore of the 'eat what you kill' variety, so it was difficult to understand how this pairing had come into being. 'Dear god, had you lost your mind? How on earth did *you* end up with her?'

'Fabulous-looking girl,' he tutted. 'Thought it was worth shooting my shot and just hoping for not too much conversation.'

'Or breakfast, lunch and dinner,' Ems added with a wry smile.

'How old is Bessie now?' Libby asked, seeing an opportunity to steer the conversation away from love lives once and for all.

'Twelve on January thirteenth. The arthritis is getting the better of her now, though, so she can't jump in the car any more, and she's awfully fat.'

'Perhaps she needs a companion?' Charlie offered. 'A whippersnapper tormenting her might be just the thing to up her activity levels.'

'Yes, there's a litter of labs in the next village to us,' Ems said. 'I could put you in touch if you like?'

Roly gave a low rumble of reluctance. 'I'd need to have a good look at the bloodline—'

Libby looked around the room as he began to hold forth on the importance of a broad head and the perils of retinal dysplasia. The old mustard velvet sofas looked sunken and crushed and the raspberry silk fabric on a pair of chairs by the window had been almost shredded by decades of exposure to direct sunlight. Small piles of books were stacked on side tables, lamps of different forms and heights throwing out uneven light, used teacups on the floor beside the chairs. Then there was the peacock . . .

She looked at her friends as they laughed and talked easily, the old dynamics of the group unchanged. Max stood out, smiling politely as in-jokes were remembered, code words reinstated, past indiscretions relived. He would have his own version of this too, of course – he had graduated from Emmanuel, Cambridge, with a first in Law and a blue in boxing – and she tried to imagine being the one standing there with a half-smile on her lips as his friends reminisced. She dismissed the thought in the next moment. These were tentative first steps into their personal lives, but she was happy with the way things were; there was no rush.

'So where's Zannah and Coco? I haven't seen them yet,' she asked, coming back into the conversation.

'They're upstairs with Archie; he's showing them to their rooms. Coco only got here this afternoon. There was an accident on the motorway so she was a bit delayed.'

'Let me guess – hers is the Porsche?'

'Um, excuse me, why would you say that? It's clearly ours,' Ems protested.

Libby grinned. With that bump to navigate, she didn't think Ems would be able to get down into the Porsche, much less out of it again.

'It's such a shame you can't stay,' Ems pouted at her sadly.

'I know, but we have to get back. Some of us haven't done our Christmas shopping yet.' She glanced across at Max and he gave a sheepish grin. 'What are you all up to for Christmas?'

'Well, we're going to Prock's sister's with all her family – she's got three kids now, can you believe it? The outlaws will be there too,' Ems replied. 'And then your brothers' lot are coming to join us there on Boxing Day. I think it was sixteen people at the last count?' she asked her husband.

He nodded solemnly. 'Cue lots of paper hats, bad jumpers and charades.'

'Your last Christmas before Bump becomes Baby,' Libby sighed. 'Do you know what you're having?'

'Yep. Apparently they've narrowed it down to either a boy or a girl,' Prock quipped.

Libby stuck her tongue out at him as she took another sip of her champagne. 'Ha ha. What about you, Charlie?' An only child and orphaned following a car crash, he had been in and out of foster care for most of his teens; Libby had always felt his phenomenal drive for success and financial security was his own attempt for stability.

'Me? Oh, I'm going to a hotel in Hampshire where someone will cook for me, no one will knock for me, I won't have to wrap a present nor feign happiness for a present I don't want.'

'Charlie, that sounds dreadful! You don't mean that!' Ems protested, sounding aghast.

'Actually, I do.'

'But . . . who will you be with? Just a bunch of strangers?'

'Ems, not even that. I may not leave my room. Nor my bed.

I might have roast turkey and all the trimmings on a lap tray as I lie in clean sheets, naked as a baby, binge-watching reruns of *Top Gear*.'

Everyone was quiet for a moment, suspended in opposing thoughts of this as the definition of absolute heaven or absolute hell.

'Nope. You're not fooling anyone, Earnshaw,' Roly said, breaking the silence. 'You'll be up at dawn for a 10k run, back for an ice bath and have speed-read three self-help books before I've even turned over with my morning glory.'

'Ew!' Ems grimaced, just as the sound of a hunting bugle started up in the hall, erupting into the room moments later. Everyone turned to see a tall, glamorous blonde in a strapless marabou-feather minidress and crystal-threaded boots dance through the doors, followed by a skinny brunette shimmying in silver sequins and a man bringing up the rear in a claret velvet smoking jacket and a lopsided coronet.

Libby swallowed as the heart of the party announced itself in typically flamboyant fashion, everyone falling back into their designated roles. She stood a little taller, reminding herself of the intervening nine years of promotions, bonuses and rapid advancement in her career; she was no longer the mousey, timid girl they had known and who she had tried so hard to shed like an old snakeskin. But as the trio fell into some sort of synchronized movement, she realized Coco was filming their entrance on her phone and that this performance was not for them, the people in the room, but her legion of followers watching through their screens.

She watched, transfixed, as the three newcomers mimed to a soundtrack. Had they been rehearsing upstairs? Was that why they'd taken so long? She watched them all perform, joking together like the old friends they were, their vibrancy that had dimmed in Libby's mind through the passage of time – memories fading like old Polaroids – suddenly exploding back into Technicolor. She had allowed them to become, in her mind's eye, mere archetypes, as her own world and ego had grown away from their long shadows. But the reality was, even if they were pastiches, she still couldn't take her eyes off them. She still wished she could be like them. Compared to their party dresses her midnight silk wrap dress looked dreary, and beside Coco's long, lean lines, she felt short and squat. Stumpy and dumpy, as her brother had always called her.

She watched Zannah too, scarcely able to recognize her old friend. Not only was she half her university weight, but her trademark wild mane of auburn corkscrew curls had been lopped and tamed with a sleek Brazilian blowout, dyed a deep chestnut and now swung above tanned shoulders and what appeared to be a very impressive boob job.

As for Archie . . . as for him . . . he was still the life and soul of every space he entered. She had cast him in her memories as an entitled wastrel enveloped in a nebulous fog of smoke, whisky and perfume, but charisma radiated from him like a second sun.

'Yes!' Coco laughed as the reel finished and she saved it on her phone.

'Thank god!' Zannah groaned, sticking her tongue out of the side of her mouth and rolling her eyes to indicate exhaustion or bewilderment at what had just passed. Libby wouldn't know – she had never done a TikTok.

Archie blew on the bugle again, one lazy, long-winded minor-key note, as he sauntered towards them. Libby could see he hadn't clocked her yet and she watched as his gaze swept the room, checking on his guests . . .

They made eye contact and she saw the jolt ripple through

him like an electric current, a short, sharp buzz that was just enough to release the bugle clamped between his lips so that it dangled on its red cord around his neck. For a moment the room contracted, bleeding of colour and noise . . . before expanding again in the next breath like a set of bellows.

'Well, well, Pugh, as I live and breathe . . .'

But his words were drowned out as Coco and Zannah rushed over to her, swamping her like a four-armed beast.

'You actually bloody came!' Coco squealed in her ear, squeezing her tightly and shaking her from side to side. Libby thought it would be a miracle if her champagne glass, and possibly a rib, wasn't crushed by the time they released her.

'Just look at you!' Zannah gushed, looking her up and down.

'Look at *you*, you mean,' Libby said, reaching out and stroking Zannah's newly sleek hair. 'When did this happen? And *those*?'

Zannah struck a modelly pose, one hand cupped under a boob as she laughed. 'Do you like?'

'Sensational. You look incredible – and so thin! Was that New York?'

'It's no place to be a size twelve, let me tell you.'

Archie brought over fresh drinks for Coco and Zannah. 'Bottoms up,' he said, clinking glasses. His gaze came back to Libby as he drank, his grey-green eyes narrowing slightly as he took her in. His face was thinner than she remembered, highlighting those fine aristocratic bones, and he had more colour in his cheeks than in their malnourished, intoxicated student days; but he was still the beautiful rake whose legend lived on in Durham's halls. What did he think as he saw her now, she wondered? Had her many successes and triumphs gilded her? Was she transformed from the pathetic girl he had known? Or would she always be a joke to him, someone to pity?

'Everyone, this is Max. Max Prince.'

'They work together,' Rollo supplied helpfully as Archie turned to greet the stranger in their midst.

'Max!' he said after a beat, greeting him like an old friend as he pumped his hand. 'Yes, indeed, of course. Forgive me! The utter shock of seeing Libby actually standing in my drawing room overwhelmed all sense of propriety. Have you a drink?'

Max held up his glass of champagne with a bemused look as Archie fell into his social persona.

'Good. Good . . . And so you and Libs *work* together?' He said the word as if it slightly baffled him.

'Yes. We have adjoining offices so we . . . see a lot of each other.'

Libby's head jerked slightly as she picked up a tremor of innuendo. She knew his tone of voice, how precise he always was with his words.

'Uh-huh . . . Well, you're a brave man. She's a machine. Or at least, she was way back when we knew her.'

'I can confirm she still is,' Max nodded laconically. 'She is seemingly inexhaustible.' This time Max met her eyes and she saw he knew exactly what he was doing, loading his replies and showing them all that this was more than a business relationship. But why?

'Well, Archie old boy, you know what this means don't you – you owe me three hundred quid.' Rollo held out his hand and wiggled his fingers expectantly as Archie gave a groan.

'Sorry?' Libby asked, looking between them both.

'We had a sweepstake running,' Rollo explained. 'Ten to one you'd be a no-show. No wonder the poor fellow just paled at the sight of you!'

'You bet *against* me coming?' she asked, looking straight at Archie.

'Of course.' He shrugged.

'Why of course? I had RSVP'd yes.'

He pulled a face. 'Mm, that wasn't fooling anyone. You've got form. Remember that empty chair at your twenty-first, Roly?'

Her mouth opened in protest. Rollo's party had been just days after—

'I still dream about it,' Rollo muttered.

'And the unused paper napkin at Glyndebourne?'

'Yup. It just blew away,' Rollo tutted.

'But I gave you notice I couldn't make that.'

'An hour's notice.'

Libby swallowed. 'My job can be very . . . demanding. Clients want their pound of flesh and I . . . I often have to cancel plans at the last moment.'

Archie looked back at her again and it was like a set of iron epaulettes had been thrown over her shoulders, making her knees buckle. 'Well, then you'll have to forgive me, but I was of the conviction that you'd rather eat your own leg than ever have to consort with us again. I thought we'd driven you away for good.' There was savagery in the words, though they were delivered in a careless drawl.

For a moment he let his words settle with his gaze, but he looked away from her again in the next instant and it was like a plaster being ripped off her skin. 'Unfortunately for me, that's three hundred quid I can ill afford,' he drawled. 'I've got a bloody big roof that needs patching. I need all the three hundred pounds I can get.'

'And what line of work are you in, Archie?' Max asked.

There was a pause as Archie considered. 'Land management and tax.'

Everyone smiled, including Max, who of course knew this

was an elegant way of saying Archie didn't really have a job, merely a position.

'Why don't you boys chat,' Coco said, steering Libby away, Zannah and Ems following after. 'And we'll catch up on our girly gossips.'

'Um . . .' Libby hesitated as she was reminded of a night, a long time ago, when she'd been bundled away by her friends in exactly this way. And look what that had led to . . .

'Oh my god, he is gorgeous,' Coco whispered excitedly in her ear. 'How long has it been going on? Tell us everything.'

Briefly, Libby caught Max's eye as she was pulled away, but he simply winked at her, looking perfectly at ease. Libby allowed herself a sigh of relief – perhaps the worst *was* over. She had done it; after nine years of exile, the ice had been broken, even if the water between her and Archie couldn't exactly be described as warm. But they could eat, drink and be merry. The world had moved on and it no longer mattered what had happened almost a decade ago. They had been kids back then, but this was the adult world now. No one was having a crisis of conscience. The sky wasn't falling in. Like the rest of them, she just had to let it go.

Chapter Five

April 2014

Libby stared at the message. *Tort is kicking my arse. Want to study together? We could get pizza to numb the pain.*

'Yeah?' she murmured as there was a knock at her door, throwing the phone on her desk and leaning back in her chair, arms stretched overhead. Her money was on Zannah; she'd gone on a date with a Classics post-grad and had laughingly sprayed her perfume on her ankles before she'd left. 'Honestly, I should just leave the condoms in a box outside the doo—'

Her words failed as Archie looked in.

'Hey,' he said with a lopsided smile.

She sat up in her chair. 'Hey,' she swallowed.

'Am I . . . interrupting?' He looked around the room, his gaze falling to her bedroom door just off this room, and jerked his thumb towards it.

She frowned, not quite understanding his meaning at first. 'Oh . . . No, there's no one here.'

'Ah. I just thought I heard you say something about condoms.'

'Ah. Well, I . . .' She shook her head dismissively. 'It doesn't matter.' She looked back at him. He had never been up to her room before. '. . . What's up?'

'I was wondering if you had a light?' He held up his roll-up and she could tell from the slight slur that he'd been drinking. 'Everyone else is out.'

'Oh, sure, um . . . I might have some matches . . .' She got up and crossed the room, looking on the shelf by her scented candle. Gone. Zannah? 'Let me just check in the other room,' she muttered, before adding, 'You can come in. You don't have to stand out there.'

'Thanks.'

She heard the floorboards creak under his weight as she rifled through her bedroom drawers and checked her toiletry bag. She was sure she had an old lighter somewhere that one of the girls had left behind after one of their gossip sessions; her sitting room, with its abundance of space, made for an obvious meeting point . . . *Yes*.

'Will this do?' she asked, walking back through and stopping dead as she saw him reading her phone. '. . . What are you doing?'

He turned back and the slight over-rotation confirmed he was even drunker than she had realized. 'Sorry, it just caught my eye . . . Who's *Ben*?'

It took her a moment to respond. Did he think it was okay to just read her private messages? She gave a small laugh of disbelief. 'Ben Parsons. He's on my course.'

He looked surprised. 'You two are a thing?'

'No.'

He looked suspicious. 'But he wants you to be.'

'No. I don't think so.'

'Of course he does. He's suggesting pizza. Pizza's always code for sex.'

She didn't reply. No doubt it was different for the Classics set but in Law, the crushing workload meant pizza equalled carbs, equalled all-nighters.

'. . . You gonna go?' he asked when she didn't answer.

'I'm not sure. I haven't decided.'

'If you have to deliberate, the answer's no.' He held his hands out in a half shrug as if this was a universal truth. 'Don't waste your time on people that don't kick you in the guts, you know?'

'Nice. Thanks for the dating advice.' She walked over and handed him the lighter. 'There you go.'

'Thanks. I'll bring it back.'

'No, there's no need.'

'Really?'

'It's fine.' She could see his eyes were greener than they were grey, and he smelled of woodsmoke and beer.

'No, no, I'll definitely bring it back,' he insisted again.

'You really don't need to.'

'But I do. It's yours.'

Libby sighed. Arguing with a drunk was like trying to rationalize with a toddler. 'Okay then. Thanks.'

He swayed a little, stepping back and turning around slowly, having a better look at her room. 'It's so nice up here.'

'Yeah.'

'I like what you've done with all the . . . the . . . papers.' He pointed vaguely towards her spider charts tacked to the walls. 'Maybe I should do that.'

'I find them really helpful.'

'You're going for a first?'

'Trying for it anyway.'

She watched as he walked slowly past her desk, stopping at the bookcase and peering at her few photos. There was one of her and her father on the beach when she was three, a bucket upturned on her head; another of her horse-riding; one of her and her brother on a slide in the park. 'Cute.'

She shrugged, feeling nervous that he was loitering. Was all this some kind of preamble to addressing what had happened between them last night? Had he remembered after all? Had it come back to him in a rush how he had kissed her, how he'd touched her and she had let him, that startling moment of connection between them when their eyes had met? Perhaps he thought her a sure thing? Maybe that was why he was here. A re-enactment, or even more . . .

He stood at the doorway into her narrow bedroom and peered in.

Libby turned away, her fears confirmed. But if she had betrayed herself last night, she wouldn't make the same mistake tonight.

'. . . Why *do* you work so hard?' he asked.

It wasn't the line of conversation she had been expecting, and she turned back to find him watching her. 'Why *don't* you?'

He slipped into a dozy smile and waggled a finger. 'Uh-uh, I asked first.'

She looked back at him. He was drunk, yes, but not crazily so, not like last night; he wore a permanently bemused expression, as if life was tickling him, but she could see a glint of that sharpness in the back of his eyes that was there in his sober moments. She sensed that – like all people with a magnetic presence – he was a good reader of people. So many wanted to be in his orbit, her included, and it made her feel pathetic to want him without hope. He distinctly had a type: skinny private school blondes with tummy piercings and Mykonos tans. Being petite, dark and curvy, with an aversion to exercise and make-up, she stood in counterpoint to everything the Hon Archie Templeton liked and there was no point in pretending otherwise.

'Because I want more than I have,' she said finally. Bluntly.

His head tipped with interest. 'Go on.'

'I'm poor, Archie.' She wondered if the word alone would make him recoil. 'My father's a mechanic, my mother works as a school administrator. They work hard to give me and my brother a good life but we're still always that bit short every month. The heating can't ever go on before December no matter how cold it is, my school shoes always had to be re-heeled to get through another term. And that's fine,' she shrugged. 'We always got by; we never needed anyone's pity. But I want a better future than that. Academia has always come easily to me, so why wouldn't I use the talents I've been given? I'm going for a first and I'm going for an internship in Hong Kong . . . Either one of those happening puts me in prime position for a job at Clifford Chance, with a starting salary three times my parents' combined income.' She gave a shrug. 'I'll be able to pay off my student loan in one year; I want to pay off their mortgage for them within five; I want to buy my brother a car so he doesn't have to get to his job on the bus. That's why I work.'

He nodded, watching her, not feeling a need to reply quickly, perfectly comfortable with the silence that opened up between them. 'You see, I knew there was a reason why I liked you.'

She gave a small snort. 'You don't like me. You never even notice me.'

'Not true.'

She looked back at him, struck by the firmness in his voice and sensing that connection flickering between them again, an electrical current trying to join up a circuit. '. . . Your turn,' she said finally. 'Why *don't* you work?'

He inhaled as if to speak but the words didn't come immediately. 'You don't have what you want . . . But I don't want what I have.'

She gave a tut and rolled her eyes. He was being flippant with her. 'It's true,' he shrugged. 'Having everything is the worst thing that can happen to a man. It rots his soul. No one should have what they want on tap.'

She leaned against the back of her chair, watching him. 'Well, with all due respect, Archie, you put on a damn good show of looking like you love it.'

He nodded. 'Because that's the role I'm expected to play: showman. What am I going to do? Expose my bleeding heart to a bunch of acolytes? I know perfectly well why people like being my friend – but it's all bullshit. There's no power in my position; the money's all tied up. It's just an illusion that people buy into. Reflected glory.'

'So then get better friends.'

'Well, I'm here, aren't I?'

She stared at him, taken aback. She wouldn't have described them as friends, not even close. They shared a postcode and a kitchen . . . 'I'm afraid I'm not buying it. You're not getting a pity party from me because you're *privileged*.'

He blinked slowly, like a cat. 'You think you're at a disadvantage to me because on paper I've got everything and you've got nothing, yes?'

'Yes.'

'Well, those are our respective inherited circumstances. But yours has given you something – a goal, drive, resilience, whatever – whereas mine has taken that away from me.'

'Oh please . . .'

He stared straight at her. 'No one ever stops to think what it's like waking up every morning with no imperative to have to do anything. I could stay in bed for a month and no one would bat an eye. There would be no loss.'

'Except muscular dystrophy.'

He didn't smile.

'That was a joke.'

'There's nothing funny about having no reason to get out of bed. Things get old really fast when every day is the same.'

'Mm. So the non-stop parties, the stream of blondes and the smell of weed coming from your room, that's you just . . . shaking up your days.'

His eyes narrowed at her tease and she saw a flash of anger in him. 'I don't expect your pity, Pugh – just like you don't want mine – but when you come from a long line of reprobates like me, when expectations for me are to be as low as I like . . .' He took a sudden inhale, raking a hand through his hair and holding it there for a moment. 'Everything's hollow. You might not have much but you've got a path. A direction of travel. No one expects anything from me. It's irrelevant if I have ambition or talent or a good heart – no one cares either way; just so long as I produce an heir someday to continue the line, I'll have fulfilled my life's destiny.'

Libby watched as he turned away, going to stand by her window and staring out. His body was tense, one finger tapping repetitively against the wall. His famous sense of humour appeared to have taken a walk. 'Surely your parents care?' she asked.

'My mother's dead,' he said flatly. 'And my father may as well be; he's drinking himself into an early grave.'

Libby watched him. 'So then do it for yourself.'

He whipped back around. 'Says the scholar with drive! Don't you see that's my point? I have no touchpaper.' He held up the joint and indicated his drunken self and suddenly she saw not libertinism but wretchedness. 'This is all I know.'

'Then try harder,' she snapped back. 'If there's more to you than this, then show it. Stop living down to expectations. There's power in being underestimated, you know.'

They stared at one another, strangers in a room. Their pasts were opposites and their futures clearly would diverge too – this moment, these few months in Mitchell Street, would be the only crossing point in their lives – and yet she felt as if she knew him better than any other person in this house. Something inside her recognized something inside him.

Or so it felt to her.

He shook his head. 'You're going to be brilliant, Libby,' he said finally. 'Your life is going to shine and you're going to hit all those marks.' He crossed the room, eyes down, stopping at the door. '. . . But don't go out with him,' he ordered, pointing at her phone and pinning her with a final rapier look. 'Wait for the kick in the guts.'

She didn't reply as she watched the door close behind him. What was there to say when she knew she didn't need to wait? She had already been kicked.

Chapter Six

22 December 2023

'Can I do anything to help?' Libby asked, peering around the kitchen door. She had heard a clatter as she was coming out of the cloakroom, followed by the sound of something breaking.

Mrs Timmock looked up from her frozen straddled position, a pool of gravy spreading across the floor from a shattered jug between her feet, beautifully caramelized carrots and parsnips scattered like marbles, a baking tray upside down.

'Oh no!' Libby ran in, reaching a hand over to the house-keeper so that she could help pull her away from the mess on the floor. 'What happened?'

'A hole in the oven glove,' Mrs Timmock tutted, her mouth downturned with pain. 'I usually remember the blasted thing but I was in such a rush . . .'

'Have you a burn?' she asked as the housekeeper pulled off her gauntlet and examined her right index finger. Both of them winced. '. . . Here, run it under the tap while I clean up. Where's the dustpan and brush?'

'In the cupboard at the end there,' Mrs Timmock said, jerking her chin in the direction of a door in the corner as she set the water running.

Libby rushed over to it and found what she needed. 'Is

there no one else here helping you?' she asked as she began sweeping the vegetables off the terracotta tiles.

'Like who . . . ? I hope you don't mean Archie,' she asked with an incredulous tone. 'He's more bother than he's worth in the kitchen. I go to great lengths to keep him *out*.'

'Quite,' Libby agreed, well able to remember his useless attempts at washing up; the girls had all been convinced he deliberately did a bad job to avoid ever being asked again. His main contribution to the house had been bringing in 'decent' wine and keep them stocked in cigarettes. 'But do you have no one to help with serving up, or putting things in the dishwasher?'

'Dishwasher?'

Libby looked at her. '. . . You don't have a dishwasher?'

'That would require money and there's a roof that needs patching.'

'. . . Of course.' Libby was reminded of Archie's lost bet with Rollo amid his utter conviction that she would never come near any of them again. Him.

She got up and tipped the ruined vegetables into the large metal bin. 'Do you have any more?' she asked, heading towards the fridge.

'No, there's no time to do the root veg again. The lamb will go over and Archie likes it pink. Grab the bag of peas in the freezer – second drawer from the top – they'll have to do.'

'Okay.' Libby hurriedly opened some drawers, looking for a saucepan.

'The Aga's going cold, that's the problem,' the housekeeper muttered. 'It's lost most of its heat from roasting the joint. If you can boil some water in the kettle, that'll help it come to the boil faster.'

'Of course.' Libby obeyed her instructions, filling up the

kettle. 'How's it feeling now?' she asked over her shoulder as the housekeeper moved slightly out of her way for a moment.

'Still a beggar,' Mrs Timmock muttered, staring at her finger with a furious expression as if it had personally betrayed her. Libby could see the skin was shiny from the burn.

'Mm, you really got good contact with the tray,' she winced.

'It'll be fine. I need to get on—'

'No, absolutely not,' Libby said firmly, stopping her from moving away from the tap. 'You won't sleep tonight from the pain if you don't keep it there. Don't move away till your finger starts going numb.' She put the kettle on and grabbed the roll of kitchen towels, absorbing the worst of the gravy spill. 'Have you a mop? I'll clean the floor.'

'That won't be necessary. We've got Labradors for that. I'll get them in from the crates and do a proper mop later once dinner's out of the way.'

'Labradors?' Libby repeated, not sure if she'd heard properly.

'Yes. They'll make short work of that mess, I can tell you, and they'll love you forever for it too.'

Libby waited for a moment to see if there was a punchline. Seemingly there wasn't. 'And where are the crates?'

'The dog room is just off the boot room on the other side of the hall there.'

'They're friendly to strangers? They won't bite?'

'Trust me, you've seen more dangerous slabs of butter.'

Libby smiled as she went through to the boot room – a large space lined with waxed jackets and mackintoshes hanging on hooks, numerous wellies on sticks and baskets piled high with knitted hats, scarves, gloves and ear defenders. A central gulley ran down the middle of the floor and towards a drain by the outer wall, catching any rainwater or mud. In the back corner, a door led through to a smaller space where what could only be disguised as an inbuilt cage was affixed to the back half of the room, three black Labradors within thumping their tails happily at the sight of her. One was deeply aged, moving arthritically, its face salted white; another, with a red collar, appeared in its prime and the last was just a juvenile, bigger than a puppy, but long-legged and bandy.

'Well, I bet the postman is just terrified of you,' she said, pulling back the bolt and opening the door. They charged at her legs, winding around her like lumpen snakes and begging to be stroked before trotting off to the kitchen, as if already apprised of their brief.

By the time she walked back into the kitchen moments later, their mission was almost accomplished and the floor, if not exactly gleaming, was certainly no longer a slip hazard.

'What are their names?' she asked, patting their backs.

'Cuthbert's the older chap. He's almost eight and getting on now. Dibble's five. And Grubb there is from her litter. She had puppies ten months ago.'

'Cuthbert, Dibble and Grubb?' Libby echoed faintly.

'I know they probably sound odd names to you but they're actually—'

'From an old TV show. *Trumpton*, yes. My father used to watch it when he was little. Because of our surname, you see – Pugh.'

Mrs Timmock smiled, her eyes lighting up and softening her entire demeanour. 'Ah, is that so? Well now, isn't that a coincidence? Not many remember it these days. It was always Archie's mother who liked it in this house. Her father had been a fireman and of course, when Archie was a boy, he was obsessed with fire engines. He always said he wanted to be a firefighter when he grew up.' She chuckled at the memory, as if it had been an impossible wish.

Libby watched the dogs trot around the kitchen. 'Do they always stay in the crate?'

'No, rarely ever, in fact. But with all the nibbles out on low tables through there and so many people, I didn't need the chaos of keeping an eye on them while I'm trying to cook as well.'

'Understandable.'

The kettle came to the boil and Libby poured the water into the pan of peas. She set it on the boiling plate, peering into the other saucepan simmering away. 'Oh, you have some left-over gravy here.'

'Yes, I always make extra, but that still won't be enough to go around everyone. We'll have to add some water for volume and thicken it as best we can in the time we've got till the peas are done. It'll be too watery, but it can't be helped. Better than nothing.'

'Okay,' Libby said, seeing a small Pyrex jug on the counter. She brought it over to the sink again.

'You should get back to the party,' Mrs Timmock said, watching as she filled it. 'He'll be wondering where you've got to otherwise.'

Libby had to suppress a scoff as she poured the water into the gravy and began to stir. Archie Templeton wouldn't miss her company if she was the only other person in the room. His tone when speaking to her had been cool and sardonic, and he had been the only person not to greet her with a hug or a kiss. She had been in his house for almost two hours now but he had spent all that time laughing and talking with the men. 'I will, just as soon as we get straight in here. It's ridiculous, you being expected to cater for so many people without any help.'

'Well, I've managed for over twenty years.'

Libby was tempted to reply that surely that meant she had earned a rest, but she held her tongue. The dogs, satisfied they had cleaned the floor to a good standard, trotted off to a water bowl and several large tweed dog beds at the back of the kitchen, under the windows.

'It certainly sounds like everyone's having fun in there,' Mrs Timmock said as one of Coco's signature screeches of delight echoed down the long hall. It sounded like someone was chasing her. Or perhaps it was just another of her TikToks. Coco had been regaling them all earlier with the ins and outs, as well as the highs and lows of her glamorous life; she had benefited from being one of the first influencers to jump platforms from Instagram to TikTok, and had a following of six million and climbing. Libby, having taken it for a glorified ego trip, had been astonished to learn that this translated into a monetization of her image that meant she could charge up to £100,000 for a single post. Her GRWMs – Get Ready With Me reels, she'd had to explain – garnered engagement rates of over eighty per cent, and brands would immediately sell out of whatever it was she was wearing. She was gifted designer clothes, bags and make-up on a daily basis and travelled first class to six-star resorts in French Polynesia and the Seychelles, where she was invariably upgraded to the best suites. Porsche had given her the car on a year's free lease and her apartment in Notting Hill was filled with gifted lifestyle products, from the sofas and rugs to her candles and coffee machine. Libby had listened on, wondering where she had gone wrong with her crushing working weeks and industrial stress levels. Only Ems's similarly dumbstruck expression had provided any consolation that she wasn't the only one floored by the revelations.

'Oh yes. Everyone's very excited to be reunited.'

'Not you?'

Had she said that? Libby glanced over to find the older woman watching her carefully. '. . . No, I am. It's great. It's wonderful to catch up with everyone's news—'

'Teabag, how are we getting on? Roly says his stomach thinks his throat's been cu—' Archie said, walking into the kitchen. He stopped dead at the sight of the housekeeper by the sink and Libby standing by the Aga, cooking. '. . . What's going on?'

'Nothing. There was a small accident,' Libby said quickly. 'But you need new oven gloves. Those ones are worn through.'

'They are?' He looked so blank that Libby wondered if he had ever seen the oven gloves before, or indeed, even knew he had any. He looked across at the housekeeper, catching sight of the glowing red tip of her finger. He winced too, just as they had. 'Tea, are you all right?'

'I'm absolutely fine. Just as soon as it's numbed I'll be able to get on again; your pretty friend here has taken me hostage in my own kitchen.'

'So I see,' Archie murmured. 'It's gone ten, that's all. And actually Libby and Max need to leave within the hour.'

'Ten? Well . . .' Mrs Timmock said with a huff. 'Then my finger is quite numb enough,' she said staunchly turning off the tap and walking over to the Aga, taking the wooden spoon from Libby's hand and shooing her off. 'Be gone now. Have fun while you can.'

'But—'

'Archie, take her away so I can get on,' she said briskly.

Archie caught Libby's eye and raised an eyebrow, seemingly as a query of whether Libby was going to dare question her.

She was not. 'Well, I'm happy to help if you need another

pair of hands for serving out,' she said, as Archie lightly took her by the elbow and ushered her out. 'It's no trouble.'

She was met with a tut.

'You were immensely brave going into Mrs Timmock's war room,' he said as they began the long walk back to the drawing room; the clamour of voices suggested double the number of people that were actually in there. 'Most people get thrown out on their ear.'

'Well, she had hurt herself. She was quite pale when I found her.'

'It was kind of you to help like that.'

'Not really. Anyone would have done the same,' she shrugged.

She felt him glance over at her as they walked but she kept her eyes dead ahead, only too aware that this was the first time they had been alone in nine years.

He seemed to realize it too because she felt an adjustment in the air between them.

'Listen, Lib, before we go back in there . . .' There was a change in his voice, his usual laconic slur dropped as the words bore more intention. He stopped walking, forcing her to stop and turn back too. 'Seeing as we're . . . Can we just have a word alone? There's something I need to say.'

She hesitated, not wanting to look back at him; he had always been different with her when it was just the two of them, and the man standing here now bore no relation to the one blowing on a bugle a couple of hours ago. 'What's up?' She kept her tone light, casual even, though she could see the tension in his face; she knew exactly what he was building towards.

'It's about Zannah—'

Memories exploded in her mind, as vivid as ever, and she

looked away. How many times had she dry-rehearsed this very scene in her head? She knew exactly how it would go, everything he would say. 'Actually, I'd rather we didn't do this,' she said briskly.

He looked back at her in surprise. 'What?'

'It was all a long time ago and I really don't care,' she said in as steady a voice as she could muster.

'But . . .' He looked confused. 'There's something I need to tell you—'

She blinked at him, wishing her heart wouldn't pound so hard. Wishing she had never agreed to come here. How could she ever have thought that it would only be a quick dinner, a convenient diversion off the motorway? It was a slip road off her life, the one she had worked so hard to build for herself. She put a hand on his arm, stopping him. 'Don't. Save us both the awkwardness. None of it matters any more, it's irrelevant.' She shrugged, turning away again.

'Lib, please—' He reached for her arm but she slipped through his grasp. Now, as then.

'Just leave it, Archie,' she said over her shoulder. 'It's all just blood under the bridge.'

The gong finally sounded at ten twenty and everyone moved in slow straggles towards the dining room. Max and Prock were bonding over the Six Nations and the new Ferrari 296 that neither of them would ever own; Charlie was listening to Ems talking about baby car seats as Grubb trotted between them, nose to the ground for any stray crisp crumbs.

Libby wandered through in a perfumed cloud with Coco, their heads bent together in gossip as they stepped into a dark-panelled dining room. It had a grand and noble ambience with huge nineteenth-century oils of landscapes and fully rigged trading ships illuminated beneath picture lights, candles flickering in ornate and heavy silver candelabras. A couple of limestone busts of historic war generals stood on grooved mahogany pillars by the windows and a still-plush Tabriz rug was laid beneath the eighteen-seater mahogany table; apparently – according to Zannah – several of the central leaves had been removed and stored to accommodate the smaller party this evening, lending a more intimate atmosphere to the space. Libby could easily imagine the Templeton ancestors in their empire-line silk dresses or Victorian crinolines, convening here just like them.

The fire was roaring away, and an arrangement of fresh ivy tendrils, eucalyptus, fir and holly berries slunk the length of the table, which was dressed with white linen and silverware, crystal glasses glowing amber as they reflected the flames from the fireplace.

'Is there a seating plan, Arch?' Zannah called over to him as he and the other men ambled into the room, their voices a low rumble.

Libby watched her, seeing how she commanded the space, quietly at home here. Already she regretted her haste in escaping Archie. What was it he had wanted to tell her about Zannah? Or could she guess?

'Oh . . . Yes,' he said, looking blank for a moment as his eyes scanned the group. He had polished off several quick drinks since they'd returned from the kitchen and he was back to being the emceé of the night: witty, lively, the Archie of old. 'Uh . . . How many are we?' he counted. 'Eight . . . ?'

'Nine,' Libby said quickly, not wanting Max to be excluded.

His eyes met hers only for a moment. 'Nine, yes. So then I think we're . . .' He cast around again. 'Boy-heavy. Right, well if I'm at the head here . . . Coco, you sit here beside me on my right. Then Prock on your other side, Lib and then Roly . . .'

Libby watched him organize their guests with effortless ease, even while drunk. How many dinners did he host a season? A week, even? Was it coincidence he had sat her as far away from him as possible? Petty revenge?

'Then Ems to my left, Max and then Zannah . . . and then Charlie. That works, doesn't it? No one's sitting next to their significant other and being bored to buggery? That is the point of coming out, after all – not having to endure another bloody meal together.'

'Oh, poor Arch,' Ems crooned pityingly, patting his shoulder. 'It's actually a lovely thing, true intimacy. You should give it a go sometime.'

The others laughed, Rollo playfully cuffing Archie about the head as Ems took her place beside him at the table. Libby turned her head slightly as Max came over to her, his hand trailing lightly over her hips. 'We'll need to leave before pudding,' he murmured in her ear. 'It's getting late; we need to be on the road again by eleven.'

'I know,' she whispered back.

She waited for him to leave but he didn't stir and as she turned back to him questioningly, he leaned in and kissed her lightly on the lips before walking around the far end of the table and taking his seat on the other side. Libby watched him, faintly puzzled. He had never done that before, kiss her in public. Or even hold her hand.

'Well, look at you lovebirds,' Roly muttered, pulling out her chair for her.

'No one on the horizon for you?' she asked, drawing her napkin across her lap as he settled himself beside her.

'Lib, the only thing on my horizon is high-flying pheasants.'

She had to grin. 'Well, are you on any apps at least?'

'Hmm. I gave Hinge a go,' he said slowly, dropping his chin to his chest, almost in apology.

'Oh?' she asked, matching his ominous tone.

'Mm. I had to complete the statement "My most controversial opinion is . . ."'

She winced. 'Oh god. What did you say?'

'That the future of the food economy lies in hydroponics and insect farming.'

She was silent for a moment. 'Right.'

'Yeah. A real conversation starter, I thought.'

'Indeed. How did you follow up after that?'

'Well, the next prompt was my *go-to* karaoke song.' He gave a laugh as though it was a contradiction in terms.

'And you put . . . ?'

'Black Sabbath's "War Pigs", naturally.'

'Naturally,' she nodded. She could still remember Ozzy Osborne's screams coming through the walls in their tiny student house. 'And . . . any matches?'

'Not really.' He looked baffled.

'No,' she nodded again. 'So you're off Hinge now, then?'

'Mm, think it's better if I don't say too much and just . . . look pretty, you know?'

She couldn't help but laugh. In contrast to Charlie's beachy, fine-chiselled features, Prock's boyish good looks and Archie's Byronesque, brooding villain vibes, Rollo had the full-cheeked, ruddy face of a man whose life was spent standing in salmon rivers and dairy barns. He had been a formidable fast bowler in his school's First XI and much legend had been attached to his scrummaging prowess at uni, but in his own words, he was 'no looker'. He typically described himself as 'gouty', a terrible self-disparagement, and the girls had all tried through the years to convince him that his hooded, pale blue eyes were beautiful and his teeth were whiter than white, in spite of the fact he drank claret like it was Ribena.

'Well, good plan, I like it.' She jogged him with her elbow. 'The right woman's out there, Roly. Don't give up.'

'I'm not so sure,' he sighed. 'I'm beginning to wonder if she got hit by a bus when she was twelve or something.'

Her attention was caught by the sight of Zannah coming in holding two plates of food, followed by Mrs Timmock pushing a two-tiered cake trolley stacked with the rest. Between them the two women set the plates down in front of each guest, moving around the table as if in a well-practised dance. Libby watched, seeing their familiarity with one another. Was Zannah just being a good guest?

'Eat up now,' the housekeeper said, setting down Libby's. 'Don't let it go cold.'

Libby looked at her plate of lamb, peas and roast potatoes. She appeared to have one more potato than everyone else. She saw Rollo notice it too.

'What did you do to get in Tea's good books?' he murmured, looking at her suspiciously.

Her duties completed, Zannah sat down opposite, fussing with her napkin as Charlie went to pour her a glass of wine and the housekeeper rattled the trolley cart back out again. 'Ah-ah, just vodka tonic for me,' she said, covering her glass quickly. 'I like to keep it clean.'

'Is that your secret, then?' Libby asked, determined to ignite a conversation between them. Despite the enthusiastic greeting, Zannah had been strangely elusive and Libby had scarcely exchanged two words with her directly. 'Spirits only?'

'That and Pilates. I swear by it. Reformer machines, though,' Zannah clarified quickly. 'Mat Pilates does nothing for me.'

'Really? I keep meaning to try that.'

'Oh you must. They're amazing. *Amazing!*'

'Well, if you're the advert then consider me influenced. I need to start trying to get into some sort of self-care regimen.'

'What are you talking about? You look incredible. A goddess!'

Libby glanced at her as she took a sip of her drink. Zannah was effusive with her compliments but they felt somehow . . . deflective. It was like talking with a promotions manager or a holiday rep. Everything was *incredible!* 'Yeah well, my days can be really long and I know it's not good for me in the long term. I do need to start taking better care of myself.'

'True that,' Zannah sighed, fussing with her napkin again. 'We're all guilty of running ourselves into the ground, aren't we?'

'Have you got any holidays coming up?'

'Actually yes. A few weeks in Switzerland in the new year. A sort of detox clinic.'

'That sounds good.'

'Mm, it's a bit hardcore though. Not much fun. But one must suffer, right?'

'Christ, it's not one of those places that makes you drink green liquid and sticks a hose-pipe up your bum, is it?' Rollo asked.

'Nicely put, Roly – and no, it isn't.'

'Everyone, time to pull!' Archie called from the top of the table, holding up a pair of crackers.

They all crossed arms and pulled on cue, Libby 'winning' both of hers. Magnanimously, she gave Prock her spare crown, plastic bottle-opener and bad joke. She pulled the purple crown onto her hair and they all began to eat Mrs Timmock's stream-lined roast lamb.

The conversation opened up across the table and Libby listened intently as Zannah, Rollo and Charlie chatted easily, with the familiarity that comes from seeing one another regularly. They seemed to know what Zannah was referring to when she discussed a conference in the summer, and they automatically knew the identity of Rollo's latest ex as he detailed their disastrous break-up. Libby felt her self-imposed isolation like a sharp pinch; she had missed so much.

She looked around the table as the conversation flowed and plates were quickly emptied, the prolonged drinks in the drawing room ensuring everyone had an appetite. The minutiae of what they discussed might have changed, but the dynamics between them all were much as she remembered: Charlie still looking up the table every few moments to steal a look at Coco; Ems still finishing Prock's sentences for him; Archie ever the louche host, always slightly bored, a restless, Gatsbyesque spirit at his own parties; Rollo masking his loneliness with innuendo and bawdy jokes; Zannah, flighty and impossible to pin down.

'Babe, can I smoke?' Coco asked Archie.

'Sure,' he said, stretching, his arms opening long and wide as he looked down the table at the convivial scene. His eyes came to rest on Libby briefly before lifting off again in the next moment.

'Have you got a ligh— Oh, don't worry, I see them.' Coco pushed her chair back and walked over to the chestnut server, where a box of matches had been left. She lit up, shaking the flame out, her gaze falling to a silver punch bowl stamped with the Templeton family crest. 'Hey, what's this?' she asked, reaching her hand in and pulling out a folded strip of paper.

'Huh?' Archie glanced back over his shoulder and gave a groan. 'Oh, that. My little cousins were over the other week, so we got into a game of Would You Rather . . . ?'

'Don't say it like that. It was very sweet,' Zannah chided.

'I love that game!' Coco breathed excitedly.

'You do?' He gave her a sceptical look.

'Yes, oh let's play a round!' Coco stuck the cigarette in her mouth and brought the bowl over to the table. 'Everyone, we're going to play Would You Rather,' she announced, the cigarette waggling up and down between her lips as she spoke.

Max met Libby's eyes in alarm, his eyebrow twitching just so to indicate that they needed to make a move . . . Libby nodded and cleared her throat. 'Guys, before you do, I'm afraid we're going to have to get going—'

'No!' Coco cried dramatically again, betraying now the too-numerous drinks she had had while waiting for dinner.

Libby met Archie's gaze again, this time with an apology in her eyes. He was their host; she knew he knew they had to leave . . .

'Just one round,' Coco insisted. 'A good game's a quick game, I always say.'

'Funny, that's exactly what I say about sex,' Rollo remarked.

'Yes, so your girlfriends have told us, Roly,' Prock rejoindered with a chuckle.

'Surely you can stay for just a few minutes more?' Ems asked, weighing in. 'We've literally only just eaten.'

Libby wanted to point out that that wasn't her fault; she and Max had been here on time for seven thirty. Nevertheless, staying for drinks and a single plate of food did feel inadequate after a decade's separation – and she had enjoyed these past few hours so much more than she'd expected, the brief step back into her past reminding her of the good times they had shared, when for nine years she had thought only of the bad . . .

'Fine,' she conceded, drawing a displeased look from Max. 'But just one round.'

'Yay! Arch, remind us how we play this,' Coco said, falling

back into her chair as if she'd exhausted herself, the ash on her cigarette growing alarmingly long.

'Everyone takes a paper from the bowl,' Archie said distractedly, reaching for the cigarette from between her lips and flicking the ash onto the dinner plate; he took a drag himself before handing it back to her, and Libby was reminded of that time long ago when he'd caught a dribble of butter on Coco's cheek and sucked it off his finger. They shared an easy, uncomplicated intimacy, but more like siblings than anything else. 'We'll take turns reading them out and you can choose who you want to ask.'

Max threw another look in Libby's direction as the bowl was passed around and he tapped discreetly at his wristwatch. Ten fifty-five, it was showing.

'I'll go first to get us going, seeing as it was my idea,' Coco slurred, opening up the first paper and reading it quickly. A small smile spread across her lips as she looked up. 'Right, um . . . Zannah, this one's for you – would you rather only ever be able to shout, or only ever be able to whisper?'

Everyone laughed. It wasn't exactly a dilemma. 'Shout, obviously,' Zannah drawled. 'As if *I'm* going to spend my life not being heard.'

'Chance would be a fine thing,' Archie quipped, winking quickly at Zannah as she shot him a glare.

'Well, haters are gonna hate anyway, right?' Zannah shrugged.

'My go,' Archie murmured, lounging back in his chair and taking the bowl from Coco. He was wearing the crown again – or was it a coronet? – from earlier, though it was slightly lopsided now, his sprawling frame and velvet jacket conjuring a careless insouciance. '. . . Huh. Okay.' He grinned. 'You can tell these were written with eleven-year-olds in mind.' He quickly scanned his guests. 'Charlie . . . would you rather have a permanent big splinter under your toe, or a permanent bad haircut?'

Ems pushed her chair back with a sigh. 'Don't mind me. I need the loo, *again*.'

Libby saw Prock watch his wife as she left the room, waddling slightly; she looked uncomfortable.

Charlie winced and laughed, lacing his hands behind his head as he considered it. 'I'd have to go with the bad haircut.'

'Wow, no hesitations! Impressive,' Ems said.

'Well, who wants to live in pain?' he shrugged. 'A bad haircut grows out. I figure it'd be a few days of shame? I hope I'm not so vain that I'd choose ego over peace.'

'Ha, we can tell you lived in California,' Zannah smiled, patting his hand approvingly.

'Yeah, style it out, baby!' Coco said, waggling her shoulders forward and inadvertently flashing a view of her cleavage. Libby watched as she reached for her drink, forgetting the joke in the next instant, unaware of Charlie's eyes still on her.

Max gave an appealingly modest smile as he unrolled his paper. 'Okay, um . . .' He gave a laugh of amusement. 'Well, I'm going to have to say Elizabeth.'

Libby saw the others startle a little as he used her given name; they had only really ever known her as Libby.

'Would you rather spend the rest of your life with your most hated enemy . . . or live on the streets?'

'Live on the streets,' she said without missing a beat and shrugging too, as if to question that it was even a question. 'To misquote Charlie, I hope I'm not so pathetic that I'd choose drama over peace.'

'Oh my god, now I want to know about your enemies and all the drama!' Zannah proclaimed, arching an eyebrow.

Libby just smiled and looked away. It wasn't something she could laugh about, not with her.

'Oh, is it my turn?' Zannah asked as Max passed her the bowl. '. . . Oh Jesus,' she snorted, looking down at Archie just as Ems came back in again. 'Um, so Roly, tell me, would you rather wash dishes with your tongue . . .'

'Ewww!' everyone recoiled.

Zannah looked up, her eyes shining with laughter. '. . . Or wash your pet with your tongue?'

The room erupted, especially as Ems started dry-heaving.

'No!' Prock protested, laughing and trying to comfort his wife at the same time. 'Please don't answer that.'

'That's so gross,' Charlie laughed as Ems fled the room again.

Rollo put a hand to his chin as he contemplated what was truly a dilemma. He looked at their dirty plates with a slightly appalled expression. '. . . I'm going to have to go with the pet.'

'Oh god, Roly, no!' Zannah cried.

'Yes, because for the purposes of this game only, I am the proud and devoted owner of a Mexican Hairless Chihuahua.'

'I don't think that's any consolation, to be honest,' Prock laughed.

'Okay Charlie, you're up,' Coco said from the other end of the table.

They all waited as he read his paper strip. He thought for a moment, then looked thoughtfully down the table. 'One for you, I think, Max . . . Would you rather . . . marry the hottest person alive? Or the smartest person alive?'

'Hmm,' Rollo breathed beside Libby, lacing his fingers together. 'This will be revealing.'

'What if they're one and the same?' Max asked, stunning Libby by looking directly and overtly at her. A collective gasp went around the women, Coco excitedly drumming her stiletto heels on the ancient floor; Libby was more circumspect. She knew Max was playing to the crowd; he was good at reading a room and he always instinctively knew the play to make. He knew her friends were watching them, assessing him; he could play the lover when he needed to.

'You've got to choose, old chap,' Prock insisted.

Max kept his eyes upon her for another moment before looking back at Charlie with a grin. 'Hottest.'

Rollo and Prock erupted, whistling between their fingers. 'Yes! Yes!'

'Interesting,' Libby grinned as Max's gaze came back to her again. He was laughing, knowing full well their 'thing' was intellectual competition; he liked that she matched him – sometimes beat him – and the sexual tension had built up between them precisely because she wouldn't let him dominate her. So to say he would ultimately choose looks over brains was provocative, to say the least.

'Roly, your go,' Zannah commanded now, but her gaze kept sliding over to Libby.

There was an expectant hush as Rollo took his time unravelling the paper, his smile slow upon his lips.

'Archie, me old mucker,' he said, his blue eyes shining. 'Would you rather . . . go back and change one thing in your past . . . or have a real Get Out of Jail Free card?'

Libby tensed, watching as Archie sat back in his chair and drummed his fingers on the table, everyone excitedly pondering on the debate. Reform something from his past – in which everyone knew there were numerous mistakes, errors and regrets – or save his possible future . . . ?

She stared at the tablecloth, feeling her heart pound as he looked at Rollo and at Zannah. At Charlie, Ems, Prock and Coco. Everyone but her.

He threw his hands up. 'Well, there's no question – Get Out of Jail Free card . . . Obviously.'

'Obviously!' Rollo cried in comradeship. 'The past is another country, my friend! What's done is done and can't be undone. And through it all, the world keeps on turning.'

Libby didn't stir, but she felt a heaviness settle within her and she wished – she bitterly wished – they hadn't stayed for this game after all; that she had quit while she was ahead and exited before old wounds could be reopened and excoriated.

'Libs?'

She looked up, feeling a hand on her arm, to find Rollo holding the bowl out for her. 'Oh.' She reached for a paper, shaken and wishing this wasn't the moment to have the room's attention focused on her. She glanced at Max to find him watching her intently, his hands pitched into a steeple and his eyes slightly narrowed, as they were in meetings.

But her upset wasn't to last, for what she read made her laugh out loud. '. . . Ha!' She pressed a hand to her mouth as she felt a giggle bubble in her throat and she looked down the table. 'Ems . . .'

'Oh god. What?' Ems murmured, her hand already reaching to her mouth.

'Would you rather buy your underwear used, or your toothbrushes used?'

Immediately Ems slapped a hand over her mouth, shoulders held high as she tried not to retch – which only made everyone dissolve into hysterics. 'Why would you ask me that?' Ems wailed when she could finally speak.

'You have to give an answer!' Coco insisted.

'Fine . . . toothbrushes . . . No! Underwear,' she corrected. '. . . No wait, toothbrushes!' She began retching again and as she jumped up, Prock wrapped his arms protectively around his wife and pulled her onto his lap.

'My darling Ems,' he sympathized, trying to keep from laughing as she kept her hand clamped across her mouth.

Libby looked around at the scene – everyone dressed in their finery, seated in this beautiful room in this historic house, silverware glittering, expensive highlights, and a baby gestating for two of them. How far they had come from their student days! Well, all apart from Archie, who had grown up at this table; he hadn't travelled anywhere. Hadn't he told her there was nothing more for him than this? But for the rest of them, for her – coming from a box room in her parents' small Victorian terraced house – they were a world away from that cramped basement kitchen, where only three could get around the table and the shelves were never full, where the front door slammed almost every fifteen minutes as someone came in and someone else went out. Back then, they had all been in their chrysalises, adults but not, thinking they were so ready to take on the big wide world and the land of law, business and tax. They had been babies, and yet how much had they really changed from those days? Ems still sat on Prock's lap. Charlie was still hopelessly in love with Coco. Rollo was still, well, hopeless. And Zannah . . . ?

Zannah was still with Archie, she was certain of it. There were no overt signs they were a couple – was it simply taken as understood by the others? Perhaps they had all known for years and it simply didn't need to be said, and yet she felt sure Charlie would have told her. Warned her. No, there was something furtive about them, even though Zannah moved through the house with the surety of the chatelaine. She was 'in' with Mrs T. And she had been here before the rest of them, when Archie's little cousins had visited the other week . . .

Libby knew she had her answer: nothing had changed in nine years. Nothing at all.

'Right, last two,' Archie said as Ems went back to her seat.

'Okay,' Prock sighed, reading it, a low chuckle escaping him. 'Coco . . .' he managed before dissolving into another fit of laughter. 'I'm sorry to ask this of you, of all people, but you haven't had a turn yet. So tell me – and blame the eleven-year-olds – would you rather suffer silent uncontrollable farting . . . or constant sneezing?'

He could barely get the words out, he was laughing so hard. Of all the questions to ask the most glamorous guest!

'Why, silent uncontrollable farting, of course!' Coco's eyes were sparkling with laughter as she took in their shocked expressions.

'*No!*' Charlie cried. '*You'd* choose that?'

'Of course I would! Constantly sneezing would be so hideous for me, but the farting would just be a trial for you! I hope I'm not so vain that I would choose ego over peace,' she grinned, quoting Charlie's own words back at him with a wink.

Archie, with tears in his eyes from laughing so hard, reached over and kissed her temple. Libby saw Charlie sit back in his chair and take a swig of his drink.

'Well, darling girl,' Archie drawled, 'it's only fitting that you should finish the first round, after such an epic response. Who are you going to pick? Everyone's had a turn but because we're an odd number, someone can go again.'

'Hmm,' Coco mused as she read the final dilemma. 'Well actually, Arch, I think I'm going to ask this of you!'

'Oh god,' he groaned. 'Me and my big mouth.'

'Ha! Serves you right, Templeton,' Prock chuckled.

'Archie Templeton, would you rather always say what you're thinking . . . or never say anything again?'

Archie's jaw slid slowly to the side, his eyes narrowing thoughtfully.

'I already know what you're going to say,' Coco laughed confidently.

'Do you?'

'Of course. You'd always say what you were thinking!'

He held up a finger. 'Actually, I was going to say I'd never say anything again.'

Coco and Ems gasped. 'You would not!' Coco argued.

'You big fat liar! You love the sound of your own voice far too much to ever shut up, Arch!' Ems admonished him.

'Thanks, both.' He winced. 'But it might surprise you to know I'm a deeply misunderstood man.'

Libby watched him closely.

'Yeah, right,' Zannah grinned, shaking her head.

'I am. People would be shocked if they actually knew what went through my head.'

'Ah, but you've got an image to protect, is that right?'

'Exactly,' he agreed. 'Far better to let people think what they want to think. There's power in being underestimated.'

Libby stared at him as he reached for his drink and drained it – *she* had said that to him once. Did he remember? But this time, he didn't look her way.

Across the table, someone cleared their throat and she looked up to find Max's stare upon her as he pushed his chair back. 'Well, everyone, that was brilliant fun,' he said. 'But I'm afraid now we really do have to leave.'

'I cannot believe you're driving back to London now,' Ems sighed. 'It'll be dawn by the time you get there.'

He shrugged. 'We can sleep in, though, once we're home.'

Home. The word seemed to vibrate. He was implying a settled domesticity to their relationship that simply wasn't the case. Was this for her benefit, in front of her friends, she wondered? Or his?

She rose too. 'I'm so sorry to break up the party, guys.'

'But we're just getting started!' Coco cried, throwing her arms in the air and sloshing drink on the rug, holding the pose for a moment as if she expected to hear the click of a camera shutter.

'Next time, I promise,' Libby said, reaching down and hugging Rollo first.

'Oh, *can't* you go back after breakfast?' Coco continued to beg. 'There's a million rooms here, isn't that right, Arch?'

He gave a lackadaisical shrug. 'If they must leave, then leave they must.' And he pushed his chair back and stood up, ready to see them out. Max began shaking hands with the men.

'I can't believe this,' Coco said, coming over to her with a sad face and dropping over her like a parched sunflower. 'I thought we had hours yet. There's still so much I want to talk to you about.'

'We'll have lunch. Or dinner. When you're back from Oman.'

'Yeah, yeah, yeah, likely story,' Ems drawled, joining in the hug. 'We've all heard that before . . . *And she was never seen again,*' she said in a dramatic voice, waving an arm towards a distant horizon.

Libby shot her a look. 'I promise, okay? I know I've been rubbish at staying in touch, but this has been *so* lovely. I've loved seeing you all. Just give me a date and I'll be there.'

'I'll walk you out,' Zannah said, turning back to the others and seeing how they moved as a huddle behind them. 'No, stay in here, guys, don't come out into the cold.'

'Merry Christmas,' Libby said, giving a small, rueful wave as she turned into the hall and out of sight.

Archie and Max were walking ahead, side by side, and talking in low voices; Archie's hands were stuffed in his pockets as if he was wandering around the vegetable garden, and Max looked like he was about to head into a client meeting. Seeing them together felt strange – Archie was all lanky silhouette, Max's physique powerful and stocky by comparison.

Zannah fell into step beside her and Libby felt again that faint hum of tension between them, of a silence weighted with unspoken words. They had talked without connection tonight, exclamations drowning out what needed to be whispered. The past sat between them like a grenade with the pin pulled out, and she sensed they were still bracing for the bang.

'It's been so good seeing you, Libby,' Zannah began. 'You look really happy. It seems you got everything you ever wanted. The career, the guy . . .'

'I guess so,' Libby agreed.

'. . . Do you think he's the one?'

Libby was surprised by the question, partly because Zannah had never believed in soulmates. 'Love the one you're with,' had always been her motto. 'I have no idea,' she murmured, anxious that Max might overhear. 'I haven't thought about it in those terms.'

'But was it like a kick in the guts when you first saw him?'

Libby stared at her for a long moment before looking away again. Words from the past kept rising up like ghosts tonight, it seemed. '. . . Well, I'm not big on love at first sight as a model for a relationship. We got to know each other first. We work together, so that can be a pretty revealing stress test.'

'Yeah, I bet.'

The men were already at the front door now, shaking hands, and Libby turned to Zannah quickly for a hug. It was brief and wooden, Zannah feeling so different in her arms to the friend she had once known as they had looped arms, drunkenly weaving up the back streets and picking each other up from sticky club floors. Now she was all fashionable hard angles and a perfect winged eye, a modern mistress-in-waiting for this old house.

'Well, it was great seeing you again,' Libby smiled. 'We must meet up in the new year.'

'Absolutely,' Zannah nodded.

She turned to Archie. 'Arch, great seeing you. And thanks for a great night. Will you thank Mrs T for me? Dinner was great.' She winced. How many times had she just said 'great'?

'Of course,' he nodded vigorously, his hand still in his trouser pocket as he leaned over and awkwardly gave her a one-armed hug. 'Good to see you, Pugh. Must do it again. Safe travels.' His gaze tangled with hers briefly and it felt like catching her hand on a rose bush, the thorns grazing her skin and drawing tiny beads of blood to the surface.

He opened the door fractionally – having to kick away a tartan draught excluder that had been laid along the base – but it was just enough for a sharp gust of arctic wind to zip in and make them all shiver. Max pulled his tailcoat closer. Once again, Libby regretted coming out in only her thin silk dress.

'We'd better run to the car,' Max called over his shoulder to her. 'Don't wait to wave us off, you two, you'll die of exposure.'

Archie nodded in agreement, opening the door wider now. He switched on a light and the old coach lantern above the door illuminated the view down the steps.

'Oh, holy fuck!'

They all looked out at the scene in disbelief. Where the giant Portland stone lions had lain, now there were only soft, white, indistinct lumps, the cars all buried into assorted mounds, thick snowflakes furiously pirouetting past in the light beams and showing no signs of slowing down.

'What . . . ? But when . . . ?' Max uttered in disbelief, his voice a croak as he looked back at Archie.

'Ah.' Archie gave a sigh and shoved his other hand into his pocket. It was a moment before anyone could speak as the reality of the situation impressed itself upon them all. Even if they could get out of the drive – which they couldn't – there was no way the long country lane leading down from here would be passable yet; the gritters would be focusing on the motorways and A roads tonight.

'Right.' Archie exhaled, his body sagging against the door. 'Well, I'm afraid that's that, then. Your escape is postponed. You're stuck here tonight, whether you like it or not,' he murmured, his gaze drifting from Max over to Libby and bouncing straight off again in the next moment, refusing – unlike the snow – to settle.

'You changed your minds!' Ems gasped, throwing her hands up in delight as they walked back into the dining room.

Charlie, Prock, Ems, Rollo and Coco had abandoned the seating plan and were now gathered in a huddle at the end of the table. Ems had her stockinged feet in Prock's lap; Roly was still wearing his orange paper crown. Coco leaped up and gave an excited squeal.

'Not exactly. The weather decided for us,' Libby said, jerking her head towards the window.

'What do you mean?' Charlie frowned, getting up and walking over to have a look outside. He had to press his face to the glass to see out into the pitch darkness. 'Oh, holy shit!'

'Yes, quite,' Max sighed. 'That's what Archie said.'

Charlie looked back in shock. 'When did that happen?'

'Apparently, in the last three and a half hours.' Max's terse tone conveyed his irritation and Libby watched as Ems pressed her hands to her open mouth, her eyes wide like Munch's *The Scream* as she looked between the two of them.

'What does it mean?' she asked quietly, sensing that this wasn't the good news they had all first assumed. Max ran his hand through his hair and began to pace. Rollo got up and poured a fresh glass of wine.

'Well, they're definitely not going anywhere tonight,' Zannah said, throwing a log on the fire and stoking it with the poker. The chatelaine again. 'Even if we could dig them out, there'd be no chance of getting down the lane.'

'Absolutely not, you'd be sleeping in the car overnight, that's for sure,' Charlie agreed, still standing by the window and watching the snow fall. 'No point risking it. It's a full-scale blizzard out there.'

'Don't worry, we're pretty used to it up here,' Prock said. 'I know a snowflake falling on Oxford Street counts as a white Christmas down south, but it takes more than that to make a Yorkshire man put his big coat on. The farmer will clear the local roads in the morning, you'll be fine,' he continued with his usual brisk optimism, jigging his leg a little and squeezing his wife's feet.

'Yep,' Max sighed. 'I guess so.' He stopped pacing and loosened his tie, rolling out his shoulders.

'Did you have somewhere you need to be first thing?' Coco asked him, as everyone picked up on his irritation.

'First thing? No,' Max shook his head. 'But I've got a lunch appointment with my father and stepmother in Richmond at one.'

'Lunch appointment?' she giggled. 'You're so formal, Max.'

Lunch? Stepmother? Libby watched him undo his top button. This was the first she had heard of either of these two things. Was he just making up excuses to justify a quick getaway?

'Well, at least you won't want for somewhere to sleep. This place has more bedrooms than you can shake a stick at,' Rollo said, handing him a brandy. 'Go on, drink up, old chap. You might as well make a fist of it and have one of these, seeing as you're not hitting the road tonight after all.'

Max took the glass, sipping it first and then, seeming to think better of it, draining the lot.

Rollo gave an approving cheer and poured him another one. 'That's the spirit!'

Charlie leaned forward and refilled Libby's wine glass too. 'Bottoms up, Libs.'

She toasted her glass towards him and took a sip, wondering suddenly where Archie was. He hadn't rejoined them . . .

Her gaze fell to the crack in the open door and she glimpsed Archie still standing out in the hall. He was motionless, staring at the floor and lost in thought.

'Hey, where's Arch?' Rollo asked suddenly, noticing his absence too; he was never long without his wingman. 'Arch!'

Archie jolted at the shout and she watched as his body straightened and he took a breath. He ran a hand through his hair and replaced the coronet at its lopsided angle. A moment later he pushed open the door and sauntered through, that hand back in its pocket. 'Right,' he announced, bringing a smile to his eyes. 'The night is young! I say we should play another game.'

Chapter Seven

April 2014

There was a light knock.

'Pugh, Pugh, Barney McGrew . . .'

She looked up to find Archie peering round her door. 'Cuthbert, Dibble and Grubb,' she replied, leaning back in her chair.

It was his turn to look surprised. 'You know *Trumpton*?' he asked in amazement. 'No one knows *Trumpton*!'

'Well, I do. It was my father's favourite TV programme when he was little. Obviously because of the name connection. He often played it to us when we were kids.'

'Huh. It was my mother's. Because of the fire engines.'

'Really?' It seemed odd to her that his mother had been intrigued by the fire engines, but they stared at one another for a few moments, amazed to find themselves bonded by such an unlikely source.

'Uh—' He broke the deadlock, holding something up. 'Your lighter.'

'You're actually returning it?' she asked, bemused. 'Even though I told you I don't need it?'

He stepped into the room and handed it to her. 'I'm a man of my word,' he shrugged. 'My word is my bond.'

'Clearly . . . Well, thanks.'

She watched as he shoved a hand into his jeans pocket and began to walk slowly around her small living room again. She spun round in her chair and waited, feeling both delighted and terrified that he was back up here and wasn't rushing straight off.

'So you're working, are you?' he asked, seeing the papers spread out on her desk.

'Is a bear Catholic?'

He gave a small laugh, looking back at her with lively eyes. 'What are you working on?'

'I'm going over the principles of the laws of restitution.'

He raised his eyebrows. 'Well, I'd offer to study-buddy for you but I could only help with spelling, perhaps.'

She watched as he walked over to her bookcase and began reading the spines of her books. 'Are you going out tonight?' she asked him.

'No,' he said after a moment. 'Charlie's bet, remember?'

'Well, yes, but it's not a bet of isolation. How can you meet anyone if you don't go out?'

'Going home alone rather takes away the fun of it.'

'As I recall, his point was that a period of abstinence might re-direct your focus onto connection, rather than endless conquests.'

Archie turned back, pinning her with a direct look. 'No, he just didn't want me getting any ideas about dating Coco.'

Libby was taken aback. How had he known that? 'Ah . . . So you know, then.'

'Naturally,' he shrugged. 'Although I'm offended he doesn't seem to realize I wouldn't go for her because he's my mate; he could have just asked.'

Libby blinked. Did this imply that he would go for Coco otherwise? 'Why did you take the bet, then?'

'Because it was a bet. And there's a grand in it.'

'Are you obliged to take every bet that's put to you?'

He shrugged, watching her. 'You approach life asking "why?" – my take is "why not?"'

'So then we're opposites.'

'Seems so.'

'Well, I'm stunned. I really am,' she said sardonically.

He threw her a ghost smile, turning back to the bookcase. '. . . You can't have read all these?' He ran a finger along the spines as if they were piano keys.

'Sorry to disappoint you but yes, I have.'

'Do you intend on *re*reading them?'

'Probably not.'

He straightened up. 'So why bring them here?'

She shrugged, having to think before she answered; no one had ever asked her that before. 'Because there's a world in each one and each time I look at them, it's like I can step back into them, like an old photo of somewhere I've been.'

'So it's a comfort thing?'

'Yes, I guess it is.'

He nodded thoughtfully. 'I find small rooms comforting,' he said after a moment. 'Like this one.'

'This is small to you?'

Her question drew a laugh, but it wasn't unkind. 'Yes . . . It isn't to you?'

'Not really.' It was the size of her front room back home.

Their eyes connected again. Opposites in every way.

He turned back to the books. 'You're so smart. You really read this?' He was holding up her copy of Goethe's *Faust*. 'For pleasure?'

'Yes. Only in English though, not the German, I'm afraid.' She cracked a grin. 'So I'm not that smart.'

He rolled his eyes as he flicked through the pages. 'But what even made you want to read it? You're not doing English; you want to be a lawyer.'

'I was just interested in the concept of a man selling his soul,' she shrugged.

'Ah,' he grinned. 'Right, yes I see it now. That is of course perfect training for law.'

She laughed out loud at the joke. He was witty. Sharp. Just from this one conversation he had betrayed that he was astute, honourable and loyal to his friends too . . . He was so much more than he showed. Why did he hide under this playboy act?

He put the book back and sank onto the arm of her reading chair, watching her. 'You know, it's my twenty-first in a few weeks.'

'I didn't know.'

'I'm having a dinner. Black tie thing.'

'Naturally.'

'. . . I want you to come.'

There was a short pause. 'Oh.'

'Oh . . . ?' He frowned. 'As in, oh, thanks, I'll be there?'

She looked away. 'Listen, it's really nice of you to ask—'

'Nice? I'm not nice!'

'—and I do appreciate it.'

'You appreciate it?'

She sighed. 'Don't waste a seat on me.'

'. . . Don't *waste a seat*?' he echoed, frowning hard. 'What does that even mean?'

'It means I wouldn't know anyone, and there'll be so many other people who would die to be there in my place.'

'I don't care whether they die or not. I want you to be there.'

'You wouldn't even see me,' she argued.

'Of course I would. I'd make sure I did.'

'Okay, fine. Maybe you'd wave across the room or something when I arrived, but the reality is I'd spend the night trapped with a bunch of toffs all talking among themselves and—'

'Hey! Just stop right there.' He held a hand up to silence her, a deep frown puckering his brow. 'I didn't take you for a bigot.'

'I'm not!'

'No? Do you know how many assumptions you've just made? One, that I wouldn't be looking for you. Two, that I wouldn't bother joining you. Three, that my friends are shallow and cruel.' He counted on his fingers. 'You've got one hell of a chip on your shoulder, Pugh.'

She swallowed. Pugh? Why did he do that – talk to her like one of his public schoolboy mates? Why didn't he call her Libby, like everyone else? He didn't call Coco or Zannah or Ems by their surnames.

'Perhaps you might want to take a moment to consider that they'd be intimidated by you.'

She went to give a dismissive scoff but he stopped her again. 'You're smarter than anyone I know – with the exception maybe of Earnshaw. You're ballsy, driven, relentless. Cut them some slack, okay?' He stared back at her with a level gaze, her heart pounding at the compliments – but it was what he hadn't said that bothered her: sexy. Beautiful. Funny . . . She was none of those things to him.

'And besides, everyone here is coming too – it's an open invitation to you all, naturally, so you'll know at least seven people there.' He gestured vaguely towards the house. 'But I'm asking you specifically because I know you wouldn't come otherwise, and I want you to be there. I'm the birthday boy, and what I say goes – for that one night, at least.' He got up from the chair and walked over to her. 'Yes?'

She stared at him, wishing her heart rate didn't spike with his proximity. Or mere presence. She wasn't used to him sober. Drunk or hungover; those were the only modes of his she had ever encountered. '. . . Why? Why does it matter to you all of a sudden? We've lived together for seven months and barely exchanged ten sentences. And now you *must* have me at your twenty-first?'

He inhaled sharply, his eyes never leaving her. 'I just like talking to you. And I didn't know that before.'

Talking. She was good for talking to. '. . . And if I tell you I have nothing to wear?'

A small light darted through his eyes and she saw his answer before he said it. *So then wear that.* It was a very Archie Templeton response.

Only he didn't say it. She wasn't a girl he'd flirt with.

He smiled and moved past her to the door. 'You're smart, Pugh. You'll work something out.'

Chapter Eight

22 December 2023

The grandfather clock chimed three times just as Libby closed the bedroom door behind her. Max was sitting on the end of the bed, slowly pulling off his tie. They were alone at last.

'Oh my god,' he groaned, falling back on the bed, his arms outstretched. 'Were they always like this?'

'Worse.'

'How is that possible?' he whispered. 'Port, chased with shots . . .'

'They do love their shots. And their port,' she added, aware she was speaking very slowly, as if that might stop the room from spinning quite so fast.

There was a short silence as they both tried to regain control over their bodies.

'. . . Still, they're good fun. And *veh* welcoming.'

'Yes,' she agreed, staggering over to the small Wedgewood-blue hand basin that Archie had said was sequestered in the closet in the corner of the room. It was very strange to her, to have a sink in a wardrobe. She stared at her reflection in the mirror. Her mascara had smudged, her hair no longer sleek but straggly and limp . . . She didn't care. They were all far beyond caring what they looked like; the real issue facing them just now had been getting up the stairs and into their beds. Prock had practically crawled and Rollo hadn't even tried – he had just 'baggsed' a sofa in the drawing room. 'I'm glad you like them.'

Now that the music was no longer playing, and they were no longer screeching karaoke hits with soup spoons as microphones, she could hear how drunk she sounded.

'Mm, they're an interesting . . . bunch.'

Her head lifted. She had sat in enough meetings with Max to know that 'interesting' was his word of choice for when he was being diplomatic about something.

'Give me your observations, then,' she said, watching him in the mirror now. He was unbuttoning his shirt, still lying down, his fingers fumbling.

'Really?' She could hear the frown in his voice.

'Sure. I'm intrigued. You're an as— ' She stumbled over the word. '–Astute judge of character.'

He gave a big sigh, as if thinking at all was depleting. 'Well . . . I think Prock and Ems are made for each other. Grounded, salt of the earth . . .' He gave a little drunk grin. 'But also wilder than they look.'

'Yeah,' she breathed, nodding in agreement, her eyes closing too.

'And I think Charlie is very interesting. Clearly a genius. But a dark horse. I'm quite intrigued by him. There's more to him than meets the eye.'

'For sure.'

'Roly is . . . lost. All bluster and bluff.'

She hesitated, then nodded again, though it made her sad. 'Coco?'

'Vivacious. Beautiful. Successful. Fragile.'

Libby watched him in the mirror as he finally unbuttoned the shirt and pulled the tails free from his waistband. His body was beautiful. He worked hard at his physique, hitting the gym almost every day. He said it was his stress buster.

'And Zannah is . . .' He mused, his eyes still closed. 'I'd say Zannah is a fraud.'

'Why do you say that?'

'Mm, she's just too . . . curated. There are no chinks. I don't trust people with no chinks.'

'She's a chinkless chick,' Libby muttered, chuckling softly at her inebriated wordplay.

He turned his head to look at her, their eyes meeting in the reflection. 'C'mere,' he murmured, waggling his fingers. She walked slowly over to the bed and climbed onto it, straddling him. She felt his hand on her thigh, his fingers slowly working their way up underneath her silk dress until they cupped her buttocks. She leaned down to kiss him, tasting the booze still on his breath.

'You forgot one,' she murmured as his hands ran up her body, pulling on the ties that held her dress together.

'I did?'

'Our host?'

'Oh.' He was entirely focused on slipping the dress off her shoulders to reveal her matching lace lingerie set; sexy but playful, she had felt when choosing it. He appeared to agree.

'*Oh?*' she grinned, placing her hands on his chest and moving her hips just a little to make him groan. 'Come on. You have to do everyone.'

'. . . Okay, fine,' he said slowly, his eyes closed in enjoyment at what she was doing. 'Well, our host . . . I would have to say I think our host is a hopeless cause. A little boy lost.'

Libby stared at him. How did he glean all these things? 'Why would you say that?'

'His *bon viveur* act doesn't fool me. He's dead behind the eyes.'

Just the phrase horrified her. 'You really think that about him?'

He moved his head to get a better look at her. 'It's just an instinct; I'm probably wrong,' he shrugged, placing his hands on her hips and moving her back and forth himself. For several moments, neither one of them spoke, lost in either their bodies or their thoughts . . .

'And as for you . . . ' he said in a low voice, thrusting his hips once, suddenly, beneath her and making her gasp.

'Oh god, no. I didn't mean me!' she laughed.

'Ah, but you said I have to give my observations on everyone. It's only fair.'

She groaned. '. . . Go on, then.'

'You, Elizabeth Pugh, are stuck. You're still who you were back then. You've got an inferiority complex.'

'I do not!' Offended, she went to dismount him but he clamped his hands to her hips, holding her in place.

'No? You don't think they're better than you? Richer, posher, prettier, wittier, sexier?' He stared up at her and she couldn't hold his gaze. Every single word was a truth. '. . . You really don't see it, do you? You don't see that you win, hands down.'

'It's not a competition.'

'No, it's not. But for the record, if it was, you would win. You need to hold that in mind when you're with them.'

'I wasn't aware I'm so . . .' She struggled for the right word. '*Diminished*, when I'm with them.' She knew she sounded defensive.

'Outwardly, you're not. I doubt they notice it.'

'Oh, but *you're* such an expert on me? Because we've been sleeping together for five months?'

He raised an eyebrow at her sarcasm. 'Because I've sat in meetings with you. I've seen you control rooms full of powerful people – mostly men, many twice your age – and you bust their balls. But with this lot? It's like a switch goes off inside you . . . Impostor syndrome.'

Libby didn't reply. If his words stung her, it was because she knew they were true; she had hoped she was more convincing than that. 'So, what? You're not into me now because I was once the ugly duckling?'

'You say ugly duckling, I say late bloomer,' he said, taking her hands in his and weaving their fingers together. 'And does it feel to you like I'm not into you now?' He gave another thrust of his hips under her for good measure, jolting a sudden laugh from her.

In the next moment, he had caught hold of her and scooped her around so that she was pinned beneath him. It all happened so fast, it took her a moment to catch up, and when she opened her eyes again, he was frozen mid-lean towards her.

She waited for the kiss, her expression changing as she watched his. '. . . Are you okay?'

'Mm . . . not sure.' He had gone very pale. Something about the sudden movement, perhaps . . .

'Oh god, you're not going to be sick, are you?' She was lying right beneath him. 'Max?'

'Of course I'm n—' But he slapped a hand over his mouth, rolling off her and sitting up quickly.

'Quick, go!' she urged him. The loo was on the other side of the corridor, an old-fashioned pull-chain job with a cistern that would take fifteen minutes to refill.

He got up, lurching towards the door and flinging it open. She heard the WC door slam shut a moment later. She lay there for several moments, feeling not much better herself.

With a sigh, she climbed off the bed and reached into her overnight bag, which Max had risked life and limb retrieving in the blizzard. She pulled out the mocha silk nightslip with baby pink lace, which had gone down so well last night but which, right now, she would gladly have swapped for a pair of flannel pyjamas and a hot water bottle; without any central heating in this room and no fireplace, it was freezing.

She rummaged through the bag and found a pair of chunky red-striped socks. She had no idea how they had made their way in, but she pulled them on clumsily and sat for a few moments at the foot of the bed, too drunk to move but also far too drunk to still be awake.

'Teeth. Sleep,' she murmured to herself, swaying slightly as she willed herself to make the final journey to the sink and then back into bed. Grabbing her toiletry bag, she tottered over carefully. She frowned as she looked for the toothpaste. '. . . Where . . . ?'

Had she left it in the hotel? She checked Max's overnight bag too, rifling through his clothes. They had both packed light for what should have been a single overnight trip. 'Come on . . . where are you?' she muttered to herself. 'I just want to get to bed—'

The word faded as her hand, and then her gaze, fell upon a flat red leather box. She fell still. It wasn't a ring or earring box, nothing so small as that; nor was it big enough for a necklace. But it covered her palm. A bracelet, then? She stared at the white satin ribbon sealing it shut, intricately tied, not something she could hope to re-do. There was no chance of peeking a look.

Questions flooded her brain. When was he planning on giving this to her? She hadn't bought him anything. She had thought . . . she had assumed 'keeping things quiet' had extended to Christmas gifts.

Across the hall she heard the sounds of more retching and she threw the box back into the bag, covering it with his clothes again. She stood for several moments, shivering in her lick of silk as she tried to calm herself. It was just a gift. Not a proposal. There was no need to panic just yet.

She grabbed a bald butterscotch towel that had been left folded on the bed and draped it over her shoulders, clutching it tight. She still needed toothpaste. Where could she get tooth-paste from, when she had no idea who was in which room? Archie had traipsed them around several rooms trying to find one that was suitable. There had been a lovely large corner bedroom that he had led them to first — but a pigeon had recently flown into one of the windows, killing itself and shat-tering one of the original single-glazed panes so that snow was blowing in and building up on the floor like a pile of sugar.

'Hmm. Suboptimal,' was all he had slurred in a slightly disappointed tone, hand in pocket, naturally, before leading them to the 'other option'. Sadly, there had been a long-standing leak in the roof of that room, and in spite of its grand Jacobean four-poster and hand-painted chinoiserie wallpaper, Max felt the continual drip-dripping into the bucket throughout the night would be akin to Chinese water torture. With seven guests in the other five guest bedrooms, they had ended up in here: the smallest bedroom in the house. It had once been the dressing room to the master suite next door but, Archie had told them in a bored voice, the sixth viscount had had it secretly converted to hide his mistress in – while the viscountess was in residence, which seemed audacious by anyone's stand-ards.

Libby went over to the adjoining door to the master bedroom and put her ear to it. Was Archie still awake? Could they use his toothpaste? There were no sounds within. Was he asleep already? She knocked, quietly at first, then louder. 'Archie?' she whispered. 'Can I come in?'

No reply.

'Archie?' She knocked louder still.

Nothing.

Slowly, she turned the knob and peered in. The room was in darkness but somehow still filled with shadows – a vast four-poster bed hulking in the gloom, the brass drop handles on a walnut tallboy catching the sliver of light that winked through from her room.

'Archie?' she whispered again. 'Can I just borrow some toothpaste?'

Her eyes began to adjust to the darkness, strewn clothes on the floor and chairs beginning to gently glow and announce themselves; the perfectly made bed too – its hospital corners still neat and precise, untouched. The bed was empty, and she felt a kick to the guts. Where was he? He had left them saying he was going to fall into bed; how stupid of her to have assumed it would be his own.

For several moments she didn't stir, pushing down feelings she would not allow to surface. She saw the en suite in the near corner, the door ajar and the light off. Tiptoeing over, she stepped in and scanned the room for toothpaste, finding a squeezed tube on the basin. Her eyes grazed over Archie's toiletries – his badger-hair shaving brush and Trumper's lime shaving cream, deodorant, a small bottle of Terre d'Hermès cologne – an intimacy she had no right to bear witness to, and yet . . .

'Elizabeth?'

She heard Max's voice in their room next door and hurried back out. He was standing in the middle of the room, looking baffled and very pale.

'Where were you?' he frowned as she came back through.

She held up the toothpaste. 'We must have left ours in the hotel.'

'Oh.'

'How are you feeling now?'

He made a small sound to imply 'not good'.

'Come on, we need to sleep.' She squeezed the toothpaste onto his brush and hers, then dashed back into Archie's room to return it. She realized she had left the bathroom light on. What would he have thought if he had come back to that? He would have known someone had been in here, snooping.

She turned back and went to switch it off, but as she did so, her gaze fell on a large framed photograph on a chest of drawers by the window. She wandered over and picked it up, pulling away the curtain to get a better look in the moonlight. It was a portrait of a young woman – incredibly beautiful, with thick brown hair and pale dancing eyes just like Archie's. His mother?

Beneath it was a trinket dish, a silver Zippo lighter nestled within, and Libby felt a small spike in her heart rate as she stared at it. After all this time . . . ?

'Elizabeth,' Max called again, sounding uncharacteristically plaintive.

Quickly setting the photograph back down, she returned to her own room. He was still getting undressed as she brushed her teeth, and they slipped into the ice-cold sheets together. They were so chilled as to make Libby gasp and tuck her bare legs up into a foetal position. She kept the towel wrapped around her shoulders as best she could, deploring the thin sheets and blankets. Was a duvet a modern inconvenience too far?

'Jesus,' Max hissed, curling up against her body as the big spoon; he always slept naked. 'How is it colder in this bed than out of it?' He shivered a few times, the contraction of his muscles rippling across the mattress towards her as he settled himself and tried to get warm. 'Maybe we should have risked sleeping in the car after all.'

'Mm,' she murmured, blinking into the darkness, trying not to think of the red box in the bag in front of her, nor the empty bedroom at her back.

Five forty-nine.

Libby blinked at the digits on her screen, both exhausted and wired. Last night's alcohol was making her restless and she had shivered most of the night; even Max's body heat and the butterscotch towel were unable to warm her enough for a deep sleep.

Beside her Max snored lightly, seemingly toasty and out cold. She looked towards the heavy chintz curtains, but there was no sign of daylight yet peeping around the edges. Peeling back the covers, she tiptoed to the window and looked out; snowflakes were still falling but nowhere near as thickly now, the landscape blanketed, puffy and utterly silent.

She stood for a moment, feeling agitated – and very thirsty. She needed water, but such practicalities had been far from her mind as they had drunkenly hunted for a bed last night. With a last look at Max, oblivious to her wanderings, she tiptoed out of the room and looked down the long corridor – all the bedroom doors were shut – and made her way downstairs. Every creak of the ancient floorboards seemed magnified in the silence, the oak handrail worn to marble smoothness in her palm.

The house was in deep slumber but echoes of the party lingered in the vaulted space: several portraits had been turned on their picture chains to face the wall, streamers hung from the antlers of the mounted stags, and the bugle was dangling from the newel post at the bottom of the stairs. She reached the bottom step, aware of a warm light radiating from around the corner, and turned back towards the grand reception hall – the fairy lights were still burning away on the Christmas tree. Just how drunk had they been to go to bed without turning them off? The timbers in this house were over three hundred years old; a mere fever and a sneeze might be enough to trip a spark and burn the place to the ground.

Detritus from last night was scattered everywhere, the sound of rhythmic snores coming from the drawing room. She peered around the door to see one of Rollo's socked feet lolling over the back of the chesterfield, the fire ashes smouldering (the fireguard was sitting uselessly off to the side, naturally). Lipstick-ringed glasses and empty bottles covered the centre ottoman, the heavy tannic smell now sour and pervasive, making Libby's stomach protest; cushions had been thrown on the floor; Archie's coronet was perched atop the stuffed peacock; various jackets were strewn about and several pairs of heels were lying on their sides. Dozens of thin little envelopes from the After Eight mints were scattered on the ground from when they'd played the chocolate game – having to wiggle one of the squares from their foreheads to their mouths without using their hands; the facial contortions required had had them all in stitches, not to mention the chocolatey snail trails left on their faces.

Vague images came back to her as she surveyed the carnage, but without sleep, her brain still hadn't processed the night's events into some sort of order – their aborted escape had given the group a second wind after dinner, Libby and Max 'playing catch-up' – and it was all a disordered, chaotic jumble. She pulled back, wearied by this confronting evidence of their excess when her hangover hadn't even had a chance to bloom yet; she was still drunk. She needed water.

Closing the door softly, she moved into the kitchen. The dogs thumped their tails lazily at the sight of her, innately sensing that she – fragile and frozen in her silk chemise, stripy socks and meagre towel – was no mortal threat, and that they could continue to lie in their beds. Shivering, Libby looked around the room in dismay. All of the dirty dinner plates and bowls were still stacked on the kitchen table, the pots and pans soaking overnight as they stood filled with cold soapy water.

'Ugh,' she groaned. She vaguely recalled Mrs T telling Archie she was 'clocking off' as she handed over the last of the puddings at eleven o'clock.

Finding a glass, Libby thirstily drank down a pint and a half of water, wandering over to the Aga and leaning into its heat. It was like hugging a bear, immediate warmth suffusing her and making her body relax at last, and she slid down to sit on the floor, her body pressed firmly against it. She sat there for a while, staring blankly at the chaotic kitchen. It was a room that had evolved without any conscious design or plan, furniture seemingly moved in or migrated from other rooms so that it had an eclectic, jumbled feeling. The pine farmhouse table was ringed with the stains of old tea mugs and wine bottles, high-backed rush chairs pushed against it. A three-metre-long prep table ran along one wall up to the sink, a navy gingham skirt hiding paraphernalia beneath; a large oak dresser unit was stacked with mismatched plates and various jugs hanging from hooks; an array of dented copper pans dangled from a ceiling pot rack. It couldn't have been more different from her own sleek black kitchen, with its dimpled brass knobs and Breccia di Medicea marble counters. She had an integrated Miele coffee machine with the pods stacked in order of strength; here, there was a jar of Nescafé with a spoon in it and an open pack of dark chocolate digestives with the top twisted off.

Her eyes fell to a navy jumper on the seat of one the chairs. From the table it couldn't be seen, but from her low perch . . . She didn't know whose it was, nor did she care as she reached for it and pulled it on, sitting instead on the towel.

She sat there for as long as she could but eventually, even with the towel, her bottom went numb from the cold floor tiles and she got up again, knowing she should go back to bed and get a few hours' sleep. They had a long journey ahead of them today. She set the glass down in the sink and went to leave, but stopped again; she couldn't in good conscience leave all this for the housekeeper. There was no dishwasher, it all had to be done by hand – not to mention the rooms needing to be cleaned and breakfast prepared. Even if she just did the crockery, and Mrs T could pick up with the glasses . . .

'What are you doing?'

Libby, standing at the sink, turned to find Archie in the doorway, looking at her with an expression that sat somewhere between irritation and disbelief. She swallowed, mortified to have been caught doing this, looking like this, even though he was dishevelled too in striped pyjamas and a dressing gown. He was pale and his hair was mussed and sticking up in places, dark circles under his eyes. He looked like he'd had precious little sleep either, though probably for very different reasons. 'I'm washing up.' She turned away again, her heart pounding.

'You shouldn't be doing that.' He came into the room, the dogs heaving themselves out of their beds to greet him as he took in the sight of cleaned dinner plates drying on tea towels down the middle of the table; there hadn't been enough room on the drainer to fit them all. 'Mrs T will be furious,' he said, looking back at Libby like she was a freak.

She was puzzled. 'I don't see why.'

'Because this is her job. Not only is she paid to do this, but she *wants* to do this. If there's one thing she can't stand, it's not being useful. This isn't helping her; she'll flip her lid.'

'I don't believe that,' Libby said, plunging her hands back into the hot soapy water and resuming her task. 'Nobody actually wants to do washing-up.'

'Oh, I have to convince you, do I? Of my own housekeeper, in my own house?'

She stopped washing again and looked at him, seeing the annoyance written all over him. 'Why are you being so cross about it? Most people would be pleased.'

'So you're doing it to please *me*?'

'No.'

'What then?'

'I'm just trying to help,' she said, scarcely able to believe they were arguing over this.

'But no one asked you to. It's inappropriate.'

She flinched at the word. Had she betrayed herself in some way? Was this a class thing she hadn't known about? She had just been trying to help!

She turned back to the sink, aware of him watching and trying to figure out why this high-flying corporate lawyer was doing his dishes. She knew she had always been a mystery to him, so unlike the *rah* girls he got with: she was too ambitious, too helpful, too plebeian. She bet Arabella Tait (wherever she was now) wouldn't dream of doing the washing up at dawn – or indeed, any time.

She let her hands drop into the water as he came and stood beside her. The tension ramped up as he picked up her water glass and refilled it for himself. She didn't move as he chugged the water down like a man in the desert.

'If you've seen the state of the dining room and the drawing room, you'll know she's not going to be short of jobs this morning,' Libby muttered. 'You might think this is "inappropriate" but I think it's unacceptable to let a woman of her age come in and have to deal with this, on her own – and by hand!' she added. 'I mean, why don't you have a dishwasher?'

His eyes narrowed at the accusation. 'Because she doesn't *want* a dishwasher,' he replied testily. 'I've offered to buy one for her dozens of times.'

'Well, people don't always know what they want, Archie,' she snapped. 'Sometimes it's only when you give it to them that they realize what they were missing.'

She felt him go still beside her, his body slumping a little at her words, and she knew they weren't talking about the dishwasher now. Neither of them spoke for several moments, the silence between them as thick as cream.

Libby turned away, feeling upset and unbalanced, everything coming out wrong – or too right, she wasn't sure which. Why were they arguing, anyway? They shouldn't even be awake; they were cranky and still drunk.

Archie stood there for another moment as she defiantly began scrubbing again; then he picked up a tea towel and began drying off the plates. Libby was stunned; she bet he'd never dried a plate in his life.

'Just tell me you didn't come down here especially to do this,' he said in a milder tone, setting down a plate and reaching for another.

She swallowed. 'Of course not. I just couldn't sleep.'

'Why not?'

'I was thirsty,' she shrugged. 'And cold.'

'You should have said. I could have given you something warmer than one of my jumpers to wear.'

This was his jumper? She felt him look her up and down, taking in the jumbled concoction of sleep clothes. 'Well, actually, I did knock on your door, but you didn't reply. I think you must have been asleep already.' She didn't know why she said it. She knew perfectly well he had been in with Zannah. Did she want to see if he'd tell her something other than what she already knew? Would he lie to her face?

He looked down as he spoke. 'Oh, probably . . . I was pretty far gone . . . Sorry.'

Yes, then.

She bit her lip. 'It's fine. I had Max to keep me warm.'

There was another silence as he set down one plate and picked up the next.

'How about you?' she asked. 'Why are you up so early?'

He inhaled deeply. Slowly. 'Just . . . restless, I guess. Too much booze. Then I heard the water running in the pipes and that woke me a little more and made me think someone was up. And I was thirsty.'

'Yeah.'

He went to reach for another plate just as she turned to set one down and for a moment they were face to face, inches apart. In a flash she was right back there, standing outside their house, his eyes hooking onto something in hers. '. . . Sorry, you first,' he mumbled.

'Thanks.'

She set it down and reached for one of the pans, beginning to scrub with the brush, grateful for something to focus on as she attacked the burned bits.

'. . . He's a nice guy, Max,' he said stiffly.

'Yeah, he is.'

'Yeah, I like him.'

'He likes you too,' she fibbed. 'He was saying last night what fun he had. Although the vodka chasers after the port were . . . regrettable.'

'Possibly not one of my better ideas,' Archie admitted.

They didn't speak for a few moments as they pretended to focus on the jobs in hand.

'I'm sorry you couldn't get away, though,' he added. 'Of all the times for the forecast to be undercooked.'

'It wasn't your fault,' she shrugged.

'Still, it must be tedious for you being stuck here.'

'Not tedious at all. Besides, you've been the one inconvenienced by having to put us up.'

'Yeah, but now look – you're doing all the washing up.' He shot her one of his signature cocky smiles. 'I call that a win.'

'You always win, Archie,' she quipped.

The smile faded. 'Yeah. That's what they say.'

She glanced across at him again. He looked like a puppy that had been kicked.

'And what kind of nonsense is this?' a sharp voice enquired behind them. Libby turned just in time to see Mrs Timmock advancing towards them with a flabbergasted look.

'I couldn't stop her, Tea,' Archie said, putting down the tea towel and holding his hands up in surrender.

'And so you thought you'd join her?' the housekeeper scolded him, before looking straight at Libby with a questioning expression.

'We made a terrible mess last night,' she explained. 'I didn't think it was fair on you to—'

'Fair? On me? Have I fallen down the rabbit hole? Miss Pugh, this kitchen is my kingdom.'

'I understand – I was just trying to help,' Libby replied, releasing the scouring brush and holding her hands up too. She had to resist a sudden urge to burst out laughing at the ridiculousness of the situation. How could her actions have caused such offence?

'Don't worry, Teabag, no harm done – we'll leave you

to it,' Archie said, reaching for Libby's arm and quickly pulling her after him as he led them from the kitchen. 'This will remain our secret. No one will ever have to know.'

'I should hope not,' the housekeeper scolded. 'Now back to bed with you. It'll be hours yet before I've breakfast ready for you all.'

Libby's mouth parted in disbelief as Archie dragged her around the corner and into the long passage.

'I did warn you,' he said under his breath. 'This is her house. I just live in it.'

'But I've never heard anything so mad in my life!' she whispered, mouth agape with shock. 'I mean, she really was cross! You weren't exaggerating.'

'Nope. She has very firm boundaries. She thinks they're good for me.' He shrugged, casting her a bemused look.

'If you were ten, perhaps.'

He smiled. 'She had a lock put on the pantry door when I was about that age because I'd come down in the middle of the night when I was back from school and eat all the cakes.'

'No way,' Libby laughed.

'Yeah, I was permanently starving back then.' He smiled, his face softening with the memory. 'Though she wasn't the housekeeper in those days.'

'No?'

'She was my nanny.'

'Ah. Well, I guess that explains her protectiveness over you.'

'Mm.' He shot her a smile that was almost shy and it took her aback; she had never seen this side of him before: nostalgic, sentimental.

They climbed the stairs like naughty children, and Libby half felt they should be trailing teddy bears or comfort blankets in their wake. They stepped up onto the landing where all the bedroom doors were still shut, except his.

'Wait till she finds out I'm buying her a dishwasher,' he whispered. 'She'll have me strung up for my impertinence.'

'So you're going to get her one, then?' she asked in surprise as they stopped outside her bedroom door. Max was asleep on the other side, oblivious to her absence.

'Yeah, you were right – sometimes people really don't know what they need till they're given it.' He looked right at her. 'But she'll thank me one day, I hope,' he murmured, the joke subsumed to the look in his eyes.

A small silence bloomed as the house breathed around them, ghosts at play as everyone else slept, the past coming alive again.

The past is another country, my friend!

Rollo's shouts echoed through Libby's mind and she re-anchored herself in the present: the little red box in Max's bag. Archie's empty bed last night . . . She stepped back. 'Well, I guess we should try and catch some sleep,' she said in a low voice. 'At least it's still dark out.'

'Yes.'

She turned to leave – 'Oh . . . and thank you for this.' She went to pull off the jumper but he stopped her with a shake of his head.

'Keep it.'

'Really?'

He just nodded.

'Okay, thanks,' she whispered, letting herself back into the room.

Max stirred as she slid back under the covers, her heart hammering as he reached for her in his sleep. His arms folded around her, but Archie's jumper was an insulating barrier between them and she could smell him in the warp and weft of it. For several minutes she lay there, replaying their encounter and how it had felt talking, alone, with him again after all this time. She closed her eyes, her body relaxed and soft; she was warm at last and able to sleep.

Chapter Nine

May 2014

Zannah gave a massive yawn followed by a strange, satisfied squeal as she lay on the floor of the dressing room, her legs up against the wall, flexing her feet as she tried to boost her lymphatic system before her date with the captain of the hockey club. 'This is *the* best way to skinny up your thighs,' she said intently, alternating her foot stretches with studied intensity.

'Your thighs are already skinny!' Ems tutted. 'Have you lost more weight?'

Zannah's eyes brightened. 'I don't know. Have I?' She gave a happy shrug.

'Did you know we have three times more lymphatic fluid in our bodies than we have blood?'

'You have three times more alcohol in your body than you have blood,' Libby quipped, glancing down at her as she pulled again on the too-tight bust of the red dress. Not that she would ever wear a red dress, even if it did fit. Not that her friends were listening to her.

'Try this,' Coco said, throwing a ruched lime silk jersey number over the door.

'Categorically not,' Libby said, throwing it straight back again. 'That looks radioactive.'

'*Try* it.' The dress came back again.

Libby gave a groan and wriggled out of the red dress. 'This is pointless. I'm not wearing anything that isn't black.'

'Which is precisely why you mustn't wear black,' Ems said, wiggling a finger at her from her cross-legged position in the corner.

'That makes no sense.'

'We are going to bust you out of your comfort zone once and for all. If black is your comfort level, then we've got to push past that and embrace colour.'

'None of this makes me comfortable. Joggers and sweats, now they're my comfort level. Slippers, my comfort level—'

'Oh yes, shoes . . . that's a whole other box of frogs.' Zannah turned her feet out, like a ballerina in first position. She craned her neck to look back towards Libby. 'What's your opinion on heels?'

'Poor.'

'Hmm. Tricky . . . It's not like you couldn't do with the extra inches.'

'Thanks.'

Zannah gave an easy laugh, her pale throat exposed and her bright hair fanned out around her. At five foot ten, extra height wasn't a concern for her; not much was: boys, romance, dresses, the future . . . none of it really seemed to matter too much, and she flitted through her own life like a butterfly, whereas Libby had to dig and crawl.

'I can't believe you've never been to a black tie do before,' Ems said with a confounded look, sipping on her coffee.

'It would make a lot more sense if you saw the village where I grew up. We think it's posh if someone has skimmed milk in their tea,' Libby shrugged, making her housemates grin as she let the red dress fall in a tiny heap at her feet – not so

127

much a puddle as a blood clot. She took the lime dress off the hanger and shimmied it up her body. 'Oh my god,' she groaned as she caught her reflection. 'No!'

'Oh my god yes!' Zannah exclaimed, lifting her head off the floor to get a better look. 'That looks incredible!'

'I look like I should be on *Take Me Out*.'

'Hell yeah, you do!' Zannah agreed.

'Zan, I wasn't saying that as a . . . ' Libby sighed. 'Ems, tell her.'

Ems considered. 'I mean, the body . . . ' She held out her hands in a *need I say more?* gesture. 'But the vibe . . .' She pulled a face. 'It's not giving Legal Motherfucker.'

They all laughed.

'Talking of – have you heard back on that internship yet?' Zannah asked, still looking at her upside down.

'Nope. Supposedly any day now.' Libby bit the inside of her cheek nervously, hoping it wasn't a bad sign that it was taking so long; the six-month placement in the Hong Kong office of her first-choice law firm was highly sought after and the odds of landing it were low, she knew that. But she had to try.

They heard feet running. 'Lemme see.' Coco poked her head round the door, peering closely. She smooshed her mouth to the side, narrowed her eyes, wrinkled her nose. 'Mmm . . . no.'

'No?' Zannah exclaimed, forgetting to flex her feet.

'The colour's off. It makes her skin tone look sallow. She needs something more . . . sober.'

'*She* is right here,' Libby retorted, not liking that she seemingly had no say whatsoever in this decision-making process. She peered more closely at the glass. Did she look sallow?

Coco disappeared again.

'– I want something black, Coco! Black, or not I'm not going.'

Fed up with looking at herself in clothes that made her look like Barbie's stumpy cousin, she slid down the mirror and clutched her feet. At least she could move in the silk jersey. 'What are you wearing, Ems? Have you decided yet?'

'It's a toss-up between the burgundy velvet or the vintage tartan Vivienne Westwood corset dress.'

'The burgundy velvet would really set off your hair,' Libby said.

'Yeah, but Prock says the Westwood makes my tits looks fantastic, so . . .' She gave a shrug as Zannah gave a throaty laugh and went back to flexing her feet.

'Honestly, the boys don't have to go through this faff.' Libby inspected her nails – unmanicured and far too short. 'All they've got to do is remember to dry clean the suit from the last time.'

'Ha! Even that's beyond most of them,' Zannah tutted. 'Besides, how boring to be stuck in the same uniform as everyone else, time after time. At least we get to have variety.'

'Yeah,' Ems agreed.

Libby didn't say anything back; she liked uniforms. Conformity made her feel safe and gave her an opportunity to blend in. When she stuck out, it was always for the wrong reasons.

'—Although I bet we can rely on Arch to put his own special twist on his DJ.'

'You mean like monogrammed slippers?' Zannah grinned.

'Exactly. Or a velvet shawl-collar jacket with *frogging*!' Ems laughed. 'Prock's got his dad's disco-dotted cummerbund.'

'I wouldn't put it past Roly to turn up in a cravat!'

Libby stared at her lime-green reflection in the mirror; perhaps this wasn't as 'out there' as she'd thought. She had never considered the nuances of black tie before. 'How many are going, do you know?'

Ems looked at Zannah as if to check. 'I think he said a hundred and fifty?'

'Yeah, pretty sure it was that,' Zannah agreed.

A hundred and fifty people were going to his twenty-first? Libby wasn't sure she even knew a hundred and fifty people, let alone liked them enough to invite them to her birthday.

Zannah nudged Libby's foot with her elbow. 'You never know, you might get lucky! I know you're fussy, but even you have got to like those odds! I know *I* do!'

Libby smiled and bit her lip, wondering whether to say anything. In the past week, since returning the lighter, Archie had visited her room several times; each time he was a little more sober, arrived a little earlier and stayed a little bit longer. Conversation flowed easily between them, not in a flirtatious way but as if they had been friends for years – trusted confidantes – and on his last visit, the night before last, he had brought Plutarch's *Life of Alexander* to read in the chair behind her as she studied. She had laughed in disbelief as he had shown her the book and insisted he was serious, he really was there to work. It had felt like a step change between them, as if he was stepping into her world. Had he noticed that she was choosing to work in her room most nights now, instead of at the library? He wasn't flirting with her, and yet a familiarity was growing between them to the point of intimacy.

It was in the silence, as they had worked, that she had felt the tension in the room – as if the air itself was being pulled tight, like a blanket. It had been so hard to concentrate, hearing the slow turn of pages, his occasional sighs, him clearing his throat. Sometimes she'd thought she could feel the weight of his stare upon her, but she couldn't sneak a look at him without visibly turning around and by the time she finally did, he had fallen asleep in the chair. She had covered him with her spare blanket and then undressed in her bedroom, shamelessly slipping between the sheets naked, her heart pounding that he might appear at the door at any moment. She had waited for him in the dark for what seemed like hours, straining to hear the sounds that would tell her he was awake again and coming over to her . . .

But she must have dropped off at some point because he had been gone by the morning. He hadn't come up last night and she'd not seen him around since. Her body felt primed and on high alert. Would he come again tonight? She felt sure they were building towards a tipping point – but what if she was wrong? Was this one-sided, or all in her head? She was distracted to the point of despair – studying felt impossible – and she'd been only too happy to agree when the girls had suggested this shopping trip. It was always an education listening to them, but even if they could give her the benefit of their considerable experience, he was their housemate. House rules. She knew no one would encourage anything to happen between them.

'This is the one!'

They all looked up as Coco peered around the door again, holding out a limp satin slip that dangled like a windsock.

'Coco, I wouldn't get my arm in that!'

'Trust me, it's bias cut, which is exactly what you need for an hourglass figure like yours. Your hip to waist to boob ratios are so insane, you'll never fit a tailored dress unless it's couture.'

'Well, that's hardly likely given that we're here trying on second-hand.'

'Vintage,' Coco corrected, pulling Libby to standing and taking her place on the floor.

Libby rose with a sigh and took a closer look at the scrap of supposed dress, trying to work out the front from the back. It was, at least, black. She pulled it on, letting it slide down her arms and skim over her body. It needed a little tug over the hips but when she straightened up, she saw that what had looked like a plain straight neckline was in fact cut low and the spaghetti straps set wide; the waistline actually dipped in where she did, and it didn't strain over the hips and bum.

'Fuck *off*!' Zannah said, dropping her legs and scrambling onto her knees.

'Oh, Lib!' Ems cooed. 'That's the one!'

Libby couldn't stop staring at herself. It was like seeing herself through a filter. Would it do? *You'll work something out*.

'I don't think you understand how lucky you are; I would kill for your curves,' Coco sighed. 'I'm bony and hard in all the places you're soft. It's not fair.'

Zannah picked up Libby's hoodie from the floor. 'Why do you insist on hiding in this shit all the time?' she asked, shaking it in her hand. 'It's an actual crime.'

'Because of precisely this. Your reaction,' Libby replied. 'I'd never be taken seriously if I dressed to show . . . *this*.' She motioned vaguely towards her reflected silhouette. 'It's a distraction and a completely unnecessary one.'

'A distraction? Yes. Unnecessary? Not always. There is a time and a place for a dress like this on a body like that and believe you me, Arch's party is that time and place.'

Libby gave a little half turn, checking out the rear view too. Could she . . . could she really wear this out? 'I'm not sure,' she murmured. It was so flimsy; she had sturdier facecloths.

Would he like it? Would he even notice? A hundred and fifty people would be vying for his attention. He wouldn't even see her . . . But words drifted back into her mind. *Do you know how many assumptions you've just made? One, that I wouldn't be looking for you. Two . . .*

Would he look for her? Libby felt her heart pound harder

132

as she tried to see what he would see. *I like talking to you.* But she wanted more.

Zannah got up and came and stood with her, resting her chin on Libby's shoulder as they both stared at her reflection in the mirror. 'You're buying it,' she said firmly. 'You'll have your pick of them in that dress. Whoever you want, done deal.'

'It doesn't work like that.'

'I think you'll find it does,' she winked.

'What are you wearing, Coco?' Ems asked.

'Well, funny you should ask. You know that YouTube I did that went viral? The one where I styled the skirt five ways?'

'Yeah. It got like fifty-k views or something?' Zannah mumbled, yawning again. She looked tired.

'Exactly. Well, I got a message from the brand and they want to send me a few dresses for free! I don't need to send them back or anything. All I've got to do is tag them if I wear them.'

'No way! Free clothes?'

'I know, it's pretty cool,' Coco agreed. 'You can make pretty good money if you break through.'

'Break through?' Ems queried.

'You know, become an influencer.'

'Right, because that's what you do with a psychology degree,' Libby scoffed. 'Play dress-up for a living.'

'Well – the thing is . . .' Coco said hesitantly.

There was a silence as her change in tone was registered.

'What?' Libby looked at her. 'What is the thing?'

'. . . I may not end up with a psychology degree after all.'

'Excuse me?' Zannah demanded.

'I've got to have a meeting with my prof to, quote, *discuss my options*, unquote.'

'. . . Because of that late essay?' Ems frowned.

'Yeah. Turns out he's not quite as chilled as I thought.'

There was a small, panicked silence. 'So what does that mean?' Libby asked. 'Discuss your options?'

Coco gave a shrug. 'Points penalty? I'm not really sure.'

'But he wouldn't . . . he wouldn't fail you?' Zannah asked.

'No!' Coco batted the suggestion away, her nose wrinkled disdainfully, but Libby and Ems swapped looks. Discussing options with half a term to go sounded ominous.

'How important was it, this essay?'

'Twenty per cent of my final score.'

'Uh-huh.' Zannah shot them an alarmed look too.

Libby tried to keep her face blank, but a shot of anger came in on the heels of her concern; this was no time for 'I told you so' but she simply couldn't believe that her friend had allowed herself to get into this position, falling at the last hurdle. Everyone teased her for her 'diligence', as if her work drive was cute, but the future she wanted was dependent upon the foundations she built here. Her circumstances might be more extreme, but surely no one could afford to attend university for three years and leave without the certificate? If Coco had just stayed in the library with her that night, instead of dragging her out for Charlie's birthday . . . And now she was out here shopping, when this was hanging over her head?

'So when are you seeing him?' Ems asked.

'Tomorrow. Seven o'clock.'

'Seven? But we've got hockey,' Zannah reminded her.

Coco shrugged. 'I'll have to miss it. He's lecturing all afternoon and he can't see me before.'

There was another silence. Twenty per cent of her final score . . .

'You all look really worried,' Coco said, seeing their pointedly blank expressions and mild smiles.

'No!' they replied in unison, fidgeting as one.

'Please don't look like that. He's always been pretty cool before. I reckon he's just trying to give me a bit of a fright . . . Which is working!' she laughed nervously. 'But it'll be fine . . . Right?'

Zannah drew herself up to her full height, rallying first, as she always did. 'Of course it will. You go in, grovel and smile. Let him rant, tell him your dog died or something. He just wants to be the Big I Am for a bit, but that's cool; you can do that.'

'You think?'

'I know. Listen, you're a girl with options. You want to be an influencer?' She winked. 'So influence him!'

Chapter Ten

23 December 2023

Libby turned over, sinking her head back into the pillow and willing herself to stay unconscious. She had fallen into a deep, motionless sleep after climbing back into bed and she didn't want it to end. The first tendrils of a hangover were beginning to climb, and if she could just sleep through them . . .

Behind her Max gave another small, sudden snore, disturbing himself so that he turned over. A moment later he was awake, jolting with a start.

'What—'

Groggily, she reached a hand back to reassure him. 'We had to stay over,' she reminded him, knowing he was disorientated. He'd probably never slept in a room with chintz curtains before. 'The snow.'

'Oh god, what time is it?' he asked, his voice a croak, as he tried to sit up. 'Ugh.' He fell back against the pillow, an arm against his face as if to protect him from the dim light.

Libby's hand flailed limply for her phone, somewhere on the bedside table. She opened one eye. 'Nine-o-seven.'

'Nine-o . . . ? Fuck!'

'What?'

He groaned. 'I'm already late. I'll never make Richmond from here in four hours.'

'No,' she agreed wanly, wondering how he had ever thought that would be possible. 'Just ring and explain. I'm sure they'll understand.'

'You haven't met my father,' he muttered, and she heard him pull himself up to an upright position. She tucked her knees up on her side, keeping her eyes closed, determined to stay heavy. Warm. Unconscious in cashmere.

'It's hardly your fault,' she mumbled.

'Mm, that's not strictly true though, is it?'

She opened an eye again. Huh?

'If we hadn't stopped in here, we never would have become snowed in. We'd have been ahead of the storm and back in London, where we're supposed to be.' From the slight increase in volume of his voice, she could tell he was looking down at her as he spoke, directing the words at her. *We* meant *you*.

She rolled onto her back, looking up at him. He had a thick stubble, his eyes puffy. 'Alternatively we might have ended up stranded on the M6, in a convertible, on one of the coldest nights of the year,' she pointed out. 'We might have died if we *hadn't* come over here.'

'Speculative,' he muttered, reaching for his phone.

Libby lay still, wondering if this counted as their first argument, as Max began texting his apology. She blinked at the intricate plasterwork on the ceiling, trying not to think of anything; but her mind kept replaying the dawn conversation by the kitchen sink, that weighted silence outside the door. She turned back onto her side and discreetly pressed the jumper to her nose.

Several minutes later, his bad mood seemingly forgotten, Max put his phone back down and shuffled down the bed again. His legs sought hers, hooking her under the sheets. '. . . Are you wearing socks?'

'I am. Is that controversial?'

He grinned at the tartness in her voice. 'No, simply unexpected.' He ran a hand across her stomach, peering under the covers as he came into contact with the cashmere sweater. 'God, are you fully dressed under there?'

'I found it when I went downstairs and nabbed it.'

'When did you go downstairs?'

'Around five-ish. I needed some water.'

'Mm, I'm pretty parched, come to think of it.' He looked across to her bedside table. 'Have you . . . ?'

'I left the glass down there.'

'Excellent.'

She turned her head fractionally. 'What?'

'Well, you didn't think to bring any up for me? You saw the state of me last night.'

'Sorry. I'm not used to babysitting.'

'Ooh,' he winced, seeing now the extent of her irritation with him. They were quiet for a moment. This was definitely their first . . . disagreement. 'Hey,' he murmured, beginning to move his hand slowly over her lower stomach. 'Sorry if I was a grouch. I'm not a great morning person, especially when I'm this hungover. I need some food to get me going.' His hand swept down her belly to her thighs, stroking gently as he began to kiss her neck.

Libby closed her eyes, exhaling slowly. Yesterday morning had started exactly the same way – minus the tiff – and it had felt exciting. Provocative . . . Right now she just felt agitated. He walked his fingers up her inner thigh just as a door slammed down the hall and bleary voices drifted towards them. Max, taking no notice, shifted position slightly, getting up on his elbows and pushing his leg between hers. He turned her face towards him and kissed her on the mouth once, twice—

There was a sudden rap on their door. 'Wake up, lazybones!' someone called. 'Mrs T says brekkie is ready. Don't let it get cold!'

'Okay, thanks!' Libby called back, feeling distinctly awkward, as if they could be seen through the closed door. 'We'll be right there.'

Max pulled back with a frustrated look. 'Really?' he muttered. 'Is this boarding school?'

'Are you willing to take on Mrs Timmock?'

He rolled his eyes. 'We don't have time for breakfast. We need to get on the road.'

'But we have time for this?'

'There's always time for this,' he grinned. 'It's a matter of priorities.'

She pulled away from him. His breath was sour and she was distinctly not in the mood. She had her own hangover to deal with. 'Well, my priority is being a good guest. If we need to get on the road then let's get on the road, but we can't stay in here and not show our faces.'

'Why? Because they'd *know* what we're doing?' he asked in a voice of mock horror, but there was no amusement in his eyes. '. . . Why don't you want them to know that we're having sex, Elizabeth?'

'What?' She stared at him in bafflement. 'That is a ridiculous comment.'

'Is it?' He blinked, holding her gaze, and she was reminded of his odd behaviour last night too – breaking their cardinal rule, touching her and kissing her in public. She could feel his erection pressing against her hip as he stared at her questioningly for several moments before he rolled off and got up.

Libby watched as he stepped into last night's trousers and left the room, crossing the hall to the bathroom. She heard the shower turn on, pipes clanking, and she stared back up at the ceiling, troubled that he had seen through her yet again. Because it wasn't disappointment or frustration she felt to have been interrupted – but relief.

'Ready?' Max pulled the door to behind him, the overnight bag swinging in his hand. They were dressed in the office clothes they had travelled up in the night before the wedding – a suit for him, wide-legged trousers and a silk blouse for her – and were looking distinctly less poised on this return leg. They had had to brush their teeth without toothpaste (Libby wasn't risking another trip to Archie's room) and she only had the merest slick of tinted moisturiser on her skin.

Libby turned from where she was standing, staring, in the middle of the corridor. 'Sure, let's go,' she said, her feet heading for the grand staircase but her eyes still on the row of doors, almost all of them ajar; everyone else was up. She glanced back to see the door to the master bedroom next door was closed. Was Archie still sleeping? Would they leave before he was awake? Her pulse spiked at the thought even though it might be a good thing. The best thing.

They stopped on the half-landing at the double-height window and looked out at the view that had been cloaked in darkness last night, and even this morning. It was still snowing, albeit more lightly now, a dazzling brightness refracting up from the pristine white blanket that spread as far as the eye could see. The hard edges of walls and spiny trees were lost to amorphous curves and the ancient cloud-clipped yew hedge rippled like a captured wave, delicate paw prints of squirrels and birds lightly kissing the pillowy surface.

'Jesus, that's got to be . . . what, a good twelve, fifteen inches deep?' Max asked, his hand resting lightly on her bottom as they stood staring out, his gaze fastened upon the distant frozen Capability Brown lake, a solitary swan walking disconsolately on the ice.

'Mad,' she murmured, distractedly.

'We're going to have a real job getting the car started in this cold,' he murmured. 'I wouldn't be surprised if the battery's flat. We can't stay for breakfast so don't get talked into anything, okay?'

'I *know*,' she sighed as they continued downstairs. Max was dragging her away from her friends at a sprint.

They looked into the dining room, as if half expecting liveried butlers to be serving out on silver platters, but it was deserted. And incredibly clean. There was no sign of last night's hedonism. Mrs Timmock had cleared, cleaned and polished the room back to a state of pristine readiness for the next dinner.

'They must be in the kitchen,' she said, leading the way down the long passage, Libby listening to the sound of her shoes clip-clopping lightly on the old floor, Max a half step behind her. Conversation was minimal between them, their mood still stunted by the morning's start.

The smell of burning toast began to drift towards them, a low hum of voices like a hive in a distant tree, and the muted good humour coming from the kitchen only seemed to highlight their lack of it.

'Well, good morning,' she said, putting on a bright smile and taking in the dishevelled scene. It was reassuring to see they weren't the only ones suffering from last night. Max's hangover kept assailing him at unexpected moments, and getting dressed had been a stop-start affair, as he was forced to pause mid-action or drop his head whenever gravity seemed to double its pull. But Coco was sitting slumped at the table in a pair of black silk pyjamas with her initials embroidered in pink, and a satin sleep mask pushed back on her head. Ems and Prock had managed to get dressed – they were in jeans and Fair Isle jumpers, looking ready to go out lambing or some such – but both were staring, baggy-eyed, into space. Ems hadn't been drinking, of course, but the late night had clearly taken a toll on her – she looked exhausted and somehow even bigger, if that were possible. Charlie was standing by the toaster in old jeans and mismatched socks, lethargically buttering the blackened heel of white farmhouse loaf, a pot of local honey beside him. Libby looked around for the others but there was no sign of Rollo. Had he moved to his own room or one of the dog beds? No Archie and no Zannah either. No doubt *they* didn't care if everyone guessed what they were doing together.

'Libs!' Coco called feebly, holding up an outstretched arm towards her as if pleading for help.

'Ah, Coco,' Libby said, wandering over and squeezing her hand. 'Feeling rough?'

'Dead. Worse than dead. Deader than a dead thing,' she croaked.

Libby reached for her half-emptied mug. It was cold to the touch. 'A fresh tea?'

Coco nodded gratefully, letting her arm slide along the dotty breakfast oilskin so that she could rest her head on the table again. Libby wandered over to the sink, emptied the mug and poured a fresh one from the teapot. There was a packet of Alka-Seltzer beside it and a jug of water with several glasses. Beside her, Charlie moved with agonizing slowness.

'There's sausages, bacon, mushrooms and baked beans in

142

the warming oven, bottom left,' Ems said in a weak voice. 'And porridge too. Top left.'

'Thanks,' Libby murmured, not bothering to look in; Max's reminders about a swift departure were still ringing in her ears. She noticed no one was really eating (yet) anyway.

'Can I have one of these?' she asked over her shoulder, holding up the Alka-Seltzer.

'Help yourself. You too, Max,' Ems said, jerking her chin towards the empty chair opposite. 'Take a seat. How are you feeling?'

The sound of scraping chair legs on the terracotta tiled floor made them all wince. Max too. 'Fragile.'

'Mm. Has to be said, in hindsight, the port-shot combo was not one of our better ideas,' Prock agreed, sliding slightly lower down into his chair. A bowl of porridge sat untouched and growing cold before him, and he looked at it suspiciously before pushing it away. 'At least we always knew where we were with a Jägerbomb . . .'

'Max, tea?' Libby asked from behind him, holding out a cup with a slightly shaky hand. He'd said no breakfast, but tea didn't count. Tea wasn't optional.

'Just a quick one, but we can't linger,' he said, his eyes flicking up towards her.

'You can't stop for breakfast?' Ems asked.

Charlie brought his toast over to the table and sat down beside her, beginning to read the newspaper in protective silence. 'That's yesterday's paper,' she whispered.

He gave a noncommittal shrug.

'We need to get on the road sharpish,' Max said. 'I fear we're going to have an absolute shocker getting back to London today. Has anyone seen the news this morning? What's it like out there? I can't get any reception on my phone; my texts aren't sending.'

Libby poured his tea for him too and set down the aspirins and a glass of water but he reached only for the tea, as if admitting to being hungover somehow diminished him.

'No, you won't get reception here; it's notorious,' Prock said, shaking his head sadly. 'This isn't so much a black spot as a black hole.'

'Oh.'

'Just about the only place you can reliably get a signal around here is a mile and a bit down the lane, near a stile. Sometimes you can get lucky if the wind's blowing in the right direction but in weather like this . . .' He gave a hopeless shrug.

'Right.' Max looked less than impressed. He'd grown up in Hampstead and had no real sense of how isolated the country-side could really be. His idea of a day in the sticks was playing golf in Surrey.

'I can't believe it's still snowing,' Libby murmured, clasping her mug for warmth as she stared out of the windows at the flimsy flakes drifting past. They had none of last night's heft or speed but they were still coming. Steady. Consistent. Endless.

'Has everyone got enough to eat?' Mrs Timmock asked, walking in carrying a heavy bucket full of hot ashes that would need to cool. She stopped dead. 'Why's no one eating?'

'We will, just as soon as we've had tea, Mrs T,' Prock said, sitting up straighter and trying to rally. 'You know your break-fasts are the only thing that keep me alive after a night with Arch.'

'Mm, you were making quite the ruckus,' she muttered, but looking at him – them – with some fondness. 'And I'm not even going to ask why there were hoofprints in the hall.'

Hoofprints? Libby looked around in bafflement but everyone was wearing the same blank expression as the housekeeper walked over and opened the back door, setting the ashes bucket down on the stone step. A waft of arctic air blew in, making them all shiver.

'There's porridge in the simmering oven too,' she said, coming back in again and this time looking at Libby and Max.

'Thank you, but we're not staying. We're about to head off,' Max said quickly.

'Are you indeed?' Mrs Timmock asked, looking put out. 'Well, you can suit yourself, but I should think you would benefit from a hot meal inside you before you go out into the cold.' She reached for a long padded coat hanging on a peg behind the kitchen door. 'Right, you can tell Archie I'll be back at four. There's a pie in the fridge for lunch and it's haunch of venison tonight, for those who are staying,' she added, shooting a look towards Max.

'You're going out in this, Mrs T?' Prock asked, concerned.

'Why wouldn't I? It's only snow.'

'But no cars can get up or down the lane till the farmer's been.'

Max's head jerked up, a look of alarm on his face. It was clear he had assumed the farmer had already been and gone.

'Indeed. Which is why I'm walking to the end of the lane, and Mr Timmock will collect me on the main road.'

'But that's miles away.'

Mrs Timmock gave a patient smile. 'Two and a half, yes. And while I thank you for your concern, it is unnecessary. Most of the walk is downhill, and by the time I get back here later, Bob will have been with his tractor and my husband can drive me right up to the door. Okay?'

Prock nodded, looking like a little boy put in his place by the teacher. 'Well, that told me,' he muttered as she went back out into the long passage. A moment later, they all heard the front door slam.

'Is Zannah still sleeping?' Libby asked, not to anyone in particular.

'Yeah, I think so,' Coco mumbled, sliding back down her arm to rest her head on the table again.

Libby looked at her friend's face in repose. She was beautiful in a delicate, fragile way; always the girl everyone noticed first in a room. It had its benefits as well as its drawbacks.

There was a small silence as everyone sipped their tea and tried to mitigate their pounding heads.

'So what are all your plans for today?' Max asked the group, finally giving in to temptation and reaching for the Alka-Seltzer.

Ems, her head resting in her hand, arm on the table, looked at her husband. 'Well we'd planned on staying for a kitchen supper but if the roads are tricky, we should probably go before it gets dark.'

'Mm,' Prock agreed reluctantly.

'Have you far to go?' Max asked.

'Harrogate's about forty-five, fifty minutes from here. Not too bad.'

'Nice. So you guys must see Archie regularly, then?'

'When he's up here,' Ems nodded. 'But he's still in London a lot. I don't think he likes rattling around on his own here too much. Hence his rather legendary parties.'

'Understandable.' Max took a sip of tea and his eyes closed with momentary relief. The journey ahead of them was not an enticing prospect. He drummed his fingers once on the table as he observed everyone in their various stages of catatonia. '. . . I'm concerned my car battery's going to be dead in these temperatures. I don't suppose anyone's got a trickle charger, have they?'

'Archie will, for sure,' Prock mumbled. 'That's a good point though. Zannah should check hers if she's heading back to London too.'

'No, she's fine. She's in no rush. She's spending Christmas here,' Ems said.

'Is she?' He looked blank.

'Yes. Remember I told you when you were cleaning out the gutters?'

Libby stared into her tea as the sound of voices came to the back door and a moment later it swung open. They stared out at Rollo carrying a dead pheasant by the neck, the black labs trotting in his wake and a loop of rope over his shoulder. Behind him, Archie was standing by the boot jack, pulling off his wellies, a sack of logs at his feet. He was dressed in a haphazard concoction of the pink striped pyjama bottoms Libby had seen him in earlier, an olive jumper with a red suede patch at the elbow and a Schöffel fleece. It was a far cry from last night's elegant dinner look but it still somehow looked good on him, and Libby felt a shot of adrenaline that she would get to say goodbye to him after all.

'Well, finally! The dead are risen!' Rollo bellowed as he took in the sight of them all. He draped the pheasant on the table beside Coco's head, making her scream and jump away.

'Oh my god, Roly!' she cried. 'I'm a bloody vegetarian! Get that thing away from me!'

'What, and being a veggie means you have no manners? Come on, just say hi to it. Say hi!' Roly teased, picking it up and swaying it in front of her as she squealed and flapped her hands in front of her face until, satisfied with her response, he went over and hung it from a hook by the window.

In an instant the energy in the room had shifted up a gear, but Libby saw Zannah wasn't with them. Where was she?

147

'Good morning, chaps,' Archie said, picking up the log sack and strolling in in his rugby socks. His brown hair was dusted with snowflakes, his cheeks smacked a bright pink and his eyes bright. He set the logs down in a basket in the far corner, beside a coal bucket and the dogs' beds. He ruffled their heads briefly as they settled back into them for the next nap before turning back. 'Everyone had some scoff?' he asked, his eyes grazing her but giving no indication – as ever – that they had stood in here together during the witching hour, bickering in one moment and giggling together in the next. Why was it that in company they scarcely spoke, and in private they couldn't stop? She saw him take in her work clothes, the indication that she was poised to leave here and head back to her own life again.

'Can't quite face it yet,' Prock mumbled.

'You should have come out with us, Prockles old boy,' Rollo said in a hearty voice, shaking some snow out of his hair. 'Nothing like a brisk walk in the freezing fucking cold to stop a hangover in its tracks.'

'What time were you two up and out?' Prock frowned.

'Mm, not sure. Eight-ish?' Rollo looked over at Archie, who was making his way over to the kettle.

'Yuh, it was about that. I needed to get some mobile reception and ring Bob.'

Libby stared at his back as he filled the kettle. The two of them had come back upstairs at half six. Had he slept at all last night?

'You went on a mile walk in your pyjamas?' Ems queried.

'What's wrong with them?' Archie asked, looking down.

'Arch, they're very clearly your *pyjamas*.'

'So? They're warm and it wasn't like I was going to see anyone. It was just me and Roly and the dogs, and they've all seen me in my PJs plenty of times before.' Libby saw the dogs were watching him from between their paws.

'I've seen you in *far* worse than that, mate,' Roly chortled.

'Arch,' Ems called over to him. 'You've just missed Teabag. She says she'll be back at four and there's pie for lunch. She's only just left.'

'Right,' he nodded.

'We didn't think she should be out walking alone in these conditions, but she wasn't having any of it.'

Archie smirked. 'No. She wouldn't.' His eyes flickered over to Libby, settling on her for a moment as their 'mischief' helping out this morning was remembered. His gaze travelled over her, taking in her work wardrobe that was so incongruous in this country house kitchen.

'I take it Bob's the farmer?' Max said.

Archie's smile faded as he looked over at him. '. . . Yeah. God, he's having a shocker. He's been out since five throwing down the salt but some of the drifts are about three, four feet deep. It's slow going. It came in far harder than they forecast.'

'Four feet?' Max asked sharply, sitting up straighter.

'Yeah, but that's only in the more exposed places that really catch the wind; the rest of it won't be too bad, certainly no trouble for him. Don't worry, I've told him you need to race off—' His eyes flicked in Libby's direction again. 'He'll come over here as soon as he's done the main roads and the school. He'll be here as soon as he can.'

'But he didn't say when exactly?' Max pressed.

'An hour or two maybe?' Archie gave a doleful shrug. 'Sorry, mate.'

Libby saw Max's mouth settle into an irritated line. He wasn't good with uncertainty. Max was a man who liked absolutes. Efficiency. He was her in male form.

Archie came over to the table with a couple of teas for him and Rollo and sat down heavily at the head of the table beside Coco, who had resumed her prone position. He fell into his own signature position, an ankle resting on the opposite knee. 'Wakey wakey, sleepyhead,' he said, tousling Coco's blonde hair. 'It's time to play.'

'I can't play,' she said grumpily. 'In case you hadn't noticed, I'm *dying*.'

'Nonsense. No one could be dying and look that pretty.'

Coco scowled but lifted her head off her arm to look at him, sticking her tongue out. She had never been able to resist a compliment.

'. . . Are you really not going to eat that?' Ems asked her husband, reaching for the porridge bowl.

'Can't,' he replied wanly.

She tutted. 'You've no one to blame but yourself.'

'I know.' He sagged a little further and Ems relented, reaching over and bringing his head onto her shoulder. 'Poor baby. Never did know when to quit while you were ahead. You know these two always take it too far.' She waved her spoon in Archie and Rollo's direction.

'Hey,' Rollo protested. 'We're not having a Christmas reunion house party just to sit around reading the papers and drinking tea, you know.' He looked pointedly at Charlie, who was doing exactly that, but Charlie was oblivious.

'Oh god, a whole day of that! It sounds like heaven!' Coco groaned.

'Now, maybe. But let us not forget, the shots were your idea,' Rollo reminded her.

'Yes, but *I* hadn't had a bottle of port first.'

'No, you'd had a bottle of Bolly. I'm just surprised you're not taking selfies, showing the Morning After the Night Before.'

'This is not my aesthetic,' Coco mumbled, vaguely waving her arm in a circle to indicate the untidy kitchen and frazzled company.

'Why not? It was last night. God knows you posted enough pictures to your stories.'

'What?' She lifted her head in horror. 'I did not!'

'You did! Don't you remember asking me to film you riding the donkey down the hall?'

'I rode a donkey?' Coco gasped.

'You've got a donkey?' Libby frowned. A vague memory fluttered out from the shadows of her mind: carrots, whiskers, wellies in the dark . . .

'Ugh, you're so horrid. I know you're lying,' Coco muttered, reaching for her phone and scrolling through it. Her mouth opened in horror. 'Oh no . . . no, no, no,' she whispered as she brought up her TikTok page. 'You let me post *that*?'

'What is it?' Ems asked.

'A disaster, is what it is.' Coco turned her phone around to show a reel of her and Zannah doing a provocative dance either side of Archie; they were all on the stairs, Archie lying back, smoking a cigar, his shirt untucked and half open, nodding his coroneted head in time to the beat as the women lay either side of him, writhing provocatively. The X-rated clip was only a few seconds long but it was impossible not to keep watching it on a loop, the image suggestive of a Gatsbyesque decadence and debauchery at odds with her carefully curated 'clean living' image. 'Oh god, it's already had seven hundred and fifty thousand views!' she remarked, sitting up with a frown; she looked like she wasn't sure whether to be devastated or delighted.

'Overnight? How many followers do you have?' Max asked her curiously.

'Six million.'

He looked impressed, but another exhausted silence settled as Coco began scrolling through the comments, deliberating whether or not to panic.

Max shuffled his chair along slightly so that he was sitting closer to Libby, and after a moment she felt his hand settle on her thigh. When she looked across at him, he gave her a wink. 'Seeing as we're here for another few hours, want something to eat?' he murmured, clearly trying to make up. Breakfast was his peace offering.

She relented. 'Mm,' she nodded. 'Just toast, though. I'm not sure I can stomach anything else.'

He reached over and kissed her for a surprisingly long moment on the forehead, before getting up and wandering over to the bread bin. She watched him go.

'How long have you guys been together?' Ems asked, looking between the two of them.

Max looked back over his shoulder from where he was slicing the white farmhouse loaf. 'It's been five months since we—'

'Yeah, something like that,' she interrupted quickly, not wanting him to detail what it was they had done on that day five months ago.

'And . . . ? Tell us everything – how did it happen?' Ems asked, a gleam in her eye.

Max leaned against the counter, his legs crossed at the ankle as he waited for the toast to pop up. '. . . Well, we were celebrating a deal,' he said when Libby didn't reply. 'I'd been trying for months to get her to go out for a drink with me but she was playing very hard to get.'

'It was hardly months,' she protested. 'You asked me twice.'

'Yes, and both times you told me you didn't think it was a

152

good idea to mix business with pleasure.' A small, flirtatious smile played on his lips and she knew he was replaying the memory of their drunken kisses in the Uber that night.

'Well that sounds like the Libby we all know,' Archie muttered, drawing her gaze.

'But now you're . . . cool with it?' Ems nodded, grinning at her.

'I'm just about managing to keep her persuaded,' Max replied with rare self-deprecation. He looked across at the Proctors. 'And you two got together at Durham, did you? Or was it after?'

'In our second year,' Ems replied for her husband, who seemed capable only of sitting up and breathing. 'Terrible cliché really; we ought to have had more imagination. We're part of the Seventy Club.'

'The what?'

'Haven't you heard of it? There's this crazy statistic that two-thirds of Durham students find their future partners there.'

'You're kidding,' Max said with a quizzical smile. 'I've never heard of that.'

'It's true,' Ems shrugged.

'Intriguing. Why should that be, I wonder? Why Durham and not . . . Exeter or Bristol? Or Oxbridge?'

Ems gave a shrug as she continued to eat. The toast popped up and Max turned away. 'So then, if roughly two-thirds of Durham students find their life partner there, your group is anomalous,' he mused, glancing over his shoulder as he buttered the toast. 'Seeing as you're the only two out of eight to be together.'

'I know, it's so weird.'

'And there weren't any . . . missed opportunities for the rest of you?' Max asked. Libby glanced at Charlie, but for once he wasn't looking over at Coco and was immersed in the newspaper. She could feel eyes upon her, though, and she knew better than to look over.

'No bloody chance,' Rollo sighed. 'But it wasn't for want of trying.'

'It would be interesting to know what the divorce rate is of this Seventy Club,' Max mused, returning to the table with a plate of buttered toast. He set it down in front of Libby, his hand back on her thigh again as he bit into a slice.

'Well, isn't this the mothers' meeting! Have I missed much?' someone said from the doorway. They looked up to find Zannah coming through. If Libby had thought she and Max were overdressed, and Archie and Coco decidedly underdressed in their pyjamas, Zannah was setting the country-house weekend guest example in blue jeans and ivory cashmere, blown-out hair and a full face of barely-there make-up. Where did she find the energy? Libby wondered. Hadn't she been drinking the champagne and the tequila they all had? Hadn't she spent all night shivering half to death in the cold?

'Only Coco's digital walk of shame,' Rollo said as Zannah walked over to the kettle and pressed a hand to the side, checking it for heat; only, instead of reaching for the teabags like everyone else, she was carrying a small clear bag of herbs. 'What the hell's that?'

'This? It's a special blend of herbs formulated especially for me by my Ayurvedic practitioner,' Zannah replied, smugly spooning several heaped teaspoonfuls into a mug.

Rollo gave a groan as he watched. 'My god, don't tell me you pay for that?'

'I do. And you'd probably die if you heard how much.'

Rollo watched with disdain as she closed the Ziploc again.

'You do realize that's just the soil scratchings from under a tree in his garden, don't you?'

'*Her* garden, actually. And I've been taking this for years. How else do you think I'm this radiant?' she asked, jokily framing her face with her hands.

'Ooh, gimme some,' Coco said, snapping her fingers lazily, still scrolling.

'Well if that's what it takes,' Rollo tutted. 'I'll take haggard and a full English any day of the w—'

His voice broke off to a sudden commotion, chair legs scraping hard against the floor as Charlie stood up; the movement was so sharp, the chair toppled backwards, hitting the ground and sending the dogs running out of the room. Everyone looked at him in astonishment, the scene made all the more startling for having been preceded by his prolonged stillness as the others had fussed and bickered around him.

'You all right, mate?' Prock asked, seeing how Charlie stood frozen, his mouth open and eyes wide as he stared down at the newspaper.

'Don't tell me your stocks have gone down, Earnshaw,' Rollo teased. 'Need to sell in a hurry? Arch, you can send a carrier pigeon to your broker, can't you?'

Archie gave a half grin but his eyes were on Charlie, who still wasn't paying any attention to them. He was reading something over and over, his lips moving as if he had to say the words out loud to make them real.

A hush descended as everyone watched him, realizing this – whatever it was – was no laughing matter. Slowly he looked up, ashen-faced. 'It's Staples.'

'. . . Staples?' Ems whispered, the spoon dropping from her hand and landing in the bowl with a clatter as he nodded.

'What about him?' Archie asked, falling out of his languid pose and leaning forward with a stern look.

'He's in hospital. It says he was attacked by three assailants.'

Silence boomed around their heads, a vacuum into which they all fell as they absorbed the news.

'Uh, who's Staples?' Max asked.

Everyone looked at him, recognition piercing their shock as his question reminded them that he hadn't been at Durham. That he wasn't one of them.

'. . . A former Durham prof,' Ems said after a moment, picking up her spoon again.

'Ah,' Max replied, taking an inventory of their stunned expressions. 'Well, that's unfortunate for him, of course, but why's that made the national news? It's hardly public interest. Townies beat up students up and down the country every day of the week.'

'It must be because he was faculty,' Archie murmured, his eyes flashing up towards Max, who was reaching for his tea, before casting a glance around at the others.

His message was understood. Looks were shared but nothing more was said, and the silence was allowed to stand at last, as their past came and sat on the table like a black cat, purring softly.

Chapter Eleven

May 2014

'Hello . . . ?' Libby called as she swung her bag onto the sofa and walked through the sitting room. 'Anyone in?'

No reply. The little terraced house had been in darkness from the street and even the smell of smoke coming from Archie's room – or 'lair', as Zannah called it – wasn't as strong as usual, suggesting he had been gone for several hours at least.

'Really?' she tried again. 'No one?' Not even Charlie? He was the only one who could be accused of – like her – having any kind of work ethic. Exams began in two weeks but she was seemingly the only one chained to her desk.

Nothing. She gave a shrug; having the house to herself was like having no one sit next to her on the plane. One of life's small wins. She walked downstairs into the basement kitchen, the strip light buzzing and flickering on. A new message had been taped to the fridge: *No milk*.

'Great,' she muttered; she'd been banking on a bowl of Frosties for her dinner. Her shoulders slumped as she opened the door and peered in: a fresh six-pack of Heineken (Prock's); a jar of pesto, a rolled bag of fresh cappelletti pasta and that half-bottle of chianti from Ems's dinner party for her tutorial group the other day; four carrots and half a tub of hummus (Coco's); a covered bowl of tuna and sweetcorn mayonnaise (Zannah?); a hoisin duck wrap and a pack of sushi (Charlie); a packet of quail's eggs and a BLT (Rollo); some blue cheese and an open tin of baked beans (Archie).

She shut the door again and reached for the cereal box. Dry Frosties it was, then. Only . . . She shook the box, trying to gauge its weight. It was distinctly lighter than she recalled. Emptier . . . 'Ugh! Bastards,' she groaned as she saw there was only the dregs left, those tiny cereal crumbs that always absorbed the milk and formed a goo that made her want to gag.

Her eyes fell to a bag of white bread pushed up against the tiles to hold the twist in place and keep the contents fresh. She didn't know whose it was and at this point she didn't care. Takeout wasn't an option; she had precisely £14.62 in her bank account and it was only Thursday. Somehow she had to get through the next three days on £4.87 daily, covering breakfast, lunch and dinner, before her next allowance came in. How was that doable when she was pulling ten-hour shifts in the library? She needed *fuel*.

She popped two slices into the toaster and boiled the kettle, swiping through Instagram as she waited. The toast popped up and she buttered it thickly, then smeared a lick of Marmite on the top, eating it at the tiny Ikea table in the corner. The tea didn't taste as good black, but it was hot and wet, and all she wanted to do was take a shower and get cleaned up. She'd been studying corporate governance all day, working with extra focus in the hope that if she was distracted by one of Archie's visits tonight, it would be time she could afford to lose.

Rinsing her cup and plate and leaving them on the side –

ignoring the stack of dirty pans and dishes in the sink – she went back upstairs, grabbing her bag from the sofa as she passed. She left the light on in the sitting room for the others. No doubt they were at Klute again and would be staggering back with tonight's 'randoms' (Zannah's word, not hers), falling over chairs, steps and their own feet in their haste to get to their bedrooms, doors slamming and then, soon enough, headboards.

She went up the first flight to the boys' floor – Archie, Rollo and Charlie's doors were all ajar – and on to the second, where Zannah, Coco and Ems resided. Ems and Prock were officially sharing, which seemed scarcely possible given the size of the rooms, but they didn't care; they liked being on top of one another. Libby's was the only room on the top floor.

She hung her coat on the back of her door and walked across to the window, staring down onto the quiet street for a few moments. It was a quarter to ten and a few bicycles were locked to lamp posts, a fox trotting between the cars, no one around. No Archie strolling down the middle of the road, as far as she could see. Did he ever glance up to check if her light was on as he came along the street? Did he look for her the way she looked for him?

She closed her curtains and began to undress. Slipping on her dressing gown and grabbing her towel, she padded down to the bathroom on the girls' floor: a 1980s white tile number with a bath that no longer had any enamel on it. She didn't care. Her shoulders were aching from sitting hunched for so long and—

She stopped suddenly.

What was that?

She looked back into the deserted hallway. The light was shining through from downstairs but there were no shadows moving on the wall, no voices carrying up.

And yet she had heard something, muffled and indistinct.

'Hello?' she asked, stepping out onto the landing and feeling her heart pound against her ribs as she strained to hear it again. Her housemates were anything but quiet; they announced themselves halfway down the street. She looked across at her friends' rooms; the doors were still ajar, just as they had been a few minutes ago when she'd come up.

She stood stock still for several moments, but the house held its breath. She peered into Em and Prock's room. The bed had been neatly made, a supermarket fleece and polo shirt strewn across the duvet by Prock, clearly in a rush to go straight out after his shift. He had taken on a part-time job as a delivery driver to start building up a deposit so that he and Ems could buy a place after graduation. It was taken as read that they'd get married.

She crossed the hall to Zannah's room and glanced in; it certainly looked like they'd been burgled – clothes, shoes and hair products everywhere – but Libby had never seen her friend's room *not* look like this. Coco's room was chaotic too, but with a different vibe. Charlotte Tilbury make-up was arranged in tiered racks on her desk, a GHD hair straightener plugged in at the wall, one of her mother's old Chanel bags dangling on the wardrobe door; heaps of clothes were draped over a chair, potted plants and dreamcatchers at the windows.

Libby felt the hairs on the back of her neck rise as she stood half in the doorway, half on the landing and waited again. Something definitely seemed somehow off, her sixth sense almost humming, telling her someone was here, in the house. She knew because she had felt this exact instinct once before when, as a little girl brushing her teeth in the bathroom, she had heard a sound in her parents' bedroom. She had gone to investigate but seen nothing. Heard it again and looked again;

nothing. On the third visit she had forced herself to walk into the middle of the room and look up at the window frames, on top of the wardrobes, the curtains . . . She *knew* there was something in there, even though she couldn't see it – bodies, even inert ones, have energy, force fields that pulse into a room just like radio waves. It was only as she had turned to leave that she had caught sight of a starling standing in the corner, utterly motionless, watching her and trying not to be seen.

So too now. She was about to walk out again when she caught sight of a dark shape squatting on the floor on the far side of the bed. Libby cried out, jumping back and into the hallway, a shot of adrenaline arrowing through her blood as she waited for the shape to give chase. She was all ready to sprint down the stairs and into the street; she could make the front door in under five seconds.

But the clamour wasn't followed up by more noise; there were no sounds of movement within, and she realized now the shape hadn't lunged at her as she had run. It hadn't moved at all.

She stepped back into the doorway and peered around. The shape was still motionless, but as Libby's eyes adjusted to the darkness she began to understand what she was seeing.

'Coco?' she whispered, moving around the bed to where her friend was sitting in a huddle, arms around her knees. 'What's wrong? Why are you sitting on the floor in the dark?'

She reached a hand out but Coco drew back, shaking her head and another sob – what Libby recognized as the sound she had heard – escaped her again. Libby took in the sight of Coco's bleeding mascara, the tension in her high shoulders, scratches on her arms that seemed to be self-inflicted from the way her fingers were digging against her own flesh. She was trembling all over, staring down at the floor.

'Oh my god,' she whispered, feeling a cold dread as she dropped onto her knees in front of her. 'Coco, what's happened?'

She watched as words rose up in her friend, falling back down again in the next moment. Unexpressed. Unarticulated. Impossible to say. 'I . . . I . . .'

'Shhh,' Libby hushed, reaching for her hand as juddering sobs wracked Coco's tiny frame. 'There's no rush. Take your time.'

Minutes passed before Coco slowly raised her eyes, looking back at Libby with a haunted expression. '. . . I . . . I . . . c-couldn't s-stop him,' she faltered. 'H-he w-wouldn't listen . . . He w-wouldn't stop.'

Libby stared at her, horrified. She shouldn't know what Coco was talking about from those few words. They should make no sense. But somehow she knew exactly what had happened.

She knew it all.

Chapter Twelve

'Are we really doing this?' Max asked as he pushed his feet into a borrowed pair of welly boots. He was wearing borrowed everything – a spare pair of Charlie's jeans, one of Rollo's tattersall shirts and Archie's cashmere sweater with numerous moth holes in it. It was peculiar to see him looking anything less than razor sharp, and Libby watched, amused, as he struggled with folding his jeans at the ankle the way she had shown him so that they didn't scrunch uncomfortably at the knees. He seemed somehow vulnerable out of his element like this – it was like watching a Great White swimming in a bath.

She was in hand-me-downs too – a pair of Coco's fleece-lined leggings and a slouchy rollneck she had been gifted and not yet worn – and they had looked at each other anew in the bedroom as they changed; they had never seen each other in casualwear before. *Off duty.*

'Well, what else would we do on a day like this?' she said. 'If we're going to be stuck here till the farmer arrives, we may as well make the most of it.'

'A walk would have sufficed. I mean, who over the age of fifteen sledges?'

'Plenty of adults sledge.'

'Yes, when they have kids!'

'Stop being such a humbug! I'm sure it'll be fun,' she hissed, worried someone might overhear as footsteps tramped up and down the hall and stairs while hats, gloves and scarves were being sought. A couple of wooden toboggans had been retrieved from the attic but Mrs Timmock had also supplied a couple of trays, which Rollo was eyeing up 'for speed'.

'He does like his games, doesn't he?' Max muttered, standing up and looking down at himself with a bemused expression. They were in the boot room opposite the kitchen, and Archie had told them to grab some of the spare Barbours hanging from the pegs; the waxed jackets wouldn't keep them warm for any sustained period outside, but at least they were waterproof.

'Who does?'

'Archie. Has he always been so . . . Peter Pan?'

A scoff escaped her. 'Nothing so wholesome! He was more like the Marquis de Sade at uni. Debauched, hedonistic—'

'Really?' Max looked surprised. 'No, you're kidding.'

'I wish I were.'

He laughed. 'But he's so . . . shambling.'

'Shambling?' she snorted.

'You know what I mean – he sort of shuffles about, always looking down. Got that self-deprecating hand-in-his-pocket thing going on. Do you mean it's all an affectation? That beneath the stripy pyjamas, he's actually a stone-cold lady-killer?'

She sighed. 'Whether he still is, I have no clue, but he always had a coven fawning over him, streaming in and out of his room at Durham. Girls went wild for him.'

'I just don't get it. He's good-looking, sure, but not what you'd call an alpha,' Max said, shrugging on a jacket that was slightly too long in the arms. He looked across at her with a curious expression. '. . . So was there ever anything between the two of you?'

Libby stopped, mid-reach for a jacket, and arched an eyebrow. 'Do I look like the type of girl who went for a fuckboy?' She watched him smile as she put on the jacket, heart pounding. 'Come on, we should get going. Let's play this one last game before we head back to the land of grown-ups.'

'Wait—' He caught her by the arm and pulled her in to him, kissing her deeply. The Alka-Seltzers had worked their magic and most of the hangovers were now just a background throb; appetites were rising once more. 'That's better,' he murmured when they finally pulled apart. 'I can't wait to get you alone again.'

They walked down the long passage and through to the reception hall, where everyone was beginning to gather. Mrs Timmock had already lit both fires, the vast chamber warming the house like a heart and the Christmas tree aglow.

'Ah good, you're kitted up,' Rollo said as they came through; then, leaning slightly as he peered past them: '. . . Did you get it?'

Libby turned to find Archie just a few steps behind them, carrying a hip flask.

'Only the one,' Archie murmured, holding it up. 'But it should do us. It's not like we'll be out for long.'

He walked past the two of them without acknowledgement and handed the flask to Rollo, who checked it for weight. Libby felt her stomach drop at Archie's stiff body language. Oh god, had he overheard them talking? Her words had been cruel, overblown and deliberately heavy-handed – sledge-hammers to the proverbial walnut. She didn't want Max to see through her on the topic of Archie. It was strictly off limits to all, herself included.

'That'll see us through,' Rollo said with an approving nod.

'Come on then!' Prock said, throwing open the door and striding out, the others running after him into the thick snow, arms aloft and filled with childlike delight. Libby watched as Archie picked up one of the trays and followed after them – still like Peter Pan, but Peter Pan when he'd forgotten how to fly.

It was a decent hike to Bombers, the Templetons' name for the estate hill with a long, steep drop and no trees, ditches, stone walls or barbed-wire-topped fences to dodge. Max marched up in front with Prock and Charlie, Rollo holding forth on a recent stalking trip to Archie, who listened with a bent head, the dogs trotting by his feet. Libby was walking arm-in-arm with Coco – the news at breakfast had given everyone an unwelcome jolt back to the past – but Zannah and Ems kept falling behind as they took frequent stops, Ems tiring more quickly in her final trimester.

The snow was almost knee deep, making the walking slow going, and Libby marvelled at how her life had derailed into this alternative reality – a world that was recognizable but not her own. She had stepped into the Other: these were her old friends, but they weren't a part of her life now. These were not her clothes and this was not her landscape. She was supposed to be back in her flat, reading *The Times* and wrapping the last of the presents. She ought to be getting a coffee from Gail's and doing a yoga class, or a face mask, or – more likely – reading over the notes for the new client her boss had passed on to her. Instead she was wearing a waxed jacket and leggings, and about to hit twenty miles per hour sitting on her backside on a silver tray.

Everyone was out of breath by the time they crested the hill and looked down on the other side. Libby saw Max's eyes widen at the gradient; the Surrey Hills had nothing on this.

'Are you kidding?' Zannah laughed as they assessed what would be classified as a red run in the Swiss Alps. 'I think I'll watch, thanks.'

'Really?' Charlie frowned. 'That's not like you!'

'Some of us are suffering more than others this morning. That walk was quite enough excitement for me, thanks. I need a sit down.'

Archie looked down at the deep snow. Sitting really wasn't an option; her jeans would be soaked within minutes. 'Here, put my coat dow—' He went to shrug it off.

'No, I don't need it.'

'But if you want to sit—'

'I don't, though. I'm fine, Arch, really,' she said quickly, straightening up and batting the chivalry away with a flick of her hand. 'Just unfit as fuck.'

Libby watched Archie watching her, seeing the tension in his face as his efforts were rejected. She looked around at the others – did they notice it too? – but no one was paying any attention; they were far more preoccupied by the near-vertical drop.

'Why don't you boys all do the first run together, and we can watch,' Coco said, also completely out of puff, her hands on her knees. 'I'm going to need to recover a little first too.'

'Lib?' Rollo asked.

She hesitated – it did look fun – but then shook her head; it seemed impolitic to abandon the girls. 'Next run. I'll let you show me how it's done first.'

'Not like you,' Max quipped, reaching for one of the silver trays Rollo was holding out for him. He knew she liked an adrenaline rush, and winked at her when their eyes met.

The men lined up on the lip of the hill and Libby looked out at the horizon. The land here was part of the livestock farming catchment of the estate, but the famous heather-dotted moors sat just beyond the pastures, the land swooping in dramatic arcs and rolling back in undulating waves. Bombers created its own miniature valley, with the land on the other side rising gently and enclosed within drystone walls now half buried, only their tops showing and criss-crossing the snowy fields like the lattice on an apple pie. A flock of sheep in one of them looked grubby in comparison to the snow as they stood in a huddle, tired eyes in black faces blinking slowly.

She turned back as Ems counted them down and the men competitively hurled themselves down the slope, stomachs down and legs kicking, on the toboggans and trays. In spite of Max's protestations in the boot room and just now, they were all ten again. Little boys. No one watching them howl and shout insults at one another would know that one of them was a father-to-be, another a tech titan; that one was a lord, one a soldier and another a corporate wolf in sheep's clothing (or, at least, a waxed jacket).

'Honestly,' Ems tutted fondly, rubbing her stomach as the women all looked on. 'They're just big kids. This baby's going to come out with more common sense than her father.'

'Her? You know the sex, then?' Coco asked, looking excited.

'No. We decided not to find out. But I'm convinced she's a girl and Prock thinks she's a boy.'

'Have you decided on names?' Libby asked.

'Yes, but we're not revealing them until the birth – in case anyone steals them.'

'Yeah, right!' Zannah protested. 'Because the rest of us are so close to having kids.'

Libby stole a look at her, trying to get a read on her situation with Archie. Not a single person had said anything about them being a couple and they 'officially' slept in separate bedrooms, and yet they acted like they were almost married – him offering his coat just now; her staying for Christmas, playing with his nephews, helping the housekeeper . . .

'Well, Max and Libs might not be a million miles away,' Ems murmured, looking at her closely. Questioningly.

'Uh, no!' Libby gave a dismissive shake of her head, shutting that conversation down immediately.

'No? He's always looking over at you.'

'Yes, because he keeps trying to leave!' Libby rejoindered. 'No offence, girls, but he had plans for today and he's pretty pissed off with me that I've put us in this position.'

'*You*? How does he figure that?' Zannah frowned. 'I didn't know weather-making was on your considerable skills list.'

It was just an off-the-cuff comment but Libby met her eyes, and for the first time during this reunion, they exchanged a rare moment of honesty. No social niceties now; Zannah had always been highly loyal to her girlfriends and, for just a moment, it felt like old times between them.

'But what would you say if he asked?' Coco pressed. 'Just hypothetically.'

'Asked me what?'

'To marry him.'

Libby looked at her in disbelief. 'I'd check him for a fever!' She laughed. 'Listen, I don't think you understand – this is the first time I've seen him in jeans! This weekend is the first time he's held my hand or kissed me in public. It's all been really casual up till now.'

'Well, it doesn't look so casual from where we're standing.'

'Because you're a romantic, Coco. Kissing in the rain is probably something you *want* to do.'

Coco looked crushed. 'You don't?'

Libby grinned. 'Things are just a lot more . . . pragmatic between us. If it started to rain, we would both run inside.'

'But that's our point! Don't you see? You're birds of a feather. He's your perfect match.'

'You do fit,' Ems agreed. 'If I had to put down on paper a description of the man I thought would be perfect for you, it would be him. Don't you think, Zannah?'

There was a pause as Zannah inhaled, thinking for a moment. 'Well, yes, in theory. But you know what they say. Opposites attract, right? There's no accounting for chemistry. Sometimes we fall hardest for people we shouldn't—'

Shouldn't? Was that a warning? Was Zannah marking her territory?

'So?' Coco pressed, refusing to let the matter drop. 'What would it be? Yes or no?'

'No,' Libby said quickly. 'It's far too soon.' But she frowned as she remembered what she had found in his bag last night.

'What? What is it?' Coco asked, watching her closely.

'Actually, I did find something in his bag earlier. A Cartier box.'

'Cartier?' Ems gasped, eyes bright. 'Oh my god!'

'No!' Libby said quickly, realizing what she was thinking. 'Not a ring! It wasn't a ring box . . . I think it's a bracelet.'

'A *bracelet* from Cartier?' Coco gripped her forearm and stared at her intently, looking even more excited. 'Well then, you know what it must be, surely?'

'No. It was ribbon-tied; I couldn't look at it.'

'You don't need to! It's a love bracelet.'

'A what?'

'You know, the solid gold bangle that they secure to your wrist with a little screwdriver?'

Libby blinked. Of course she had heard about them. It simply hadn't crossed her mind that he might have bought her one. 'How do you know it's that?'

Coco pressed her hands to her chest. 'Because I know luxury, and that's what you get from Cartier. If it's not an engagement ring, it's the love bracelet. Trust me.'

'Clearly it's a precursor to an engagement ring, though,' Ems added. 'They're bloody pricey. You don't drop on one of those unless you're serious about someone.'

Libby stared at them all, taken aback by their certainty. Was that true? Were the girls right and she was missing clues? Were things further along for Max than she had thought? 'Right.'

There was an expectant pause as they watched her absorb this news.

'Well, you don't look too happy about it!' Ems laughed.

'I'm just . . . shocked,' she mumbled. She really was. 'We . . . We haven't had any discussions about next steps.'

'Discussions? Next steps?' Coco smiled. 'Love isn't a negotiation, Libs. It isn't something you need to have a meeting about. If he wants to take things to the next level, this is how he'll do it – he'll just surprise you. At Christmas. It's perfect!'

The others nodded in agreement as the men's voices began to carry over the crest, and Libby felt relieved to have been saved from further interrogation when Ems pressed a finger to her lips. A few seconds later they reappeared with flushed cheeks and bright eyes, some with a headful of snow.

'Oh no! They're back in their witches' coven!' Prock laughed, holding his fingers up in the sign of the cross at the sight of them standing in a huddle. 'They're casting spells again.'

'You're hilarious,' Zannah said drily.

'How was that?' Ems asked as Prock came up and planted

a kiss on her mouth, as if he'd missed her for the few minutes they'd been apart.

'Brilliant! I caught air on a molehill.'

Libby looked for Max, bringing up the rear. He was smiling as well, snow in his hair too, but there was tension in his face. Unlike everyone else's unbridled enthusiasm, he looked merely polite. Was his patience being pushed to the limit as he was forced to play childish games while they waited for the farmer to dig them out? She knew London, and his own life, had probably never felt so distant.

'Right, your turn, girls,' Rollo said, holding out his tray. 'Zannah? Ready now?'

She held her hand up again. 'No, and I'm not sure I ever will be.'

'What? Nonsense! What's wrong with you?'

'Roly, I fully admit I'm not the girl I used to be,' Zannah shrugged. 'But I'm perfectly happy watching you behave like lunatics.'

'But—'

'Leave it, Roly,' Archie said sharply, cutting him off with a terse shake of his head.

'Libs, how about you?' Charlie asked. 'You'll love it, I promise.'

She smiled. 'Sure,' she said, reaching for Rollo's outstretched tray.

'No, you should have this one,' Archie snapped, snatching it before she could take it and handing her the wooden toboggan instead. 'It's more steerable.'

'But the tray is faster,' she protested.

'Precisely.'

She stared back at him, waiting for some kind of explanation but seeing only a hardness in his eyes instead; a hardness that hadn't been there standing outside her bedroom earlier, nor even at breakfast. 'I don't see what your point is,' she said uncertainly.

'When was the last time you sledged?'

'I don't know exactly . . . ' She shrugged. 'When I was nine, ten, maybe?'

'There you go then, you won't know what you're doing on it. Most people don't sledge after the age of fifteen.' He looked at her with an even, inscrutable expression, telling her in no uncertain terms that he'd overheard her terrible words.

Her mouth parted in dismay and she felt instantly sick, but he turned away and walked over to Charlie, who had possession of the hip flask and was offering Prock a shot. Archie took a deep swig too, shrugging his shoulders just once as the whisky burned his throat.

Max trudged over to her, shivering somewhat in his uninsulated jacket.

'Surviving?' she asked, trying not to show her upset.

'Just about,' he muttered, watching on as the boys had their warming nips; there was no chance of him having a snifter if he was going to be driving shortly. 'Although I got taken out by our host towards the bottom and faceplanted. He cut right across me . . . Looked pretty deliberate to me.'

'I'm sure it wasn't. It's hard to get much control over the trays.'

'Well, he had none.'

Libby bit her lip, wondering if it really had been an accident. 'It looked fast.'

'It is.' He looked at her. '. . . Perhaps you should sit it out.'

She raised an eyebrow. 'Why? Because I'm too fragile to play with the big boys?'

He didn't reply, but there was a gleam in his eyes again

and she felt a faint frisson of their chemistry, the tension that had built up at work over the weeks and months. He knew exactly how to play her.

'Game on.'

'Good,' he smiled, reaching over and planting a lingering kiss on her lips – just as a snowball whistled past.

'Now, now, you two,' Ems called with a mischievous smile. 'No heavy petting in the snow!'

It was the cue no one had needed and within moments a full-scale snowball fight had broken out. Libby screamed as she took several direct hits, her own attempts either pathetically short or off target. Sport had never been her thing.

Coco squealed, her long legs almost goose-stepping through the snow as Charlie chased after her and lobbed a snowball at the back of her head, the snow catching in the hood of her coat and trickling down her back. She wriggled like she was dancing as Charlie loaded up for the next round, but Zannah loyally caught him with a face-on shot that had him spluttering for several moments.

'Yes!' the girls cheered, just as Rollo returned the favour with a swift left and right double attack, his cricketing prowess on full display and sending Zannah toppling over her own feet. Libby watched in amazement as Archie rushed over, sweeping the snow off her and pulling her up again.

'Archie, I'm fine!' she laughed as he fussed.

Libby watched them. She had never seen him like this before: seductive, attentive, intense, yes. Obnoxious, arrogant, cocksure, that too. But never chivalrous, never gentle – and there was no doubting it now: whether it was supposed to be a secret or not, she knew the impossible had finally happened. Archie Templeton was in love.

Chapter Thirteen

May 2014

Footsteps on the stairs made her look up. She hadn't heard the sound of a key in the lock, nor the heavy click as the door shut. Beside her, Coco's breath juddered deeply and her fingers dug into Libby's arm. Libby looked back to find her friend desperately shaking her head, understanding they had to stay quiet.

They both listened as the sound of a door closed on the floor below. For several moments they could hear only vague sounds of movement; then footsteps came again, this time coming upstairs to where they were sitting in the dark. Coco flinched, but the footsteps passed by on the landing and then turned up to the final flight, heading for the top floor. Libby's room.

They heard the sound of knocking on her door . . . 'Pugh?' Archie's voice.

In spite of the circumstances, her heart skipped in her chest. So he had come for her after all, then? The thing she had wanted more than anything had happened – but she could never have foreseen it would play out like this.

There was a pause, then another knock. 'Pugh, Pugh . . . ?'

She remembered she had left the door ajar, intending only

to come down for a shower. Her lights were on, her bag on the desk, her clothes on the bed . . .

'Lib?' She heard the creak of the hinges as the door was pushed open and the sound of his feet on the noisy floorboards as he crossed the space into her tiny bedroom, looking for her. 'Are you here?'

She wondered what he would be thinking. Everything suggested she was home. Would he think she had come in and rushed out again – joining the others at Klute? Or did he know her better than that?

His footsteps sounded on the stairs once more, but he didn't pass through this time as he had on the way up, and she heard him knock on Ems's door. 'Anyone in?'

Coco's fingers pressed harder again on Libby's arm as she realized he was going to look in here after all, just as she had. Could he sense their presence, even in the silence? They watched as his silhouette came into the doorway, backlit by the landing light.

Slowly the door swung back further. 'Coco . . . ?'

He fell quiet as he took in the sight of them huddled together on the floor. Libby hadn't been able to get Coco to move; they had been here now for over half an hour. His eyes moved to hers, as if asking her to make sense of the image – Coco gripping her and shivering like she'd been caught in the rain, her mascara bleeding down her cheeks . . .

He seemed to immediately understand this was no hoax. He looked quickly around the room, as if searching for someone. 'Is anyone else here? In the house?' His voice was low but urgent.

'No,' Libby replied quietly.

He looked back at them, seeing again the way Coco clung to her, staring down at the floor. 'Do I need to call an ambulance?'

'She says she doesn't want one,' she almost whispered, as if words alone might break their friend's bones.

She? Not we? He looked at her and something like relief crossed over his face. Relief, followed by guilt. '. . . Police?'

Libby shook her head. 'Not them either.'

There was a long pause and Libby could see him beginning to guess what this was, piecing together this scene of a traumatized young woman huddled on the floor. He looked at her and she saw the question in his eyes: what next? If there was no ambulance, no police – what next? It was the very question she had been asking herself as they sat in the dark.

'. . . Is it okay if I come in?'

Libby looked at Coco, who was staring at her knees. 'Would that be okay if Archie comes in?' she whispered.

Coco nodded.

Slowly he walked in and came over to the far side of the bed, where they were crouched. He got down on the floor with them and placed a hand on Coco's foot.

For several moments, there was only silence, a dreadful yawning abyss of sound as horror overlaid the domestic scene, stripping them all back. But then a long, low moan emanated from somewhere deep in Coco's chest and all the agony she had been trying to hold back, to suppress and muffle, erupted in heaving sobs. As if kindness was undoing her.

Archie gripped her foot harder, anguished by her torment, and in the next instant, Coco crawled into his arms as she cried and cried. He looked at Libby over Coco's shoulder, his eyes burning with clarity and confusion, pain and anger. She knew he wanted to know what. Who. When. Why. But he didn't speak, just shushing her instead and gently rubbing circles on her back.

The three of them sat there for a long time. Every time it

seemed like Coco's sobs were subsiding, a new wave would come along and flatten her. Libby could see Archie's cheek was wet with Coco's tears, his own eyes reddened as he tried to remain calm for her sake.

Eventually, her breathing settled. Her head hung heavily on Archie's shoulder, exhaustion suffusing her body. Libby got up – stiff from holding her awkward position on the floor for so long – and went over to the bed, pulling back the duvet and turning and plumping the pillows. 'She should try and get some rest,' she murmured.

Archie stroked Coco's hair. 'Coco, I'm going to lift you and put you into bed, okay? Sleep will help,' he said, not making any sudden movements, not doing anything at all that might alarm her. Libby watched as, slowly, he got to his feet, carrying Coco the short distance and setting her down like a baby. Immediately she curled onto her side, still weeping. He tucked the duvet around her and straightened up, looking at a loss.

'I'll stay with her till she drops off,' she murmured.

'Try to sleep, you're safe now,' he whispered, looking down at Coco, a fragile curl in the bed.

Libby got onto the mattress beside her and met Archie's gaze one more time before he left them alone together in the dark. She cupped her body around her friend's, feeling how she shivered and shook like the last leaf on a winter oak.

All they could do now was wait for the wind to die down.

Archie was sitting on the stairs when she emerged over an hour later. He looked pale, the book he had been carrying when he'd first come in untouched on the step beside him. She looked at it, thinking how their evening might have been so different. Had he shared the same hopes as her, or had he really just wanted to read?

'She's asleep,' she whispered.

'Lib, are you . . . ?' His scattered gaze over her betrayed his fear she had been hurt too, but she shook her head quickly.

'I'm fine. I wasn't there.'

She saw his body physically ebb and she pressed a finger to her lips, pointing to the ceiling to indicate they should talk upstairs in her room. He stood aside for her to go first, his eyes following her as she passed by him, and they climbed the stairs in silence.

He pushed her bedroom door to, but didn't close it fully; they needed to hear if Coco woke up, not to mention they would need to stop anyone barging into her room 'for jokes'.

A sour silence, like a cloud of acid rain, settled in the room as he waited for her to tell him the grim truth. She hugged her arms close to her chest as she tried to order her thoughts, to make sense of the words that had tumbled from Coco in fits and starts, but there was nothing that could ever make them make sense; it was incomprehensible.

She turned back to him and swallowed hard. The words had to be said anyway. 'It was her professor,' she said. 'He did it.'

'. . . What?' Archie blinked once. Twice. 'Her . . . ?'

'She had missed an important deadline for an essay. It was worth twenty per cent of her total marks. So she had to meet him this evening to discuss "options".'

'Options?' he frowned.

'That was how he put it. She thought it meant she might have to repeat the year.'

There was a pause as he tried to process all this information. '. . . Okay.'

'So she went to his house this evening—'

'She went to his *house*?'

179

KAREN SWAN

Libby took a breath, hearing anger under his disbelief. 'He'd been in lectures all afternoon and he was having to fit this meeting in; she said she was inconveniencing him because of her fuckup. She figured he just wanted to get home, eat . . .'

'And rape a student.'

Libby winced and looked away. He was upset; they both were.

'. . . Sorry.' He turned, raking his hands through his hair and taking a breath. 'Sorry, Lib . . . Go on.'

'She said he offered her some wine and that they talked. He confirmed she would fail and have to repeat the year, unless . . . unless they could find some sort of compromise.'

Compromise. Archie fell very still at the word, his jaw bunching. They could both imagine how the conversation had played out. She saw the horror that she felt reflected in his eyes.

Suddenly he exhaled as if he'd been punched, then walked over to the window and stared out, shaking his head. One arm was stretched out above him, his hand pulled into a fist as the streetlights cast a warm glow on his face, but she knew he saw nothing.

'She needs to go to the police,' he said finally.

'I know. I've tried telling her that but at the moment she's adamant she won't. She says he'll say it's his word against hers.'

He half glanced back. 'Fine. So it's her word, then. Why wouldn't she be believed? She's reputable, highly educated, smart. No . . . no criminal record, nothing to discredit her. If she says her professor raped her, why shouldn't anyone believe her? She needs to go to the police and let them do their tests—'

Libby took a sharp breath. 'There wouldn't be much forensically. He didn't beat her. And he wore protection.'

Archie wheeled around. 'So then he planned it? He actually planned it?'

She put a finger to her lips, reminding him Coco was just downstairs. 'Possibly.'

His eyes shone with anger. 'Possibly? What do you mean, possibly?' he hissed. 'Of course he did! You're a law student, you know how this goes! He had a beautiful student in a compromised situation and he used his position to get what he wanted from her! There's nothing unequivocal about that. It was an abuse of power. At that moment, her entire future rested in his hands and he knew it!'

'I know. I fully agree with you. But in the eyes of the law, proving force, proving lack of consent, proving premeditation is hard. And it does all have to be proven.'

He stared at her suddenly with a new look. '. . . Whose side are you on?'

'Archie, of course I'm on her side,' she whispered, hardly able to believe he could doubt it. 'But Coco's traumatized and incredibly vulnerable right now. I have tried convincing her to come with me to the police, but I can't make her, and we have to respect what she wants to do next. She knows how this will play out – she went willingly to the house; she accepted the wine; there were no witnesses, no force, and there's very little forensic material. I can't give her false hope of a straight-forward court case when the percentage of convictions is so depressingly low. The system is hugely flawed—'

'It's barely fucking working!' he snapped.

She swallowed, calm in the face of his attack, understanding that it was part of the process for him as he absorbed what had happened – although that didn't make it any easier for her to play devil's advocate. 'I agree. It may not be in her best interests to go through the legal channels, and we only want what's best for her from this point forward, don't we? Whatever *she* wants goes.'

'Christ, I can tell you're a lawyer,' he muttered, realizing she had closed the circle on her argument.

'I'm not one yet.'

'Oh you are, Lib,' he said quietly. 'You are.'

It didn't sound like a compliment.

They stared at one another for several long moments before he turned away again, breathing heavily, his usually languid body brittle with tension.

'What are we going to do about the others?' he mumbled, standing at the window again and staring out. 'Do we tell them?'

'. . . I'm not sure,' she hesitated. 'But I think it's going to be almost impossible to keep it from them. There's no way Zannah and Ems won't pick up that something catastrophic has happened.'

'Mm.' The sound was more of a breath dragging on the ground. A grunt, barely able to lift itself.

'Is she going to leave?'

'I don't know that either. She's saying she doesn't want her parents to know.'

'But . . .' He looked at her, ready to argue again. She shrugged.

'At the very least, we need to keep everyone out of her room tonight. Try and keep the house as quiet as possible.'

'Good luck with that,' he muttered.

'I'll text the others and put a sign on the door saying she's got a migraine or something. If she can sleep tonight, it will help her with getting through tomorrow. We can decide a plan of action then.'

'Mm,' he grunted, turning away again.

She stared at his back, seeing the way his ribs flared, his breathing coming heavily as his body was overridden by its stress response; he was lashing out at her, as immersed in Coco's trauma as if he had picked up her body covered in blood. Libby watched him, knowing he had nowhere to place his rage; but didn't he see she felt it too? Coco was her friend as well – maybe not as close as the two of them; they had been friends for longer and shared a lazy intimacy with one another that she had always envied – but woman to woman, what had happened resonated with Libby in a way he could never understand. She needed comfort too. Even if she was pragmatic in a crisis, she wasn't the bad guy.

She walked over and slipped her hands around his waist, resting her head on his back and hearing – for a brief moment – the rapid clatter of his heart.

Immediately she knew it was the wrong thing to have done, breaching his personal space. She felt his muscles tense and, after a few seconds of awkward silence, he pulled away.

'I'll text the others,' he murmured.

Libby watched, stung by the rejection, as he crossed the floor. It was the first time she had ever instigated personal contact – in fact, it was the first time they had actually touched since that night by the front door – but he couldn't get away fast enough. She had embarrassed him and humiliated herself.

He stopped with a hand on the door but he didn't look back at her. 'Goodnight, Libby. We should all try to get some sleep while we can.'

Chapter Fourteen

23 December 2023

The walk back was slow but spirited. Laughter came easily, as if their adult edges had been chipped away, and the joy of playing gave way to jokes and stories as they walked in dynamic groups, falling behind and catching up with one another.

Libby had caught a bad case of the giggles. Ever since graduation she had been on a treadmill to corporate success and there had simply been no room in her life for snowball fights or sledging, for house-party games or lounging hungover in a kitchen and playing Pass the Porridge; now, even Max was growing more relaxed by the minute. The first run on the sledge had been terrifying and she had screamed all the way down, water streaming from her eyes as she flew at speeds that made the scenery a blur, but she had loved it. And on her second run, they began the races. The men, on account of their weight advantage and velocity, agreed on giving Libby and Coco ten-second head starts – but it still wasn't enough to stop them pulling ahead with metres to go. Ems and Zannah had been wise to sit it out: the trays were loose cannons, spinning if they hit a bump and – Archie had been right – far harder to steer.

They must have run up Bombers Hill ten times before the

farmer's text came in, and in spite of her utter exhaustion, Libby felt loose-limbed and revitalized. She couldn't say things were normal between her and Zannah, and Archie wasn't even looking at her now, but with the others it felt almost like the old days. Despite everything she had said to Max – and everything she had promised herself about not getting entangled again – she wanted more time here.

She and Coco were walking either side of Charlie, their arms looped through his, as Coco mooted a ski trip to Italy. She was certain she could get a deal with a five-star hotel in Cortina – 'They'll upgrade us for sure,' she promised. 'We've got to do it! If we can have this much fun with five inches on the Yorkshire moors, imagine the Dolomites!'

'There's a joke in there somewhere,' Charlie had muttered, sending Libby off into hysterics again and prompting Archie – walking just ahead with Prock – to glance back and check on the cause of their amusement. His gaze intertwined with hers, making the giggles die in her throat. She knew there would be almost no chance for her to apologize to him before they left. She would leave here with her renunciation of him in the boot room as her final word, and the impasse of the past nine years would still stand as their lives diverged once more. They were never supposed to have been in each other's lives—

'Oh my god!' Zannah cried, stopping walking suddenly and making everyone turn. Archie immediately looked ready to sprint over to her – an action hero in Barbour – but hesitated as he saw her pointing a finger in the other direction. On the far side of the Bombers valley the flock of dirty-looking sheep was running, scattering, in the field opposite. Was a dog worrying them?

Rollo and Archie stood on high alert, knowing especially well the damage that could be done by an out-of-control dog, but there was no sound of barking, no sign of a chase. Just escape.

Libby looked out over the polar landscape, unable to work out what was spooking them – until the first spark flew, jumping like a firework from the pylon standing in the middle of the field.

'There it is again!' Zannah cried.

The pylon, though massive, had been invisible to Libby's eye as she had scanned the view beyond it, admiring the trees, the fields, the lights in the distant towns . . . Only now did it sharpen into focus; only now did she see the fat sleeves of frozen snow clinging to the transmission lines, bowing them down.

More sparks crackled and spat, making everyone recoil even at this distance. What was . . . what was happening? Sparks were flying at a gathering speed at each of the conductors between two pylons, where a line was hanging so low it almost kissed the ground. Libby became aware of a low, constant buzz. Had that always been there . . . or was it growing?

'We need to ring the power board. Has anyone got reception?' Archie asked quickly, grabbing his phone and holding it up towards the sky. 'Fuck, I've got nothing. Roly?'

Rollo did the same and shook his head. 'Nothing.'

'Charlie?' Archie asked, just as there was a deep groan, as though the ground itself was yawning open. It was like waiting for the first spew of lava from a smoking volcano; they could sense the shift in energy, that pause before disaster, the dragging of waves back out to sea to greet the tsunami already barrelling in.

Suddenly Libby understood what was about to happen. Her hands flew to her mouth as she watched the pylon slowly begin to topple, like a dinosaur felled by a meteor. Coco cried out as they watched it thunder to the ground and set off a huge, dazzling shower of sparks, flames flickering against the snow. 'Oh my god, it's exploding!' she cried, turning on the spot in terror. Charlie grabbed her and put an arm around her.

'We're perfectly safe over here,' he reassured her.

But were they? The metallic buzzing was growing louder and Libby saw more sparks crackling on the pylon beyond as the fallen tower now pulled on that electricity line instead, ratcheting up the tension between the two posts. Tightening, straining . . .

'Oh shit,' Charlie murmured. 'Dominoes . . .'

The neighbouring pylon came down too with a deathly groan and a crescendo of crackles and sparks; it abruptly slammed into the ground – followed by the next . . .

Two more pylons came down. Of course they did. They would. Each tower was connected to the next. Where one fell, so it would pull on all the others in turn. It might go for miles!

Libby saw Archie's head suddenly whip round, looking over in the direction of the fallen pylons. The direction of the house. 'Oh shit, no. No.'

'What is it?' Coco asked, trepidation in her voice as she watched him.

Archie looked back at her, all his high colour gone. '. . . The road.'

They ran for what felt like miles but, in fact, could only have been one. Ems fell behind, of course, unable to sprint in her condition; Zannah stayed back with her but Archie was especially propelled by an adrenaline surge that saw him pull ahead of all the others, and he was standing with his hands on his knees, his head hanging, by the time they caught him up.

'Fucking hell!' Rollo exclaimed as they approached. The upper section of a pylon had fallen across the lane, blocking it completely. Sparks were still flying from the conductors. 'Oh Jesus Christ!' he cried, staggering forward in disbelief at the sight. Up close, seen from ground level, the scale of the pylon was colossal.

'Stay right back!' Archie ordered, his voice flexed with strain. 'Those lines are live. They've got four hundred kV running through them.'

Libby stared at the lines as if they were venomous snakes capable of striking out at her, and even though she was a good distance away, she took another few steps back. She looked around, unsure of exactly where they were. The house was still out of sight from here and the single-track lane was nondescript in this section, flanked on one side by a drystone wall and on the other, a wooded bank that rose steeply. It wasn't possible to see how far the dominoes had fallen beyond the bank, but surely there had to be a break in the chain somewhere? A tree breaking a fall, perhaps, and catching just enough in its canopy to reduce the angle and strain on the transmission lines?

But even if there was, it didn't help them here. The road was still completely blocked.

'Is there . . . ?' Max turned on the spot, looking behind them, his hands on his hips as the same thoughts occurred to him too. His body was rigid, his movements stiff, all playfulness forgotten. 'Is there another road into the Park?'

Archie seemed unable to reply, his hand now slapped across his mouth as he tried to think. Rollo gave a small shake of his head instead. 'This is the only road into or out of the estate.'

'And how big is the estate?'

'Thirty thousand acres.'

'*Thirty . . . ?*' Max spluttered. He tipped his face to the sky and leaned back a little, his eyes closed, striving for a calmness he did not feel. He was visibly irritated, even though this clearly wasn't anyone's fault; certainly not Archie's. But Libby's, maybe? He had certainly thought so this morning, when the snow had been the sum total of their problems. If only they hadn't made this detour . . .

She watched as he fell into a crouch, arms folded over his head, and stayed there for several moments before getting up and beginning to pace.

'Come on, you fucker,' Archie hissed, scrabbling up the bank a little and holding his phone aloft. 'You can usually get a bar here,' he said, scowling at the screen.

'Power to the masts must be out as well then,' Charlie said, checking his devices as well. He had no fewer than three phones in his pockets.

'What are those, your burner phones?' Prock quipped flatly. 'Don't tell me MI6 signed you up after all?'

Charlie shrugged. 'They were persistent. And the holiday allowance was too good to pass up.'

The two of them swapped dry smiles but their amusement was brief; this was no time for jokes. The stress was plain on Archie's face. Libby watched as Zannah walked over and placed a hand on his shoulder. He didn't shrug her off but turned towards her, nodding as she said something to him quietly.

Libby looked away again, biting her lip as she stared at the pylon that had become their captor. There was no way in and no way out. And no safe way of crossing over those grounded power lines . . .

Power lines.

'Oh,' she breathed, as for the first time the full impact of what had happened occurred to her; suddenly the extent of Max's anger and Archie's despair was explained. This wasn't just an immovable obstacle blocking their path out of here. It wasn't just a tree that needed to be cut up and removed. There would be a resulting power cut too, and these mammoth structures would all need to be either repaired or replaced before electricity could be restored. None of that was going to happen quickly. This was a disaster on an industrial scale. Her Christmas was cancelled. And Max's. Everyone's. No one was getting out of here soon.

A dismayed silence blanketed them all as they realized no one could even make a call to let their families know where they were or what had happened. There would be no emails, no landlines, no mobiles. No heat, no light, no hot water . . .

Libby thought of her parents and brother awaiting her at home in Herefordshire, their small fire laid for her return, the tree set up in the corner of the sitting room as it always was, a new bottle of sherry on the drinks tray.

Prock, who was stroking his jaw, trying to self-soothe, looked up. 'No offence, mate, but this is a . . . this is a real bummer.' He slid his mouth to the side. 'If Ems's waters break . . .'

Archie stiffened. '. . . Is that likely?'

'She was thirty-seven weeks two days ago; technically she could go into labour any moment now. That's why we brought the hospital bag with us.' He was outwardly calm but his discomfort reverberated in his words; panic hovered, waiting to land.

Rollo leaned in. 'Wait – so you mean, if she gets a fright or she sneezes too hard, we'd find ourselves delivering the baby on towels on the floor?'

'Um, *she* is right here,' Ems replied tartly. 'And the thought of you lot, down at the business end with a couple of old towels, is in itself all the motivation I need to keep this baby cooking for a while yet, thanks very much.'

'No guarantees, though,' Prock added with a sombre look.

'I'm really sorry, mate,' Archie muttered, looking down guiltily as he stuffed his hands into his pockets and they all sank into thoughts of their broken plans and the cold, dark Christmas that awaited them here.

It was Rollo who broke the silence.

'But you've got a turkey, right?'

Archie's blink was the vaguest of assents.

'So then it's . . .' Rollo gave an uncharacteristically weary sigh, trying to summon an optimism he didn't feel. 'It's not all bad.'

'Right, we've got about three hours of daylight left,' Archie said as they pulled off their boots on the back step and traipsed back into the kitchen. The sledges were propped against the outside wall; mementoes of an already bygone time, everyone shrugging off their coats, hats and gloves. Ems walked over to the fridge and pulled out the pie Mrs T had left for them; she popped it straight into the baking oven, checking the flame on the Aga and throwing a small shovel of coal in too. The range radiated its usual comforting warmth, and Zannah and Coco went over to huddle beside it, shivering as they blew on their frozen fingers and pressing their socked feet against the cream enamel doors.

'Libs,' Coco said, motioning for her to join them.

She shuffled over in her socks as Archie began to draw up plans.

'We need to get set up for the night so that we're all warm enough and can actually see. The scale of the house will work against us and this place gets very cold, very quickly. Chaps, we'll start with bringing in the logs and filling every basket to the brim; that includes for the bedrooms. We'll probably need to split some more too. Roly, you can help me with that; I know you know your way around an axe and the last thing we need is anyone requiring an A&E trip with their toes in a freezer bag . . . Girls, go to the pantry and boot room and find every candle you can, plus boxes of matches. Make sure there's at least one candle in every room and on the stairs as well. You'll find some glass hurricane lamps somewhere there. Use those for the stairs.'

'Okay,' they all murmured, watching him intently. Archie was rarely serious – some might say rarely sober – and now his mood set the tone. No one was joking or laughing. Even the dogs were forlorn, picking up on the down energy and heading straight for their beds.

'Then go through the pile of newspapers in the baskets round the back there and make paper scrunchies and twists as the base for the fires. That also means for the bedrooms.'

Charlie wandered over to the sink and ran some water. He looked back at them all. 'Another thing we should probably do,' he said thoughtfully, 'is fill every bucket we can find with snow.'

'Why? It'll just melt,' Coco queried.

'Exactly. And if the water goes off too – which it might well do, because they need electricity to power the pumps – then at least we've got something for flushing the loos, as well as cooking with.'

'The loos?' Coco asked, looking aghast.

'Plus we'll be able to make tea,' Ems said, holding a finger up. 'I'm a cockroach, I can survive a nuclear winter – but I refuse to exist without tea.'

'Okay, so then we'll fill every bucket we can find,' Archie said. 'Good call.'

'Will we be okay for food?' Coco asked, looking pale. Breakfast seemed like a long time ago now and their exertions sledging, plus the run towards the road and the long walk back, had depleted them all.

'Yeah. The Aga's solid fuel so we can cook as long as we keep it stoked up; and thankfully Teabag had already got all the food in for the next week, so we'll not starve.'

'Oh god, Mrs T!' Ems said, shooting him a concerned look. 'She said she was coming back at four. What if she comes up the lane and tries to cross the power lines?'

There was a momentary pause, a look of pure panic crossing Archie's face. Libby remembered Mrs Timmock had been his nanny first, housekeeper second; it was clear he cared about her.

'. . . No, she won't,' he said slowly, thinking it through. 'Bob was already making his way over here when the pylons came down, so he'll see what's happened and raise the alarm in the village. Word spreads fast there. And she knows we've got food, so she won't be worried about us for a few days.'

'She always worries about you,' Zannah said, looking at him.

'Well, at least Bob can report that the pylon's blocking the lane,' Max said. 'The power board will have to prioritize it if there's live power lines on the ground. Right?'

Everyone nodded, but none of them knew how things worked in a scenario like this, or where priority was given. How many more pylons had toppled? Had any come down near the village, where the local kids might play? Or fallen on a house? There was always someone who had it worse. How much attention would be given to a house party on a grand estate at a time like this?

'Ems, how long will that pie take to cook?' Archie asked.

She blew through her cheeks. 'Forty minutes?'

'Right then.' He clapped his hands. 'We'll get started on the logs and you find the candles. Let's make life as easy for ourselves as we can while we've still got light. We'll reconvene here in just over half an hour.'

The men turned back and began pulling their boots on as the women went off in search of candles and matches. Everyone keeping calm and carrying on.

'Lunch!'

Ems's voice was distant, and Libby sat back on her heels, wiping her brow with her sleeve. She was setting the bedroom fires while Zannah and Coco dispersed the candles around the house; Ems was self-appointed 'lunch monitor'.

No job was easy in a house on this scale. The rooms were so large, with such high ceilings, that a single candle – come nightfall – would make very little inroad into the darkness; each room needed two or three church candles at a bare minimum. As well as the rooms, they needed to light corridors, stairs and any passageways they would be using. They didn't have anywhere near enough candles for all that, but Zannah had made the good point that the fires in the bedrooms would throw out light as well as heat, so they could get away with only one candle in those spaces.

Libby rose, putting the small guard in front of the hearth, and let herself out of Prock and Ems's room. It turned out they were in the room next to hers, should she need more toothpaste – which of course she would now.

She heard the sound of a door opening and looked up to see Archie letting himself out of the corner bedroom at the far end of the hall.

'. . . Hey.'

'Hey.' He seemed startled to see her there and an awkwardness settled over them.

'I was just setting the fires.'

'Right, yes.' He walked towards her. 'I was bringing up the kindling.'

But there was no bucket in his hand and though she hadn't yet gone in there, she had worked out through a process of elimination that the room at the end must be Zannah's. Within a few strides, he was upon her.

Then past her. As earlier in the reception hall.

She looked at his back, then hurried to follow after him.

'. . . You heard Ems calling for lunch?' she asked, feeling her nerves mount at his continuing frosty demeanour. There was no sign of his signature dozy smile; even his hand wasn't in his pocket.

'Yes.'

He hated her, and why wouldn't he? What she had said had been unforgivable.

They headed downstairs, passing the glass-cased storm lanterns that had been set out on the staircase.

'Those should do the job, don't you think?' she tried again.

'They'll be fine,' he said shortly.

'. . . I expect you must be used to power cuts here, being so remote.' She was almost having to jog to keep pace with his long-legged strides.

He sighed, as if bored by the conversation. 'Reasonably.'

'We can all pull together, though – and at least we're somewhere warm and dry.'

He made a scoffing sound, seemingly making no attempt at all to even be polite. 'That very much depends on which room you're standing in.'

He walked a step ahead of her down the hall, not bothering to keep the conversation going. In the kitchen, the others were already taking their seats at the table as Ems divvied up the pie, a pan of steaming peas and carrots sitting on the warming plate.

'Arch, hair of the dog?' Prock asked him, holding up a bottle of red.

Libby was astonished as she saw almost everyone else had a glass too – Max included; he gave her a hopeless shrug as she looked at him. 'Are you serious? After last night?'

'Yeah, go on then,' Archie said with a nod.

Charlie walked past her carrying two plates and set them down at the table. Libby felt her tummy growl appreciatively. All morning she had been regretting not eating more at breakfast when she'd had the chance.

'Right – how many more are left, Charlie?' Ems asked him, the knife hovering in her hand.

'Uh, we're . . . nine, aren't we, so three more.'

'Actually, Zan's not coming down,' Archie said, taking his glass from Prock. 'She's sleeping.'

Zan?

'*Sleeping?*' Rollo huffed. 'While we're all breaking our backs, she's sleeping?'

'Hangover's still bad,' Archie shrugged. 'She says she'll be fine after a nap.'

Ems rolled her eyes. 'If anyone should be daytime sleeping, it's me!'

Zan? Libby stared at the back of Archie's head as he took a place at the table.

'This looks great, Ems, well done,' he said with significantly more appreciation than he'd given for her job setting the fires.

'Don't thank me. It's all Teabag's hard work. I'm just the finisher.'

'My wife, the finisher,' Prock mumbled in a dramatic film voiceover voice, making them all smile.

Ems handed Libby the last plate and she slid into the empty spot beside Max. Immediately he put his hand on her thigh, keeping it there as he ate with a fork. No one spoke much to start, their meagre appetites at breakfast now coming back with a roar as hangovers gave way to the munchies.

'So all the log baskets are filled now, are they?' Ems asked.

'Mm-hmm. Coal buckets too,' Archie mumbled.

Libby ate her pie, only half listening to the roll call of completed chores. *Zan*.

She felt a squeeze on her leg.

'You're jiggling,' Max murmured as she looked at him questioningly. 'You okay?'

'Sure.'

'Tense?'

'A bit.'

He squeezed her leg again, sliding his hand further up her thigh. 'I have a remedy for that,' he whispered.

She blinked in surprise. For a man who had displayed utmost discretion for the past five months, he was becoming sloppy to the point of brazen. She thought again of the red box in his bag and the decision behind it. *Had* a switch flipped in him? Did he want to make this official? Could the whole world now know?

Did she want it to?

'. . . Arch, did you hear what I said?'

Libby tuned back in to find Archie turning back to Ems. 'Huh?' He went to take another bite of pie.

'I said I think the water pressure's dropping,' she said with an apologetic grimace.

His fork stopped mid-air. 'Really?'

She nodded. 'I noticed it just now when I was rinsing the spoons.'

He dropped his fork onto the plate and rubbed his face in his hands, keeping it there. 'Right.' He was quiet for a moment as everyone swapped looks. Losing running water had been a worst-case scenario. He finally looked up with a sigh. 'Well then, in which case, no more showers or baths today and we'll have to restrict loo flushing to the minimum.'

'Oh Archie, come on!' Coco complained. 'First no wifi and now no baths?'

He gave her an incredulous look. 'What? How is this my fault? This could go on for days, or even—' He cut himself off, not wanting to say it. How long did it take to remove a pylon? Until it was removed and the lane cleared, they were not only without power but without exits.

'Thank god you've got a decent wine cellar,' Rollo said staunchly. 'Otherwise I might start to feel sorry for myself.'

'Sorry for –?' Coco huffed. 'Roly, this isn't a joke! You might think I'm being a princess but I'm not sure you quite understand what the fallout is for me from this. Burberry is paying me eighty k to post on three consecutive days while I'm up here and I've only done one – which, as you'll recall, was completely off brand.'

'I thought you said it got a good response?' he frowned.

'Maybe it did, or maybe the tide turned – I wouldn't know, seeing as getting wifi here is like catching a fly with chopsticks.'

'Aah, great scene,' Rollo grinned, looking over at Prock, who nodded enthusiastically. 'Mr Miyagi, what a legend.'

'No, don't start going off on tangents,' Coco huffed crossly. 'Burberry are banking on my posts as one of their major lead-ins to Christmas. They want all the country house vibes! What am I going to tell them now?'

Archie's head snapped up. 'Wait – so you pitched to them that you were coming here?'

There was a pause.

'. . . Nooo,' Coco said slowly. 'Not specifically. I simply mentioned in passing during a meeting that I was reuniting with my old uni housemates at a historic country estate and they thought it would make a great synergy of their brand and that whole typical English heritage thing . . .'

'In my home? You monetized my home?'

Coco swallowed. 'It's not going to mention anything about Drewatts, Arch.'

'So you mean it's just a backdrop?'

'Yeah.'

'Like a fucking Ralph Lauren store?'

'Well, no—'

'Well, yes! Is that why you came this weekend, Coco? To earn money off me?'

'Archie!' Coco looked taken aback by his abrupt tone. It was so unlike him. 'Of course not.'

Archie threw down his fork again and pushed back in his chair. 'How about anyone else? Any more hidden agendas I should know about?'

Tension breathed among them as Libby fell very still, Max's hand squeezing more tightly on her thigh. Archie was looking at everyone but her; talking to everyone but her; since he'd overheard her in the boot room earlier, he'd barely been able to look at her. But she knew it was all targeted directly at her.

She looked down. He had every right to be angry. She had taken his hospitality and trashed it; trampled upon the tentative shoot of friendship that had briefly broken ground during their dawn talk.

'Mate,' Rollo began, 'you know none of us here have an agenda—'

But Archie got up, his lunch scarcely touched. 'I need some air,' he muttered, stalking across the room, the dogs immediately at his heels.

No one stirred until the back door clicked shut again.

'Oh my god,' Coco whimpered, tears shining in her eyes. 'I didn't mean to—'

'Shhh, of course you didn't,' Ems reassured her. 'He knows that really.'

'It's just . . . the stress is real, you know? For as long as I'm off grid, I'm losing traction, followers . . . the algorithm will overlook me. I have to post at least once every day; I can't just ghost my fans. It's taken me so long to get to this point . . . Just to lose it over a weekend?' Her eyes were wide as she implored them all to understand the catastrophe staring back at her.

'Of course not. We get it,' Charlie said, appeasing her, reaching for her hand and squeezing it.

'You do?' She looked at him gratefully as he nodded.

'Arch is just stressed.'

'But Archie never gets stressed.'

'Yeah, but he's never had to look after nine people in a place like this over Christmas, with no power, no housekeeper and no known end in sight, either,' Rollo said, defending his old friend.

'Should I go after him and apologize?'

'No. Give him a minute. He's just got a lot on his mind. I'll check on him after this.'

'Yeah yeah, anything to get out of the washing up,' Prock teased, trying to lighten the mood.

'Well, eat up, everyone,' Ems said with her usual placid stoicism. 'This pie will knock the hangovers into touch once and for all. Plus it's fuel to warm us, which is more important than ever now. I expect we'll be sleeping in our coats tonight.'

Libby stared at her plate, knowing she had to go after Archie and apologize for her part in this. She knew she had made a bad situation worse. Did he not have enough to deal with, without whispered character assassinations? Her muscles braced as she went to stand but Max's hand tightened on her thigh, as if he could read her mind. As if he knew.

'Just eat up,' he murmured. 'It's going to be a long day.'

Libby set down the kindling bucket, hoping it wouldn't take too much to get the hall fires going again. Without Mrs T's careful attention this morning and after their protracted time outdoors, the morning fires had long since gone out and a frigid chill was beginning to set in this, the biggest of the rooms. At her back, in the middle of the space, the giant Christmas tree brooded like a dark spirit, giving Libby the spooks. Without fairy lights to impart a glittering festivity, it stood like a pantomime dame in the stage wings, both mawkish and grotesque.

Everyone had dispersed again after lunch. With most of the chores completed, Rollo had gone to find Archie; Ems had gone to have a well-earned and much-needed nap; and Coco, Charlie and Prock were in the drawing room, having taken the wine bottle with them. Coco was lounging on the sofa reading old copies of *Country Life* and *The Field* while the boys played backgammon. Max was having a lie down upstairs – he had tried to get her to join him, but she was too restless. She felt a need to move about, to keep ahead of her thoughts.

Outside, dusk was beginning to creep, a grainy haze peppering the sky and the snow beginning to glow ultraviolet. Night shadows were already spreading; an owl calling from one of the great oaks. Libby felt the polar chill begin to grip the house and hoped it was a whisper that wouldn't become a scream.

A low heat was still breathing in the grate, so she carefully prodded the cinders with the poker, increasing air flow, before throwing in some paper twists. She blew on them gently, seeing how they smoked, small flickering flames leaping up suddenly like tiny orange butterflies. Then she stacked a tepee of kindling around them and banked them with the quarter-sawn logs. Within a few moments, the hall was enlivened, a gentle crackle and golden light breaking the incipient gloom.

Satisfied with this small token of life, she rose, picking up the empty log sack and heading for the kitchen.

Rollo looked up as she came in. 'Ah, Libs . . . mercy has been granted in the form of an Aga kettle! We *shall* have tea!' he cheered. 'And I've found a fruit cake in the tin too.'

'How civilized!' she smiled as she walked straight through to the back door. 'I'll come and help you with it in a sec.'

'Where are you going?' he asked, as she opened the door and reached for the nearest set of wellies; it didn't matter if they fit or not. She only needed to walk a few metres.

'Just to get some more logs. I want to finish up in the bedrooms before it's dark.'

'No, don't do that.'

'Why not?'

'I'll go for you.'

She gave him a quizzical look. 'But you're making the tea. And I'm already togged up. I don't mind getting my hands dirty,' she shrugged, closing the door and descending the steps. The cold hit her like a hard slap and she looked up to see the sky was deepening to a plum, light leaching away fast. She shivered, thinking she should have at least put on a coat.

'. . . Wait . . .'

She turned back to find Rollo charging down the steps in a pair of sheepskin slippers that could only belong to Mrs

Timmock. They were several sizes too small, meaning he was almost on tiptoe.

'Roly!' she laughed. 'What's got into you?'

'I'll do it!'

'And I'm a big strong girl, thank you very much. I don't need you to carry a bag of logs for me.'

'It's not that.'

'What then?' She waited as he tottered over in the snow. 'Have you gone quite mad?'

'. . . Archie's still chopping,' he panted, reaching her.

'So?'

'He's just letting off some steam. Give him some space, Libs. This is tough on him.'

'Of course it is. Which is why I'm trying to help.'

'No, not that!' he sighed, looking exasperated.

She waited for an explanation but seemingly none was forthcoming. 'Then what, Roly? What's tough on him?'

'I mean *you*. You being . . .'

She stared at him, seeing the frustration in his face, a resentment surfacing that she had never noticed, or even suspected. He looked around them furtively, as if checking they were alone. 'Look, I know, okay?'

'Well, clearly you know more than me then,' she said tightly. 'Because I'm at a loss.'

A silence opened up as he stared at her, his cheek twitching with discomfort. Deep and meaningfuls were not his forte. 'I mean, I know what happened back then.'

Libby stared at him, stunned by the revelation.

'Look, this is a difficult situation for everyone. Maybe more difficult than any of you anticipated, I don't know . . .' He shrugged, as if he was all out of words. 'Look, I'm just trying to keep the peace, Lib.'

'I wasn't aware war was about to break out.'

'No? You think Max is oblivious too?'

Libby swallowed. It was true Max had become increasingly affectionate – but jealous? Was her friction with Archie (and by extension Zannah) really so evident that everyone could see it?

Rollo held out his hand for the log sack. 'Just let me collect the logs, okay?'

She stared at him for another moment, appalled to think that everyone had been watching on as she struggled through her interactions with them, striving so hard for civility, benign friendship, and seemingly failing . . . 'Sure,' she muttered, handing it over. 'If it's so important to you.'

'Thanks.' And he turned and walked – tottered – towards the log store in the housekeeper's slippers. Vaguely it occurred to her that Mrs Timmock would have something to say about her house slippers being returned with tide marks all over them; distantly, she heard the sound of an axe swinging onto a block.

Rhythmic. Repetitive. Exhaustive.

Frustration being spent.

Memories being crushed.

Chapter Fifteen

May 2014

'I'm an arse.'

The whisper fluttered through the darkness like a bright ember, stirring her dormant mind. She became aware of a gentle movement beneath her body, a feeling of constriction against her arms.

She startled slightly, eyelids fluttering, consciousness rising and falling with her breath.

'Shhh. It's just me.' His voice was so low against her ear, it tickled her.

'Archie . . .'

'Mm.'

'What time is it?'

'Late. Or early I guess—'

She remembered then, her body jolting, but his hand pressed down on her quickly. 'She's still sleeping, don't worry, I've left the door open.'

'. . . What are you doing here?' Her words were slurred with sleep but she could feel, now, his arms around her.

'Hugging you back.'

'. . . Why?'

'Because I was an arse. I'm sorry.' She heard him swallow. 'It just wasn't how I wanted it to be.'

Her mind felt muddled. 'How you wanted what to be?' she mumbled. If she could move, if she could see him, then she would wake up. This might make sense. But she was pinned on her side, her duvet pulled tight and his arms heavy upon her as if holding her down in sleep. Was she dreaming? Was this a dream? Him here at last?

'Us. Our first . . . touch.'

'I don't understand.' She felt him lift her head and his arm snaked under her neck. She sank again into the pillow.

'I didn't want it to be tainted by what's happened . . . I wanted something to be good, for once.'

'. . . Oh.' Not a dream? This couldn't be real . . .

'Go back to sleep,' he whispered.

She felt herself sink into the mattress once more, barely awake but vaguely aware of the distance between them, him on the wrong side of the duvet still. 'You'll get cold.'

'I'm fine.'

'Come under the cover.'

'No.' He swallowed again. 'Better not.'

'You don't want to.' The words were a whisper, barely formed. This wasn't real. She was dreaming.

'I do.' She heard a swallow, and then a sigh. 'More than you know, Lib. More than you know.'

Chapter Sixteen

23 December 2023

'Zannah can't still be sleeping, can she?' Coco asked, pinching the last of her cake crumbs from her plate. 'She's been off for hours.'

'You know Zannah,' Rollo muttered. 'Sleeps like a hibernating bear.'

'That reminds me – I was woken up by the sound of someone's snores through the walls last night,' Coco said.

'I bet it was her,' Rollo said ungallantly.

'Could've been Max,' Libby offered.

'I wasn't snoring, was I?' He looked sheepish, glancing up from the cryptic crossword.

'A little bit,' she shrugged. 'But in your defence, you were completely off your head.'

He rolled his eyes. 'I didn't think I ever snored.'

'Well, you have to have *one* flaw, Max,' Coco said with a cheeky wink. 'Otherwise you'd be hatefully perfect.'

Max gave a small, abashed smile, catching Libby's eye. He winked at her and reached over to squeeze her thigh, his mood improved again since several glasses of wine at lunch and his power nap.

'Back in a bit,' Archie muttered, setting down his plate and flicking crumbs off his fingers. His cheeks still had the deep stain of a good Bordeaux from his exertions and there were wood shavings stuck in his jumper and hair, although he appeared oblivious. He looked shattered.

Libby watched him go, before becoming aware of Rollo watching her. She turned away again.

'We should probably start lighting the candles soon,' Charlie murmured, looking out of the windows. The fire was throwing out so much light – as well as heat – that everything felt deceptively okay, but within half an hour the sky would be black and the house plunged into an absorbing darkness.

'Then I really have to finish the bedroom fires,' Libby said with a sigh. 'That tea and cake was good though, thanks Roly.'

'No worries. Need a hand?' he asked, watching her cross the room, heading for the log sack which he had left for her by the door.

'I'm fine. But thanks,' she said pointedly. What did he think she was going to do? Harass Archie in his room?

She went upstairs, pausing on the half-landing and looking out again at the view. The pristine perfection of this morning had been punctured now, the snow dotted with whirling Labrador paw prints. Life had continued as normal for them at least today; they had enjoyed their extra-long walk, romping through the snow to Bombers this morning, and the house party meant there was always a free hand to pet them. They knew nothing of the calamity affecting their two-legged friends.

She turned down the corridor to Zannah's corner room, her hand held up to knock on the door, but she heard voices coming from within.

'—should tell them.' Archie.

She froze.

'Not yet,' she heard Zannah reply.

'But it's the elephant in the room.'

'Is it?' Her voice suddenly inflected with alarm. 'Has anyone said anything?'

'No, but I mean . . . they must suspect. It's a hard thing to hide, especially when we're all here together and you know we can't keep it a secret forever. We have to tell them.'

'I know,' Zannah sighed. 'It's just . . .'

'Just what?'

There was a silence and the creak of floorboards suggested one of them was walking. Pacing . . . ? Coming over here? Heart pounding, Libby went to turn away. She could come back in a few minutes. Her phone still had some charge in it; she could set the fire by the torchlight function if she needed to.

'. . . It's Libby.'

She stopped again at the sound of her own name, her heart rate skipping into a full gallop. She pressed her ear closer to the door again.

There was another pause.

'What about her?'

'Things between us feel . . . strained. Off.'

'Well, it was always bound to take a bit of time. She has been MIA since graduation.'

'Yes – and we both know why . . .'

There was no immediate reply but someone sighed.

'. . . Let's not rake it all up again,' Archie said finally.

'I just thought that after all this time, it would be easier, than this . . . What if she hates me, Arch?'

'Don't be ridiculous, of course she doesn't. She seems fine to me. Every time I look at her she's in cahoots with Charlie or mucking about with Coco and Ems.'

'Precisely. Because she has no issue with them. They didn't do what I did.'

'What *we* did,' he corrected.

'. . . I don't think she's forgiven us.'

'Has she said that?'

'No, but I can feel she doesn't trust me. There's this . . . awkwardness between us. It's like we can't quite meet each other's eyes.'

There was another pause and Libby heard what sounded like a bed creaking.

'. . . Look, she's with Max now. She doesn't care about the past, Zan. It was probably naive to think things could go back to exactly how they used to be between you – all of us – but people change, they move on.'

'You know I asked her if things were serious with Max?'

'I didn't know,' he sighed.

'I thought if she was loved up with him it would be proof she *had* moved on.'

'And what did she say?'

'She was noncommittal, said it's not serious. But then this morning she revealed he's bought her a Cartier Love bracelet. I mean, that's one down from a ring.'

'. . . Right.'

'Which means it *is* serious – she just doesn't trust me. Not with anything. Not even that.'

There was a small silence.

'I don't know, Arch, it feels wrong to share this with her when things are like this.' Zannah's voice had dropped, as if she was mumbling. 'Maybe she won't even care, I don't know . . . My instinct is to wait.'

'But that's been your instinct for the past nine years and at some point, people have got to know—'

Libby winced at his words, feeling the scab ripped off and the wound as pink and soft as it ever had been. She was right back there, to that night . . .

'—You're over-thinking it. Libby's moved on, stop torturing yourself. Forget about the past and focus on the future; that's all that matters now.'

The past is another country.

There was a long silence.

'. . . Yeah . . . Maybe you're right.'

'Of course I'm right. Come here.'

Libby closed her eyes as she heard footsteps and the sound of a kiss.

'So we'll do it then, yes?' he murmured. 'Tonight? We'll just tell them.'

'If the right moment comes up.'

'Zan!'

'No, I will, I promise – but if not tonight, then definitely tomorrow.'

He gave a frustrated groan. 'Not last night. Not today. Definitely tomorrow . . . You're procrastinating!'

'I'm not, I promise. When the right moment comes, we'll do it.'

'You're a bloody nightmare,' he muttered.

'Yeah, but you love me.' Her voice was muffled.

'I do . . . More than you know.'

BLACKOUT

Chapter Seventeen

May 2014

Almost the entire household had convened in the kitchen, and it was a tight squeeze. It would have made more sense for them to move to the sofas in the sitting room, but it felt more natural jostling together in here, as if they could pretend this was just another morning. As if life was continuing on the same path as yesterday.

Coco was still in bed – she didn't want to get up – but she had asked Libby and Archie to do this for her. 'I won't be able to hide it,' she had whispered in the dawn light, her face as pale as a moonbeam. 'I can't fake my way through this.'

It was almost lunchtime, and Archie had gathered them together on the WhatsApp chat under the auspices of a house meeting. Prock, Rollo and Charlie were sitting at the table, eating sausages and beans on toast. Ems was making a sandwich, Zannah sitting on the worktop with wild hair and last night's make-up, white as a sheet and looking wrecked. She was nursing a mug of tea but looked like she too would be better off in bed.

Libby watched them, all loafing about in their usual manner and oblivious to the horror she was about to reveal. She herself could still hardly believe that this was a conversation they had to have. She remembered the desolate look in Archie's eyes when Coco's message had lit up her phone around four and she had risen – Archie still lying on top of the duvet – to go down and lie in bed with her. The pillow had already been wet with tears.

Libby glanced over at Archie, who was standing in the corner of the kitchen by the basement door, uncharacteristically quiet and still. Rollo, like an obedient spaniel, kept looking over quizzically at him as he ate, clearly suspecting something.

Archie, as if sensing her stare, looked back at her and gave a tiny nod. They had agreed she would lead; that this was information best revealed by another woman.

She cleared her throat, loudly enough that the others glanced up.

'So guys,' Libby said quietly, her sombre tone making them all turn towards her with concern. '. . . The reason we asked you all to come down here this morning is because . . . well, I'm sorry to say that something terrible has happened . . .' She saw the frowns already on their brows, cutlery held in a pause, mid-air. 'And it's not something we're going to be able to keep a secret. At least, not within these walls.'

She looked at Charlie. 'I'm afraid it's about Coco.' He paled before her; it was like watching blood run down a drain and she knew she had to get the words out quickly. 'She was sexually assaulted last night . . . She was raped.'

Silence boomed through the tiny room like a thunderclap. Ems's eyes were instantly shining with tears, her hand slapped over her mouth. 'No.' The word was barely a breath.

For several long moments, no one stirred as the shock of her words whipped up silent storms in their hearts.

'. . . Do we know who?' Prock asked finally, looking ashen. 'Her professor.'

'What?'

Libby just nodded.

'Where is she now?' Zannah asked. Her voice had lost its usual colour, all its signature force; her tea pooled on the counter as the mug tipped in her hand.

'Upstairs in bed. She's asked us to tell you but she's not ready to talk yet. And obviously this news isn't to leave this room. Not under any circumstances.'

For several moments no one moved at all, then Charlie suddenly pushed his chair back and ran to the bin. Holding up the lid, he threw up.

Archie went to the sink and poured him a glass of water. 'Here,' he said, handing it to Charlie as he finally straightened up again. Charlie accepted in silence, looking buckled.

'She's been to the police?' Zannah asked, but it wasn't actually a question.

Libby shook her head and braced for the response. 'At the moment she's saying she doesn't want to, although we've been trying to convince her.'

'Why not? She's got to go!'

Libby took a breath as she glanced at Archie; the smoke of the same argument still lingered between them. 'In theory, yes. But in practical terms, it's not so cut and dried.' She saw everyone's eyes harden slightly at her words. 'The problem – from a prosecution perspective – is lack of forensic evidence. It looks like it was largely premeditated. Coco had a prearranged meeting with him at his house to discuss missing a term paper, where he said she'd be failed for the year . . . unless they could come to an arrangement.' She swallowed, hating how *straightforward* it had all been for him. Had he been anticipating it all day, lecturing to a theatre of students, knowing what he was going to do in his own kitchen that night? 'He didn't need to use physical force when he could blackmail her. That meant it wasn't violent and he used protection.'

'All rape is violent,' Ems said in a hushed voice, her eyes burning.

'Yes, it is,' Libby agreed. 'But without bruising or any kind of defence marks, there's nothing to suggest – from a purely forensic point of view – that it wasn't . . .' She could hardly bring herself to say the word. 'Consensual.'

There was another sound and Charlie turned back to the bin, throwing up again.

'. . . This all adds the burden of proof onto the victim.'

'Don't call her that,' Charlie croaked, his head still hanging over the bin.

'Sorry,' Libby murmured. '. . . Coco herself is arguing these points. I do personally think she should go in and make a statement, but the last thing any of us can do is force her to do this against her will. She is traumatized and she has to feel she has control of the next steps.'

There was another silence until Rollo cleared his throat. '. . . If burden of proof is the issue, then if she goes to the police they would have to arrest him, yes? Bring him in for questioning? He might have a record. This might not be the first time. It probably isn't.' His voice was hoarse and flat as if ribboned. 'There's got to be weight in numbers.'

'I agree that from the way he . . . managed the situation last night, it's improbable this is the first time he's done this. The question is whether anyone else has reported him.'

'Well then, that's exactly why the university needs to be told too,' Zannah said, a little strength returning to her voice now, though she still looked dazed. 'Other women are at risk. How do we know he hasn't got someone else lined up for exactly the same thing tonight? Or tomorrow? Or next week?'

'Agreed. He's a danger to women and he needs to be stopped, but it all comes back to the same issue: Coco needs to agree to the next steps. This didn't happen to *us*. We're all on the outside looking in; it's easy for us to talk theoretically. She's the one who went through it and right now, the thought of anyone knowing what happened to her is only adding to her trauma.'

Everyone fell back.

'Do her parents know?' Ems asked.

Libby bit her lip. 'No. Not yet.'

A small silence bloomed, everyone lost in their own thoughts. No one was eating, drinking. Stirring.

'. . . What if an allegation was made anonymously?' Prock asked.

'You mean to the uni?'

'Yeah. Could we somehow prompt an enquiry but still keep Coco's name out of it?'

'I'd have to check but possibly not. He will have rights to make a defence.'

'*He'll* have rights?' Prock scoffed, a look of disgust on his face.

'Innocent till proven guilty,' Libby said quietly. 'It would be incumbent upon her to show that it was rape.'

'So you're saying everything – be it with the police or university – will in effect come down to her word against his?' Zannah said flatly.

'Yes.'

'And we've all seen enough *CSI* to know his barristers would try to discredit her: she's a student, she has casual hook-ups, ergo she's a slut . . . ?'

Libby recoiled from the angry words. '. . . Testifying in court would be challenging.'

'Challenging?' Zannah whispered. '. . . And that's *justice*?' She pulled her feet onto the counter and hid her face.

'This is why she's resisting it,' Libby said to them all. 'She knows she would be forced to relive the ordeal in painstaking detail, when all she wants to do is forget.'

'But that would mean he'll get away with it,' Ems hissed, her lips blanched with fury.

The silence was heavy in the room, a black storm cloud pushing against them all and chilling their bones.

Charlie looked up from where he was standing, his arms folded tightly across his chest. 'What's this guy's name?' He had been staring into space the whole time everyone had been talking.

'Staples. Richard Staples. He's a psychology professor.'

Everyone frowned, trying to place him, but Coco was the only psychology student in the house. How many professors were there in the teaching body?

'And where did it happen? Where does he live?' Charlie asked.

'Alandale Gardens, I think she said.' Her face changed as she saw the expression on his face. Charlie was a judo dan. '. . . Charlie, no. It would only make things worse.'

'How?' He looked up at her, his mouth drawn into a flat line, his cheeks pinched. 'How does it get worse for Coco when the worst thing has already happened?'

'She wouldn't want *you* to get into trouble. You could be arrested for battery, assault. GBH.'

'Fine. And I'd be more than happy to tell the police, when they arrested me, exactly *why* I knocked ten bells out of him—'

'Wait,' Prock interrupted, looking up. 'You said Alandale Gardens?'

She looked back at him. 'Yes. So?'

'Sasha Staples . . . 26 Alandale Gardens . . .' he muttered. 'I deliver to her every Wednesday evening between seven and eight.'

'What?'

'Is he married?' Archie asked, looking over at Libby, but she could only shrug.

'She's about early, mid-forties? Does that sound about right?' Prock asked.

Libby nodded. She had questioned Coco through the dawn hours as gently as she could, trying to gather information. Staples himself was, at Coco's best guess, around fifty.

'Well, if she is married to him, it's not happily,' Prock muttered.

'How do you know?'

'Let's just say she's one of these fairly . . . predatory older women. I always feel like she's hitting on me.'

Ems flinched, looking shocked. 'Sorry? Predatory how, exactly?'

'It's just little things – like she always remembers my name and talks to me like we're friends or something. And she's often in just her dressing gown or something low cut,' he muttered. 'One time, she was in a towel.'

'Are you fucking kidding me?' Ems cried.

'Listen, I just bring the bags in, set them down and try to get the hell out of there as soon as I can.'

'But . . . ?' Ems frowned. 'What's the but?'

'Well, I have to wait for her to unpack first and give me the bags; she's signed up to the recycling scheme and she takes *so* bloody long 'cos she won't stop talking. She always offers me a beer – I mean, I'm driving a fucking great van! Why does she think I want a beer?' He shook his head. 'But I have to stand there and wait for her, and every week it makes me late for the next drop.'

'Have you ever met *him*?' Archie asked, bringing the conversation back to the point.

Prock swallowed and shook his head. 'No, never seen him . . . But it wouldn't surprise me if she books the slot precisely because she knows he's out then.'

'Oh my god!' Ems cried. 'What does she actually think is going to happen between you? That you're going to shag her on the kitchen table?'

Prock grimaced. 'Don't.'

'Just wait, though . . .' Archie bit his lip, musing on something. 'Maybe that's something we could work to our advantage?'

'What do you mean?' Rollo asked, watching his old friend closely.

'Well, there's more than one way to skin a cat, right? Libs's right – we can't force Coco to go to the police, but if we tell this woman what her husband did, *she* might shop him? She might even know about other girls and Coco's name may not need to come into it.'

'You know, that's not a bad idea,' Rollo said, leaning in. '"Hell hath no fury" and all that . . . If she finds out the man she's sleeping next to at night is raping his students, she's better placed to wreak merry hell on him than anyone. She could destroy his career with one email, blow up their marriage, throw him out of the marital home . . . He can still lose everything, even without a criminal record.'

'But what if she doesn't believe us?' Zannah asked. 'Some women can be really fucking delusional about their men.'

'We'd *make* her believe it,' Archie said, looking straight at Prock.

Prock looked nervous. 'What?'

'If she's so keen on you, mate, let's use that.'

'How?'

'Get into a deep and meaningful with her, flirt back, drink the damn beer; make her think she might be getting what she wants with you—'

'Erm!' Ems interrupted. 'Excuse me?'

'She won't, obviously,' Archie reassured her. 'But if he can get her onside . . . Prock already gets to stand in their kitchen anyway, every Wednesday evening . . . Why not make the most of it? We hurt Staples via his wife. No risk of GBH charges derailing anyone's future careers. No mention of Coco's name . . .'

Everyone looked at one another, eyes locking, brains whirring as they tried to process a plan that – even twenty minutes ago – would have seemed laughably disconnected to their lives. Libby looked across at Charlie. Out of everyone, he had been the quietest. He was staring into space at a spot on the floor, deathly pale.

'Charlie, are you okay?' she asked in a low voice.

He looked up slowly, though he offered no reply. He looked broken, as if every bone in his body had been crushed.

'Do you agree this might be the best option if Coco doesn't want to press charges?' she asked.

'Just so long as there's something,' he said finally. 'He can't be allowed to get away with it.'

'Exactly,' Archie said beside him, placing a hand on his shoulder.

'He just has to pay,' Charlie said, his voice wavering, his lips thin with anger. 'One way or another, we have to make sure of it.'

Chapter Eighteen

23 December 2023

The first candles were flickering, the fire roaring in the hearth as the sun gave up its fight for the day and night won out. It wasn't yet five but they had started drinking anyway. 'There's nothing else for it,' Rollo had shrugged, popping the cork on a bottle of Bollinger. He had used the very last of the light to quickly strip the brace of pheasants he'd brought in from the cold store earlier – and terrorized Coco with – and they were now neatly stored in the fridge. It had been felt 'some refreshment' was much deserved.

Ems was still upstairs 'gestating' (Prock's description) but Zannah had finally surfaced from her recovery sleep, skipping lunch and afternoon tea to move straight on to her streamlined vodka tonics. She had changed into an ivory cashmere lounge set with yellow cashmere socks and immediately bagged the chair nearest to the fire, staring into the flames like a gypsy queen reading a future.

Libby tried not to dwell on her even though Zannah seemed to glow in her peripheral vision like a hot coal, impossible to ignore. Archie wandered back through, his gaze skipping over everyone and making sure they were happy. He seemed pleased that bodies were spread long and languid over almost every surface, a louche expression of their collective intimacy with the house now. Last night's raucous mood, and even this morning's childish frivolity, had segued into an insider's *ennui*.

Everyone was tired, the chores completed for today at least, although more logs would need to be chopped tomorrow when, again, they would have to make the best of the daylight while they had it. It was easy for things to feel more normal by day, but it was at night when the deprivations announced themselves. It wasn't easy going cold turkey from their daily tech addictions – it wasn't just Coco fretting over her lost link to TikTok. Charlie was edgy without his stock reports, Rollo wanted the racing news . . .

'Let's play a game,' Coco said, sounding bored.

'Scrabble?' Charlie suggested, moving over from the window to join her on the sofa. Coco folded her legs up like a flamingo to give him space.

Charlie sat beside her, glancing over at her huddled form, then reached for her foot and placed it on his lap. 'You can stretch out,' he said quietly. 'It's fine.'

'You can't play Scrabble with this many people,' Archie murmured. He had dropped himself into the fireside chair opposite Zannah, his legs splayed. His eyes went to her every few moments and Libby couldn't stop watching the silent communication that travelled between them. It was almost constant, and made a mockery of Rollo's fears outside earlier: Archie wasn't remotely troubled by her presence here. She didn't understand what he was so concerned about.

'How about Two Truths and a Lie,' Coco suggested.

'Ooh,' Prock said, looking up from his card game with Rollo, a glint in his eye. 'Now that's always amusing.'

'Okay then. You go first, Coco,' Archie drawled, reaching for his glass.

'Fine.' There was an easy silence as she drifted into thought. '. . . Okay. Well, I was once arrested for shoplifting.'

There was a titter of disbelieving laughs.

'I have cheated death twice in my life.'

Eyebrows went up.

'And I'm ambidextrous.'

'Hmm.' A collective murmur swept around the room, everybody thinking hard.

'I'm going to say the first one's a lie!' Zannah said. 'Flagrant lie. There's no way you've ever nicked anything. You're too clumsy for one thing, and you'd probably have blushed madly for another. You used to look guilty as hell just for using my shampoo.'

Libby smiled; Zannah was spot on in her assessment. 'I agree,' she chipped in.

'Hmm,' Coco murmured. 'Okay. Anyone else?'

'I agree with Zannah too,' Prock said.

'. . . I'm going with the second one being the lie,' Archie said thoughtfully. 'I reckon it's a lie in that it's a manipulation of a truth. I think you have cheated death – but only once.'

'Or possibly four times.' Rollo shrugged.

'Why four?'

'Like Zannah said, she's clumsy.'

Archie nodded. 'True. Either way, second one's a lie.'

Coco hitched up an eyebrow. 'Charlie?'

'Last one,' he said firmly, no hesitation. He had begun squeezing her feet, though whether or not he was even aware of it wasn't clear.

'Really? You seem pretty certain of that,' she replied.

'You write right-handed, smoke right-handed; you shoot your right hand in the air whenever you're asking for a cup of tea; you pull your hair back off your face with your right hand when you're twisting it up with that fabric thingy; you text right-handed and you always paint your left hand first when you're doing your nails. In fact, I don't think I've ever seen you do anything with your left hand. So no, I don't think you're ambidextrous. I'm calling that out as a lie.'

There was a long silence.

'What?' he asked, looking around at their faces.

Zannah sat up a little. '. . . Can I change my answer?' she asked as everyone looked at Coco expectantly.

'Well,' she said, looking taken aback. 'I can confirm that Charlie is in fact . . . correct. The third one is a lie. I'm not ambidextrous.'

'You're hella observant, Charlie,' Zannah said, her eyes narrowing slightly.

'Who wants to go next?' Archie asked, casting a look around the room, his gaze settling upon Max, who was absorbed in the crossword. 'Max, how about you?'

Max set down the newspaper slightly. 'Me?'

'Sure, why not?'

'Well, none of you know me well enough to judge, surely?'

'Libby does, surely?' Archie said coolly. 'Besides, the fun is in trying to make a snap judgement.'

Max glanced at Libby. 'Fair enough. Well, then . . . let me see . . .' He lapsed into deep concentration, falling very still, his profile especially handsome in repose. Libby was pretty sure she had first caught feelings from sitting downwind of him in too many meetings.

'I . . . Okay, well, I suffer from globophobia.'

'Globo-what, old chap?' Rollo frowned.

'Globophobia.' He looked down, a small smile playing on his lips. 'And I believe in love at first sight . . .'

Coco whooped as she looked over at Libby and winked excitedly (and very unsubtly).

'And . . . and . . .' he said, waiting for the room to die down, 'I have had dinner with Barack Obama.'

'Oooh.' Prock sat back in his chair, whistling between his teeth. 'Interesting.'

The room was quiet for several moments, everyone ruminating.

'I'm feeling the Obama thing could well fly,' Charlie said pensively.

'Yeah,' Prock chimed. 'My thoughts too . . . I'm going with one's a lie, whatever the hell it means.'

Max smiled, looking around the room. 'Okay. Anyone else?'

'. . . I'm with the boys,' Coco agreed. 'One's the lie.'

'Zannah?'

She was watching him intently, her fingers pressed together in a steeple. She looked across at Libby, then back to him again. 'I'm saying . . . three's the lie. You didn't eat with Obama.'

Max just nodded. 'Archie?'

'Yeah, sure,' he replied noncommittally, as if he couldn't be bothered to think about Max himself. 'Why not? I'm with Zannah.'

It was a moment before she realized Max was looking at her and awaiting her answer. 'Elizabeth?'

'Elizabeth,' Zannah echoed with a small laugh, as if trying the word for size. She saw Libby look over at her. 'What? It's just so *odd* hearing you called that.' She struck Libby as being on her old feisty form tonight. She really had slept off her hangover. Or perhaps it was the empty stomach and the vodkas.

Libby looked back at Max. 'I'm going to say . . .' Their eyes locked and she was immediately reminded of the tension between them in the office, the excitement that had come from keeping it secret. '. . . Two. I don't think you believe in love at first sight.' He was like her – a tactician. Pragmatic, rational, controlled (mostly). That statement had been intended for the room; he was playing them again. And she watched for the look that came into his eyes – shock, followed by bemusement that she had put a pin to his romantic statement.

'Ouch,' he winced, but a small smile played on his lips too.

'So what was it, Max?' Coco asked.

'Well, the lie was actually . . . number three.'

'Ugh!' Libby laughed, covering her face as Max lunged for her, grabbing her and cuddling her close.

'How could you think I had dinner with Barack Obama?' he asked, kissing her cheek, but she knew what he was really asking was, how could she rebut his belief in love at first sight? Had it been intended as a public proclamation, of sorts?

Everyone laughed.

Almost everyone.

'Lord, what a racket! How am I supposed to grow a baby through that? You could wake the dead!'

They looked up to find Ems coming through, bump first, her hand pressed against the small of her back. Immediately, Prock held his arms out for her to go to him.

'That was a solid sleep, baby,' he said, kissing her cheek as she sank onto his lap. 'You were off for at least three hours.'

'Really?' She gave a small stretch, her face still puffy with sleep, before sinking against him. She really did look very pregnant indeed. She seemed to get bigger every time she left the room. 'Well, that's good. I think I would have slept for another three if I hadn't been so rudely torn from my slumber.'

'Sorry, Ems,' Coco cried, pulling a sad face. 'But things were getting exciting down here. Max was just revealing he's actually a romantic at heart.'

Max gave a groan. 'Oh god, I knew I shouldn't have said that!'

'Actually, it wasn't you lot that disturbed me.'

'No? What then?' Prock asked, stroking her hair.

'I got woken up by Archie's dratted ghosts haunting the bedroom.' She shot their host a pointed look.

'Shit, it wasn't my father, was it?' he asked darkly. 'If I'd known he was wandering the halls, I'd have asked you to ask him where the hell he left the key to the gold vault I'm still hoping he has hidden in a Swiss Alp.'

Ems chuckled. 'More like Ten Ton Tessa, from the noise she was making. Rattling the windows, hitting all the creakiest floorboards.'

'Mm. Pretty much impossible to avoid those in this place.'

'*Have* you ever wondered if the house was haunted, Arch?' Coco asked him interestedly. 'Have you ever seen a ghost?'

Archie merely raised a sardonic eyebrow in reply.

'No? No one's ever reported seeing things moving out of their place? Mrs T hasn't felt a ghostly presence when she's stripping the beds?'

'She *is* the ghostly presence!' Roly laughed. 'She just appears from dark corners with a tray of cheese and crackers. Or stands at the foot of the bed with fresh towels.'

Archie grinned.

'Well, *I* definitely heard something, so you can log me as your first witness,' Ems said. 'I thought you'd come in to get something?'

Prock shook his head. 'No, I've been down here all afternoon.'

'Plus, the phone wasn't where I left it. I swore I put it on the side table, but when I woke it was on your pillow.'

'Well, that's not too odd,' her husband said gently. 'You did put it in the fridge last week.'

'True. The baby brain is real.' She looked around at their scattered scene. 'So what was causing all the fuss down here, anyway?'

'We're playing Two Truths and a Lie,' Charlie said.

'Ah, always a bit of an eye-opener.'

'Indeed.'

'Max,' Zannah said, pinning him with a curious look, 'what exactly is globophobia?'

He gave a rueful grin as he glanced across at Libby. 'Please don't think less of me . . . It's the—'

'Fear of balloons,' Archie supplied for him.

The two men shared a look.

'That's right,' Max nodded, a twitch of displeasure flashing across his face. Somehow, Archie's hijacking of the definition stripped it of comedy value.

'How did you get *that*?' Zannah asked, her gaze sliding over to Libby too.

'Over-enthusiastic blowing at my seventh birthday party. One popped in my face and a bit of the balloon went straight in my eye and scratched the cornea. I had to wear an eye patch for a month afterwards.'

'Hmph, I think I'd dislike them too after that,' Charlie said sympathetically.

'What happened to your party?' Zannah asked.

'It went ahead – without me.'

Zannah chuckled. 'That sucks.'

'Ems, do you want a drink?' Archie asked, sitting straighter in his chair as he realized she was still without one.

'No, I'm fine, I'll have one when I come back. I'm going to slam the venison in first and get the veg going.' She rose from her husband's lap. 'Anyone want to give me a hand? I'm not sure I want to be all the way down there in the kitchen on my own. It's pretty spooky out there now.'

Libby threw a questioning look in Zannah's direction but she was resting her head back on the chair, eyes closed again

231

as the firelight warmed her face. Really? Was she really going to do nothing at all? She had slept all afternoon as they'd carried out the chores to ready the house for the cold and the darkness tonight. She couldn't help with the meal either?

'I'll come and help you,' Libby said, after a moment. Irritated, she turned to go, but her gaze tangled with Archie's; he was watching her watch Zannah and she saw protection in his eyes, as if he could read her resentment.

She turned away.

'So what were the two ways you cheated death?' she heard Charlie ask Coco as she and Ems walked out.

'Yikes, it's *so* dark out here,' Ems said, starting down the long passage. 'Old houses are way creepier in the dark, don't you think?'

'Yep,' Libby nodded, although she thought maybe it wasn't so much age as size that was the determining factor. She had grown up in an isolated rural village where power cuts were fairly routine, but her home had never felt creepy.

Church candles had been set on saucers every twenty metres, emitting low orbs of light, but the ceiling was far too high for the light to illuminate the upper reaches, and it lay untouched above them like a midnight sky.

Libby saw the hurricane candles on the stairs hadn't yet been lit. 'I'll catch you up in a sec Ems. I'll just light these,' she said, reaching for the box of matches that had been left specially on the bottom step. The lamps had been set on every fifth step and by the time she reached the last one on the bedroom corridor, the flickering view back down was beautiful. Almost romantic. Elongated shadows were thrown up the walls, the family portraits and stag heads enriched by the period lighting.

She set the matches back down on the top step and was

turning to head downstairs when she froze. In the corner of her eye she was sure she had glimpsed a movement at the far end of the passage. For several moments, she didn't stir.

'Hello?' She stared into the darkness – no candles had been set to line this corridor – waiting for someone's head to bob out from one of the bedroom doorways. '. . . Who's there?' she asked, trying to think who it might be. Everyone had been in the drawing room when she had left, hadn't they?

She blinked, waiting for some kind of response, the hairs on her arms standing up and her heart rate beginning to speed up as the silence drew out. She had that feeling again that she had had several times before, an instinct of a hidden presence. Someone was there. She was sure she could hear breathing – it was drawing closer – but there was nothing she could see. No silhouette, no shadow, no creaking floorboard.

Something touched her arm and she whirled around with a cry.

'Jesus!' Max exclaimed, almost falling back down the stairs. 'You almost gave me a heart attack!'

'*Me?* How d'you think I feel?' she gasped, pressing her hand above her heart and closing her eyes.

'What's got you so jumpy?' he laughed.

'Nothing, I . . . I thought I saw something, that was all.' She looked back down the unlit hall; everything was inert, not even so much as a potted fern to indicate life.

Max followed her stare down the corridor. 'It wasn't Ten Ton Tessa, was it?' he whispered.

'Ha ha.' She smacked a hand to his stomach, feeling embarrassed that the thought had actually crossed her mind.

'I hadn't credited you with a vivid imagination,' he grinned, pulling her in by the waist and kissing her cheek. 'A brilliant mind, yes, but a vivid imagination? Not so much.' He kissed her. 'Mm. Why don't we take advantage of all these dark corners?' he murmured, his hands beginning to wander.

She pulled away. 'I can't. I promised to help Ems with dinner. She's waiting for me . . . What are you doing up here anyway?'

He gave a sigh. 'I was coming to check for messages on my phone, while it's still got some juice left.'

'But there's no reception here. And the power to the masts is down.'

He shrugged. 'I'm an optimist.'

'You're delusional, is what you are,' she smiled. 'Did you manage to get that message out to your father this morning? Does he at least know we're snowed in up here?'

He shook his head. 'It didn't send. We weren't in the right spot before the power went.'

'So then he has no idea where you are?'

'Nope. Hence my frustration. They'll be worried.'

'I'm sorry.' At least her parents knew about her detour here; she had mentioned it to her mother on the phone as they had discussed Christmas plans. She was supposed to be arriving tomorrow lunchtime, but if they were watching the news they'd see how badly Yorkshire had been affected . . . They'd be able to guess what had happened, surely?

'It's not your fault,' he shrugged, clearly in a more generous mood than he had been first thing.

'Isn't it, though?' She arched an eyebrow. 'A quick dinner has turned into you spending Christmas with my old house-mates.'

He sighed, his smile fading. 'Yes, well, it would be easier to accept if things were better with our host. I thought I was imagining it at first but I am sensing distinct hostility.'

'Really . . . ? No,' she demurred. 'Surely not . . .'

But Max just stared at her. He was an expert reader of behaviour; it was what made him so good at his job. 'Are you going to tell me what's going on? Why am I like Monday fish?'

She swallowed. '. . . I think . . . no, I'm pretty certain, actually, that he overheard us in the boot room this morning.'

Max frowned as he tried to think back. 'You'll have to refresh my memory. What happened in the boot room?'

'Well, you called him Peter Pan. And I likened him to the Marquis de Sade.'

'Ah. That's unfortunate.'

'I also called him a fuckboy, for good measure.'

'Well, he was, wasn't he?'

'Whether he was or wasn't, we're guests in his home. It was unforgivable of us to talk about him like that. Me. I shouldn't have said those things.'

'It was a private conversation, Elizabeth. People are entitled to their own opinions. Obviously we wouldn't have said those things if we'd known he could hear.'

Libby looked away. 'It just doesn't sit well with me. I really feel like I need to apologize.'

'Well, don't do it on my behalf,' he said sharply. 'Trust me, he's been getting his revenge, taking pot-shots all day.'

'Pot-shots?'

'Yes – cutting me up on the sledges; then when we were getting the logs, he gave me a carrier with a broken handle. And then the way he tried to embarrass me just now with the whole balloon thing . . . Plus, he's staring daggers any time I catch him looking my way. The guy is not a fan.'

'Oh.'

'There's not going to be much festive cheer around here if

he carries on like that, I can tell you. This may be his home, but I'll only put up with so much.'

'I'll have a word. Try to clear the air.'

Max stared at her.

'. . . What?'

'I was just thinking back . . . When you called him a fuckboy, it was in direct response to my question as to whether anything had ever happened between the two of you.'

'Yes. And I told you it hadn't.'

He blinked, still watching, a question in his gaze.

'What?' she asked again, even more defensively now. It was one thing working alongside him, but being interrogated by him was a daunting proposition.

'I don't know, Elizabeth, it just . . . I feel like there's something you're not telling me.'

She gave a shrug. 'Nothing happened between us. I was never with him. I don't know what more I can say.' It was technically true.

'Maybe he wants it to happen and he resents me getting in the way?'

She gave a small, dry laugh. 'He's with Zannah. You must have noticed how they are with one another?'

He frowned. 'No, not really.'

'Well, we've barely seen her, of course. She's been pretty elusive.'

'You say elusive, I say lazy,' he shrugged, still watching her closely.

Libby swallowed. 'Anyway, I think they're going to announce their engagement this weekend.'

'*Really?*'

'I'm almost certain of it.'

He caught her chin with his finger and made her look at

him again. 'So you're telling me he's *not* secretly in love with you?' He said it as a joke but she saw the scrutiny in his eyes.

She arched an eyebrow as she released herself and headed for the stairs. '. . . Now whose imagination is running riot?'

Chapter Nineteen

May 2014

'Cut it all off.'

The stylist, holding Coco's long hair in her hands, paused, making eye contact in the mirror. 'When you say all . . . ?'

'All of it. I want it gone. I want a short back and sides, like a boy.'

The hairstylist made eye contact with the rest of them, perched forward on the chairs in a huddle.

'She means Kate Moss's pixie cut era,' Zannah supplied.

'Oh! So really short-short then.'

'Exactly,' Coco nodded, staring at herself in the mirror with wide eyes. She had come into Libby's room exactly two hours earlier, asking if she had any scissors. She didn't want to look like the girl *it* had happened to any more, she had said; she wanted to be someone new.

Libby's first impulse had been to resist – she didn't think she could bear the thought of Coco's hair clippings in the kitchen bin, a symbol of her anguish and need to cleave away from herself – and it had taken her a moment to gather her thoughts and propose that they go, all the girls together, into Newcastle instead (going into town ran the risk of seeing Staples, of course). If her hair was to be cut, it should be cut well and in a decisive, empowered way, not a wretched one. They would all get cuts. All for one.

'Well, you've got the bones for it,' the stylist said, fluffing out and draping Coco's magnificent mane, then pulling the ends against her head. 'And it'll improve the condition for sure.'

'Yes. It's what I want. It's the best thing.'

Another stylist came over. He was heavily pierced and holding a coffee. 'Okay, who's up next?'

Ems, Zannah and Libby looked between one another.

'She is,' Zannah smiled, placing a hand on Libby's arm and volunteering her.

Great. She'd been hoping to have a quick look at the magazines on the coffee table for some inspiration first.

'If you'd like to take a seat here, then, next to your friend.' He held out a black nylon cape and fastened it around her before she sat down. Libby settled herself as he began holding up her hair from the tips and letting it fall in heavy chunks back onto her shoulders. She always found having to stare at herself in the mirror like this so challenging. 'So when was it last cut?'

To her embarrassment, Libby realized she couldn't remember. 'About six months ago,' she fibbed.

'Uh-huh,' he murmured, and she sensed her split ends were betraying her. 'And what are you looking for today?'

'Um, well to be honest, I'm not really sure.' It wasn't like she'd woken up that morning with this in the diary. 'I'm happy to be guided by whatever you th—'

'French au pair,' Zannah said authoritatively, leaning forward in her chair again to make sure of being heard.

'What?' Libby asked, trying to make eye contact with her in the mirror, but Zannah was determinedly looking solely at the hairdresser.

'Hmm!' he said more brightly. 'Yes, that could work. Really freshen your whole . . . look.'

'You know what that means?' Libby asked him nervously. How did 'French au pair' translate into a hairstyle? What were these references Zannah was able to pepper around so freely and be understood?

'Of course! I think it's an inspired decision.'

Libby wasn't aware she'd made a decision. She caught Zannah's eye at last and her friend gave an assured nod.

'Just trust me,' she winked.

An hour later, the transformation was complete. Apparently the shift between lawyer and French au pair wasn't the ability to understand tort, but to rock a long, thick fringe and feathered layers that magically sculpted cheekbones. Libby blinked at the young woman staring back at her, brazenly more insouciant than uptight now. She shook her head lightly from side to side, admiring the sensuousness of the cut as it tickled her face. Could a haircut really engender a whole new identity?

She looked across at Coco in the next chair and had her answer. Where before her friend had belonged to the tribe of blonde, long-haired private-school girls with ring stacks and North Face puffas, now she looked like a Paris model. The elfin cut revealed a long slender neck and emphasized her doe eyes, her coltish limbs more prominent without the distraction of a tossed mane. She looked redrawn. Burnished. Purified. No relation to the chaotic, drawn creature who had walked in.

Zannah and Ems were in the adjacent chairs now, Zannah having a keratin treatment to relax her curls and Ems going for a long bob.

'How do you feel?' Libby asked, reaching a hand over to

Coco as she blinked back tears, absorbing this new version of herself. Able, now, to look at herself.

She looked at Libby. '. . . Better.'

It was a small word, but it felt like a landmark moment. Not only was this the first time in five days Coco had left the house – it had only been yesterday that she had left her room. A horror had entered their household and no one was untouched; the girls were taking it in turns to sleep in with her but even the guys heard her shouts in the middle of the night, her whimpers and cries as she woke up sobbing; the sound of the shower going on at odd hours as she tried to wash herself clean. They had moved as a pack since their meeting in the kitchen and there was a tacit agreement to keep the place quiet and secluded: no guests, no loud music, no weed. Even the sun didn't dare peek into the rooms, the curtains largely remaining drawn.

Libby had taken to studying at home full-time, abandoning her treasured spot at the Billy B library window to remain on hand at all times, and each day the boys brought back food from campus. Archie had even said he was cancelling his twenty-first, and only Coco herself had been able to talk him out of it. As much as the chaos of daily life was largely being put on hold for her recovery, she had insisted it couldn't and shouldn't be stopped altogether (although clearly she would not be attending).

Archie. He hadn't come up to Libby's room since the night of the attack, when he had slept with his arms around her – but at a distance. It was a distance that had held, a breach they couldn't seem to span. Sometimes, when they were all sitting in the living room or they would pass in the kitchen, their eyes would catch and she would feel that small hitch in the pit of her stomach, as if she was being physically hijacked from one reality to another. She thought he felt it too; there was always a slight spasm across his face whenever he saw her, but they were stuck in a lull. Caught in a pause. Life was on hold and love – or lust, whichever it was – was distinctly inappropriate, transgressive even. Nothing could happen and yet she felt his absence every minute; as if something fundamental was missing from her now.

'Girls.'

Libby looked up at the word. It had an inflection in it, a call for attention, and she looked across to find Zannah, freshly defrizzed, looking back at them with a smile. '. . . I may have just had a brilliant idea.'

The train pulled out of the station and Libby let her head press against the glass, the platform hoardings beginning to rush past in a blur. Commuters waiting for the next train stood with their heads bent, reading the paper or scrolling on their phones, oblivious to the faces flashing past them with empty eyes. It was rush hour, and after a bright, breezy day that carried whispers of summer within it, the sun was smudging itself against the sky, pigeons cutting a dash to chimneys and nearby treetops.

Coco was sitting to her left, staring into space; Ems opposite her on her phone; and Zannah fast asleep in a sprawl against the glass. Shopping bags were scattered at their feet. The lights of the next station shone into the carriage, and she nudged Zannah's foot with her own. 'Wake up, sleepyhead,' she murmured. 'This is us.'

The others began gathering their bags but Zannah didn't stir. Libby nudged her again.

Nothing.

'Hey,' Ems said, jogging her with an elbow as the train began to slow to a stop. 'Earth to Zannah? Hello . . . ? Welcome back,' she grinned as Zannah blinked at her blearily. 'You were sleeping like the dead.'

Libby grabbed all the remaining shopping bags.

'Wait – are we there already?' Zannah mumbled as they rose to standing.

'Hurry up!' Ems said as the doors whooshed open. Zannah staggered off the train as Libby set the bags down on the platform and rearranged them.

'Yours,' she smiled, handing Zannah her new shoes and the haul of Charlotte Tilbury make-up.

'Thanks,' Zannah sighed.

'You look wiped,' Libby said as Ems trotted ahead and looped her arm through Coco's.

'Yeah, I feel it.'

They fell back into single file to allow an elderly lady on a mobility scooter to pass.

'I could do with one of those,' Zannah muttered enviously. 'Imagine being able to sit down all the way home.'

'It's only a five-minute walk.'

'Yeah, but I'm a lazy cow.'

They turned onto the street, heading for home. It was that time of day when the residents were coming in and the students going out. A changing of shifts, a changing of the guard.

'. . . Have you still not heard back on that internship?'

'Oh god, please don't remind me,' Libby said, feeling her nerves pitch at the mere mention of it. 'I really thought I'd have heard by now, and I'm so nervous. I don't know what I'll do if I don't get it.'

'But you will,' Zannah said assuredly. 'There's no question of it. No one works harder than you.'

Libby didn't reply. There was no point in saying that everyone who applied was the hardest-working of their friends – that it wasn't enough to have a brilliant mind and the work ethic of a beaver; there still had to be an extra edge. She also didn't want to admit that during the past week, her unwavering faith in her chosen profession had taken a bad knock. She could still remember the scorn in Zannah's voice that terrible morning: *And that's justice?*

She had been right to be angry. Archie too. Their friend had been subjected to a traumatic attack and the legal redress was not fit for purpose. Everything was stacked against Coco. Innocent till proven guilty protected the rights of the accused – but overrode those of the victim until fact and truth could be proved beyond reasonable doubt. The wound was left to fester as an open sore till judgement was given. Was this really a system she could believe in – and become a part of – when, as an involved bystander to a crime, vigilantism appeared to be their better option?

They walked past the fish shop and the bookie's, the off-licence and the twenty-four-hour local food mart. They turned into their street, their little house looking somehow shrouded and set apart from all the rest now; their neighbours might be forgiven for thinking they'd moved out or else were lying in there dead. There wasn't even so much as the *EastEnders* theme tune humming through the walls.

Zannah slid the key into the lock and they walked through to the sitting room. Archie and Rollo were on the sofa, going through a wine list for the party; Charlie was coming down the stairs with his laptop. They all looked up as the girls walked through with their bags.

'Bloody hell!' Charlie exclaimed in surprise as he caught sight of Coco.

'. . . Is it okay?' Coco asked apprehensively, stopping dead, her eyes wide at Charlie's evident shock.

'You look . . . amazing.'

Her body softened a little at his response. 'Really?'

'You really do,' Rollo agreed, leaning back on the sofa cushions.

Her hands fluttered to her bare neck. 'I just felt a change would be good.'

'Change is always good,' Archie agreed.

'. . . Hungry?' Charlie asked her. 'I was just about to cook.'

'Oh . . . What are you making?' Coco asked, following him towards the kitchen stairs.

The others watched them go.

'I'm going to put my trackies on,' Ems said, trudging upstairs.

'Nice haircut for you too, Ems,' Rollo called after her.

'Ta, Roly.'

'Well, that looks like a successful outing,' he said in a hushed voice. 'We couldn't believe it when we came back and found Coco gone. All of you, gone.'

Libby registered Archie's double take as he clocked her new hair.

'Pugh,' he drawled, his gaze travelling over her like a hot poker and a smile flickering on his lips as he saw her blush. 'You're made-over too.'

'We all got our hair done, actually, thanks for noticing,' Zannah tutted, collapsing in the armchair. '*And* we got tattoos.'

'What? Even you?' Archie asked looking at Libby directly.

'Well, don't look so shocked!'

'What did you get?'

'We all got a little star outline,' Zannah sighed.

'Show me,' Archie said, still looking at Libby.

'Show us then,' Rollo said at the same time.

'Can't,' Libby shrugged.

'Why not?'

'It's somewhere . . . discreet.'

'*Where*?' Archie asked, even more intrigued now.

Zannah pressed a finger to her lips. 'Uh-uh-uh, nosy. That would be telling. We girls have got to have some secrets, isn't that right, Lib?'

'Yep,' she replied, seeing Archie's eyes widen as he scanned her. Did he have X-ray vision? He looked like he wished he did. He seemed heavily invested in seeing that tattoo for himself and the look was loaded when he made eye contact with her again.

Another set of keys slid into the front door lock.

'Hey, Prock,' Libby smiled, best positioned to see him first and grateful for the distraction.

'Mate, what are you doing here?' Rollo asked, lolling his head back on the sofa cushions again as their housemate rushed through. 'I thought you said your shift finishes at nine.'

Prock was out of breath and still wearing his supermarket uniform. 'It does, but I had to come back,' he panted. '. . . I did it.'

Everyone straightened up, more in response to his frantic mood than his words. They made no sense.

'Did what?' Zannah asked, confused.

'I drank the beer. I flirted . . . And then I told her.'

'What?' Archie almost leaped from his seat. 'But . . . you said . . . you said Wednesdays!'

'I know, but for some reason, this week she changed it to today. So I bit the bullet and just did it. I figured it was best not to overthink it.'

Everyone was staring at him, open-mouthed. Their plan, such as it was, hadn't yet been talked-through in fine detail. They had thought they had a few days to finalize tactics.

'And?' Zannah bit her lip and pressed her hands together in a prayer position. 'How did it go?'

He swallowed hard as he shook his head. '. . . She didn't believe me.'

'*What?*'

Prock looked crushed, as though he felt he'd failed. 'She said he's always fucking his students. Those were her words. Said they wouldn't think twice about giving him a blow job for a grade increase . . .'

'But . . . no! This wasn't that!' Zannah exclaimed.

'Obviously I told her this was . . . I said it was . . .' He stopped himself from saying the word too loudly, glancing quickly towards the stairs. '. . . Rape,' he mouthed. 'But she wasn't having any of it. Complete denial.'

'Fuck,' Archie hissed, sitting forward and resting his elbows on his knees.

Libby sank onto the arm of the chair. She couldn't believe it either. There had been so many reasons why this was the best course of action – it would spare Coco *and* still deliver a form of justice against Staples.

'Oh god, so that idea's fucked, then,' Rollo sighed, resting his head on the cushion back and staring, unblinking, at the ceiling. '. . . And meanwhile almost a week's gone by and she hasn't reported it . . .' He turned his head to look at Archie. 'So then we have to go over there and kick the living shit out of him, or we have to accept he's going to get away with it. Those are our only two options.'

'No, no,' Prock said, still looking wild-eyed. 'That's the thing, you see. That's why I came back . . .'

'What is?' Archie asked, looking up through his fingers.

'When I was in the kitchen with her, before I told her, she asked for my number, so I . . . I gave it to her, because you know, why not? I was trying to pretend I was interested at that point and obviously I can just block her later.'

'But?' Libby prompted, watching him closely.

'I wasn't even at the end of their road when she sent me this.' Prock reached into his pocket and pulled out his phone. The screen was opened to an explicit image which took them all a moment to process.

Archie looked back at him in amazement. 'She sent you a fucking nude?'

'Several,' Prock replied, swiping the screen.

'Jesus,' Zannah murmured. 'She's no prude.'

'So then . . . ' Archie looked back at Prock. 'What's your idea?'

'Well, if she won't confront the truth about her husband, what if we turn this on its head and confront her husband with the truth about his wife. We could threaten to publish these; say we'll send them round the student body if he doesn't do as we say. He may not give a shit about other women, younger women, but his own wife . . . ?'

'You mean, good old-fashioned blackmail?' Archie asked.

'That would be risky,' Libby said quickly, nervously, seeing how her housemates were all leaning in, thinking it through. 'Blackmail comes with a custodial sentence. Up to fourteen years.'

She felt a new fear flutter through her chest. Them appealing to Sasha Staples's better nature had been one thing, but if she was linked to something like this, actual criminal behaviour, her career would be in flames before it was even started.

'Of course we're not actually going to publish these,' Archie said, pointing to the phone. 'Our only involvement would be threat, not action.'

'That's not the point,' she argued. 'It doesn't matter that Staples doesn't know we wouldn't do it. From a legal perspective, just as long as he believes we would, that's blackmail.'

'It's leverage,' he said evenly. Somehow they were pitted against one another again. 'How could he risk exposing us, without shining a light on his actions too?'

Libby bit her lip, seeing the dark gleam in his eyes. The gambler's buzz as he assessed the risk.

'What would we be demanding from him in return – hypothetically speaking?' Zannah asked, interrupting them.

Prock shrugged. 'Whatever Coco wants – immediate resignation? Moving away and leaving the area? Handing himself in to the police? I don't know; she'd get to choose. The important thing would be that we'd have him over a barrel this time; we'd not be relying on someone else's goodwill. With these pictures, we can force him to surrender. He's a cornered rat.'

Zannah looked over at her. 'What do you think, Lib?'

Everyone waited for her response; the one who knew the consequences of any potential fallout, she seemingly held the veto on this action. But if she was the star lawyer-in-waiting, she was also a friend and fellow housemate.

She thought of Coco, renewing herself by trying to look like a boy; of that man in a lecture theatre just waiting for the next desperate girl . . . Her mind raced through the possibilities of the different ways this could come back on all of them, too, their own futures and incubating careers hanging in the balance if they were to be implicated. If Staples called their bluff, it could be their worlds that fell apart too. She saw her parents, proudly anticipating a better future than their past, the promises she had made them . . .She saw Coco, sobbing in the dark . . . What other options did they have? In this instance, doing the right thing meant doing the wrong thing. Slowly she gave a nod. 'We should do it.'

Chapter Twenty

23 December 2023

Supper was served in the kitchen. It made no sense to be using more rooms than were strictly necessary when candles and log fires were the basic prerequisites for inhabiting any space tonight. In spite of the double hall fires and the one in the drawing room, and despite the Aga throwing out as much heat as its small furnace could possibly generate, the house was growing cold fast. Everyone was wearing sweaters – or in Coco and Zannah's case, two.

Both Ems and Libby were perfectly warm enough from their efforts making dinner; Libby had been the *chef de partie* to Ems's *chef de cuisine*, taking her instruction willingly as they had roasted the venison haunch – checking the pinkness by candlelight – and blindly reducing a red wine jus to the perfect consistency. The beans were al dente, cooked in water from one of the melted snow buckets, and the potatoes fluffy inside. 'Ha! What power cut?' Ems laughed triumphantly as she drained the pans and they served out. She made it look easy, even while heavily pregnant, and kept putting it down to the nesting instinct, but Libby was concerned – didn't pregnant women experience a burst of energy just before they went into labour?

Christmas by Candlelight

They could hear the others all the way down the hall, noise levels rising with their wine consumption. Rollo was playing on the piano, banging out some Elton John, but occasionally a lone voice or two warbled into earshot as well, Zannah's laugh carrying like a bugle down the long passage.

Archie had earlier decanted 'a particularly good Malbec' to accompany the meat, and as Ems yelled 'Supper!' Libby admired what they had managed to pull together, against the odds. She had pinched some of the greenery from the dining room and wound it around the flickering church candles as a table centre; some napkins and old rattan placemats had been found on a shelf in the pantry. The room had a cosy, atmospheric festivity to it, and as they set down the plates, it was almost possible to believe they had *chosen* to be without light and heat.

Coco gasped as she came through first. 'Oh you guys! This looks so pretty.'

'Smells pretty amazing, too,' Prock said, coming in sniffing the air.

Rollo slung his heavy arms over Libby and Ems's shoulders. 'You're good in a crisis, girls,' he said solemnly. 'I can offer no higher compliment.'

Chairs were dragged back and everyone sat with sighs of relief that they could fill their stomachs at least, draping napkins on their laps – or in Rollo's case, under his chin.

'Well, cheers, everyone!' Archie said as Ems sank heavily into her chair. She looked immediately exhausted again, and Libby caught Prock watching his wife anxiously too. What if her exertions triggered the labour? If the baby started coming now, how exactly could any of them help her? No one had any medical experience and, not for the first time, Libby shot another irritated look in Zannah's direction. How could she just sit around and watch?

Archie raised his wine glass. 'A toast to the chefs for giving us a Christmas Eve eve dinner by candlelight. It'll take more than a blizzard to bring us down.'

'To the chefs!'

'It is so reassuring to know that even when we have nothing, we can still be civilized,' Rollo said with conviction. Libby half expected him to start singing 'Jerusalem'.

'I'm not sure a haunch of venison and a bottle of malbec counts as "nothing",' Charlie quipped.

'Quite. And only my wife could have us eating like kings when the national grid is down,' Prock said proudly.

'Indeed. Thank god for your wife – and solid fuel Agas,' Archie smiled. 'Teabag was having none of it when I suggested we get an electric model. Quite right too. She always knows best.'

'Do you think they'll have got word out about the pylon blocking the lane?' Coco asked no one in particular.

'Of course. Bob would have raised the alarm within minutes, I should think. He was already on his way over here when they came down, so that will have helped with getting any recovery effort mobilized quicker.'

A tut came from down at the opposite end of the table and eyes swivelled towards Max. It took another moment for him to notice. 'Sorry,' he said with an eye roll. 'I was just thinking it was such sod's law with the timing and all – given Elizabeth and I were already waiting on him getting over here to dig us out so we could leave. If he'd just come a half hour earlier . . .' He looked around, seeming to read the room. 'Well, you'd have two fewer mouths to feed, is what I'm getting at. I'm thinking of the extra burden on you, Archie, having a houseful at a time like this.'

'Generous of you,' Archie drawled.

'. . . What's that?' Prock frowned, sitting up a little straighter in his chair, fully alert and looking like the black labs when they heard the sound of a knife on the chopping board.

'What's what?' Ems asked distractedly, not breaking off from eating. But a sound gradually came to her ear, too: the distinctive beat of rotors.

'It sounds like a helicopter.'

'Probably the army,' Archie nodded. 'They come over a lot; the MoD is constantly doing drills on the moors.'

'I wouldn't be surprised if they've been drafted in,' Rollo chipped in. 'A chain of pylons down is a whole other box of frogs to your common or garden power cut.'

'Do you think they're coming to rescue us?' Coco asked hopefully.

'Do we need rescuing?' Archie asked, pointedly dipping his venison in the jus and sipping his wine.

'Mm. Doesn't sound like the army,' Max said, concentrating on the noise, which was growing ever louder. 'It sounds smaller than a Chinook.'

Libby saw Zannah set her knife and fork together on the plate and lean back. Was she really finished already? She had eaten maybe a third of her food. She saw Archie notice it too, skimming a look in Zannah's direction, but she winked back at him and patted her flat stomach.

Oh god. Was that . . . ? Libby felt the floor drop beneath her chair. Was *that* their news? Suddenly it all made sense – Zannah's refusal to go sledging, her slow walking in the snow with Ems, her seemingly excessive need for sleep . . . Libby felt a heaviness in her chest, her appetite suddenly abated too.

She stared at them, feeling a desperate need to hear them say the words – she had to know for sure – but the noise was closer now; it sounded like the helicopter was going to pass directly over the house. For ten or so seconds it felt as if it must be right overhead, the sound almost unbearable as the low thud of the blades displaced the air and made the windows rattle in their frames. The dogs whined in their baskets; the glasses vibrated slightly on the table.

'What on earth . . . ?' Prock pushed his chair back suddenly, his gaze upon the window.

Libby, staring unseeing at her plate, looked up at precisely the wrong moment as a bright light shone straight in through the glass, blinding her. The cutlery dropped from her hand as everyone stood in a panic, the house trembling in the disturbance.

'It's landing!' Prock cried, whipping open the back door and running out, oblivious to the cold.

'Oh my god, they *are* rescuing us! We're saved!' Coco cried, throwing down her napkin and following after him.

Everyone clustered on the lawn, Coco and Ems holding onto each other's arms and jumping excitedly as snow was blown everywhere, the landing rails twitching left and then right as the pilot hovered, then touched down.

Libby wandered over to Max, who was watching with a look of undisguised open-mouthed delight. 'My god,' he grinned, pulling her close and dropping a kiss on her cheek. 'Talk about leaving it to the bell!' He checked his watch. 'Nine fifteen. Nine fifteen. Where do you think they'll drop us?'

'I . . . I have no idea,' she replied, feeling more shaken than elated by this sudden intrusion. She wanted to get back to her family for Christmas, of course she did.

And yet . . . She stole a glance back towards Archie, standing with Rollo, hands in their pockets and both of them watching the helicopter land with benign expressions. She had thought he might look happier to be rid of his unexpected houseguests. She had thought she would feel happier to go.

'Where's the next village? No, town? Somewhere with a station?' Max wasn't listening for an answer from her, she realized, his mind running on a stream of consciousness. 'Will the trains be running, that's the thing . . . ? We'll never get a hire car now, not at this time on Christmas Eve eve. Or . . . I guess it depends if their IT systems are down,' he mused, his eyes narrowed in concentration. 'God help us if it's a manual booking system . . .'

The sound of the engine cut out and the rotors began to slow. Libby could see the relief on Prock's face, his hands clenching and unclenching as he waited for the pilot to jump out.

When he finally did, he was greeted almost as a hero.

'Oh thank god you've come for us!' Coco exclaimed as he ran towards them. 'You don't know what it's been like! We've got no heating, no light, not even running water! We're having to throw buckets of melted snow down the loos!'

Archie and Rollo swapped looks, their eyebrows hitched up at the sob story. 'More venison, anyone?' Rollo muttered. Archie just tutted and shook his head.

The pilot hesitated, looking alarmed by the frantic reception. '. . . Mr Earnshaw's party? Drewatts Park?'

Charlie?

Confused, everyone turned back to him. Libby realized for the first time that Charlie was standing further back from the rest of them, still in the light-spill from the kitchen. 'Um, yes,' he said, walking forward reluctantly to the pilot. 'I'm Charles Earnshaw.'

'I've got here . . . one passenger, to Hampshire?' the pilot asked, referring to his log.

'One . . . ?' Zannah queried. 'Charlie, what does he mean, one?'

Eyes narrowed as the accusation hung, unarticulated, in the air.

'I booked this long before I came,' he shrugged.

'You booked a helicopter? In advance?'

'It was the only way to make the timings work.'

Libby remembered his Christmas Day plans at the spa hotel. He had detailed staying in bed all day and eating his turkey on a lap tray but he had failed to mention that he would be travelling there by helicopter. A small detail, perhaps, but a pertinent one now.

'And you didn't think to say anything when we were panicking about what to do?' Zannah persisted. 'About Prock and Ems if they went into labour?'

'Honestly, I had just completely forgotten all about it.' Charlie swallowed, looking embarrassed.

Zannah was incredulous. 'You forgot? You forgot you'd booked a helicopter?'

Charlie looked over at the pilot; there was no point in discussing his oversights now. 'In light of the recent weather, we're going to have to have a change of plan,' Charlie said. 'How many passengers can you take?'

'Three, sir,' the pilot replied.

Coco looked panicked as everyone exchanged glances.

'Well, clearly the Procks, you *must* go,' Charlie said quickly, looking at them both.

Libby saw the relief ripple across both their faces. 'Really?'

'Naturally. There's no question of it. Can you drop them in Harrogate?' he asked the pilot. 'As you can see, we could have a medical emergency on our hands otherwise.' Ems stuck her belly out for good measure, lest he should be in any doubt as to the imminent nature of the birth.

'Shouldn't be a problem, but I'll need to run it past ATC.'

'Sure.' Charlie sighed. '. . . So then, that leaves one more space.'

'You mean you're not going to take it?' Libby frowned.

'Well, I suspect my need to get back isn't as great as someone else's.' He looked back at Archie. 'Assuming you're happy to put up with me a little longer?'

Archie grinned, looking genuinely pleased. 'As long as you like, mate.'

Libby looked back at the others. So then, who . . . ? This was practically a second home to Rollo, so Libby didn't think he'd feel in any desperate rush. And with Zannah staying here, the obvious candidate had to be Coco, surely? Her worry about the damage to her career, with every passing day that she went *sans* wifi, had already caused one argument. And with eighty thousand pounds hanging in the balance if she didn't post today and tomorrow too . . .

'. . . Well, if no one else minds, my need to get back *is* actually fairly great.'

Libby's head whipped up as Max cast an apologetic smile around the group. She felt everyone's eyes lift off him onto her, and back again. Was he being serious . . . ? He had heard as clearly as everyone else that there was only one seat left. Did he really intend to leave her behind?

No one responded immediately, and she knew their shock mirrored hers.

'Well, uh . . .' Charlie looked straight at her, trying to gauge her response.

'You don't mind, do you, Elizabeth?' Max asked, turning to her, dropping his voice. 'It's just that . . . it's obviously a bit different for me here, than for you.'

Logically, she got it; but emotionally? He didn't seem to register that even if he was only escaping on account of her friends, she was nonetheless seemingly no incentive for him to stay. 'Sure,' she nodded, trying to hide her hurt and praying

257

no one could see how humiliated she felt. 'Of course you should go.'

He smiled. 'And at least that way, you get the fun of driving the car back too. I'm pretty jealous.'

Was he, though? 'Well, we'll see,' she said shortly. 'Obviously with my own plans so up in the air, I can't promise anything. You might need to make your own arrangements on that score.'

'Sure. Sure,' he nodded, registering the immediate drop in temperature between them – but still looking happier and more relaxed than he had at any other point in the past twenty-four hours. He rubbed his hands together, though whether with glee or from the cold, Libby wasn't sure. 'Well, I'll just get my bag, then . . .'

'Yes, I'll bring ours down too,' Prock said, looking a little stunned as he followed after him. Libby watched as they both walked back into the house. She was painfully aware of eyes landing on and off her like flies.

'And there's really no way you can take another passenger?' Coco asked the pilot, putting a hand on Libby's shoulder. 'She's just a pocket person. There's not much of her.'

Libby looked at her friend, surprised that *she* wasn't trying to strong-arm a lift. After all her panic about being offline at breakfast this morning, she now seemed curiously resigned to staying here . . .

'None at all, I'm afraid – insurance,' the pilot said firmly. 'I'll just make contact with ATC and file the new flight plan. Three passengers to Harrogate, then, is it?'

'Um, it'll be two to Harrogate and one to London,' Charlie said quietly.

'That will affect the quote, you understand, Mr Earnshaw?'

'That's fine,' Charlie said quickly. 'Just add it to my account.'

'. . . You have a *helicopter account*?' Coco whispered, looking amazed.

Charlie met Libby's gaze with an inward groan.

'Any chance you can get back here again tonight?' he asked the pilot. 'We might be able to do another leg.'

'Sorry, Mr Earnshaw, the roster is completely full. I'm booked to a drop in Jersey after this one. The first availability is the twenty-eighth of December now, I believe.'

'Right.' Charlie stepped back, looking irritable, and they watched as the pilot headed back to the helicopter. 'If ever there was an argument for buying your own . . .' he muttered under his breath, prompting another staggered look from Coco.

Libby turned away quickly, realizing she was shivering from standing outside in just a sweater and no coat. She walked back into the kitchen. Ems, Rollo and Archie had already gone back in, the boys seated back at the table to finish eating as Ems – unable to sit still – stacked the dirty pans and began washing up. Archie, a glass of wine in his hand, paused as she walked back in.

'Ems, for heaven's sake stop; I'll deal with that later,' Libby said, taking the scouring brush from her and moving her away. 'You've done your bit. Is there anything lying around the house that you need to pack? Shoes, jumper . . . hot water bottle?'

'No, I don't think so,' she murmured. 'Oh wait, no, my phone is beside the green chair in the drawing room. I left it there, charging, last night. I'll just go—'

'No, *I'll* get it. You sit down and take the weight off your feet. You're doing far too much. You've got to slow down.' Libby walked down the long passage, through the flickering darkness. The dramatic lighting seemed to suit the house somehow, as if the shadows conveyed the weight of history and all the many lives that had been lived within these walls.

Archie's family. Ancestors. The ones responsible for his straight nose or the slight curl in his hair or his lofty height . . . She found the phone, threw another log onto the fire while she was in there, and was heading back when Max bounded back down the stairs.

'Hey,' he said, catching her by the elbow and swinging her around to him. His eyes were bright and he had changed out of Archie's loaned clothes and back into his suit. He looked like her lover again – urban, dynamic, thrusting; the embodiment of corporate power. 'You do understand, don't you?'

'Understand?'

'These aren't my friends; let's be honest, no one really cares if I'm here.'

'No one?' She arched an eyebrow, hurt to be lumped with strangers, as if that made her one.

'No one but you, naturally,' he corrected with a smile. 'To be honest, I think they'll be relieved that I'm gone. Having an interloper always changes the dynamics with really old friends, no matter how polite they are about it . . . Not to mention, the Archie situation is looking unlikely to improve.' He took in her unsmiling demeanour. '. . . You're cross with me.'

'Embarrassed is more like it. Purely as a gentleman you should have offered the seat to Coco first.'

He gave a small smile as if to say, 'Is that all?'. 'You may be right, but somehow I think she'll be perfectly fine staying here, now she realizes Charlie travels by helicopter.'

She frowned. '. . . That's a terrible thing to say.'

'Is it though? Really?' He arched an eyebrow.

'She's not a bad person because she likes the finer things, Max! She may be highly strung but she's not shallow. Coco has a big heart. You don't know the half of what she's been through in her life; what matters to her is people. Friendship.'

'Which is why she'll be happier celebrating Christmas here, with all of you,' he shrugged. Winning an argument with him was almost impossible.

Libby turned to walk off, exasperated, but he caught her again and pulled her in for a kiss. 'Look, don't be mad with me. I'll see you back in the office in a few days and make it up to you then, okay?'

She stared back at him, feeling that actually no, it wasn't okay – his ungallant behaviour smacked of the First Class men rushing for the lifeboats on the *Titanic*, and he seemed diminished in her eyes now – but they heard Prock coming back down the stairs, and both stepped apart slightly.

'All set?' Max asked him.

Prock looked so loose-limbed, it was only now Libby realized how tense and distracted he had been all day. The worry of his wife potentially going into labour without hope of any help must have been terrible. 'I think so. Hospital bag. Medical notes. Toiletries . . .'

'Ems's phone,' Libby said, handing it over to him. 'Oh – and could I have your toothpaste, seeing as you're going home? We left ours in the hotel in Durham.'

'Yeah, sure,' Prock said, rummaging through the bag to hand it over.

Libby took it gratefully, a talisman that would protect her from having to run the gauntlet to Archie's bathroom again.

They walked back into the kitchen to find the goodbyes had begun. Ems was standing with Rollo, who was comparing the size of their bellies. The whir of the helicopter could be heard outside as the rotors started up and the pilot ran through his checks. The harsh beam of the lights shone straight in through the windows.

Charlie turned to her. 'Lib, Ems has just had the very good

idea that they can pass on messages, once they get back home, to anyone who is waiting to hear from us.'

'Oh yes, that's a great idea!' Prock agreed. 'Why didn't I think of that?'

'Do you think you'll have power?' Libby asked him.

'No idea, but we're almost an hour from here, so hopefully that should be far enough away. But don't worry, even if we don't, I'll find a way once we're over there. I'll drive as far as I have to, to get a connection. Just consider it done, okay?'

'That would be amazing,' she said gratefully. 'My parents and brother will be so frantic.'

'Here you go, then.' Charlie handed her a pen and a sheet of paper with everyone's names underlined and some mobile numbers and emails beneath. Libby added her family's details.

'And you'll explain to them what's happened?' she asked as she scrawled.

'Everything. We'll make sure they're not worried about you.'

'Uh, Zannah, before these chaps depart, is there anything you'd like to say?' Archie asked suddenly.

Libby looked up to find Coco and Zannah both with their hands on Ems's bump; the next time they all saw her, Ems would be a mother, but Zannah looked particularly emotional as she looked back at him.

Libby felt another rush of fear at what was coming.

'I mean, I know it's a rush like this,' he said, looking tense. 'But . . . do you want to?' It was a not-so-subtle prompt, and everyone looked between the two of them expectantly. Libby held her breath, waiting for the axe to fall. Just say it, she willed.

But a silence bloomed.

'What's going on?' Coco asked as everyone waited, intrigued. Zannah looked at the Procks, at Ems's bump . . . they were about to head for the door. This was it. Now or never for her big announcement.

Max shot a look at Libby, a small nod confirming she had been right after all, but Zannah looked frozen, her mouth parted, as if the words couldn't travel from her throat.

'Well, I only really wanted to say that . . .' She faltered. '. . . Susannah is a *great* name—'

Libby frowned as Zannah gave a weak laugh.

'—I mean, I'm not saying you have to, I'm just saying think about it! No pressure, I'll still like you. Just food for thought.'

'Oh . . . okay!' Ems said, looking bemused. 'And what if she's a boy?'

'. . . Well, Zane, clearly.'

'But then everyone will think I was a One Directioner.'

'Weren't you?' Zannah looked scandalized.

'Good point. I will give it due consideration,' Ems grinned, going to hug her.

Libby watched Archie's expression. Zannah had clearly wriggled off the hook, again. What had got her so spooked?

'As for you,' Ems said, coming over and hugging her too. 'No more disappearing acts. I fully expect you to visit me when I've had this baby.'

'I promise.'

'Yeah well, we'll see, won't we?'

Max shook hands with the men, managing even to smile as he thanked Archie for being 'the consummate host'. He came over and kissed her once more, lingeringly on her lips. 'Happy Christmas, Elizabeth. Let me know when you're back, okay?'

She nodded, watching as he jogged outside, looking like a prisoner released.

'I've never been in a helicopter before,' Ems said, sounding daunted as they stepped into the snow, Prock laden with their bags. '. . . How will you get me in?'

But the men easily helped her into the helicopter, and in another few moments the blades were turning faster, becoming a blur. Snow flurried upwards, the downdraft making every-one's hair fly as their faces peered out from the windows, ear defenders on. Libby could see Max saying something to Prock and making him laugh, back to being his ebullient, charismatic self now he was getting away.

Everyone was waving, even the dogs coming out to bark at the commotion – and they were rarely stirred to action. Libby watched the helicopter rise up, fast becoming a dot, so that soon all that could be seen was the blinding white beam splitting the dark sky.

Max was gone.

She had been left here. Left behind.

She understood his reasons, and yet it still felt like aban-donment.

Like goodbye.

Would things really be the same between them when they got back to the office after this? He had stepped into her life and – there was no other way to put it – rejected it.

She realized she was the last one out there and she turned to go back in but Archie was waiting by the back door for her, watching.

'Are you okay?' he asked as she moved past him on the steps.

'Of course.' But just from that question, she knew he regarded Max's departure as a desertion of her too. Their great love story had been exposed as nothing of the sort. It was an office affair – risky and exciting, yes, but also simply . . . conven-ient.

'Well, I guess that's something,' Rollo said, rubbing his hands together as the stragglers reconvened in muted mood. 'At least none of us have to worry about delivering a baby on the kitchen floor now . . . And our families will have some peace of mind.' He looked back at Charlie. 'Astonishing though that you had *forgotten* about your helicopter, Earnshaw.'

Charlie looked sheepish. 'My assistant booked it,' he shrugged. 'And I haven't been able to access my diary since we lost wifi, so . . .'

'Still. A helicopter, mate.'

'Shall we sit soft, then?' Archie asked, seeing how Zannah was clutching her vodka tonic and staring into space. Regretting her missed opportunity after all?

Everyone began filing out. Libby looked at the pile of dishes that needed to be washed.

'Don't even think about it,' Archie said in a warning voice.

'Well, they're not going to wash themselves.'

'No,' he sighed. 'But I'll do them with the boys later. It's only fair when you and Ems cooked—' He cleared his throat. '—Not to mention your efforts this morning as well.'

Her eyes met his. Had it really only been this morning that they had stood in here, dodging ghosts and stepping over secrets? It had been a long day in which nothing at the end of it was the same as at the start. She was trapped here and yet Max was gone; he had left her alone and now, standing in this kitchen, she felt it acutely – not because she missed him but because he had been a buffer. She had used him, she knew, as a physical barrier between herself and her past. He was proof, in human form, that her life had moved on.

But had it – really? Almost a decade had passed. It shouldn't upset her that Archie was with Zannah. It shouldn't be difficult for her to look him in the eye. She shouldn't look for him every time she entered a room. He shouldn't be the one in her thoughts as she fell asleep.

And yet . . .

She looked away as if worried he might read her thoughts. 'We should join the others.'

'Yes. It's never a good idea leaving Roly in charge of the drinks.'

He stood back to allow her past and they began walking down the long passage. They were quiet for a moment, watching the silhouettes of the others ahead, already turning into the drawing room.

'Good that the chopper can drop Max in London,' he said, politely keeping the conversation going.

'Yes, isn't it.'

'Had you planned on spending Christmas together?'

'No.'

They listened to the sound of their footsteps, in step with one another. 'He seemed very agitated to leave,' Archie muttered. 'I'm sorry, I think that may have been my fault.'

'Why would that be your fault?'

'I probably wasn't as . . . hospitable as I could have been.'

She swallowed, knowing that this was her chance to salve her conscience. 'Actually I disagree. I think under the circumstances you've been incredibly tolerant.'

'Tolerant?' He looked across quizzically at her strange choice of word.

'Yes.' She took a deep breath, keeping her eyes dead ahead. 'I know you overheard us talking in the boot room this morning. You're fully entitled to hate us both after the awful things we said.'

There was a pause. 'I could never hate you, Pugh.'

Pugh. '. . .Well, that's very generous of you,' she said with deliberate blandness.

'It's not generosity.'

He was looking at her, she could feel it, but she kept her gaze on the pool of candlelight puddling outside the drawing room door. 'Well, I just want you to know I really am sorry. I should never have said such things.'

He cleared his throat. 'If it's how you feel about me—'

'But it's not.'

'No? Why say it then?'

They were almost at the drawing-room door now and she felt his hand close around her wrist suddenly so that they stopped short in the darkness, their friends' voices a low murmur in the next room. The others were barely ten feet away and yet as they stood toe-to-toe in the shadows, it felt like ten years.

'Lib?'

She looked back at Archie, knowing she couldn't tell him she had been scared Max would see straight through her; that if he had had the slightest inkling of their past, her carefully constructed facade would have come crumbling down. And if she couldn't tell Max that, she certainly couldn't tell *him*, because standing here now, looking into his eyes, she realized nothing had changed for her. All this time she thought she had sprinted away from him, but in truth, she'd been running on the spot.

'Lib? Talk to me.' He was standing close and she felt the pressure in his grip betraying stronger emotions in his body than he was showing. Did he feel it too—?

Of course not. She dismissed the thought with a blink, knowing she was being irrational. He was with Zannah now; he loved her. Libby had heard him say it. He just wanted an answer for her cruelty, but as she tried to avoid his gaze, her eyes lifted off him and fell on something behind him.

She frowned. Was she going mad?

'What?' he asked, half turning back. 'What is it?'

It made no sense. She distinctly remembered doing it only an hour before.

'What's wrong?'

She looked back at him. 'Archie . . .' she murmured, feeling a chill trickle down her spine. 'Who blew out the candles on the stairs?'

Chapter Twenty-One

May 2014

It was almost midnight when she heard the knock at her door. She looked up in anticipation of seeing Coco's face.

'Hey,' Archie said, peering in.

Her fingers fell away from the keyboard as she absorbed the sight of him, suddenly there. She had longed for it but no longer expected it. Coco came first now.

'Still working,' he tutted, but there was a smile in his eyes. 'Of course you are. Why did I ever think you might be done for the night?'

'You should know by now,' she sighed. 'I am nothing if not predictable.'

'Says the girl with a tattoo.' He watched the proud smile grow across her lips as she was reminded of her momentary wildness. '. . . Are you going to show it to me?'

'Can't.'

'Why not?'

'It's not for public consumption.'

'Ouch. You're saying *I'm* public? Part of the proletariat?' He gave a look of mock hurt but she wouldn't be drawn into saying what he was exactly. '. . . Hmm, your poker game must be formidable, Pugh,' he murmured, leaning against the door.

She sat back in her chair. 'Is this a flying visit or are you coming in? Don't tell me, you've just realized you've got to read Plato's *Republic* in a single night?'

'Well . . .' He stepped around the door and into the room. In his hand he was holding a Jaffa Cake – or rather, two Jaffas sandwiched together with marmalade – with a candle in it. 'I thought we could celebrate me becoming a fully paid-up member of the adulting club.'

She looked at it, then back at him, her mouth open with a half-smile. 'Strictly speaking it's not your birthday yet.'

'It will be, in . . . ' He looked down at the time in the corner of her laptop screen. 'In two minutes.'

She smiled. He wanted to see in his birthday with her?

'Well, that is . . . that is a very special birthday cake,' she said, getting up and inspecting the Jaffa Cake cupped in his palm.

'My mother always made it for me. I never had a birthday at home – I boarded from the year dot – so she'd come into school instead, and we'd sit on a bench under this massive beech tree and eat it together. It always reminded me of home but then, after she died, it reminded me of her; so Teabag would make it for me instead.'

Libby watched him, seeing shadows pass at the back of his eyes. For someone who was always surrounded by people, he seemed so alone. 'I'm sorry.'

He shrugged off her pity. 'Long time ago.'

'Who's Teabag?'

'My former nanny, but she's our housekeeper now.'

'Right.' She regarded him closely, seeing a tiny muscle twitch in the outer corner of his right eye. He looked back at her. 'Well, if you're to blow that candle out, then you're going to need a lighter. Again,' she smiled, turning away and retrieving the old Bic on her bookcase. 'Thank heavens you returned this one after all.'

'That's what I was thinking,' he murmured as she cupped a hand around the candle and flicked on the flame, angling it onto the wick.

'There.' She looked back at him. 'And would you like me to sing Happy Birthday to you too?'

'Yes.'

She went to laugh, but there was no devilment in his eyes and she felt herself blush instead; she had only been joking, of course, but something in his expression stopped her. She looked down for a moment, her new haircut providing some protection at least, the fringe and long layers folding in around her face as, quietly, she began to sing.

At first she couldn't look at him but as she got to 'dear Archie', she looked up and felt his gaze hold her there.

'That was really nice,' he said in a low voice. 'No one's sung that to me since I was ten.'

She frowned. 'That's so sad. Everyone should have Happy Birthday sung to them.'

He gave a tiny shrug.

'Well, happy birthday, Archie . . . You'd better make your wish, then,' she said, seeing how the wax was melting and dripping down the candle in fat globules. He glanced at her, blowing out the flame with a small puff.

'Did you make one?'

'Of course.'

'Are you going to tell me what it was?'

A small smile climbed into his eyes. 'Are you going to show me your tattoo?'

'Ha. Touché.'

'. . . You have first bite,' he said, holding up the tiny cake.

'Really? You know it's going to go everywhere,' she laughed, attempting to take a small nibble.

'You can do better than that!'

She took a larger bite so that the candle toppled towards her and rested on her nose. She looked at it cross-eyed and then back at him as he laughed. He removed the candle and took a bite too.

'Mmm,' she said appreciatively as he offered her another bite.

'Good, right?'

'Very. I think I may have been missing out with my Colin the Caterpillars.'

'Definitely.'

'. . . Oh.' She saw some of the chocolate had melted against the skin of his hand and without thinking she wiped it off with her finger and sucked on it. 'Yum.'

She hadn't intended it as some sort of provocative gesture but there followed a pause and she felt a shift nonetheless, the space between them becoming charged. Was he going to kiss her? Finally?

She felt the blood rush in her veins, time slowing to a half speed.

'Pugh . . . There's something I want to tell you,' he said. His tone had changed, becoming serious.

Libby felt her blood slow again. 'Okay.'

'It's about the night you . . . helped me out of the middle of the road.'

Libby felt her stomach drop. Oh god. She didn't want to talk about that. Not now! She shifted her weight. 'What about it?'

'I . . . know what I did . . . ' He looked apprehensive. 'I remembered.'

'You mean your argument with Belly?'

He frowned. 'No, not her.' He sighed and she waited as he tried to gather his thoughts. He looked nervous and it made her anxious in return. 'I mean, you. What I did to you. I . . . jumped on you, mauled you, like some kind of fucking . . . animal.'

She looked away, mortified. '. . . Maul isn't the word I'd have used,' she said quietly.

'Okay, but . . . I kissed you and I touched you and it should never have happened. I know that and I'm sorry. I swear to god, I was off my head. That isn't a defence, I just had no . . . impulse control and it was impulsive. Or instinctive.' He frowned again, as if trying to discern the difference between the two. He looked back at her, desperate that *she* should understand anyway. 'What I'm trying to say is, suddenly it was like you were there, right in front of me, and it was as if I'd never seen you before.' He blinked. 'You looked at me and . . . I didn't know I was going to do it, I swear.'

'Okay—'

'I realized what I'd done when I saw you in the kitchen the next morning and I couldn't believe I'd fucked up so badly. Even by my standards.'

'Archie—'

'I kept waiting for you to hit me or scream at me for what I'd done. I didn't know how to face you . . .'

Libby remembered how he had stood with his back to her almost the entire time. She had felt invisible, small, utterly forgettable.

'. . . So when Charlie offered that ridiculous bet, I thought it might be a chance to show you that I *can* control myself.'

She blinked in surprise. What? He had taken the bet for her? 'I know you can.'

'Well, now you do, maybe . . . I hope, anyway . . . But back then you didn't, and we both know my reputation. I came off like some kind of crazed sex fiend, and after everything that's happened with Coco . . . I need you to know I'm not like that.'

'Of course you're not. Archie, I know.'

'Really?'

'Yes! You're clever and thoughtful and funny and loyal and sensitive.'

'You forgot handsome.'

'Handsome too,' she grinned. 'To be honest, I don't know why you hide behind this image you've got. You're so much better than that.'

He hesitated. 'It's just easier.'

'You mean because it keeps people away?'

He shrugged again, and she wondered whether this tied back to losing his mother. 'But I don't feel that with you. I don't want you to be at a distance from me.'

'That's why you've been making these visits up here.'

'Well, you call them visits. I prefer pilgrimages.'

She gave a low laugh, feeling the energy shift up again now that his conscience was clear. 'Why are you telling me all this?'

He inhaled sharply. 'Because I'm going to kiss you now and I wanted to forewarn you this time, so that you can run – or punch me in the face – if you want to.'

She felt her breath catch as she looked into his eyes. 'No punches . . . And I'm not running anywhere.'

His gaze laser-locked on hers as his hand went to her waist, pulling her nearer. Slowly he leaned towards her, his eyes only closing as their lips touched. She felt his body relax, the pressure in his fingertips increasing as Libby felt herself fall through the fathoms of lifetimes and epochs. It was exactly as she had dreamed, everything she had hoped it would be, and when he pulled back, looking at her like she was something wondrous, she knew he felt it too. She was weak with longing, immediately wanting his mouth upon hers again. Now that they had started, she never wanted to stop—

'I should go.'

She stared at him, not understanding the words at first. What? '. . . What?'

'I should—'

'*Why?*' Had she done something wrong? But as she asked the question, the answer came to her. He wanted the money still? '. . . Is it the bet?'

She went to step back but he held her firmly. 'No.'

'No? A grand is a lot of money.'

'Lib, think about it,' he said calmly. 'The terms are, I hold out till I find someone there's a connection with . . . So if I stay here now, I'll *win* the money.' He blinked. 'It's not about the bet.'

Oh . . .

'So then what?' She felt so confused. On the one hand he was saying there was a connection here, that she was special; on the other, he was rejecting her again. Just as he had the other night, when he had slept on top of the covers.

'It wouldn't feel right here, not at the moment, in this house. And because today is my twenty-first, I want this to mark my new start of doing things right.'

'Oh.'

His fingers pressed on her waist again as he touched his forehead to hers. 'I want it to happen between us after the party, when I can take your dress off you – the one I'm hoping you bought especially for me; just like I hope this was especially for me too,' he murmured, twirling a strand of her newly cut hair. 'And then, when I've got your dress off you, I'm going to find that tattoo and kiss it.'

She swallowed.

'Does that sound . . . acceptable?'

She nodded. 'Perfectly,' she whispered.

'Good. So then I'll book a room at the hotel for us?'

'Okay,' she breathed, wishing he'd kiss her just one more time.

'I'll leave your name at reception,' he murmured, pressing his fingers gently against her lips as if testing their pillowiness, his eyes grazing her a final time. '. . . Only one more sleep.'

She nodded, though she was breathless with anticipation. She could do that.

One more sleep.

Chapter Twenty-Two

23 December 2023

'Well, it's a bit like being in an Agatha Christie novel,' Rollo said as they reassembled in the drawing room. It was warm in there now, the fire roaring hot. 'And then there were six.'

Charlie and Coco had reclaimed their positions on the yellow sofa, including Coco's feet making their way into Charlie's hands. Zannah and Archie were back by the fire, leaving Libby and Rollo to the other sofa. She was finishing the crossword Max had been working on; it had been strange coming in and seeing it folded in half from when he'd thrown it down to go to supper. Here one moment, gone the next . . .

'Lib, I was just telling Charlie he's a hero getting the Procks to safety like that,' Coco said, watching him as he sat in profile to her.

'Hardly. It wasn't like I planned it,' he demurred.

'Still, you didn't have to give up your seat.'

'I think you'd struggle to find anyone here who wouldn't have done the same.'

'You're determined not to take a compliment, aren't you?' Coco said, jabbing his thigh with her big toe. 'I'm saying you're a good man.'

'Hmm,' he said, still squeezing her feet. 'Well, don't think too highly of me. Perhaps I just had more reasons to stay than to leave.'

Libby fell still for a moment, hearing the gentle probe in his words – a tentative first approach to Coco after all these years – but she also heard the implication that Max had had more reasons to leave than to stay. She resumed looking for the clue for twelve down and a small silence settled over the room, the mood muted by their diminished numbers. They were the stragglers, the ones stuck in the cold, dark house, surrounded by thirty thousand acres of frozen Yorkshire moorland.

'. . . Well, it's a pretty bloody poor show that there's not one present under that enormous tree,' Rollo declared to no one in particular. 'If my six-year-old self could see me now, he'd be sorely unimpressed.'

'Believe it or not, Teabag doesn't put the presents out until Christmas Eve,' Archie said, not in the least offended.

'Why not?'

Archie pulled a face. 'Let's just say I used to find it very difficult resisting temptation.'

'Ha!' Rollo laughed. 'What's changed?'

In her peripheral vision, Libby saw Archie glance her way. 'Well, we could always do Secret Santas,' he suggested after a moment, changing the subject.

'How?' Coco puzzled.

'Everyone pulls a name from a hat and has to find something in the house or garden to give to that person.'

'*Give* give?'

'Yeah, why not?'

'But what if they choose something valuable? Some historic heirloom?'

Archie considered the point. 'Okay, fine. Everyone's forever saying it's the thought that counts – which is clearly complete tosh – but on this occasion, let's go with that and it's the intention that's the gift, not the gift itself.'

Libby stood slightly to tuck one leg beneath her, shifting her weight and collapsing back into the cushions again. 'So when you say choose something in the house or garden – you mean literally look anywhere in the house or garden? Bedrooms, cellars . . . ?'

'Probably not the bedrooms,' Archie said quickly. 'Or at least the ones that are occupied.'

'Yeah. It'd be a drag having to hide the sex toys,' Rollo drawled.

'I'm not sure all of us are up for another game,' Libby said, pointedly looking at Zannah, who was dozing again, basking in the heat of the fire. The glass looked like it was about to drop from her hand and Archie reached for it with a wince.

'Well, unless you can think of anything better to do,' he replied, checking his watch. 'It's only just gone nine. We've got hours yet.'

'It's so dark now, though,' Libby murmured, looking into the shadowy corners of the room. Even with a blazing fire throwing out light, the darkness hovered just above their heads like a witch's veil.

'Yes, but everything's more fun in the dark,' he replied, holding her gaze; she felt herself startle at his sudden boldness, a heat coming to her cheeks. Beside her, Rollo's head snapped up at the comment and Archie began drumming his fingers on the arm of his chair. 'Besides, you can always take one of the hurricane lanterns from the stairs if you want. In case you're worried about the ghosts.'

It was a deliberate tease. They had come to the conclusion, standing in the hall, that a strong draught – perhaps from when the helicopter was blowing up a hoolie outside – must have sent a freak wind through the house and blown the lanterns out. Like Max upstairs earlier, Archie had been bemused by Libby's jumpiness; she had just been grateful for the distraction it had afforded, allowing her to get away without giving an answer to his question. What *did* she feel about him?

'I'll get a pen and some paper then, shall I?' Rollo said in a funny tone, shooting Archie a look before getting up from the sofa and leaving the room.

Libby went back to the crossword, refusing to make eye contact. Archie was still for a moment, then he leaned over to Zannah and squeezed her knee.

'Hey, wake up, sleepyhead.' He rubbed her thigh gently. 'You'll not sleep tonight if you go off now.'

Zannah stirred, looking startled to discover she had dropped off. '. . . What?' she murmured. 'What time is it?'

'Not bedtime yet. Want another drink?'

'Mm.'

They spoke in hushed tones, Libby watching in her peripheral vision as he got up and threw another log on the fire.

'Libby? A drink?'

She nodded, just as from the other room they heard a shout, then a succession of curses.

'Ten quid says he just walked into the desk,' Archie chuckled, wandering over to the drinks table.

'I'll have another too,' Charlie said, leaving Coco's feet for a moment and getting up. She made a little mewl of protest. 'I'm coming back. I just need to stretch my legs.'

'Cabin fever?' Archie asked over his shoulder, his back to the room as he poured.

'Well, I'm not sure cabin's quite the word. You're a lucky bloke calling somewhere like this home.'

'As I understand it, it's well within your means to be able to call something like this your home too.'

Libby watched as Charlie fell still. '. . . Ah. So you know then.'

'Of course I do. Roly too,' Archie grinned, placing a fresh drink in his hand. 'We've been waiting for you to share the happy news all weekend. Any reason why you're playing coy?'

Charlie shrugged and pulled a face. 'Didn't want to be a dick?'

'Well, the chopper was a bit of a clanger, if you were hoping to go stealth mode.'

'Yeah, my PA really didn't think it through.'

They laughed and Archie slapped him on the shoulder. 'Happy for you, mate. It's well deserved.'

'I'm not sure that's true. I just got lucky.'

'Yeah, much like that saying: the harder I work, the luckier I get.' Archie gave Zannah and Libby their drinks and raised his in a small toast. 'To your continued good fortune, mate.'

'Good fortune,' Zannah echoed.

Libby took a sip – and almost choked. 'Oh my god!' she spluttered, as Zannah did exactly the same. 'That's not vodka. It's . . . water!'

She pulled a face that made the others laugh at the irony.

'Apologies! Wrong way round.' Archie quickly swapped her glass with Zannah's.

'But I thought you were drinking vodka?' Libby winced.

'I am. I just alternate with water so I don't get too smashed.'

Libby didn't question her further but her suspicions had been fully raised again. Zannah hadn't specified she wanted water; Archie had just poured it for her, unasked. Had he been doing that all weekend? No one would have questioned it. If Zannah said she was drinking vodka, then vodka it was, but there were enough other clues to support Libby's hunch that her friend was indeed pregnant. Her stomach may still be pancake-flat but if it was still early days, if she wasn't yet out of the first trimester, that would also explain her hesitance to tell everyone. Lots of women kept the news under wraps till they passed the twelve-week mark . . .

Libby stared at the floor, dismayed but also bewildered by Archie's confusing behaviour. That comment just now—

'Right,' Rollo said, walking back in with a limp and the art supplies.

Archie grinned. 'Walk into the desk, did you?'

'Damn near broke a toe!' Rollo sucked through his teeth, looking pained. 'But that's nothing to the frostbite. Christ, it is perishing through there! Fully arctic.'

'Mm.' Archie frowned. 'Problem with big houses.'

'I don't suppose you've got any polar bear rugs rolled up in the attic? Or at least some mothballed minks? Fuck knows how we'll sleep tonight.'

Libby remembered something. 'Damn. I'll be right back,' she murmured, setting down her glass.

Archie looked up as she went to leave. 'Was it something we said?'

'I'm coming back,' she replied, not looking directly at him.

'Where are you going?' Coco whispered, catching her hand as she went to pass by.

'Just to set the last of the bedroom fires. I kept getting distracted earlier.' She would have to do it by the light of her phone torch now and she only had two per cent power left.

'Need a hand?'

'No, I'll only be a few minutes.'

Coco arched an eyebrow. 'It'll be spooky up there in the dark though.'

More ghost jokes. 'I'll be fine, thanks for your concern,' she smiled, rolling her eyes.

282

She retrieved the log basket she had left in the hall from her aborted attempt earlier and, grabbing one of the hurricane candles from the stairs, made her way into the darkness. Rollo had been right – she could feel the temperature drop a degree with every tread. The house itself seemed to shiver, wearing its flickering shadows like black lace, a widow's mantilla.

In spite of her brave words to Coco, she hurried quickly down the corridor towards the corner bedroom, her eyes darting nervously to the dark corners and her imagination playing tricks, making her think shapes were shifting and walls breathing. It was something of a relief to get to her destination.

Upon opening the door, her first thought was that in nine years, nothing at all had changed. She could have been walking into Zannah's old room in their shared house. The bed was unmade, the pillows arranged in such a way as to suggest Zannah had been reading before getting up earlier. A laptop and some books were on the covers, a stack of jumpers folded upon the armchair at the foot of the bed; numerous mugs sat on the bedside table, her phone charging – but not charging, of course. But it wasn't so much the mess Libby noticed as the smell. It was cloying and almost fetid, as if the room hadn't been aired for days.

The room was much larger than the others, decorated with a cream blooming hydrangea chintz, double-aspect windows and a matching pair of large plum-pudding mahogany armoires either side of the fireplace. She lifted the fireguard away, her fingers immediately becoming covered with thick soot.

'Ugh,' she groaned, holding her hands up, looking around her and seeing the door to the en suite in the opposite corner. She would need to wash her hands now.

She was halfway across the room when she heard footsteps in the hall – someone was running – and she immediately tensed, all her paranoia bearing out. Who the hell—?

'Pugh?!'

Archie. Thank god.

She sighed, telling herself to get a grip. 'In here! Zannah's room!' she called back, reaching the bathroom as the bedroom door swung open and he burst in.

'Libby, no!' he said, just as she opened the bathroom door and looked in. This was no mere shower room; not for Zannah a handbasin hidden in a cupboard. In fact, her en suite was roughly the same size as the bedroom Libby had shared with Max last night, the viscount's former dressing room. A claw-footed bath stood in the middle of the room opposite the west-facing window, and a contemporary walk-in shower with a glass screen dominated the far corner. There were deep fitted wardrobes down one wall and the ivory carpet – contrary to Libby's own mother's exhortations that carpets had no place in bathrooms – was deep and plush and unashamedly luxurious. The whole space looked newly fitted out.

But it wasn't the scale or the sumptuousness that caught her eye and she was only vaguely aware of Archie coming up behind her as she took in the paraphernalia that had no place in a country house.

'Libby, please,' he said, trying to turn her away; but it was already too late and she looked at him with an expression that made his arm drop.

For several moments she couldn't speak at all as the truth was revealed through a series of vignettes. She knew exactly what she was seeing.

And yet still, the question had to be asked – confirmation must be given.

She looked at him, tears in her eyes – and his, she saw – as she was able to hold his gaze for the first time that evening. 'Are you going to tell me what's going on?'

Chapter Twenty-Three

May 2014

'Wake up!'

Libby felt a hand on her shoulder and she jolted as she realized where she was. She lifted her head, blinking and bleary-eyed. 'Huh?'

'Have you been here all night?' Ems asked, walking over to the window and drawing open the curtains. Libby sat up in her chair, looking down at the creased pages of her reference book; she put a hand to her cheek and felt the same crease imprinted into her skin.

'I was . . .'

'Don't tell me! Finishing a paper? You're *always* finishing a paper,' Ems sighed, standing there for a moment with a hand on her hip.

'It's my final paper and I won't be able to do it tonight.'

'Damn straight. We've got some partying to do, and even you have been issued a cease and desist order.' Ems gave a pleased smile. 'See what I did there?'

'I do,' Libby nodded, giving a lazy smile as she stretched. '. . . What's this?'

She looked over to find Ems holding the pale blue candle

from Archie's Jaffa Cake last night. Memories rushed in. *Take it off you . . . find that tattoo . . .*

'Oh, um . . .' Libby stalled, unable to produce a convincing explanation for having a chocolate-dipped candle in her room. 'I don't know.'

'It's a candle, Lib.'

'Yes.'

'But why's it here?'

'. . . I don't know; it must have been in the bottom of my bag or something,' she mumbled.

There was a baffled pause. 'Well, just so long as you've not been eating cake without me. You know my views on that.' Ems winked and crossed the room. 'Come on, everyone's downstairs. Archie's waiting to open his pressies.'

'Oh god, really? What's the time?'

'Ten something,' Ems shrugged.

'. . . *Ten?*' Libby gave a weary sigh and rubbed her face in her hands. What with staying away from the library to be near Coco, and the distraction of Archie's visits, she was falling off the pace. She still needed to get her final essay finished by mid-afternoon – with the party this evening she needed to get ahead. She desperately didn't want to have to curtail her night (and hopefully, morning after) with him on account of a deadline. 'Okay, I'll be right there.'

Three minutes later, she was. Everyone had taken their usual positions in the tiny room, and she had been greeted on the stairs by the welcome aroma of a full English. Charlie, Rollo and Prock were knocking knees under the table as ever; Ems was cooking sausages and bacon at the stove; Coco was sitting with her feet up on the counter beside the sink, looking even more like a pixie on a toadstool thanks to her new cut; Zannah was sitting on the tall stool in the corner by the bin, on her phone. Archie was leaning against the worktop in a pair of striped pyjama bottoms and a grey t-shirt, and she felt his gaze land upon her as she walked in. His head tipped up, his arms folded across his chest, a smile stretching across his lips like a lazy cat.

'Ah, Pugh,' he drawled. 'Sleeping at your desk, we hear.'

'Happy birthday, Templeton,' she muttered, meeting his gaze and matching his drawl as she wandered over and gave him a hug, her arms around his neck. She felt his body instinctively lean in towards her as she held him close for a moment, allowing him to feel her bare curves under her sweatshirt, and she felt the pressure in his fingertips as she pulled away. The air between them was supercharged, and she felt sure it must be obvious to all the others what was unfolding between them. '. . . Here you go.' She held out a small box, neatly wrapped in newspaper but tied with a red ribbon.

'For me?' He looked genuinely surprised, even though they were specifically gathered for the purpose of him opening his presents.

'Of course. I couldn't let your twenty-first go uncelebrated.' They shared a private look. 'I hope you like it.'

He looked suddenly at the others, as if remembering they were still there, and shook the box. 'It's not a library pass, is it?'

Everyone laughed as he opened it, pulling out a small silver Zippo lighter. His mouth parted in genuine surprise and pleasure.

'I had it engraved, see?' she said, taking the opportunity to lean close again and show him the inscription down the side: *Barney McGrew.*

'Barney McGrew?' Coco queried, leaning over to read it too. 'What's that?'

'Pugh, Pugh, Barney McGrew. It's from an old kids' programme in the seventies. It was my parents' nickname for me growing up, and Archie happened to know it, too.' She gave an easy shrug but she could feel his stare upon her, and the temptation to sink into him, to rest her head upon his chest, was almost overwhelming, a gravitational pull she had to actively resist. 'Something for him to remember me by, lucky chap.'

'*Remember* you?' Archie queried, a flash of irritation in his voice at the hint of some unspecified future separation. '. . . As if I'm likely to forget you, Pugh.' He held her gaze in his own, seeming not to care who noticed the intensity between them. What had started up last night still simmered this morning, and she had a feeling today was going to feel endless. All she wanted was to get to tonight already, to be in that hotel room with him.

'That's super cute,' Ems said, looking over her shoulder as she stirred the baked beans.

'Well, thank Christ you've finally got a lighter of your own!' Rollo declared. 'You can stop nicking mine now. Don't lose that one.'

'No chance,' Archie murmured.

'Is there a charger in here?' Libby asked, forcing herself to turn away from him. Having fallen asleep at her desk, she hadn't charged her phone overnight and it was completely dead.

'There's one by the toaster.' Ems pointed.

'Great.'

Libby plugged it in, glancing at Zannah, who was being uncharacteristically quiet. Hungover? Libby touched her lightly on the shoulder, a question in the gesture, but Zannah looked back at her with blank eyes. Hangover confirmed.

'Is mine the only present?' she asked, tuning back again and noticing the lack of presents on the table.

'The only physical one,' Archie replied, eyes glittering at the private double entendre. 'Roly and Charlie have bought me tickets to Royal Ascot.'

'Steward's enclosure,' Rollo purred. 'My uncle's got a runner from his stud this year.'

'And Ems and Prock are standing me dinner for two at the River Cafe.' He caught her gaze and widened his eyes fractionally. It was just a micro-movement but his meaning was clear: they would be going there together.

'Wow. That all makes my little lighter look very meagre by comparison.'

'No,' he said simply, holding eye contact.

She swallowed. Much more of this and their secret would be out.

Coco cleared her throat. 'I promise I will sort something, Arch,' she said quietly. 'I can't believe I was at the shops yesterday and I didn't even think—'

'Hey.' Archie walked straight over to her and clasped her face between his hands, like a big brother to his little sister. 'All I want is to see you smiling again, okay . . . ? That's literally all I want.'

She nodded, looking down as *it* came into the room again and settled itself between them all.

'But as for Zannah,' Archie said with a sly, playful look, turning in a slow half circle back to where she was sitting in the corner. 'Well, I'm disappointed, I can't pretend otherwise.'

Several seconds passed before Zannah looked up from her phone, as if she hadn't even heard him. She looked at him – them all – blankly. '. . . Huh?'

'His present?' Rollo prompted.

'Oh, yeah . . . I did get you one.' A small frown puckered her brow as if the thought hovered just out of her reach.

Everyone waited.

'Oh but . . . yeah, I need to go collect it.'

'Uh-huh,' Archie grinned. 'Sure.'

'No really – I meant to do it yesterday.'

'Uh-huh.'

'Archie!' Zannah's voice cracked with protest.

'I'm just teasing you. Don't worry about it,' he chuckled. 'It's not deep.'

'But I'm telling the truth. I just forgot to pick it up! . . . There's so much going on right now.'

Archie's grin faded as they strayed back into uncomfortable territory again. Everyone snuck a look at Coco, but Libby looked at Zannah. Something was off with her.

'I'll bring it tonight.'

'Okay, great,' Archie nodded, looking like he wished he'd never brought it up.

'Right, well, this is ready,' Ems said, shutting off the gas and reaching for the plates stacked in a tower beside her. She bent down and pulled out a baking tray with mushrooms and scrambled eggs warming in the oven.

'That is looking like some top scran!' Rollo remarked without any trace of northern dialect, rubbing his hands together as she began to serve out.

Libby went over to where her phone was charging and turned it on. It only had three per cent charge, but it was enough to be able to check whether she had missed anything this morning.

She waited as it loaded, plates being piled high behind her as Ems started serving out.

'Lib, yours,' Ems said, handing one over.

'Great, ta!' she said, clicking on her emails as she took it. Her eyes grazed over the perfectly chargrilled sausages before flicking back to her emails, and back to the sausages again . . .

She caught her breath as she glimpsed a name in her inbox.

'Oh my god,' she whispered, still holding the plate in her other hand but already utterly oblivious to it.

'What?' Archie asked, his attention back on her.

She looked up, her eyes wide and bright. 'I got it!'

'Got what?' Prock asked, pouring the orange juice.

'The overseas internship.'

'*What?*' Ems shrieked, throwing her hands in the air so that a few baked beans flew off the wooden spoon she was holding and splatted the wall. 'The Hong Kong one?'

'Yes! Oh my—' She pressed a hand to her heart and tipped her head back, eyes closed, as she realized what it meant. 'Oh my god,' she whispered. She had been up against almost ten thousand applicants; they only took two hundred globally. With this on her CV, her chances of securing one of the ninety graduate entry positions at Clifford Chance in London had just skyrocketed. She was on her way. Everything she had promised her parents was beginning to happen.

Ems took the plate from her and hugged her hard, Coco too.

'Bloody amazing!'

'Never doubted it!'

'Of course you got it!' the boys cheered, high-fiving her.

'When does it start?' Charlie asked, munching on toast.

'How long is it for?' Rollo asked at the same time.

'Um, six months and it . . . uh . . . it starts, well, immediately after graduation. I would fly out the next day.' Her mind was racing. There was so much to organize. She had to tell her parents.

'Bloody well done, Pugh.' Archie said. Their gazes connected as he smiled, forking a sausage and 'toasting' her with it. 'No one deserves it more than you.'

She felt her smile fade, her excitement popping like a champagne bubble as she realized what else it meant. How could she have both? How could she have him *and* this internship? They wouldn't survive six months on opposite sides of the world when they hadn't even moved past their first kiss yet.

Archie's phone rang, but Rollo reached for it. 'Archie's phone. Roly speaking,' he said brusquely, chewing on mushrooms. '. . . Ah, Jake. Jake. How are you, fellow?'

Libby looked again at Archie as they all ate in silence, the boys chowing down as if they were in a timed race, allowing Rollo to take the call in peace.

'. . . I absolutely hear you, mate. Trouble is, it's a hundred and fifty bums on seats and Archie's old man has made it clear if we go a single arse over, he's dumping the bill on the birthday boy . . .' He gave a chortle as Jake said something down the line. 'Exactly, he's rightly fucking scared. But I tell you what I can do, old boy – if we get a cancellation I can let you know. How does that sound? I mean, obviously it's highly unlikely and I don't want to get any hopes up, but if anyone does drop out . . .' He nodded. 'Mm . . . Yeah . . . Great stuff, will do then . . . yuh-yuh, later mater.' Rollo disconnected the call and gave a sigh. 'Fourth already this morning,' he tutted.

'Thanks, mate,' Archie muttered, not looking up.

Libby watched him. She suddenly had no appetite.

'We'll need to get a shift on too if we're going to get to the station in time for the 11.27,' Rollo continued.

'What's happening at the station?' Charlie asked.

'We've got a rather good consignment of wine coming up from the Drewatts Park wine cellars for tonight.'

'Nice.'

Archie dropped his knife and fork on the plate with a clatter as he sat back and pressed a hand to his stomach. 'Stuffed,' he announced. 'Ems, you're a star, thanks for that.'

'My pleasure. A little birthday treat for you.'

He pushed his chair back. 'And thanks, all, for my presents, and making this such a good start to my birthday.' He reached over and squeezed Coco's hand, then threw a quizzical look at Zannah, who was pushing her baked beans around the plate. Finally he looked at Libby again – and she could see already that things were different. He had realized the same thing: whatever was happening between them had nowhere to go. She was about to travel to the other side of the world. 'I'm going to shower and hopefully get all the hot water for once.'

'Ah, we love you Arch,' Ems smiled, and he winked at her as he got up.

Libby watched him go, understanding now that her bright new beginning would be prefaced with an ending, all her joy turning to ashes in her mouth.

Libby sat on the end of the bed, trying to still her mind. Her thoughts were racing, along with her heart, as her panic mounted. She had never felt this way about anyone before. She knew she couldn't call it love, not yet – not when so little had been articulated or done. 'They' existed in an emotional realm only, a dark pocket at the edges of their lives, a promise or a hope at the end of every day. And yet, in spite of that, those quiet hours had somehow been so much more than any of the flesh-and-blood encounters she had ever had. Something deep inside her recognized something deep inside him.

The door swung open as if it had been pushed too hard,

and she looked up sharply as Archie stopped dead at the sight of her there, in his room. She had never come into his room before; he always came to hers. A towel was wrapped around his hips, his hair slicked back from the shower.

She stood. 'Can we talk?'

He missed a beat. '. . . Sure,' he said, closing the door behind him. 'What's up?'

What's up? That question alone told her he was already retreating and it was more than she could bear; the cracks were already spreading over her heart like a crazy glaze and she realized it wasn't talking that would help them. In silence, she walked over to him and threw her arms around his neck, her face burrowed in the nook as she smelled his skin. He stiffened at the unexpected embrace as if determined to hold himself back, just as he had the night Coco had been attacked, but then she felt his hands upon her waist too, pulling her close. For several moments they stood there, heart to heart, his breath in her ear and hers in his as they silently acknowledged what was coming for them.

She began to kiss his neck and she felt his shoulders drop as she nibbled his earlobe. She knew he had wanted this to be a certain way between them, that he wanted it to be perfect, but she didn't care about perfection; she only wanted him – and now there was a timer ticking, already counting down all the minutes and hours they would get to have together.

'We can make it work,' she whispered, leaning back slightly and pulling her sweatshirt and t-shirt off in one fluid action, knowing she had to get instinct overriding logic. He looked down at her and she heard him groan as she pushed herself against him again – skin on skin – picking up where she had left off. 'It's only six months.'

'. . . Lib.' There was caution in his voice but his hands began to move over her back, his breathing quickening as his urgency rose with her kisses. She combed her hands through his hair, twisting her fingers so that she was connected to him, kissing his throat.

'I'll come back whenever I can . . . long weekends . . . even if it only gives us a few hours . . .' she murmured. '. . . And we can Skype or FaceTime; we can see each other every day if we want . . .' she whispered, hearing him gasp as her mouth travelled along his collarbone, her hands tracing the top of his towel. '. . . People do it all the time . . . long distance is nothing now—'

'Ready, mate?!' They both froze as Rollo's familiar bellow came through the wall. Or was he approaching the door?

In a flash, Archie spun her around so that his back was to the door and she was blocked by his body. 'Don't come in!' he yelled back.

She stood close to him, feeling his heart hammering against her chest.

'. . . All right,' Rollo replied with a slightly baffled tone, clearly now on the other side of the door. 'But you ready?'

'Yep. Just give me two.'

'Okay, but the train's coming in in ten minutes. We need to shift.'

'Yup, will do.' There was another pause and then they heard Rollo's footsteps going downstairs. Archie looked down at her, his expression pained as all the longing between them raged without hope of relief. He stepped back and turned away, raking his hands through his hair and trying to slow his breathing. Logic was intruding again, she could feel it.

'I've got to go,' he said quietly after a minute, reaching for the jeans on his desk chair and pulling them on. 'We can't miss that train.'

'Of course.' Libby picked up her tops from the floor too and held them against her. She watched as he shrugged on a shirt and stuffed his feet into his Nikes, his movements stiff with tension.

'Look, I'll see you later; we'll talk then,' he said, stopping in front of her and kissing her lightly on the lips; it was a casual, familiar move that she could only have dreamed about this time yesterday but which already felt so natural and so right. And yet she was already losing him.

'I don't have to take it,' she blurted out as he walked away, his head down.

He stopped at the door and turned back. 'What?'

'It's not a deal-breaker, the internship. My hopes at Clifford Chance are still really strong without it . . . I don't *have* to go to Hong Kong.'

She saw something that looked like hope flicker across his face. He swallowed and gave a nod. He didn't say anything at all for several seconds. 'We'll talk tonight.'

'Okay, yes,' she murmured, feeling the executioner's hand stayed, the ticking clock falling silent. 'Tonight then.'

Chapter Twenty-Four

23 December 2023

Oxygen canisters. An IV saline drip beside a small chaise longue. More blister packs and pill bottles on the vanity unit than she could count. A thermometer. Blood pressure machine. Syringes . . . Wig tape.

'She's dying.'

Libby saw Archie say the words, she heard him say the words, but they fell like rocks off a high cliff, falling against the stone face with violence but dashing only themselves, splintering up and becoming smaller until they rolled out of sight.

No. They made no sense. He was mistaken. Zannah was the most alive person she knew. She had more life force in her little finger than Libby had in her entire body. Dying simply wasn't an option for someone who had so much to *do*. Perpetual motion, that was Zannah's life philosophy. She couldn't be caught if she didn't sit down.

More words were coming but she couldn't catch them now. She felt herself sinking – or was it a numbness rising?

'Lib?' She felt something and looked to see Archie had put a hand on her arm and was looking at her with the expression of someone awaiting an answer.

'. . . What?' Her voice sounded strange, as if she was hearing it underwater, or through a wall. How could it sound so distant and disembodied?

'Come and sit down.'

She found herself being walked, his hand under her elbow, guiding her to the bed.

A house of cards was falling down, one deck after another, as she saw her friend through a new gaze: her tiredness on the walk to Bomber's not a hangover after all; her long recovery sleep afterwards, not pregnancy. Her lack of appetite, not fashion. Her constant distractibility, not somewhere more important to be . . . That sleek hair Libby knew now to be a wig. And the vodka, which was actually water . . . The boob job? Libby was guessing a mastectomy. The tan . . . ? Chemo.

She had got everything back to front. Upside down. Inside out. She couldn't get her bearings. '. . . How long has she got?' Her voice was tiny, as if she had been miniaturized.

'They think maybe a year. Maybe a little more. She's steady at the moment but it can – it will – change quickly.' She heard a rasp undercutting his voice, as if the words contained razor blades, the pain serrating him on the inside. He really loved her.

She looked at him. 'How long have you known?'

'Since the day she found out.'

'And when was that?'

He took a sharp intake of breath. 'Nine years ago.'

Libby recoiled. 'She knew at *Durham*?' But even as she asked the question, she remembered Zannah's chronic fatigue, the weight loss, her paleness . . . all mistaken for a burned-out student partying too hard.

'Look,' he said, looking down at the floor. 'I shouldn't be

talking to you about this; she wants to tell you herself. She's been trying to find the right time but it never quite happens.'

'Why not?' she demanded, suddenly angry. 'How do you put off telling your best friends you have cancer?'

'Because back then, we were all helping Coco deal with her shit,' he said calmly. 'And this time, with the Procks about to have a baby . . . she didn't want to trauma dump on them.'

'So you're saying we're always either too sad or too happy to be able to help her with this?'

'I'm not saying anything, but you know what she's like – vulnerability isn't her strong suit.' He swallowed. 'And she especially didn't feel she could tell you after . . .'

She stared at him, wanting him to say it. To admit what he'd done. Zannah had called and called her in the weeks afterwards, but all she had received from him was pure and perfect silence.

He looked away again. '—Well, you know what. She thinks you hate her.'

She stared at his profile, wanting to hate him. Even now he wasn't sorry. He didn't see that it wasn't Zannah she had blamed back then, but him. Zannah had done nothing wrong because she had never known about them – not at the time, anyway; no one had. They had been a secret.

'Who else knows?'

He hesitated. 'No one, but I think Roly has his suspicions. Obviously she's always over here.'

She looked away, heartsore at the references to *them* on top of all this. She could only take so much.

She rose abruptly. 'I need to speak to her.'

'Lib—'

But already she was out the door and running down the

corridor, the shadows not holding any fear for her now. Zannah's cancer had been right there in plain sight, and she'd never seen it. Never even suspected it. She had failed her friend.

'Lib, wait—' Archie said, chasing after her, but she knew she was uncatchable. She had escaped him years before and even now, right next to him, she was too far away. She ran down the stairs and into the drawing room, stopping abruptly at the sight of Zannah standing by the fire. She was staring into space, her glass of water held in her hand as Roly scrunched up the paper strips on which he had written their names. Ready for the next game.

Perhaps it was the suddenness of Libby's stop that caught her attention, but Zannah's head jerked up and Libby saw, in the way she stiffened, that she knew she knew. She saw it in the way Zannah's mouth dropped open a little, the slight slump in her shoulders. Tiny details in a failing body.

The space between them contracted, years of silence that had built up like a wall beginning to topple. The past was indeed another country, all the hurt and jealousy sluiced away by the sabre swipe of her disease. Her tough, ballsy, shake-it-off friend was dying. She was going to lose her, properly and irrevocably this time. Nothing else mattered.

Without a word, Libby crossed the room and threw her arms around her, feeling Zannah's tears on her cheek and the bones beneath her skin; she felt the tremors in Zannah's muscles as she sought to retain self-control against a lava spill of emotions.

She pulled back and looked Zannah straight in the eyes. 'You should have told me. I would have been there for you.'

Zannah swallowed. 'Even . . . ?'

'Even then,' she murmured. 'No more secrets.'

Zannah nodded and Libby thought how tired she looked, up close. 'No more secrets.'

'Lib?'

She turned to find Coco watching them, evident concern in her eyes. '. . . What's going on?' she asked quietly.

Libby looked at Zannah for confirmation, then turned around so that she was facing the room. She kept her hand on Zannah's waist, seeing how Charlie and Rollo were watching on from the sofa with disquieted expressions too. Archie was standing in the doorway, looking stricken.

She pressed her fingertips into Zannah's waist for encouragement. 'Zannah's got something she wants to tell you.'

The questions and tears came thick and fast.

'The pain's manageable at the moment,' Zannah said, as if trying to reassure them. 'I have a pretty decent set-up now. Almost a hospital ward up there.'

'Is there anything you need?' Charlie asked. 'Anything . . . anything I can do . . . ?' He faltered on the words.

Zannah smiled. She was curled up in the fireside chair again, her favourite spot. 'You're a peach, Earnshaw,' she winked. 'But I'm already VIP. I was selected for a trial at the Northern Centre in Newcastle. Early signs are promising . . . it's not going to give me a different ending, but I might get an extended finale.' She spoke with signature bravura. 'There's another three weeks to go there, then I'll be going back to a clinic in Switzerland for a rest . . . And Archie will get a well-deserved one too. He's been incredible.'

'Hardly,' he scoffed, looking away.

'Yes you have,' she insisted. 'You've been ferrying me to my appointments, making sure I'm eating properly, resting enough.'

Libby watched Archie stare at his feet, his jaw clenching. He had known for all these years, been caring for her whilst the rest of them had got on with building their lives. How was he going to fare . . . afterwards?

'You have to tell the Procks,' Roly said.

'No,' Zannah said with a strong shake of her head. 'It would be like announcing your divorce at someone's wedding. Ems has a birth to deal with at the moment; I'll not give her a death too.'

'She would want to know; they both would,' Libby said. 'Life is rarely clean. Everything overlaps and meshes. It's always a mess. Timing is never perfect.'

'Only after the baby comes,' Zannah repeated staunchly. 'Which, from the looks of her, won't be too long anyway.' She looked at them all, seeing their averted eyes and downturned mouths. 'Don't look so sad. There are upsides.'

Charlie looked appalled. 'There are no upsides to cancer.'

'How would you know?' she challenged him. 'I get to always be right now, did you know that? No one argues with you if you have cancer – and even if they do, you always win. You always get the last word. I can be a prize bitch and no one can call me on it because when you're declared terminally ill, you're suddenly a saint. You must be handled with kid gloves and no one must ever upset you. *Don't upset the cancer lady! She's dying, you know!*'

Libby saw Archie flinch at the dark humour and there followed another small pause.

'That's why I was in no rush to tell you all, do you see? Once people know, everything changes. It doesn't matter how much you say you just want to be treated normally, people can't do it. All they see is the cancer and so all you become is the cancer. You end up behind a glass wall—'

A sudden sound upstairs made them all look up. It sounded as if something heavy had been dropped.

'What was that?' Coco frowned.

There was a silence as everyone waited to see if it came again, trying to make sense of it. They were all in here, in this room. There was no one else in the house.

Or at least, there wasn't supposed to be. Mrs T was back in the village.

'. . . Which room is above us here?' Charlie asked as the silence lengthened.

'The green room,' Archie murmured, his eyes on the ceiling.

'The one Prock and Ems were in?'

'Yes . . . It's odd. I'll go check.'

They struck Libby as mild words for what seemed to her an alarming occurrence. Things didn't just randomly throw themselves on the floor. Archie swapped looks with Rollo and Charlie, the slight tip of his head almost imperceptible – but Libby caught it.

'I'll come with you,' Rollo said.

'Me too,' Charlie muttered.

'I'll come t—' Libby began but Archie wheeled round, a pointed finger outstretched towards her.

'Wait here.'

'But—'

'Pugh. Wait here,' he commanded, leaving the room.

Chapter Twenty-Five

May 2014

'I am literally going without you!' Charlie yelled up the stairs. He had been waiting for at least forty-five minutes now, sprawled on the sofa in his black tie, the scent of his cologne beginning to sink into its middle notes. 'I am *literally* going out the door!'

'You *literally* are not,' Libby thought to herself as she stared at her reflection in the mirror, smoothing the black silk dress down over her hips, the dress Archie had told her in the first few minutes of this morning that he would be taking off her tonight. She shook her head, loving how her new layers always fell into a perfect frame around her face and admiring again the winged eye Coco had done for her; she looked sultry and dramatic and nothing like the girl usually sitting at the library window in jeans, trainers and an Adidas hoodie. She wondered if Archie would like it – she still wasn't one of his Fulham blondes – and how he would greet her. Would this be the first public proclamation of what was happening between them?

She hadn't seen him since he had left for the train station earlier – there were so many last-minute jobs to complete before the guests arrived, and if he had come back to shower and change, she had missed it. She spritzed her perfume –

Narciso Rodriguez, a Christmas gift last year from her mother – and walked through it, feeling the droplets fizz slightly on her skin. She grabbed her bag, took a last look in the mirror and strode out.

'I mean it!' Charlie yelled again, now lying on the bottom step. 'You do realize there's a seated dinner? I would like to get some booze down me before—'

Libby peered over the balustrade. 'I'll get them,' she said calmly, seeing his cheeks were pink with frustration. He sagged with relief.

'Thanks, Lib.'

'Ems, are you ready?' she asked, pushing on the door and walking into the bedroom. 'Charlie's about to have a coronary.'

Ems looked up from where she was lying on the bed, wriggling herself into a pair of control tights. 'Just . . . give me . . . a sec,' she panted, falling back as she caught sight of Libby. 'Oh bloody hell! Look at *you*!'

'Do you like?' Libby gave an excited twirl.

'Like? Lib, you're a whole new woman! That dress *and* with your hair too! Who even are you?'

Libby gave a delighted smile. 'Well, I can't wait to see your dress on. I'll go and corral Zannah. I can't believe she got back so late. Like, why go to the library today of all days? Even *I'm* not there!'

'At least her hair's already done,' Ems said, standing up and doing some donkey kicks to ease out the tights.

'Yeah, I guess.' She slipped out and crossed the landing into Zannah's bedroom. 'Hey, you rea . . . ?' The words died in her throat.

Zannah, standing motionless in the middle of the room, was staring blankly at the wall. It took her another moment to register Libby's presence. '. . . Huh?'

Libby frowned. 'Zannah, are you okay?'

'Sure. Why?'

'You seem really preoccupied.' This morning at breakfast she had been distracted too.

There was a small pause before Zannah turned away, fussing over something out of Libby's sightline. 'I'm fine. Just a bit stressed. Exams, Coco . . . It's all a bit shit.'

'Yeah, it is,' Libby agreed. They would all miss Coco tonight. She was the social butterfly who connected groups and made everyone feel a little more beautiful as they basked in her reflected glory. No party was complete without her.

'Probably Mercury in retrograde or something,' Zannah muttered, standing back up again and bringing her focus onto her reflection in the mirror. Libby saw her reinhabit her body again, drawing up and standing taller as she appraised her image. She looked striking in her newly purchased vintage peacock dress; it had a low back and a full lamé skirt with sunray pleats that swished as she walked. Her long reddish hair was still beautifully sleek and she was wearing a couple of gold cuffs at each wrist, with gold strappy sandals. '. . . I can't decide whether to add earrings or not.'

'Hmm . . . no, you don't need them. The cuffs are so strong. You look incredible.'

Zannah glanced over at her and nodded approvingly. '*Et toi, ma petite.*' She gave a wink.

'*Je suis une au pair française,*' Libby muttered. French had never been her strong suit.

'Mm. It's going to be interesting watching people's reactions to *you* tonight.' She reached for the hot pink suede pouch on the bed and they walked out of the room together.

Ems was already halfway down the stairs, Charlie jangling the car keys impatiently by the front door.

'Finally! If I'd known you were going to take the mick like that, I'd have let you take the bus,' he grumbled without much conviction.

'Oh, Charlie,' Ems pouted, chucking his chin. 'You're so cute when you're cross.'

'Have we got the 'pre' booze?' Zannah began, her eyes falling to a carrier bag on the sofa. 'Yes, good. Here.' She began handing out pre-mixed cans of passionfruit martinis. 'Bolt.'

'How many have you got in there?' Libby asked, hearing them clatter.

'Not enough,' Zannah said, opening hers and downing almost half in one go.

'Woah!' Charlie exclaimed. 'Steady there, cowgirl!'

'Nope.' Zannah smacked her lips together and raised the can to her lips again. 'There's been enough misery to deal with lately. I want to forget everything. All of it. Tonight, we've got one mission – we are all going to get absolutely wasted! Yes?'

Libby and Ems swapped amused looks. '. . . Sure. Archie would expect nothing less.'

Twenty minutes later, Charlie drew up to the hotel, a gracious Georgian limestone country house with curved bay windows and a colonnade that gave onto mature grounds. Impossibly green lawns nudged up against abundant islands of rhododendrons and azaleas, and ancient yews were clipped into the shapes of acorns. There appeared to be a wedding going on in the westerly side of the house, hatted guests mingling and cream bunting hanging in swags from wooden posts as a bride and groom posed for their photographs during golden hour.

Charlie followed the drive round to the car park, which

boasted a curious mix of glossy 4x4s on the one hand and dented Micras on the other.

'Well, I think we know which party we belong to,' Ems chuckled, finishing her second can as Charlie looked for a place to park.

'So Prock's coming straight here from work?' he asked her.

'Yeah, I've brought his suit so he can just get changed in the loos and not lose any more time.'

'Oh shit!' Libby gasped as she remembered far too late the small overnight bag, left on her bed.

'What's wrong?' Ems flinched, looking alarmed.

'Oh . . . uh, nothing,' Libby murmured, drawing a suspicious scowl from Zannah who was already on her fourth can. It wasn't a disaster, she supposed, but it would mean doing the walk of shame through the hotel lobby tomorrow, in what was clearly a Night Before dress. 'It's a shame he has to do you-know-what, today of all days. It's not exactly an ideal start for coming on to something like this.'

'Don't worry about that,' Charlie scoffed. 'Roly will have a special line-up of shots behind the bar especially for him.'

'I reckon he'll need them,' Ems sighed. 'He barely slept last night. He's bloody nervous.'

Everyone shared apprehensive looks. They had managed to get hold of Staples' teaching schedule and agreed today's lecture presented the best opportunity for confronting him. Plotting a criminal endeavour was very different to actually going through with it, and there had been several whispered conversations in the past few days, running through the numerous ways the confrontation might unfold and the various threats Prock might deploy. They wanted to cover all the bases, but there was no textbook for blackmail. Coco had no idea of their plan, naturally, but Libby's nerves had been rising all day: with the Hong Kong offer now confirmed and her final essay submitted, her starry future was twinkling before her, within touching distance. If this backfired . . .

'He should have let me do it,' Charlie said, gripping the wheel more tightly as he found a parking spot.

'How could he, though?' Ems argued. 'Sasha Staples sent the nudes to *his* phone. He was the one who talked to her. He has to be the one to confront him.'

'Well, at the very least he should have taken me and Roly with him, for backup,' Charlie said, reversing into the space.

'It won't get physical,' Ems said calmly. 'Prock's a twenty-one-year-old flanker and that bastard's a fifty-two-year-old geek.'

'Yeah, I guess . . . From the looks of it, he's only got a fifteen-inch neck.'

Libby looked at him in surprise. 'You mean you've seen him?'

Charlie hesitated as he cut the ignition. 'I may have kept an eye out for him recently.'

'Charlie,' Libby said in a warning tone. 'Have you been following him? We need to make sure we can't be implicated. Harassment and stalking are—'

'Relax, he had no idea I was there. I just wanted to see if he had any routines or a favourite place for lunch, things like that. I'm not intending to jump the guy . . . At least, not yet. It's just helpful to know a bit more about him, you know, in case this doesn't work.'

'Well, it will,' Ems said confidently, undoing her seatbelt and opening the car door. 'He risks explicit images of his wife being circulated to all his colleagues and the entire student body. Like Prock said, he's a cornered rat.'

Libby bit her lip, forcing herself to stay quiet. She really didn't like that analogy. It made her nervous.

Surely everyone knew cornered rats attack?

It was like walking into Babylon. The party had only begun half an hour ago but the place was already rammed and a hedonistic air prevailed, conversation at shouting pitch and screamed laughs carrying over the music. The space was appropriately grand with a coffered ceiling, marble columns that stood at opposing ends of the vast room and floor-to-ceiling windows giving onto the colonnaded terrace they had seen from the car.

Navy and gold balloons hung in extravagant clusters, like bunches of grapes; on closer inspection, they were printed with *Older not wiser!* and *Birthday bastard*. Rollo's hand was everywhere, it seemed, and not just at the bar – the waiting staff were all wearing black t-shirts printed with Archie's face.

Libby scanned the room for the man himself. She was alone already. Charlie had promised to get her a drink, but she wasn't hopeful of seeing him again; he was too popular by half, no one would let him past without a chat. Ems had gone off to find the reception desk and hand them Prock's dinner suit, and Zannah, well, she had peeled away almost immediately, diving into the crowd with joyous abandon. She had managed five cans in the car on the way over, compared to Ems and Libby's more modest two.

But Libby could feel the alcohol working its magic. She felt looser-limbed already, and as she squeezed past the bodies, she noticed people making space for her, doing double takes as if they recognized but couldn't quite place her; she wasn't the creature who blinked through the darker hours of the twenty-four-hour library tonight.

'*Libby?*' She had just squeezed past a dark-haired guy with curls and glasses and he caught her by the elbow. 'Bloody hell! I never would have recognized you!'

Libby blinked several times in surprise to see her law course-mate here.

'Ben!' she exclaimed. 'What are you doing here?' She backtracked quickly. 'Apologies, that came out wrong! I only meant . . . I didn't know you knew Archie!'

He laughed. 'To be honest, I don't! Never spoken to the guy, I had no idea he even knew my name! One of my housemates shoots with him so he was coming here and . . . I dunno, maybe he put a word in for me. But I'll be honest, I was pretty surprised when I got the call this morning.'

'He called you this morning?'

'Yep.' He rolled his eyes. 'I know. Obviously I'm a stopgap because someone else dropped out at the last minute, but do I give a shit? No!' he laughed. 'Just look at this place! Let's be honest, Archie Templeton's twenty-first was always going to be iconic. To hell with my pride, there was no way I was missing out on this.'

He took a swig of his beer, his eyes upon her as she took it all in. This morning she had heard Rollo fielding calls for Archie as people rang and begged for entry. But now Archie had personally rung Ben and invited him?

Her eyes scanned the crowd again, but there was still no sign of Archie that she could see. 'I don't suppose you've seen him?'

Ben shook his head. 'No – although isn't it a bit like following the seagulls to find the herrings?'

'Huh?'

'Look for the flock of girls?'

'Ha, right.'

He took another swig of beer. 'By the way, I heard congrats were in order.'

'Sorry?' she shouted, struggling to hear him over the crowd.

'Hong Kong! Congratulations! That's incredible.'

'. . . Oh! Thanks,' she said, puzzled. She hadn't told anyone but her housemates – not even her parents; she needed to talk to Archie first and discuss their options. Nothing was yet set in stone. 'Who told you?'

'Archie mentioned it when he called. Said you were made up about it. I'm not surprised.'

'It's . . . yeah, it's great . . . It hasn't really sunk in yet, though.'

'I've been trying for Madrid. Still waiting to hear back.' He gave a grimace. 'Maybe it's not good news if you've heard and I haven't.'

'I'm sure it's not like that. They must all have different processes.'

'Hopefully.' He inhaled deeply, trying to remain optimistic. 'I'm—'

'Oh, Ben, I can see my housemate bringing over my drink,' she interrupted, catching sight of Charlie. 'I'd better go help him before he sloshes most of it of himself! But great seeing you!'

'Oh . . . s-sure. And listen, if ever you fancy that pizza—?'

He faded out as she dipped through the bodies, grateful to get away. She just wanted to find Archie. To see him. '. . . *I'd be looking for you.*' Memories kept lighting like flares in her mind – how he would pace her room like a caged tiger as they talked, his jeans hanging low on his hips, eating his Jaffa Cake cake together at midnight, the way he had struggled with his self-control in his bedroom this morning . . .

'Here, Lib!' Charlie was heading towards her, holding the

champagne flutes aloft; she had been right, most of it was on his jacket, everyone jostling.

'Charlie, you're a superstar,' she said with relief as they met in the sea of bodies. '. . . Cheers!'

They clinked glasses and gulped down the champagne; it was good stuff, doubtless still dusty from Archie's father's cellars. Libby had to stop herself from draining hers; she felt strangely anxious. 'Ahh. You just saved me from the most dull guy.'

'Well, sorry I took so long, something of a scrum at the bar. This place has gone demob happy. Looks like Zannah's not the only one on a mission tonight.'

'Yeah, I lost her almost immediately. And I still haven't seen Roly or Archie yet. Have you?'

'No, but I overheard someone say they were over in that corner, or thereabouts. No doubt getting mobbed . . . ' He looked around quickly, a good head and shoulders taller than her, a smile beginning to play on his lips.

'What is it?' she asked. 'Who are you looking for?'

'Bella Tait,' he said in a conspiratorial tone. 'Apparently she's been telling everyone she's getting back with Archie tonight.'

'. . . *What?*' Libby felt the floor drop beneath her feet.

'She wants him back. Apparently she can't believe he went no contact on her. She assumed he'd chase but he hasn't . . . Our boy's done good on the bet so far but I reckon I might be a grand up by the end of tonight.'

Libby's heart felt like it was going to leap out of her chest. Archie had told her he'd taken the bet to show her he wasn't – in his words – 'an animal'; he'd had a point to prove. But Bella Tait was the queen of campus and his ex; if she was determined to get him back, who could stop her? Not Libby. And probably not even Archie himself.

She saw his shoulders slump suddenly, his smile fade as he looked around the glamorous crowd. 'What is it?' she asked him.

'. . . Coco should be here,' he said in a pained voice. 'It's not right. She should be here.' He threw his head back and drained the glass.

'Oh, Charlie.' Libby put a hand on his arm just as a gong sounded and everyone turned to find Rollo standing on a chair. He was wearing a mustard velvet dinner jacket and looking particularly florid.

'Ladies and gentlemen! Eyes right and quick march to the next room, if you will! Dinner is served!'

A cheer went up as Charlie groaned, holding up his single empty glass. 'Oh great! You see? That's what comes of getting here late. This is my first drink. We're about to eat and I'm as sober as a bloody judge.'

'Sorry, Charlie,' she grimaced, trying to keep sight of Rollo as he jumped back down into the crowd. Where there was Rollo, there would be Archie.

'Come on,' he sighed. 'Let's find our seats. At least there's wine on the tables. I'm going to have a bottle to myself.'

Libby grabbed his arm so she didn't lose him in the crowd again. The tide of bodies had turned as one and they were being swept along into the adjacent room where fifteen large round tables had been dressed with navy linen and gold chairs. There was a dance floor and DJ decks through there, and more balloon arches bobbing overhead.

Everyone clamoured to find their names on the seating plans set up on huge boards.

'. . . Right, you're table nine, Lib,' Charlie said, using his superior height to check on her behalf.

'Nine?' It sounded like she was almost in the garden! It

wasn't as if she'd expected to be top table with Archie – or at least, she hadn't even given the matter any thought – but . . . *nine*?

'And I'm table five.'

Libby scanned the tables – they were marked out by navy balloons floating on gold ribbons from the floral centrepieces and printed with gilded numbers. Sure enough, number nine was set towards the back of the room in the corner; it appeared to be diametrically opposite to table one, where Archie would surely be sitting. They couldn't have been further apart.

'Earnshaw!'

Libby and Charlie looked up at the shout. Prock was weaving his way through the crowd, still dressed in his supermarket uniform. Ems was trying to catch his attention from the far corner, no doubt to tell him his suit was at reception – but from the look on his face, he wasn't here to party.

They all met in a huddle behind one of the boards, Ems breathless from swimming against the tide.

'So?' Charlie asked him intently, tension pulling down the corners of his mouth; it was like waiting for a jury's verdict. 'What'd he say?'

Prock shook his head slowly. 'It's all fucked.'

'What do you mean?' Charlie frowned. 'How can it be fucked?'

'I showed him the photos. Said everything we agreed.'

'Yeah? And?'

'He laughed in my face and said he didn't give a damn what I did with them. Told me to give them to Pornhub if I wanted!'

'What?' Ems cried. 'He does understand this was his *wife* you were talking about?'

'Yup. He said I'd be doing him a favour, he's been – his words – trying to be rid of her for the best part of a decade!'

315

They all stared at one another in disbelief.

'He's a fucking sociopath,' Ems whispered.

'Of course he is. He's a rapist,' Libby said flatly, glancing at Charlie. He was ashen-faced.

'He's a rapist who's moving among all of us every day – working here, living here . . . He's a potential danger to every single girl in this room.'

'And an actual attacker to the girl who is *not* in this room,' Charlie spat, bringing it back to Coco again. Everything came back to her, for him. He looked back at Prock. 'Did you tell him you knew exactly what he'd done to her?'

'Yes.'

'And?'

Prock seemed to freeze for a moment. He looked away with a slight shake of his head, his hands coming to rest on his hips. 'He said prove it.'

'*What?*' Charlie looked destroyed. 'That son of a bitch!'

Prock watched him, looking apprehensive. 'There's worse—'

Libby felt her heart drop to the floor. What could possibly be worse?

'I lost my temper when he said that. I just saw red and went off script . . . I told him we could.'

'But we can't!' Ems cried.

'I know. But the way his face changed . . .' Prock looked at Libby. 'He asked me what I'd seen.'

'Seen?'

'Yeah. Not what I knew. What I'd seen.'

Libby swallowed. There was surely only one thing to infer from such a comment?

'. . . You think he filmed it?' she whispered. It made her feel sick even to think of it. Was it a trophy for him? Something to go back and revisit? To *enjoy*?

'I'm not sure. He was careful in everything he said, but I definitely got the feeling that made him nervous. He was probing, trying to see what I knew.'

'Did Coco mention any of that to you?' Ems asked her. She had grown pale, a pain flickering in her mascara'd eyes.

Libby shook her head. 'No, but . . . that doesn't mean it didn't happen. She wouldn't necessarily have known. He could have hidden the camera, set it up before she got there.'

They all looked at Charlie but he was as frozen as if he'd been carved from marble. Libby put a hand on his arm; he didn't even blink.

'What do we do?' Ems asked her, as if a law degree was a manual for how to manipulate a sociopath. Libby tried to think but her brain was blunted with booze and there just didn't seem to be an obvious weakness, a chink in the armour where they could drive a fatal wedge. *He* didn't care about his wife's reputation and *she* didn't care about his 'womanizing'; she certainly didn't recognize it as a rape . . . Professor and Mrs Staples, though clearly unhappily married, were both utterly immutable and locked in a stalemate that protected them both.

'If there is film footage, clearly that would be proof of the assault. Admissible evidence. But we can't know for sure and even if there is, *we* don't have it. He's called our bluff,' she said finally. 'We either have to act on what we threatened or . . . we don't; that's it. We're at the end of the road, so far as I can see.'

Ems looked back at Prock. '. . . And he really wasn't fazed by being blackmailed? You're sure it wasn't a double bluff?'

Prock shook his head. 'He's a cold fucker. I swear to god, I was so psyched. Everything was perfect – I caught him at the end of the lecture when there was no one else around.

I had all the time in the world to do it. I had the photos ready . . .' He gave a bitter laugh. 'Do you know what he said to me at the end?'

'What?' Ems whispered.

Prock pinched his work top. 'He said that if I didn't get off university property, he'd have security throw me out. I told him to his face I know he's a rapist and he hit back with fucking *trespass*. He honestly thinks he's untouchable—'

'Excuse me.' A couple of waitresses tried to get past him, plates stacked along their arms, and he stepped aside, out of the way.

Libby looked around them to see that most people were now seated at their tables. 'Look, there's nothing more we can do now. We'd better sit down and not call attention to ourselves,' she said quietly. 'Let's just take some time to think and talk about it later.'

'Yeah,' Ems said, guiding a disconsolate Prock away. 'You need to get changed too, babe . . .'

Libby looked back at Charlie. 'Don't worry,' she said, seeing how he was still staring into space. He looked utterly crushed. 'We'll think of something else, I promise.'

It was another moment before her words appeared to reach him. 'Yeah . . . Sure,' he mumbled.

She watched as he drifted away too. Libby couldn't imagine how hard it must be for him to have had this happen to the girl he loved and be able to do nothing about it. They were all utterly impotent – and clearly not gangsters.

Libby sighed and headed over to table nine, feeling none of the alcohol buzz and only the melancholy. There was only one empty chair left at the table and she stopped short as the guy to her right turned around.

Surely not—

'Well, well, well – you're like buses, Libby! Nothing for weeks and then twice in an hour!'

Libby raised a weak smile as he patted her chair beside him. '. . . Hi, Ben.'

Chapter Twenty-Six

23 December 2023

The girls stood in a huddle around the fire, blaming their shivers on the cold as they waited for the men to return.

'Well, that escalated quickly. We've gone from playing Secret Santa to Burglar Bill,' Zannah murmured, rubbing her hands. She seemed grateful for the diversion, excusing her as the topic of conversation – at least for the moment. 'Although I suppose they aren't really very different – either way, there's a strange man creeping about the house . . . Let's just hope it doesn't become Murder in the Dark.'

Libby wanted to laugh in spite of her alarm – Zannah's dark sense of humour had always appealed to her – but Coco was pale and ominously quiet. She couldn't joke about a strange man being in the house.

'It'll all be fine, Coco,' she said, as reassuringly as she could. 'The boys are just being extra-cautious.'

'But that sound . . . we all heard it.'

'It was probably just a picture frame toppling over or something.'

'On its *own*? No.' Coco wouldn't be dissuaded that the threat was real.

'Yeah, you know how draughty these windows are; they rattle all the time.'

'Not enough to knock something over, though.'

. . . Nor to blow out hurricane candles either? Libby bit her lip as she suppressed the thought. Her imagination was getting the better of her in the dark again; she wasn't used to buildings of this scale and age. They creaked and groaned; they trembled and seized.

'I reckon a bird's got in through that broken window,' Zannah said, looking wholly unperturbed. 'Or maybe even a squirrel, driven in by the snow.'

'You think?' Coco sounded a little more hopeful.

Zannah nodded. 'Honestly, this place is like a menagerie. I came down and found a badger in the kitchen once.'

Libby swallowed at the casual reminiscence, a careless allusion to memories made here. Even knowing what she now knew, the words felt like acid on her skin, burning away to a deep tender spot.

They heard the sound of footsteps in the room above them, the low timbre of the men's voices vibrating through the floor as they searched in the dark for . . . what? Who? They had no idea.

Suddenly there was a silence – then the footsteps quickened, leaving the room again.

They heard creaks on the stairs and were staring, open-mouthed, at the door when the men burst through a moment later.

'What is it?' Zannah asked. Even she was looking concerned now as they came in, thin-lipped and eyes darting like fireflies as if searching for something. Rollo was still carrying one of the hurricane candles from the stairs.

'What's happened?' Coco breathed.

Archie swallowed as he saw her fear and when he spoke it

was in a hushed voice. 'Someone's in the house – or they were. We found a couple of notes.'

'*Notes?*' Zannah exclaimed. 'What kind of notes?'

'They were left on the pillows in some of the rooms,' Archie murmured, glancing at Coco.

'Which rooms?'

'Mine and Prock's,' Charlie said.

Libby tensed. The Procks? Hadn't Ems been convinced someone had been in the room with her earlier?

Archie cleared his throat and straightened to his full height. 'But look, it's probably just a prank. Local kids larking about. They've probably gone already. We need to go around and check but you just need to stay all together in this room, okay? It's a big house and it's fucking dark. We need to know you're safe in one place while we search.'

'Surely it would be better if we all looked together?' Libby suggested. 'We could split into pairs.'

Archie blinked at her. '. . . I think it would be better if you just stay in here.'

Libby read the subtext – he was saying one thing, doing another, and she knew he didn't believe what he was telling them. If he really thought these notes were just a prank or that the person who had left them had gone, he wouldn't be insisting on their seclusion. She guessed he just didn't want Coco to be any more frightened than she already was.

So what wasn't he telling them?

Libby frowned as she remembered the passing shadow in the hall upstairs, just an hour ago. It had been around the same time that the candles on the stairs had been blown out – as if someone was deliberately taunting them. As if wanting their presence to be known . . .

'What did the notes say?' Zannah asked.

'That doesn't matter,' Archie said. 'You don't need to—'

'We're not children, Arch!' Zannah snapped. 'Show them to us.'

Archie looked at Charlie, who stalled for a moment before pulling two small, folded squares of paper from his pocket. He watched Coco as the women peered closer; the handwriting was difficult to discern clearly at first, in the dim light, and Rollo held up the hurricane candle so they could read more clearly.

There's blood on your hands
I know what you did

Instinctively, they stepped back again, chilled.

'But what does that mean? What *did* we do?' Coco asked Charlie.

'. . . Nothing,' he shrugged. 'These are generic, playground threats. *I know what you did* – I mean, come on, it's a Netflix series! It's just a prank.'

But Libby knew no one was going to come all the way out here, in these extreme conditions, on account of a prank. She looked towards the windows and saw that the curtains were open. Although there was only the flickering light from the fire and a couple of candles illuminating this room, it struck her that from out there in the darkness anyone could easily look in and watch them, unseen. From outside, they would be like actors on a stage.

Without saying a word, she walked over and drew the curtains shut.

'We're going to finish checking the rooms,' Archie said, watching her. 'Just do not leave this room. Close the door behind us. Maybe push a chair against it till we get back.'

'That's a bit much, isn't it?' Zannah asked. 'If it's just a prankster.'

'Perhaps. But until we know exactly what's going on, we shouldn't assume anything. Remember, we've got no way of contacting the emergency services. We're on our own out here.'

Everyone fell quiet at his words, not sure whether to scoff at the threat or quail at it. Why was someone in the house? Libby looked at Charlie again, sensing he was holding something back.

'We'll be back shortly,' Archie muttered. 'Stay here.'

'We're like fish in a barrel,' Coco whispered as he led the men's exit once more. 'Just waiting for the bullets.'

'We're safe, babe,' Zannah murmured, holding her by the arm. 'The boys won't let anything happen.'

'I'll be right back,' Libby said to them, following after the men.

'No, you can't!' Coco quailed. 'Archie said—'

'I'm only going to stoke the fires in the reception hall,' she said quickly, striding across the room. 'They mustn't go out. They're keeping the house at a subsistence level of warmth. Don't worry, I'm right outside the door.'

She slipped out into the long passage, only just managing to grab Charlie by the arm. Rollo and Archie were already out of sight up the stairs.

'Hey,' she whispered.

He looked angry. 'What are you doing?' he hissed. 'We literally just said—'

'What are you not telling us?'

'Me?'

'Yes. I know you're hiding something. There's something you don't want Coco to know.'

He stared at her, and she knew from the way he balled his jaw that she was right.

'Charlie, tell me. You don't think this is a prank?'

'. . . No.'

'You think someone is actually threatening us, specifically?'

He swallowed. 'I don't think it's a coincidence that the notes were on my pillow and Prock's.'

'Because . . . ?' she pushed.

'Because we were the ones who confronted Staples.'

That name again. A cold shiver trickled down her spine. She'd not heard it in years and now twice in a single day?

He nodded. 'Remember at breakfast, when I read out that Staples had been attacked?'

'. . . Yes.' Her eyes narrowed.

'And Max thought it strange that the national press was reporting on the assault of a retired university professor?'

'Yes,' she said slowly. Max's instincts were always razor sharp. Any anomaly, he noticed. What had she missed?

'Well, that's because the assault wasn't the focus of the piece – but as soon as I remembered he was sitting with us, I dropped it. Obviously it wasn't something we could discuss in front of him, for Coco's sake.'

'No.' She felt her anxiety mount. 'So what did you leave out?'

'The full story was that Staples was doing voluntary work at a bike shop in Acklington as part of an initiative between HMP Northumberland and this rehabilitation enterprise. He was jumped by three men, hospitalized with his injuries . . .'

'Oh god,' she murmured, a hand flying to her mouth as she guessed what was coming next.

He nodded. 'And now he's absconded.'

She stared at him, appalled, for several moments. Staples was free?

'But how could they have let him out at all?' she hissed. 'He's a serial rapist! Wasn't it obvious to anyone he encountered how dangerous he is? He was a psychology professor! He understands human behaviour. He knows how to manipulate people!'

Charlie pressed a finger to his lips, his eyes darting towards the drawing-room door. Neither of them wanted Coco to overhear this. 'He was a Category C prisoner; considered low risk on account of his age and good behaviour credits inside.'

Libby blinked back at him, hardly able to believe it. 'So he's been on the run since yesterday?'

'Actually, the day before. I was reading an old newspaper. There were no deliveries this morning, obviously.'

Two days, then.

'But . . . I mean, it can't be *him* that's here, surely?' she whispered, incredulous. 'How would it even be possible? How would he know we're here, together? We're in the middle of nowhere, in a blacked-out house that can't even be seen from its own garden right now.'

It made no sense that he could have found them, especially in these extreme conditions . . .

'Coco's TikToks last night,' he said in a low voice. 'She tagged this place and had on her geolocation.'

'Oh god.' So then Coco had unwittingly led her own attacker right to her door? Where it was dark and cold. Where no one else was around. Where there was no escape.

'She can't know it's him, Libby,' he murmured.

She stared at him, knowing he was right. There couldn't be any suggestion to her that the man who had ruined her life had come back for his revenge. But how could they protect her? For as long as Staples was in the house, they were sitting ducks.

Chapter Twenty-Seven

May 2014

She couldn't eat. She couldn't even drink. She could only stare across the room, watching in frozen horror as Archie ate and drank and talked and flirted with Bella Tait, sitting on his left. She watched their heads tilt towards one another in close conversation, excluding everyone else; she saw Bella push back his hair as it fell forward, her fingers tracing down the side of his face afterwards. She saw how Archie didn't lean away.

Did he know where she was in this room? Did he know she could see this? His eyes never strayed from the table, even though all eyes were on him, not just hers.

Beside her, Ben was holding forth on his upcoming travels to Colombia, where he was working with a pro bono charity; he seemed not even to have noticed that she'd barely said a word. Her gaze sometimes travelled the room, scanning desperately for rescue. Charlie, at his table, looked much as she felt – mute, inert, depressed. Libby couldn't tell if he was dead drunk or stone-cold sober. Ems and Prock (still in his polyester work clothes; he hadn't bothered changing after all) were faring slightly better, holding conversations and laughing at appropriate points; but though Prock was tucking into the wine, he looked pale and tense, his fingers tapping against his glass.

Zannah was the life and soul at her table, leading everyone in rounds of shots and drinking games; she wouldn't be so carefree once she heard their foray into the criminal under-world had fallen flat on its face. Rollo too was set for a crash; he was seated at Archie's table and every inch the bon viveur, making sure his best friend's party was an unmitigated success.

The courses came and went with impressive speed – Rollo was of the opinion that sitting too long eating would sober everyone up, an utter disaster for any party. The waitresses looked at Libby quizzically as her plates were returned as they had come out. She didn't care. She could feel her anger building as she watched the seduction playing out across the dance floor

What the hell was he doing? Even by his standards, it was surely unimaginable that he was doing this? Had every word from his mouth been a lie? What had the past few months been if not a slow falling in love? The growth of an emotional connection, the likes of which he had admitted he had never known before.

Had she been played? Had their encounters last night and this morning been enough to show him that he could have her if he wanted to – he had broken down her famous reserves – and that knowledge was all he had really needed? Wanted?

The pain weighed like a leaden ache in her chest, leaching poison into her veins so that it circulated and spread into every part of her body. Heartbreak. So easily said; so hard to endure.

People were getting up now, the lights beginning to flash on the dance floor and the DJ ramping up the volume. She saw Archie rise and whisper something into Bella's ear, a small jerk of his head upwards that made her nod and smile in return, looking happy and victorious. He went to turn away but something – an instinct – made him look up, his eyes finding hers upon him immediately. As if he had known she was right there. Watching.

Neither one of them moved; they didn't even blink as his message was silently conveyed across the span of the room. No words were needed. She understood they were over, even if she didn't understand why.

'. . . Libby, I swear you haven't heard a single word I've said.'

She tuned back in to Ben, but she didn't even see him. Her entire body felt made of glass. She was hollow, fragile and entirely transparent – surely every emotion could be seen in her right now? She was utterly exposed.

When she looked back again towards Archie, he was gone.

'. . . Would you excuse me?' she murmured.

'But—'

She pushed her chair back and it toppled behind her, but she didn't stop to pick it up as she walked slowly to . . . she didn't even know where. She needed air. Something terrible was happening, she could feel it, as if her life was tapestry and the threads were being pulled.

'Lib!' Someone wheeled her around, catching her by the arm.

'Charlie!' Relief overwhelmed her when she realized she was facing a true friend and the word came out as a sob; she was already beginning to collapse inside.

Then she saw him. In contrast to his earlier despair, he looked wild – his eyes wide and tension radiating from him in waves. 'Oh god, what?'

'It's Coco. She's just rung me . . .' His breathing was hard and fast, like he'd been running. 'She's freaking out. Staples is there! He's outside the house!'

'*What?*' The word was almost a shout and she slapped her hands over her mouth.

'I'm leaving right now.'

'I'll come with you!'

'No,' he said firmly. 'I need you to tell the others and get over there with them. We'll need witnesses, we can't do this on our own.'

'But . . . how will we get there if you've gone?'

'Take Archie's car. I saw it parked outside.' He stopped suddenly, thinking hard. 'Get his keys but don't tell him. Or Roly.'

'Why not?'

'Because if either of them leaves this party, people will notice and ask why and what happened to Coco will be around uni in minutes. Just get Prock and Ems and Zannah. That's enough of us.'

'Okay.'

'You'll come immediately, yes? *Immediately*. You won't waste a minute?'

'I promise.'

With a single nod, he turned on his heel and ran through the crowd. Libby looked around, desperately trying to find one of the others – Prock in his polyester polo shirt, Zannah's bright hair – but there were just too many bodies and even in her heels she wasn't tall enough to see clearly. She began to push her way through with shoulder barges, the intrusive thoughts of Coco's sheer terror giving her an assertiveness that made the crowd part for her.

She found herself back in the cocktail bar. It wasn't as rammed now, but still there was no sign of her housemates. Were they all in the loos? She ran through to the hall and down to the ladies' toilets.

'Ems! Zannah!' she called, ignoring the queue of girls waiting for the stalls. 'Are you in here? It's urgent!'

Nothing.

She ran out again, aware of the curious looks at her back as she made a scene. She was about to dive back into the bar when she saw the reception desk. A few guests from the wedding in the other wing were wandering around—

Archie's car keys. He wouldn't have them on him, she surmised. He wasn't leaving here tonight.

'Hi,' she panted a few moments later. 'I believe there's a room booked for me? Libby Pugh? I'm with Archie Templeton, he made the booking.'

The receptionist checked her system. 'Ah, yes, Miss Pugh. You're in Room Sixteen.' She tapped the keyboard. 'That's a corner room on the second floor. Take the left at the top of the stairs and it's at the end of the corridor on the right.' She reached for a keycard in the drawer. 'Would you like someone to bring up your bags?' The receptionist looked around blindly for them.

'No, no bags,' Libby panted, grabbing the card from her. 'Thanks.'

She sprinted up the stairs, following the receptionist's directions so that within a few moments she was standing outside the door. She slid the card in and watched the red light flash green, walking in and stopping almost immediately as she heard sounds. Distinctive sounds.

She was in a narrow corridor off the bathroom and unable to see the whole of the bedroom from where she stood; only the headboard, plumped-up pillows and a bedside table were in sight. She could see a phone, coins and the car keys on the table and she kept her gaze fixed upon them as she slowly put one foot in front of another.

The sound of heavy breathing, of rapid panting grew as she approached the threshold to the bedroom and it felt as though her heart had forgotten how to pump, her lungs couldn't inflate.

She stared at the keys, six feet away; she just had to reach forward and grab them. Not look left. Just dead ahead.

But it was an impossible task. Even just in her peripheral vision, as she stepped through, she saw Archie sitting in a chair in the corner, a girl astride him and kissing his neck. She was still fully clothed; the pleated skirt hiked up over her thighs and her hands in his hair, the light from a table lamp making her gold cuffs flash.

Libby cried out – the sound like a fox's whelp – as Archie looked straight at her, his eyes red-rimmed and glassy, a look she had seen in him many times before – wasted, vacant, desolate.

He held her gaze as Zannah straightened up and looked back; her response was chronically delayed. 'Lib!' she slurred. She looked a mess, her mascara smudged like she'd been crying.

Libby took a step back, gulping for air. She felt like she couldn't breathe. Like she couldn't live. How could Archie just sit there and make no move? Wasn't he supposed to rush towards her and tell her this was all a terrible mistake, that she'd got it all wrong and it didn't mean anything? That she was the one he loved and he'd do anything to win her back?

Because it could have just been anything; she'd accept whatever breadcrumb he gave her; she was that pathetic, that broken over him. But even that was more than he was willing to give. He didn't stir.

Coco . . . immediately. She remembered the wild look in Charlie's eyes, his desperation to protect Coco, to save her. *That* was love. He would never do something like this. He was a good man. A better man.

A sob escaped her as she took a last look at him before tearing her eyes away from the squalid scene. She grabbed the keys from the table and, without a word, ran out.

'Come with me,' Libby said in Ems's ear. 'We need to leave right now.'

Ems looked up in surprise. She was back at her table, in conversation with a group of people Libby didn't recognize. 'What?' She gave a small laugh, waiting for the joke – but then she saw Libby's face. 'What's wrong?'

'I'll tell you outside. Where's Prock?'

'Over there.' Ems pointed to where he was standing with a few of the rugby boys. 'But—'

'Grab him. We need to hurry.'

'But Lib—'

Libby turned away and began heading for the doors, the car keys pressed tightly into the palm of her hand. There was no time to explain.

'Shit . . . Prock!'

They caught up with her by the main entrance, the three of them running down the steps together, or in Prock's case, staggering. Seemingly he had caught up on the drinking after his late start.

'Lib, what's going on?' Ems asked, trying to keep up as Libby strode towards the car park, searching for Archie's car. She held out the beeper, looking for lights to flash.

'Over there.'

'But that's Archie's car,' Ems said in bafflement.

'Yes. We have to get back to the house right now. Coco rang – Staples is outside the house.'

'*What?*' Prock almost shouted.

'Exactly. And she's terrified out of her mind. Charlie's

already gone over there but he needs backup. Witnesses. We know what Staples is like now. It's going to take all of us together to move against him.'

'Holy shit,' Ems cried. 'Where are the others?'

Libby swallowed, trying to banish the image of Zannah straddling Archie, but it was seared in her mind. 'Charlie said not to alert Archie and Roly, and I agree. If they leave the party, word will spread like wildfire about why. We can't do that to Coco.'

'And Zannah?'

'She's wasted. No good to anyone right now.' Only Archie was benefiting from her inebriation.

'But you've seen her? She's okay?'

Libby glanced at her. 'Just now. And yes, she was having a great time.'

They were at the car now, a tatty black Golf with a Badminton Horse Trials sticker on the back window, and they all jumped in.

'Lib, are you insured to drive this?' Prock asked, only just clicking his seatbelt in as she reversed at speed.

'Nope. But I am sober, which is probably the only good news we'll have tonight.' She calculated it had been an hour and a half since her half glass of champagne and another forty minutes before that since her two canned margaritas.

Everyone was quiet as she sped down the long drive, catching a little air over the speed bumps. She was aware of Ems and Prock swapping looks; she was also aware of the tremor in her hands. Her entire body was in fight or flight mode, adrenaline pumping hard.

'You know . . . this could be a good thing, Staples being over there,' Ems said cautiously.

'*How?*' Prock scoffed.

'Well, you might have felt your encounter with him failed, but it clearly got him rattled.'

'Or riled,' Prock warned.

'Either way, he's going to make a mistake if he's that upset. If he says something and there are witnesses, this could be for the best.'

'I think Coco would disagree right now,' Libby muttered.

'Yeah, but he has no way of getting to her. Just so long as she doesn't open the door . . . She wouldn't open the door, would she?'

There was a slight pause. Panic could make people do stupid things.

'. . . Charlie's there already,' Libby said quietly. 'She'll be safe with him.'

'So then, yes,' Ems said, as if comforting herself. 'If Charlie's there and Staples is . . . upset enough that he's actually gone over to . . . confront her, there's a good chance he'll slip up and do something that we can use.'

'Like what?' Prock asked, groaning as Libby took a corner in third gear. '. . . Shit. I might throw up.'

'Feel free,' Libby muttered. 'But I'm not slowing down.' A car full of vomit was the very least the Hon. Archie Templeton deserved.

'I think we should set our phones to record, in case he says something to incriminate himself. Don't you agree, Lib?' Ems looked over at her and she gave a single nod.

'That's not a bad idea. Let's all do it to maximize chances of a full recording. It wouldn't be admissible in court, but all we really need is leverage against him. That, plus his wife's nudes, should definitely make him think twice about calling our bluff . . . My phone's in my bag, Ems.'

Libby gripped the wheel tightly as she drove. How had her

life come to this point? She was driving uninsured in a car she technically had stolen; to all intents and purposes she was joyriding, barely below the alcohol limit, trying to rescue one housemate and escape another two. What had happened to her small, stable existence, moving between the three points of her bed, her library chair and the lecture hall? What about the promise she had made in earnest to her exhausted parents and how quickly she had been prepared to risk it for a man she knew to be spoiled, weak and broken, unreliable and undisciplined? She had fancied herself the girl who would save him. She had told herself she would scoop up the pieces of his broken heart and put them back together again, but a shattered heart could never be remade whole. It would always be patched, scarred and intrinsically weaker.

As they turned into their road, they all leaned forward in their seats, craning their necks to get a glimpse of the scene. What would they see? Staples standing in the middle of the street, shouting obscenities? Blue lights? Neighbours standing around in their pyjamas?

But all was silent. All was still. There was no sign of a madman anywhere.

'Where is he?' Ems breathed in bewilderment. '. . . Has he gone?'

'That or he's inside the house,' Prock said grimly.

The girls swapped horrified looks. Libby parked at a skewed angle, not even bothering to correct it, and they all jumped out and ran up the path.

Ems struggled to get her key in the lock, her hands shaking with panic.

'Coco, it's just us,' Prock said, bending down and calling through the letterbox. 'We're back . . . Coco, it's just Prock and Ems and Libs – okay? You're safe now!'

They got the door open and burst through. The sitting room was blazing with lights but no one was in there. 'You check upstairs,' Prock said, running towards the basement kitchen.

Ems was up the stairs first, bounding up two at a time and heading straight for the girls' second-floor bedrooms. 'Coco?' she called, heading straight for Coco's own room.

Libby did a preliminary scan of the boys' rooms, flinching as she returned to the scene of this morning's suspended seduction in Archie's room. The towel was still where he had dropped it on the floor, his jeans and shirt tossed on the bed.

'Anything?' she asked, getting to the second-floor landing as Ems came out of Zannah's bedroom.

'Nope.'

'She's not down here!' they heard Prock yell up the stairs. 'Is she up there?'

'No,' Ems yelled back. 'Just trying the top floor now.'

Libby burst into her own room. Her papers and books were still spread across the desk as she had left them earlier, her clothes strewn across the armchair, the little blue candle still felled on the bookshelf . . .

The bedroom door was shut. She didn't recall having closed it, though she couldn't be a hundred per cent certain . . . She put a hand to the handle but it wouldn't move. She tried again; the handle was jammed.

'Coco?' she frowned. 'Are you in there? It's me, Libby.' She looked behind her again and realized her desk chair wasn't there. Had Coco barricaded herself in?

Or had Staples locked them both in?

She tried to keep the panic from her voice. 'Coco, are you alone? Just knock once on the wall if you're alone.'

Libby waited, her ear against the door. She pressed her

finger to her lips as Ems came tiptoeing into the room, Prock just behind her.

One knock came and Libby felt the relief wash through her. It reminded her of being a little girl on the beach, the surf knocking at her knees and threatening to swipe her feet from under her. 'Okay, good. Now, Coco, are you unharmed? Knock once if you're unharmed.'

There was another silence. Then the knock.

'Okay, Coco, listen to me. I'm out here with Ems and Prock. We've checked the entire house and we're the *only* people in here. Everything is locked and secure. He's not outside either. You're safe . . . So we're just going to sit out here and wait for you to come out when you're ready, all right? There's no rush. Just come out in your own time.'

She looked back at Ems and Prock. Ems was biting her nails, Prock standing limply and looking utterly helpless. Libby went over to where they stood and moved her clothes from the armchair. 'Sit down, Prock,' she whispered. He looked like he needed to lie down.

For several minutes they waited, no one talking, everyone thinking about how terrified Coco must have been to have run to the furthermost room in the house and barricaded herself in. Had anyone called the police? Had the neighbours had the faintest inkling of the terror playing out in this sleepy street?

The sound of something shifting came from behind the door, and they looked up. Coco appeared a moment later, ghostly and shaking. All three of them embraced her as she came to them, eyes like moons. 'You're safe,' Libby whispered.

'He's really gone?' Coco asked.

'Really and truly.'

'Can you tell us what happened?' Ems asked quietly.

'I was . . . I was watching TV. I had gone down to make a

cup of tea and when I came back, I heard a knock at the door. I put the tea down and was just about to answer it – I thought it might be you,' she said to Prock. 'Coming back to change. But just as I put my hand to the latch, the letterbox suddenly flipped up and—' A sudden sob escaped her. 'There he was. He was right there.'

'Oh my god,' Ems whispered. 'You poor thing.'

'He saw me. If he could have got his hand through, he could have grabbed me. I don't know if he'd been knocking while I was in the basement and he'd lost patience, but suddenly he wasn't knocking any more, he was pounding on the door. I thought he was going to knock it down. He kept telling me he could see me. He called me a lying bitch. A whore. Told me I didn't know who I was dealing with, that I was out of my depth . . .' She looked back at them with shining eyes. 'I didn't know what to do. So I called Charlie.'

'And that was exactly the right thing to do,' Ems reassured her softly.

'It was?'

'Yes. You got yourself up here to a place of safety, alerted us and created a barrier that would have given you time if he'd got in. You're brilliant, do you hear me?'

Coco nodded, childlike and obedient; the fawn response, Libby knew. 'Where is he?'

'We don't know, but he isn't here and that's all that matters. Don't worry,' Prock said quickly. 'He's gone.'

'No, I don't mean *him*.' Coco swallowed. '. . . Where's Charlie?'

Libby looked at her. 'You mean he's not here?'

Coco shook her head. 'No.'

Libby looked at the others as she realized the glaring omission. In all their panic and rush, how could she have failed to spot that Charlie wasn't here? 'And there's definitely no sign of him in the other rooms?' She had checked both sides of the beds in the boys' rooms, plus their bathroom.

'None.' Prock shook his head.

'Definitely not,' Ems concurred.

Libby frowned. Charlie had had at least an eight-minute headstart on their departure. She tried to think back to their conversation. *I'm leaving now . . .* That wasn't the same, she realized now, as saying he was *coming here*. She had simply inferred it.

Leave immediately. Immediately, yes?

Had he needed them to get here, so that he could be elsewhere?

'Shit, Charlie,' Libby muttered to herself. 'Where the hell are you?'

Chapter Twenty-Eight

23 December 2023

'Go back in there and don't say a word about this,' Charlie murmured. 'With any luck, we'll find the bastard and get him out of here and Coco won't ever have to know Staples was the intruder.'

'Get him out of here? You can't just . . . let him loose,' Libby hissed. 'If he's gone to all this trouble to get here in these conditions, he'll just come straight back.'

'We'll find somewhere to detain him on the estate till we can get the authorities out here, don't worry.'

But she did worry. The man had spent eight years in prison, nursing a contempt that was clearly alive and kicking. If they were the first people he came to see in his freedom, he wasn't going to be satisfied with just a conversation. She could still remember the derision with which he'd treated them back then as they'd sought, in a floundering way, some form of justice for their friend.

She watched as Charlie started climbing the stairs. 'Go!' he hissed, looking back down at her on the turn of the staircase and pointing towards the drawing room.

She nodded, glancing down the flickering hallway. The wicks were already beginning to burn low in the candle stacks, reducing their field of glow. It was atmospheric, moody and beautiful. Also utterly perishing. She gave a sharp exhale and saw her own little breath clouds.

Hurrying into the reception hall, she threw another stack of logs onto the grates, prodding the ashes to get some more air circulating; no one else seemed to notice that these two fires were vital for keeping the worst of the chill out of the house. She replaced the poker on its stand and turned to go back to the drawing room, the Christmas tree seeming to barrel its chest at her as she passed. She looked up at it, still sulking without its resplendent lights and emitting that same cold, resentful energy that it had been uprooted from where it belonged to have to stand here, pointless in the dark. But the revitalized firelight caught on one or two of the old coloured-glass ornaments, delivering a flash of beauty, its intended purpose—

And something else, too.

Seemingly something else that didn't belong in here.

Libby stood stock still, peering through the sweeping fronds, her heart beating faster as her eyes tried to discern what instinct had caught. It wasn't immediately obvious in this dim, dancing light, but slowly her brain began to attune to the lowered frequency and she understood what she was seeing on the far side of the tree.

A pair of feet.

'Archie!' Libby screamed as the feet suddenly moved, sprinting around the tree so that she was caught on the wrong side of the hall, between the fireplace and Staples.

What . . . ? She stared in disbelief as they looked at one another . . . *What?*

She heard footsteps stampeding overhead and tearing down the stairs; a similar commotion coming from the drawing room.

Archie and Rollo reached her first, their own feet stopping dead at the sight of the standoff. Staples was cradling the puppy, Grubb, and in one hand glinted a knife. Immediately Staples made a half turn, outnumbered, looking quickly between Libby and the men.

'Where is she?' Staples demanded. 'Get her out here. I want to see her.'

'Who?' Archie asked coolly, stepping forward.

'Don't play games with me. You know who.'

'. . . Coco's not here,' Archie murmured, stuffing his hands into his pockets and removing any sense of physical threat from the situation; at least from his side. Rollo sidestepped away from him once, twice, falling still as Staples made another visual sweep of the scene.

'Bullshit. I saw those ridiculous posts. I know she's here.'

'She was here but now she's left, along with three others. You may have seen the helicopter . . . ?'

'I just *heard* her.'

'I'm sorry, but you're mistaken.'

Grubb began to wriggle in Staples's arms, as if detecting the rising hostility.

'Could you put him down, please?' Archie asked in his most civilized voice. 'We can still talk, but you're frightening him and he's done nothing to warrant being in this predicament. He's just a baby.'

Staples raised an eyebrow. 'A baby? Oh, you mean an innocent?'

'That's right.'

'And who else was an innocent in all this?' Staples sneered, flashing the knife towards them in jerky gesticulation.

Archie blinked but didn't waver. 'Coco. Only Coco.'

'Me,' Staples snapped. '*I* was innocent and you ruined my life. All of you.'

'No, this was not started by us. You know that,' he murmured. 'Just put the knife down and let the puppy go. We can talk reasonably.'

Libby watched the tip of the knife as Staples waved it distractedly in her direction. She could see Archie watching her intently all the while, as if anchoring her with his eyes, keeping her in his sights.

'You're not listening to me,' Staples said in a low voice, making the puppy whimper as he was held in an ever tighter grip. 'I have no interest in being reasonable.' As if to prove the point, the knife slashed through the air in a wide, savage arc. 'Now get that little bitch out here. I'm only talking to her.' They all stood in silence as the blade of the knife pressed against the puppy's neck. 'Or do you need proof that I'm being serious?'

For several moments, only the fires and the tree breathed. Then came the sound of footsteps – light, slow, halting.

'I'm h-here,' Coco said, stopping short in the doorway at the sight that greeted her. '. . . *You?*' she cried.

There was another long pause.

And then Sasha Staples smiled a cold smile.

'Why are you here?' Coco whispered, tears springing to her eyes. She was pale and wraithlike.

'Because I want you to admit your lies. I want you to understand what they have cost me.'

'*Lies?* Everything I said was the truth!' Coco cried. 'You just refused to see that you're married to a rapist!'

'Don't you think I saw dozens of girls, just like you, all thinking you could manipulate him? All thinking you were so much better than everyone else, above the rules just because you were young and pretty?'

344

'You enabled him – don't you see *that*? By turning the other cheek, you let him get away with it. He only stayed with you because it gave him the veneer of respectability.'

'I don't expect you to understand. Richard loved me in his own way. No one ever knows what goes on behind closed doors.'

'That's true – what went on behind *your* doors was far worse than anyone could have imagined.'

Sasha Staples's mouth flattened. 'It was a set-up.'

Libby stepped in. 'How? Was it a set-up that a police report had been filed, only a few days before he was arrested, by a neighbour of ours alleging he was standing on the street harassing Coco – one of his students – at her home address? Was that a set-up? Or did he go round there of his own volition because he was so arrogant and so enraged that he had been confronted with his crime, that he believed it was his right to terrorize a young woman he had already traumatized?'

'I'm telling you it was a set-up!'

'Not according to your computer's hard drive.' Libby gave a shrug. 'Your husband's crimes were all neatly laid out in a file. He was so arrogant he didn't even bother trying to hide it.'

Sasha looked wildly around at the men, her eyes narrowed as she scrutinized Archie and Rollo. 'Where is he? I want to hear him say it!' She spun round, the blade of the knife flashing in the firelight. 'Where is he? The one who came to my house?'

'Prock actually did leave earlier. On the helicopter,' Archie said calmly. 'You remember him – Jack Proctor? He had a job at your local supermarket back then and you kept throwing yourself at him?'

'No, not him,' she snapped. '. . . The other one.'

They all exchanged baffled glances. Who? What other one?

Libby looked at Archie and Rollo. Prock had gone, of course, but . . .

'Do you mean me?'

Archie saw Charlie step into the reception hall. Had he been standing on the stairs, listening in?

'You,' Sasha whispered, examining him intently, her eyes brightening as her conviction was confirmed. 'Yes . . . you were dressed up.'

'Was I?'

'You were wearing a tuxedo.'

The boys all winced.

'Oh, you mean dinner suit . . . ?' It was unlike him to be a snob but Libby could see the uncharacteristic coldness in his eyes; the intervening years had done little to dim his contempt. 'Yes, I do recall there was a brouhaha back at our house, when your repugnant husband's actions interrupted Archie here's twenty-first.'

'*You* came into my house!' Staples insisted, growing agitated in the face of his provocative calm.

'Did I?' He was deliberately taunting her, it seemed; playing coy and not admitting to anything. He was far too clever to incriminate himself.

Libby thought back to that awful night, trying to remember the exact details herself. She'd been reeling from discovering Zannah and Archie together, her own world coming crashing down. Everything had been such a jumbled mess . . . But they had arrived home before Charlie. A flat tyre, he'd said . . . Staples had already left, of course, scared off by the neighbours coming out to check on the commotion.

'Don't play games with me! You pretended your friend had sent you. You said he'd lost his watch last time he was over and he asked you to look in on your way past.'

Charlie simply blinked. 'If you say so.'

'I do say so! But that was just you getting your foot inside the door. You had me checking through carrier bags in the back, while you gained access to our home computer.'

'Wow. And did I do that in a matter of mere minutes? I assume it was password protected?'

'You know damn well it was!' Staples sneered. 'You did something – I don't know what, but you . . . you jammed the computer somehow. It wouldn't work that night. I couldn't get it to log on.'

'So now you're accusing me of breaking your computer, too?'

'You logged in long enough to access what you wanted on it.'

Charlie nodded. 'I'm impressed with myself. And did I do this while your husband was at home too?'

'You left minutes before he got back. You must have done it remotely!'

'I see.' He looked thoughtful. 'So I managed to hack into your personal computer within a matter of minutes of entering your house; then fled before your husband came home and worked overnight remotely hijacking it – doing what exactly?'

'*You* sent that video to the Vice-Chancellor in Richard's name – the one you pretended was sent in error. You knew he would report it to the police, that they would get a warrant to seize the computer and find all the others.' She was breathing heavily, her eyes blazing. 'It never should have been admissible in court! None of them should. The entire case should have been thrown out. It was built on information that was procured unlawfully! The warrant itself was unlawful!'

Libby listened in disbelief. *That* was the root of her grudge? Not that her husband had raped these girls and filmed himself doing it, but that the entire case against him had been built on a hacked email? The incongruity echoed within her and she remembered Richard Staples himself – the night of the party, when Prock confronted him – countering an accusation of rape with threats of trespass.

Like husband, like wife. Richard and Sasha Staples were of the same mind.

'My god,' she murmured. 'You did know. You knew exactly what he was doing to those girls. You knew he was raping them . . .' She took a step towards Staples and, over her shoulder, saw Archie step forward too, like her shadow. 'Did you watch the videos together afterwards, was that it? Was that your *kink*? Just like he liked you sleeping with other men and sending them nudes?'

Staples didn't reply, but Libby could see she was on the back foot as truth bombs were lobbed. All these years she had been given the benefit of the doubt, dismissed as a wronged wife, pathetic and weak – when in fact she had been an accomplice?

'What exactly is it you've come for?' Libby's eyes scanned her. 'Are you recording this conversation? Do you think that you can get Charlie to admit to something and that the verdict will be overturned on a technicality?'

'I know I'm right,' Staples hissed.

'Well, there are two things you should know,' Libby said quietly. 'And I speak as a qualified lawyer. The first is that based on what you've just said, I believe there would be enough for the CPS to charge you with aiding and abetting your husband in his crimes.'

'I never did anything!'

'Precisely. Even when you were in full possession of the facts,' Libby said coolly. 'The second thing you should know is that there isn't a statute of limitations for rape allegations in the UK. And although *you* knew and your husband knew what Coco was alleging, she never formally reported her assault. It turned out that she didn't need to once the files of the other rapes were discovered on your home computer and the police ran with those charges instead. It may not have been justice for Coco specifically, but she took a lot of comfort in knowing that at least it meant he wouldn't be free to hurt anyone else. Back then, she didn't feel strong enough to go through a court case.' She glanced over at Coco, who was standing ever taller. 'But now, nine years later, well . . . How are you feeling now, Coco?'

'Strong.'

'Strong, yes,' Libby smiled at her before looking back at Staples again. 'So if she did decide to come forward with her allegation, well . . . sentencing recommendations for rape are anything between four and nineteen years, depending on offence category and any aggravating factors. Of course, your husband is already registered on the sex offenders' list for life, but having just absconded from hospital will lose him any brownie points he may have accrued. When they capture him – and they will – this, along with a new allegation of sexual assault, wouldn't bode well for him – or you, as a *de facto* accomplice.'

Staples took a step back, the knife dragging through the air. 'There'd be no case to answer. There's no proof. She didn't report it at the time, and the police didn't find a film of her.'

'No,' Charlie said coolly. 'They didn't, did they.' He locked eyes with Staples, communicating without words. Did she have any idea who he was, Libby wondered – a man who had just sold his tech business for £100 million?

'You slippery bastard,' Staples hissed. 'What did you do with it?'

Charlie simply stared at her, uncowed. 'It would be a mistake for you to think you're the only person in this room who would go to extreme lengths to protect the person they love, Mrs Staples.'

Libby caught her breath. Was that an oblique admission that he had found the footage? Done something with it? It had always been strange that no footage of Coco had been found when there had been so many others.

There was no time to consider it. Something shot through the air; Libby gasped as there was an impact and Staples screamed. Everything seemed to happen in slow motion then. The missile – a phone? – had hit Staples's hand, knocking the knife from her grasp, and as she instinctively recoiled she sent Grubb hurtling towards the ground, where he scrabbled into a gallop towards the kitchen. Libby saw Rollo correct himself from a fast bowler's hunch and pitch into a rugby player's dive. In under three seconds, Sasha Staples was flat out on the floor and pinned under his considerable weight.

Archie crossed the space to her in five steps. 'Lib, are you okay?' he asked, roughly checking her over with his eyes, looking panicked. 'She didn't do anything to you before we got here?'

She swallowed. 'No. I'm fine.'

'It's just, when you screamed my name like that . . .' He shook his head, his jaw pulsing again.

'Did I?' she asked distractedly; she could scarcely remember now. Her mind was still whirring from what had transpired. She looked at Charlie, who had gone over to Coco and was holding her close; Libby could guess now what had happened that night, why he hadn't gone straight back to their house from the party. As long as Richard Staples was rampaging

350

outside the front door, he was guaranteed not to be at home – which had given Charlie a narrow window of opportunity to get inside the Stapleses' house and find the video of Coco. Charlie had probably just intended to delete it. It must have been terrible for him, finding all the others too.

'Why did you call for me?' Archie pressed, and she realized he was holding her arms. As if her wellbeing mattered to him. As if he cared.

But he never had.

She looked back at him. '. . . I don't know, Archie. Because it's your house, I suppose.'

She looked again at Charlie and Coco on the other side of the hall. Coco was hugging Charlie tight, her face pressed into his neck. That was love. That was the love she wanted.

'What are we going to do with her?' Rollo asked from his position on the floor.

Archie stepped away and considered for a moment. It was almost midnight on the night before Christmas Eve, and they had no way of contacting the police, or anyone. They were surrounded by thirty thousand acres of snowy dales and moorland – 'releasing' Sasha Staples into the night wasn't exactly an option. 'There's only one door with a key lock on it in this house,' he murmured. 'Just give me a minute.'

'You can't do this to me!' Staples cried as Rollo stepped back and Archie locked the pantry. 'This is false imprisonment!'

'No, you've been placed under a citizen's arrest following your trespass, illegal entry and aggravated harassment with a knife under the 2019 Offensive Weapons Act,' Libby said calmly through the door.

'No. N-no . . . Let me out, I'll just go!'

'For your safety, we can't let you leave here. You'd die if

you got lost out there in these conditions. And for our safety, we can't let you stay freely here either. You threatened us with a knife, Sasha.'

The tiny room had no windows, only air vents, and no radiator, but Archie had dragged a single mattress down from somewhere which they had piled high with blankets; they had even filled a hot water bottle for her. 'You'll be warm enough tonight with the bed we've made up for you, and you've got water too and a bucket, should you need it. Our intention is not for you to suffer, but to keep everyone safe in the current conditions.'

'Please!' Staples begged, hammering on the door as they turned and walked back into the kitchen.

'She'll calm down in a bit,' Rollo murmured, though he looked rattled. No one felt comfortable with this situation. 'What should we do with her in the morning, though?'

'No idea, mate,' Archie sighed. 'I've never had a lunatic locked in my pantry before. We'd better just hope for her sake that Teabag doesn't make it up here and find her in there. She'd definitely have her guts for garters.'

'Ha!' Rollo chuckled at the thought but it slipped into a sigh. 'Lunatic's definitely the word. What the hell possessed her to come all the way up here and do this?' He ran his hands over his face, looking pained.

'People suffer when they don't have answers to their questions.' Libby shrugged, and she felt Archie's glance towards her like the snap of a rubber band against her skin.

'But no one would ever have suspected her involvement before tonight. She just blew up her own life,' Rollo continued. 'I don't get it.'

'Well, Staples is on the run but he doesn't appear to have gone running back to her, does he? She's lost him.'

Libby looked around the kitchen and saw the washing-up still needed doing, but she was too worn out to care. She watched as Archie locked the back door and petted the dogs – Grubb was perfectly happy curled in her bed beside Dibble, unaware she'd been in a hostage situation – and blew out the candle in there. Darkness shimmied down over the room like a velvet dress.

The others looked up as they all walked back into the drawing room. Zannah was curled up and almost asleep on one of the sofas, a wool throw draped over her, as Coco, sitting on the floor beside her, stroked her hand. Charlie was perched on the far arm of the sofa, looking pensive.

'Sorted?' he asked, standing as they came in.

'Yep. She's screaming blue murder at the moment but hopefully she'll settle down in a bit,' Archie said.

'She's quite comfortable in there,' Rollo said. 'It's a damn sight better than the accommodation we had at school.'

'And she definitely can't get out?' Charlie asked.

'Trust me – Teabag was determined to keep me away from the chocolate cakes,' Archie smiled.

Everyone smiled at the little quip, but it was difficult to lighten the mood after the evening's events.

'How are you feeling, Coco?' Libby asked.

'Better, actually,' she responded after a moment. 'It felt good to confront her, I guess. I mean, I know *she* didn't actually hurt me but . . . I got to say words I've needed to say for so long.' She looked at Charlie. 'And I got to discover that you got justice for me – you got him sent down and never said a word about it?'

'Don't look at me like I'm a hero. I only went over with the intention of wiping the footage of you,' he said quietly. 'I didn't expect to find what I found . . .'

He looked away, biting his lip. Libby watched him.

'You're conflicted about the choice you made that night,' she murmured. 'Sending that email showing the attack on another girl?'

Charlie stared at her, before nodding. They had always understood one another. 'She had never reported it. Like Coco, she wanted it all to go away. She never asked to be "saved".'

'No, she may not have asked but you helped her get justice. You knew that if you pushed one domino, the rest would come falling down. Staples had incriminated himself – you just had to choose between exposing her or Coco.'

She could see the shame on his face as he glanced at Coco nervously.

'Of course you chose to protect Coco. It was why you risked everything to go over there. If Staples had come back and found you, in the state he was in that night, god knows what might have happened!'

Charlie shrugged, like that was no consolation.

'You just need to remember, Charlie, that the girls on the films testified against him in the end. Every single one of them. They chose to do that. Your actions that night made it possible for them to do that.'

'And you deleting my film allowed me *not* to testify,' Coco said quietly. 'Because I couldn't have done it back then.'

He nodded. 'I know. I wasn't going to let you go through that.'

Libby saw the look that passed between them and she sensed Charlie wouldn't be sleeping alone tonight. Rollo saw it too, widening his eyes with barely concealed delight.

'Don't mind me,' Zannah murmured quietly, lying between them. 'I'll just quietly lie here dying while you two get it on.'

There was a stunned silence, both Coco and Charlie visibly paling – before Archie burst out laughing.

'You're not dying yet!' he protested as Zannah grinned into the cushion.

'God, can't you just let me have this one thing?' she complained as he tossed another cushion at her.

Libby watched them tease like an old married couple, Archie looking down at Zannah with a sad smile. All the emotions, all at once. Comedy in one moment, heartbreak in the next.

'. . . We do need to get you to bed, though,' he said, reaching down and scooping her up.

'I can walk,' she protested.

'I know, but I can carry, and it's been a hell of a day,' he replied. 'Just for once, stop being such a hard-arse.'

'Fine,' she exhaled, dropping her head against his shoulder as he carried her out. 'Night all,' she said over his shoulder.

'Night all,' Archie said too. 'You'll blow out the candles for me?'

'I'm on it,' Rollo said, walking over to fetch the fireguard.

Libby listened to the sound of Archie's footsteps disappearing upstairs, the low murmur of their voices. 'I'm so ready for my bed,' she said quietly, feeling exhausted and rolling out her shoulders. She hadn't exactly had a great sleep last night. 'This feels like the longest day ever.'

'Agreed,' Rollo said, placing the fireguard in front of the hearth. 'But let's try to make tomorrow a good one, for Zannah *and* Archie's sake.'

'Tomorrow has to be better, surely?' Charlie sighed, just as Coco walked over and slipped her hand in his. Another look crackled between them as she tugged him towards the door.

'Night, guys,' she murmured, throwing Libby a shy wink.

They slipped from the room and Libby waited for Rollo to blow out the candle.

'He's so good for her,' she murmured.

'Yes, but in a funny way, she's been good for him too. It's been cathartic for him. It's healed some old wounds, letting him do for her what he couldn't for his mother.'

Libby frowned, confused. '. . . Sorry?'

'Well, his mother died of the same thing.'

'Charlie's mum died?'

'What?'

'Wait, who are you talking about, Roly?'

'Archie,' he said glancing over at her. 'Why – who are you?'

'I was talking about Charlie, being good for Coco.'

'Oh.'

They began walking up the staircase together, blowing out the hurricane candles one at a time, but her mind was stuck on Archie now. Again.

'. . . His mother died of cancer too?' she asked quietly.

'Yes.'

'I never knew that.'

Rollo was quiet for a moment. 'She was lovely. Doted on Arch, of course; he was her only baby and I don't think the marriage was particularly stable.'

'No.' Libby had been able to glean that just from the way Archie referred to his father.

'Poor Arch; it all happened very quickly. Teabag said she was dead within five weeks of diagnosis. She hadn't even had a chance to tell him – apparently she'd been waiting for the holidays. The first he knew of it was when he was called out of Latin to the headmaster's office and told that she'd died.'

Libby gasped, literally pained by the thought of it. 'Oh my god!'

'I know. Explains quite a bit about him, don't you think?' Roly murmured. 'He lost his mother without warning. He was . . . unmoored and shell-shocked for years really. Who wouldn't want to escape if that was their reality?' They were at the top of the stairs now and he looked across at her. 'But he's a good man . . .'

She blinked at him, hearing the defensiveness in his voice. Who was he trying to convince?

'Night, Lib.' He squeezed her arm affectionately and she watched him walk towards his bedroom, down the corridor. But she wasn't seeing him. An image was flashing through her mind of Archie's glassy eyes as Zannah had kissed him in that hotel room the night of his party – wasted, desolate, little-boy-lost. But she remembered his defiance upstairs in Zannah's bedroom, too, only this evening – an adult now and still refusing to take responsibility for what he'd done to her. The hurt he had caused . . .

No, people had to take responsibility for their actions. At some point, even Peter Pan had to grow up. He may not be a bad man, she thought, turning towards her bedroom too, but that didn't make him good.

Chapter Twenty-Nine

23 December 2023

Libby turned over, hugging her knees into her chest and shivering. How could it be this cold? Was there ice inside the windows? She was wearing Max's socks with her nightie again but she had stupidly returned Archie's sweater to the kitchen chair where she had found it; an efficiency decision she was bitterly regretting now. She stared at the wardrobe, wondering if it was too much to hope for an Edwardian mink to be hanging in there, as Rollo had suggested earlier. It was the sort of house where one might expect to find random furs, as well as ghosts . . . Bracing herself for the chill, she threw back the bedcovers and tiptoed quickly over to the wardrobe, the floorboards creaking and the door swinging open with a loud groan. Immediately something fell towards her from an upper shelf and she gave a small shriek as she jumped back.

She looked down and saw an old, tall Locke hat box at her feet.

'Ugh,' she groaned, standing on tiptoe as she carefully replaced it. She peered in, her hopes rising as she saw there was something in there, but it was so dark she couldn't see clearly. She reached for the hanger, pulling out—

She stared in dismay at the lilac taffeta strapless ballgown.

'God,' she sighed, juddering with cold. A top hat and a ball-gown. 'Just my luck.'

'Lib?' There was a quick knock at the door and she turned – not to the main door, but the jib that led into Archie's quarters – to find him peering in. 'Are you okay? I heard—' He stopped at the sight of her hiding behind the taffeta mass. 'What are you doing?'

She stared back at him. His entry into the room, any room, always disturbed her peace. As if he was a molecular agitator, changing the very substance of a space.

She kept the dress held up in front of her, for decency's sake. 'I was looking for something w-warm to put on the bed,' she said. 'I'd been h-hoping for a fur coat or maybe a rolled-up t-tiger rug or something, like Roly said. Instead I g-got this and a top hat.'

'Jesus, it's bracing in here,' he frowned, stepping in. She saw him remember there was no fireplace in the room. He looked back at her, appalled. 'Fuck, why didn't you remind me? No wonder you're frozen.'

'It's fine. I'm f-fine.'

'No, you can't sleep in here.'

'I did last night.'

'Yeah well, you had Max with you then,' he muttered. He gave a shiver too, even though he was in his flannel pyjamas, socks and a cashmere sweater; no bare limbs for him, at least. 'We'll swap. You go into my room. I'll sleep in here.'

'Oh, so you get to freeze in your own house after the day from hell with a madwoman locked in your pantry? I don't think so. I'll be completely fine if we can just find a blanket from somewhere.'

He gave a bemused laugh, seeing from the set of her jaw that she wasn't going to be budged on the matter. 'Fine. Go and stand next to the fire in my room and warm up, while I get a blanket. Or ten.'

She waited for him to turn and walk off first before she returned the dress to the wardrobe and followed him into his room. Her body immediately eased a little into the ambient temperature. The space glowed golden, the four-poster looking sumptuously soft and warm, the room enlivened by the quiet crackle of the logs. She placed her hands towards the fire, warming herself.

Several minutes later, he returned with a pile of blankets in his arms. 'Right, we have blankets—' He stopped at the sight of her. She was wearing little more than a handkerchief, a ridiculous getup in the circumstances, and without a ballgown to protect her modesty now, she felt exposed.

'Thanks,' she said quickly, walking over and going to take them from him. '. . . Thanks?' she said again as he didn't release them to her. A look had come into his eyes that she recognized, that tension that was always there between them beginning to tighten its grip now that they were alone.

'Uh, no.' He cleared his throat, holding them aloft, easily out of her reach. 'These are for me. You're sleeping in here.'

'Archie, don't be ridiculous. That's not what we agreed.'

His eyes flashed. 'This isn't a negotiation, Pugh.'

Pugh? Calling her by her surname had always been charged; calling her Lib or Libby was something he did when he was being polite or public or distant. She felt the fizz of static in the air, feelings from long ago shifting from the shadows.

'My house, my rules. You sleep in my bed.'

She watched as he began to cross the room. 'No!' The word burst from her, surprising her as well as him.

'*No?*'

'You say that to all the girls,' she snapped, reaching for self-control. 'You don't get to say it to me.'

The past had exploded at their feet and he stared at her for what felt like an age, an inscrutable look in his eyes. '. . . No, I guess not.'

She snatched the blankets from his hands, refusing to look at him. Her heart was pounding and she felt shaky. 'Goodnight,' she muttered.

He watched her turn to walk towards the other room. 'Downstairs just now, you said something . . .' he said to her back, deliberately pausing until she turned around again.

'What did I say?' she asked flatly.

'You said people suffer when they don't get answers to their questions.'

'So?'

'Don't you have questions with answers you want from me?'

She clutched the blankets closer to her, summoning the lie. 'Not really, no.'

She saw him wince slightly at the knockback. 'I don't believe you.'

'Fine, don't then,' she shrugged, going to leave again, but he crossed the space between them and caught her by the arm.

'You really don't want to know about my twenty-first birthday? Why I sat you next to the guy I wanted you to avoid? Or why I sat next to my ex? Why I avoided you all night even though I said I'd find you?'

She blinked back at him. 'No.'

He clenched his jaw, frustrated with her. Didn't he realize, as a lawyer, she was paid to stonewall? 'Why not? You really don't care any more?'

'Why should I? You chewed me up and spat me out that

361

night for reasons I didn't understand then – and that I don't want to try to understand now. There is no justification for what you did. None. But I'll bet you're just dying to tell me.'

She stared back at him, the firelight flickering over his face, looking more handsome than he could possibly know.

'So that's why I won't let you,' she continued. 'I will not ask. You want me to tell you I forgive you, because at heart, you want to believe you're a good bloke, right? You're not *him* any more. You're not like your father; you didn't live down to expectations after all.' She shook her head. 'But I don't believe that. You still want to have your cake and eat it.'

'Not true.'

'No? Last night, playing that game at dinner, you chose the Get Out of Jail Free card over changing something in your past. You and I both knew what you were doing. You were telling me you don't regret it.'

'Not true. I *do* regret it – I've regretted it every single day since you walked out of that room – but I still wouldn't change what I did.'

Word games. Admission and denial in one sentence. She stared at him, hating him for his cavalier defiance. Why was he doing this? Was he poking the bear, trying to see if she still cared, even though he was with someone else and so was she? Was his ego so monstrous that he had to have her devotion, even after all this time? She knew he wouldn't be talking to her like this if Max were still here. 'You know, Zannah deserves better than you,' she said quietly.

'What?'

'After everything she's been through – and is still going through – she deserves to be loved by someone who isn't seeking validation from—'

'What are you talking about? I'm not *with* Zannah. Not like

362

that.' He looked taken aback, staring at her with outright puzzlement. 'We're just friends. Best friends. I've been the one supporting her throughout all this.'

'Oh yes, I saw your "support" the night of the party.'

'That was different!' he argued. 'She had literally just got the diagnosis.'

'What?' Libby stared at him, remembering the mission Zannah had been on that night, fuelled by a desperation for hedonism that bordered almost on anger.

'She'd been told she was Stage Three. She was a wreck! She wanted to escape.'

Libby let his words settle. They had the ring of truth to them. It made perfect sense of her actions.

But there was no such justification for him. She looked back at him with a sneer. 'Whereas you just wanted . . . ?'

'Anyone.'

The word, swift and direct, pierced her like a poisoned dart. 'Anyone,' she repeated, a whicker of disgust escaping her.

He nodded. 'It didn't really matter who.'

'Wow.' Callous was an understatement. She looked away, feeling the tears press; even after nine years, the emotions were right there, hair-triggered. He would never have any idea of the tears she had cried over him, the dead weight that pressed on her chest every morning when she awoke, the hollowness in her heart as she won case after case. 'God, you really are a piece of work, Templeton . . .'

'It had to be done.'

'It *had* to b—?' she echoed in disbelief, feeling her anger surge as her self-control finally crumpled. 'Oh did it really? Why? Because you didn't like that I'd fallen in love with you? Was it an unseemly display of emotion?' she spat. 'Or was I just the wrong sort of girl for you to fall in love with?'

She stared at him, hating that she had asked the very questions she had promised herself she wouldn't. But she craved the answers and perhaps, she realized, she could never truly move on until she had them.

'It was the only way to stop you from doing what you were going to do. You were going to pass up Hong Kong for me, and I couldn't let you do that. I knew I wouldn't be able to talk you out of it so I pushed you away instead. You had to reject me.' He spoke slowly and calmly, but every word felt like a bomb.

'. . . *What?*'

'I played to type, Pugh . . . Because I knew you'd believe it.' He stood there, staring back at her, eyes burning, and she saw for the first time that people didn't suffer just because they couldn't get answers, but sometimes because they couldn't give them, too.

'Tell me it wasn't the right thing to do.'

The right thing? She stared back at him, feeling shaken. She had never anticipated this. Of all the explanations that had run through her mind over the hours and weeks that had followed . . .

'Have you paid off your parents' mortgage?' he asked.

She didn't reply.

'. . . Well, have you?' he pressed.

'. . . Maybe.'

'That means yes. And your student loans?'

'. . . Maybe.'

'That means yes. How about your brother's car?' He arched an eyebrow, prompting her to respond.

'Possibly.'

'That means yes. Are you ahead of your contemporaries on your career path?'

'Perhaps.'

'That means yes. And I imagine you've got a great place too, yes . . . ? Not to mention Max is perfect for you, right?'

She blinked, seeing his jealousy, his pride—

His love.

It would be a mistake for you to think you're the only person in this room who would go to extreme lengths to protect the person they love . . . For the first time, she saw his intentions and not his actions.

'He's perfect for you, right?' he insisted.

She nodded, seeing how his mouth grew tight at the reply. On paper, Max was perfect for her.

'Right. So then you get it. You see it now. You're brilliant, Pugh. You shine, just like I knew you would. But you would have risked all of that on account of me, and I wasn't going to let it happen.'

There was a pause, and that same hesitant look came onto his face as he realized that for once she wasn't arguing back. 'You can blame me and hate me all you want, but I know I did the right thing,' he said stubbornly. 'Your life is exactly where it was always supposed to be.'

There was a small pause as they both took a breath.

'. . . Exactly?' she queried.

'Yes.'

'I was always supposed to be here? Right here?'

Uncertainty came into his voice. '. . . Yes.'

'Naked, in your bedroom?'

He blinked, openly confused. '. . . You're not . . . naked . . .' he managed, just as she dropped the blankets at their feet and pulled her silk slip over her head. He swallowed. '. . . What are you doing?'

'It's called making my own decisions.'

She saw his breathing become deeper and in a flash, they

were both standing in his bedroom in Durham again. He met her eyes. 'What about Max?'

What about him? She remembered the red box, and knew she and Max had never really been 'together'. Nothing founded on a secret could truly be real, and if he had left here without giving her what was clearly a very expensive present, then it wasn't to her that he was giving it. His urgent need to leave here had been down to having other secrets too.

'We broke up.'

'. . . *When?*'

'Do you really care?'

He shook his head. 'No,' he swallowed.

'Good. So then, kiss me all over,' she murmured, slowly wrapping her arms around his neck. 'And see if you can find my tattoo.'

Chapter Thirty

24 December 2023

They slept with the curtains open, the moonlight and firelight tussling like kittens on the floor and walls as they lay, limbs intertwined, in the antique bed. If they had slept four times, they had made love five – unable to get enough of each other as the promises that had been made nine years earlier were finally delivered.

Libby didn't ever want to leave this room. She didn't want the lights to come back on or for the lane to be reopened. She wanted to stay here with him, in the whiteout, in the blackout, where the real world couldn't reach them.

'What's that?' she murmured as they dozed, sated again, his body cupped around hers.

'Hm?' He was almost asleep.

But she recognized the sound as it drew closer. '. . . Is it a helicopter?'

'What?' He was awake again, throwing off the sheets and moving over to the window. Libby admired his physique as he peered out, wondering at the turn of events that had brought them together against such unlikely odds.

'It looks like they're landing,' he said, turning back to her and stopping in his tracks as he caught sight of her, lying on her side and watching him with a smile. 'God, you are a vision.'

He came over and kissed her again and she could feel him want to fall back into bed. But the downdraft of the blades was making the windows rattle and he pulled back with a groan.

'Charlie, do you think?' she asked, as he went over to the chair and pulled on his jeans.

'Who else?' he shrugged. 'They must have had a cancellation or found another charter.'

'I wonder if he'll take Coco with him,' she mused, watching as he pulled his shirt over his head.

'Well, if he's had a night as good as ours, he'll never let her go again.' He winked at her as he pulled his socks on, making the butterflies in her stomach take wing again.

'I'll come down too. Make some tea,' she decided, climbing out of bed too and walking over to where his dressing gown was hanging on a hook on the back of the door. He watched as she shrugged it on, ridiculously oversized for her petite frame.

'It is my personal ambition to keep you out of clothes as often as is decently possible,' he said, kissing her as they walked down the hall.

It felt strange, in the cold light of morning, to see the hurricane lamps on the stairs and the candles on saucers dotted along the long passage. They would need to get the fires going straight away again, to minimize any drops in temperature from when they'd gone out overnight.

The knock came at the back door as they walked into the kitchen, the dogs getting out of their beds to greet them. Archie went to open the door as she wandered over to the kettle; there was a half-full bucket of melted snow on the worktop for the sole intention of making tea.

'Good mor—' Archie's voice died in his throat as he took

in the sight of the police officers. Surprised, too, Libby tightened the dressing-gown belt more tightly.

'Archie Templeton?'

'. . . Yes.'

'We've had a report of a possible intruder on the property.'

Libby gasped, glancing across at the pantry. For a moment there, in her blissful daze, she had completely forgotten about the woman they had locked in with the pickled onions and flour.

'How on earth did you know that?' Archie asked in amazement.

'So there is an intruder?'

'Yes, but . . . it's all settled for the moment. We've . . . we dealt with it the best way we could in the circumstances.' He glanced over at Libby. 'Come in. I'll take you to where she is.'

'She?' The officer looked surprised.

'Yes. Her name's Sasha Staples. She's the wife of Richard Staples.'

The police officer recognized the name. 'The convicted rapist who absconded from hospital?'

'That's right.'

The police officer's eyes narrowed. 'I see. Has there been any damage to your property? Any threatening behaviour?'

'Mainly what you would call mischief, but she did threaten us with a knife,' Archie said quickly. None of them were going to forget that Sasha had all but admitted her complicity in her husband's crimes.

'Officer,' Libby said, stepping forwards. 'How did you know someone was here? We've been cut off without any communications for almost twenty-four hours now.'

'Yes. We had a call from a Mr Proctor last night. I believe he had been staying here too?'

'That's right. He and his wife. They're good friends of ours.'

'Well, on his return home, Mrs Proctor powered up her phone and discovered some images on it that had been taken of her while she was sleeping. There was also what appears to be a selfie of an unknown person standing in the room. It was dark so the figure was shadowy and couldn't be identified, but she was adamant it wasn't anyone in the house party. She was very concerned for your safety, especially given your current isolation.'

'She gave us a fright more than anything else.'

'Where is she now?'

'Well,' Archie said, blowing out through his cheeks, his hands on his hips. 'This might sound funny, but there's actually only one room in this house with a lockable door . . .'

25 December 2023

'Happy Christmas!'

They raised their glasses as they sat around the fire, cushions from the sofas thrown onto the floor. Everyone had wrapped their Secret Santa presents in yellowing newspaper and put them in a pile on the floor, ready to distribute. All the chores had been completed before lunch, while they had the light; more snow had been collected in buckets. Three days in to the power cut and they were becoming a well-oiled machine.

Libby leaned back against Archie's chest, her eyes closing happily as he kissed her hair. Everyone's reaction at breakfast yesterday morning to finding her sitting on his lap, wearing his dressing gown, had been the sort of cheers and back-slapping usually reserved for bagging the snipe on a shoot. It was much the same with Coco and Charlie, who kept taking advantage of all the dark corners and talking in whispers.

'I'll pick, shall I?' Rollo asked. He had been playing carols on the piano any time there was a lull in activity – 'to keep the festive spirit going' – and was suitably dressed as Father Christmas in an ancient costume he had pulled from the dressing-up trunk. Libby had long since run out of clean options too, so she was wearing one of Archie's mother's evening skirts and another of Archie's sweaters.

'Now who is this for?' Rollo asked, reaching for something very large and flat and straining to find the name written on the wrapping. 'Ah, for Coco, from Charlie. How fitting.' He lifted it gingerly, everyone intrigued by the scale of it; even Archie looked perplexed, although technically it belonged to him, having come from his house.

Coco looked at Charlie happily. 'Is it romantic?'

'Um . . . well . . . I don't know if you'd call it romantic, exactly . . .'

She tore the paper wrapping off and held up a longbow and some arrows. Her face fell. 'An archery set?'

'Ah, but not just any archery set!' Archie said, stepping in to try and save his friend. 'That's actually a bow that was used in the Battle of Tippermuir in Scotland in 1644. Supposedly it was the last time bows were ever used in battle in the United Kingdom.'

Coco turned back to Charlie, looking distinctly underwhelmed. 'And you looked at that and thought of *me*?'

He nodded. 'Yeah . . . You're a warrior.'

Instantly her expression changed. It was like watching butter melt. 'Oh, Charlie,' she sighed, clasping it to her heart. 'That really is romantic.'

'You think?'

'I know,' she sighed, leaning in for another kiss.

'Don't mind me,' Zannah quipped again. 'Just single and dying over here.'

It was becoming her catchphrase and everyone groaned, protesting at her dark humour, but also grateful for it. Ever since her condition had been revealed, it was as if she had been released from a straitjacket and the blunt, ballsy girl Libby had known at university was among them again. No more studied manners or polite distance; Zannah was back to being herself. No one fussed if she went upstairs to lie down, and she did the drying up – now reserved as her own special chore – at her own pace; sometimes she had to rest in between, but they were all determined no glass wall should spring up between them. Normality would rule.

'In which case, you should open yours next,' Rollo said, reaching for a paper-wrapped shoebox with her name on. 'In case you suddenly pop your clogs.'

Zannah grinned at him, appreciating the joke. 'Who's it from?'

'Me. I hope you like it,' Libby said, feeling nervous.

Zannah took it with a hooked eyebrow. 'Hmm,' she said suspiciously, giving it a rattle. 'I can't hear a glug.'

Libby bit her lip as she watched Zannah carefully unwrap the newspaper, as if savouring the process. She tried not to think that this might be Zannah's last Christmas, her last ever gift, but the thought was right there, impossible to forget. They might laugh, but they were all going to cry, too; they knew harder times were coming.

She saw how Zannah's mouth dropped open as she opened the box. There was a long silence and Zannah swallowed hard as she reached for the red suede shoes.

'Dancing shoes,' Libby said quietly. 'Because you love to dance.'

There was a long silence as Zannah turned them over in her hands. '. . . Bitch, you've made me cry,' Zannah whispered as a tear rolled down her cheek.

'You like them, then?'

Zannah looked up at her. 'I love them! Are they yours?'

'No, they were Archie's mum's.'

Zannah stroked the pristine soles. 'But they've never even been worn.'

Archie cleared his throat. 'No. Teabag told me she got them as an incentive for getting better.'

Zannah brushed her fingers against the unblemished surface, her bottom lip wobbling at what that meant: an intention unfulfilled. A dream dashed.

'Will they fit you?' Archie asked her, looking apprehensive. It had been difficult for him, seeing the shoes again after so many years.

Zannah nodded. 'Perfectly. They're my size.'

'Good. So then, after dinner, Roly's going to tinkle the ivories, you're going to put them on and we're all going to dance.'

Zannah smiled at Libby. 'Just like the old days, huh?'

Libby nodded. Zannah had always been the last man standing on the dance floor.

'Well, I promise not to wreck them,' she said, looking over at Archie.

'Actually, Zan, I want you to keep them. Wear them as often as you can. Wear them till they've got holes in.'

Everyone knew what he was saying – live till the last moment – and Zannah looked back at both of them, more than one tear skimming her cheeks now. 'Thank you, bastards.'

Libby couldn't help but laugh as she kissed her cheek.

'Right,' Rollo said, rubbing his hands together. 'Well, that's two corkers! I pity the fool who came up with this rather unimpressive-looking attempt!' He held up a flat package the size of his hand.

'Great. Thanks for that, mate!' Archie groaned, rubbing a hand over his face and stretching back. 'That would be my gift. For Lib.'

Libby smiled as Rollo handed it over. 'Don't worry, you were reassuring me earlier that all the best things come in small packages,' she teased, Archie's eyes widening in disbelief at her blatant lie.

'I said no such thing!' he protested as everyone laughed. 'I didn't say that!'

'Yeah, yeah, tell it to the judge,' Zannah sighed, stroking her shoes.

Libby tore off the newspaper to reveal a huge, very rusty old key.

'Hmm,' Rollo grunted. 'Interesting. A reminder for your tetanus booster?'

Libby looked at Archie and saw the look in his eyes. She knew perfectly well he meant it as the key to his heart, even though it would almost kill him to say it in front of everyone.

'I love it. I've always wanted this very key.'

'Yeah?' His eyes shone.

'This exact one, no other key in the world for me,' she murmured, twisting back to kiss him again—

Suddenly, there was an electronic symphony of beeps ricocheting, appliances switching on: phones charging, the Sky box rebooting . . . The lights flickered once, twice, three times, before settling on and drenching the room with bald light.

Everyone squinted. Candlelight had a gentleness to which they had quickly become accustomed.

'Ahaha, yes!' Rollo cheered, punching the air.

'We've got power?' Coco asked with relief. 'Oh my god! My phone!'

'Joy. Now you can post your TikToks,' Charlie said, bemused.

'No, now I can FaceTime my parents!' she smiled, kissing him as she scrambled to stand up.

'Let me quickly check the fuse board, and I'll see if we've got water too,' Archie said, kissing Libby once more on the mouth before getting up and running down to the kitchen.

Libby got up too as everyone sprinted for their phones, wandering into the hall as she saw that the entire house was ablaze with electric light; seemingly people must have tried every single lamp when power had been lost, a futile exercise in hope over expectation. She turned into the reception hall and stared at the Christmas tree, magnificent once more as it shimmered from base to tip, no longer a shadowy interloper here, but fully and magnificently at home. Born to stand in this space. And yet, something of its brilliance was lost in the glare. She turned off the wall lights, darkness resumed as she stared at it.

'All is good with the world. We have water *and* we have power again,' Archie murmured several minutes later, coming up behind her and slipping his hands around her waist. He gave a small, bemused chuckle in her ear. '. . . Now why would you want to stand in the dark?'

'So that it shines more brightly,' she replied. She understood now that like a star in the night sky, it was the contrast with the darkness that gave the light such radiance. One couldn't exist without the other, just as she and Archie couldn't have had this present moment without living through their past.

He turned her to him, seeming to understand what she was saying, and clasped her face in his hands, gazing at her with appetite again. 'Very well then, Pugh,' he murmured, pressing his lips to hers. 'Christmas by candlelight it shall be.'

Epilogue

Drewatts Park, Yorkshire, April 2024

The church bells rang out into a bright sky, fast-scudding clouds throwing down speeding shadows that ran over them all like laughter. Cuthbert, Dibble and Grubb were weaving between the clumps of daffodils, tails aloft, enthusiastically nosing the grass; the gated graveyard wasn't an area they often got to explore, the chapel so rarely used these days.

Libby stood at the east door and looked over the low stone wall, absorbing the view. It was her first visit back here since Christmas and it seemed hard to believe now that they had endured the privations of light and heat with such high spirits. The backup generators that had been installed as a temporary fix while the network was repaired had been removed only the other week but the snow had long since melted away, the harshness of winter just a memory. The endless rolling moors she had only seen in a black-and-white filter were now a bright, sappy green, pin-dotted with primroses, budding trees and bleating sheep. Everything was waking up; it felt like life was just beginning.

The helicopter didn't sit quite so naturally in the landscape, but it made her happy nonetheless, bringing back Charlie and Coco from a four-month honeymoon that had made everyone wonder if they would ever return. They had eloped on New Year's Eve, just the two of them exchanging rings on a beach in Fiji. No one had resented being deprived of a wedding – they'd all witnessed this slow-growing love affair over the years – and besides, Charlie had promised to throw a party to make up for it now they were back.

'A photo with the godmothers now.'

Libby turned back to where the photographer had set up the camera on the tripod. It afforded a view of the house in the background, but it was also open to the wind there and the vicar's cassock was blowing in the breeze to reveal Easter Bunny socks.

Coco and Zannah were already standing either side of Ems, all of them gazing down at the bundle in her arms. All for one . . .

'Lib, our turn!' Coco said, glancing up and beckoning her over.

Arms snaked around her, pulling her close into the group as the four women smiled for the camera. The shutter snapped several times, a tiny mewl from the blankets making them all look down again. Ems gently shook the silver Tiffany rattle the Earnshaws had brought as a christening gift as Libby peered, smiling, at the swaddled form of her god-daughter, Stella Susannah Proctor. Stella, meaning star of course, after the matching tattoos denoting their friendship; Susannah, well, that was self-evident. Zannah the First, as she had taken to calling herself, was holding steady. No one fooled themselves that getting better was an option, but she hadn't deteriorated either, and every day that passed in that state of abeyance was a win. The clinical trial had ended in January and she had been resting in Switzerland with her parents ever since, though there was talk of her coming back to her London apartment in May to see how she'd 'get on'. Normality was something she was determined to hold onto for as long as she could, and her red shoes were already well worn.

'And now the godfathers, please.'

The women stepped back to join Ems's and Prock's families as Charlie, Rollo and Archie were summoned, all of them handsome in their suits. Archie reached for her as she passed, the way he always did. It was seemingly impossible for them to walk past one another without stopping for a kiss.

He clasped her head in his hands and smiled down at her. 'Getting broody?'

'Perhaps,' she smiled back.

'But first things first, right?' he said, taking her hand and kissing it, the engagement ring – which had been his mother's – sparkling in the sunlight.

'You know me so well.'

'Yes I do, Pugh.'

'Come on, Templeton! Put her down for just a minute,' Rollo shouted.

Archie drew away with a laugh, standing with the others with his signature slouch, one hand in his pocket and the breeze flashing the yellow silk lining of his suit.

His eyes darted back to her every few moments, as if checking she was still there, but she would never leave. They might not make sense on paper but they fit together, two parts of a whole. Even Max had simply nodded when she had seen him in the office and replied: 'I thought as much.' He read people the way Charlie read code, and he had seen what she had hidden even from herself; he had perceived Archie as a threat long before she'd even known he was an option. They had parted on good terms before he left for his new role, headhunted to a rival firm, and the news of his engagement to his long-standing girlfriend wasn't a surprise when it came – Libby had guessed as much from the Cartier box in his bag. She was simply a little sad for a woman she hadn't known about in time to stop herself getting involved with him in the first place.

'And now everyone together,' the photographer said, beckoning the women back into the frame along with the doting grandparents, uncles and aunts.

Everyone shuffled themselves into a vaguely tiered crescent shape. Libby naturally had to stand at the front; she was far too petite to ever make the second row, and she noticed Rollo standing at the far end, somewhat on his own.

'Can you scrunch in a bit?' the photographer asked.

'Maggie,' she said quietly, turning to Prock's younger sister standing next to her. 'There's a space in front of Roly. Do you want to stand with him?'

'Oh, uh . . .' Maggie hesitated.

'Or I can. It's no problem,' Libby suggested, feeling Archie's hand immediately reach for her arm.

'Oh no, it's no problem,' Maggie said quickly. 'I'll go.'

'Great.'

Maggie smiled, making her way over. Libby watched as she positioned herself in front of Rollo, his eyes brightening as she made a comment, her ready laugh as he cracked a joke in reply.

'Pugh, what are you up to?' Archie murmured, pulling her in closer as everyone took their positions.

'Nothing,' she murmured back. Could the fact that she'd caught Rollo repeatedly glancing at Maggie in the chapel be taken as admissible evidence for a possible attraction?

'Do you want the dogs to make an appearance in this?' the photographer asked as Grubb sniffed a patch of dandelions front and centre of the group.

'Yes!' Ems shouted, looking so happy that Libby expected she wouldn't mind the sheep and cows joining in too.

Rollo called them over with one of his obscure commands, positioning them expertly to face the camera; Libby noticed Maggie's admiring look. Rollo had been working with the gundogs intensively since leaving his brother to run the family farm and coming here to head up operations instead. With Archie still mainly based in London, Rollo was tasked with setting up the new commercial grouse shoot. 'Diversifying the income streams' was his new mantra and under his steward-ship there was going to be significant building activity on the estate throughout the spring and summer, transforming the many workers' cottages that had fallen into disrepair into boutique holiday rentals. The plan required liquid capital that Archie simply didn't have but, after much persuasion, Charlie had finally convinced Archie to let him be their sleeping investor, and Libby had talked Coco into being their interior designer.

Teabag was back at the house, preparing a feast for their return and revelling in having another house party to keep her rushed off her feet. She kept grumbling about the new dishwasher, but they had a full house – the old housemates were all staying for the long Easter weekend – and Libby had come into the kitchen this morning and found her holding up the gleaming glasses with an admiring look; Libby had been certain the housekeeper had flashed her a wink as she turned away with a tut.

The next time they would all be together like this, standing outside the chapel, would be at their wedding in June. Libby felt Archie's arm hug her tighter, as if he could read her mind, while the photographer clicked away. She looked across at her friends, windswept and smiling, and realized something else too: the Procks, the Earnshaws and of course the two of them, the soon-to-be Templetons . . . It might have taken their group almost a decade of trying and failing, of falling apart and falling back together again, but they had finally made the Seventy Club after all.

Read on for an extract of

The Last Summer

The start of a major new series by Karen Swan

'**Powerful writing and a wonderful premise make this a novel you'll simultaneously want to savour and race through**'
Jill Mansell

Summer 1930 on St Kilda – a wild, remote Scottish island.
Two strangers from drastically different worlds meet . . .

Wild-spirited Effie Gillies has lived all her life on the small island of St Kilda, but when Lord Sholto, heir to the Earl of Dumfries, visits, the attraction between them is instant. For one glorious week she guides the handsome young visitor around the isle, falling in love for the first time – until a storm hits and her world falls apart.

Three months later, St Kilda falls silent as the islanders are evacuated for a better life on the mainland. Effie is surprised to be offered a position working on the Earl's estate. Sholto is back in her life but their differences now seem insurmountable, even as the simmering tension between them grows. And when a shocking discovery is made back on St Kilda, all her dreams for this bright new life are threatened by the dark secrets Effie and her friends thought they had left behind.

Available now

Chapter One

13 May 1930

The dogs were barking on the beach. The old women came to stand at their doors, looking out with hard frowns across the curve of the bay. The tide was going out and there'd been a testy wind all day, whipping up the waves and making the birds wheel with delight.

Effie didn't move from her position on the milking stone. She had her cheek to Iona's belly and was filling the pail with relaxed indifference. She knew it could be another twenty minutes before a boat nosed around the headland, though it would probably be sooner today, given these winds. Her collie Poppit – brown-faced, with a white patch over one eye – sat beside her, ears up and looking out over the water, already awaiting the far-off sea intruders, though she wouldn't leave Effie's side.

She watched the movements of the villagers from her elevated perch. The milking enclosure was a good third of the way up the hill and she always enjoyed the view. It was a Tuesday, which meant washing day, and she could see the younger women standing in the burns, skirts tucked up and scrubbing the linens as they talked. They wouldn't like having their sheets flying in the wind if visitors were coming. None of the tourist boats were scheduled to come this week, but if it was a trawler, it wouldn't be so bad; most of the captains were friends.

The indignity of airing their linens before strangers was taken seriously in a village where privacy was merely a concept. The layout alone meant anyone could see the comings and goings of the villagers from almost any point in the glen; it was shaped like a cone with smooth but steep slopes two-thirds of the way round, leading up to towering cliffs that dropped sharply and precipitously on the other sides to the crashing sea below. The cliffs only dipped, like a dairy bowl's lip, on the south-easterly corner, skimming down to a shingle beach. There was nowhere else to land on the isle but here. The seas were heavy and torrid all around but by a stroke of luck, the neighbouring isle, Dun – no more than a bony finger of rock – almost abutted the shores of Hirta, creating a natural breakwater and rendering Village Bay as a safe haven in the churning grey waters of the North Atlantic. During some storms they had as many as twenty ships taking refuge there.

Trawlermen, whalers, navy men, they all rhapsodized, as they took shelter, about the welcoming and cosy sight of the village tucked beneath the high-shouldered ellipse, chimneys puffing, oil lamps twinkling. The grey stone cottages – interspersed with the older traditional blackhouses, which had been steadily abandoned since the 1860s – sat shoulder to shoulder and fanned around the east side of the bay, bordered by a strong stone dyke. Looking down from the ridges on high, they were like teeth in a jaw. Giant's teeth, Effie's mother used to say.

The village's position afforded the best protection from winds that would funnel down the slopes at speeds that lifted rocks and tore the steel roofs from the stone walls (at least until the landlord, Sir John MacLeod of MacLeod, had had them strapped down with metal ties).

The Street – and there was only one – was a wide grassy path, set between the cottages and a thick low wall that topped the allotments. It was the beating heart of island life. Everyone congregated there, protected further from the wind by their own homes and able to bask in the sun on fine days. The old women sat knitting and spinning by their front doors; the children ran along the wall, cows occasionally nodding over it. Every morning, the men would meet outside number 5 and number 6 for their daily parliament to decide upon and allocate chores; and after tea, the villagers would amble down it to pick up from their neighbours 'the evening news'.

In front of each cottage, across the Street, was a long, narrow walled plot that ran down towards the beach. It was here that the villagers planted their potatoes in lazybeds, hung their washing and allowed their few cattle to overwinter. During the summer months, the cows were kept behind the head dyke, whilst the many sheep were grazed on the pastures of Glen Bay, on the other side of the island. Separated from Village Bay by a high ridge, Am Blaid, Glen Bay spiralled down to a sharply shelved cove. There was no beach to speak of over there, for the northerly waves were relentless and though the villagers kept a skiff there for emergencies, heading out and coming ashore were only possible on the rare occasions when the prevailing wind switched and the sea lay fully at rest.

Iona stopped munching and moved with a twitch of irritation. Unperturbed, Effie reached down for the pile of dock leaves she had picked on her way up and wordlessly passed her another few. The cow gave a sigh of contentment and

Effie resumed milking. This was their usual morning routine and both were accustomed to its gentle rhythms.

A few minutes later, the pail was almost full and Effie sat up, patting Iona on the flank. 'Good girl,' she murmured, standing up off the milking stone and looking down the slope. As predicted, the prow of a sloop was just nosing round the headland of Dun.

She watched keenly as the ship slipped silently into the embrace of the bay and threw out an anchor, sails drawing down. Not a trawler, then. The women would be displeased. This vessel with its slim-fingered triple masts and low curved hull was a finessed creature, more likely found in the azure waters off France than the outermost Hebrides.

'Friend or foe?!'

The question echoed around the caldera.

The crew were just black dots from here but she could see the locals already readying the dinghy; the men would need to row powerfully against waves that were pounding the shore. The passengers aboard the sloop had chosen a bad day to sail. The open water would have tossed them like a cork and although Dun's presence granted mercy, it was no free pass; a south-easterly made the bay's usually sheltered water froth and roil like a witch's cauldron and there was no guarantee they would be able to disembark.

Only one thing was certain: if the men were able to land them, no one would be coming back dry, and the villagers knew it. Already faint twists of grey smoke were beginning to twirl from the chimneys, people rushing in and out of the arc of low cottages that smiled around the bay and taking in their washing, sweeping floors, putting on shoes, moving the spinning wheels to their prominent positions so that their visitors might watch.

They all knew the drill. Catering to the tourists had become a quietly profitable sideline. It couldn't help feed them – with not a single shop on the isle, they had little use for money on Hirta itself – but it was useful for asking the more familiar captains to bring back treats when they were next passing, or to give as extra credit to the factor when he came wanting the rents. Or in Flora's case, to purchase a brightly coloured lipstick she'd once seen on one of the well-heeled lady visitors – even though it would be wasted on the three hundred sheep she was currently herding in Glen Bay for the summer.

None of the villagers understood quite why the world at large took an interest in them, but the postmaster, Mhairi's father, Ian McKinnon, had been told by colleagues on the mainland that a St Kilda-stamped postcard was now considered desirable, if not valuable. Their way of life, they were told, was being rapidly left behind by the rest of the world. Industrialization meant society was changing at a more rapid pace than any other time in centuries and they were becoming living relics, curiosities from a bygone age. Some people pitied them, perhaps, but the St Kildans cared naught for sympathy. They had learnt to play the game to their advantage – Effie chief among them.

She lifted the pail and began to walk down the slope, her eyes never fixing off the black dots as they transferred from one heaving vessel to the other. Once they'd dried off and recovered from the swell, she knew they were going to want a show. And she was going to give it to them.

'Where'll they do it?' her father asked gruffly as she finished with churning the butter. He was standing by the window, looking out, his pipe dangling from his bottom lip.

'Sgeir nan Sgarbh, I should say,' she replied, closing the lid of the churn and going to stand beside him. 'It'll be more protected from the wind round there.'

'Over the top, aye, but will they get the dinghies round on the water?'

'Archie MacQueen's got the arms on him,' she murmured. 'Just not the legs.'

'No, not the legs.' She watched a trio of men walking down the Street. One she recognized by his distinctive gait – Frank Mathieson, the factor, their landlord's representative and the islanders' de facto ruler – but the other men were strangers. They were wearing well-cut dark brown suits and wool hats, but from beneath one of them she caught the gleam of golden blonde hair and a tanned neck. She willed him to turn around, wanting just to glimpse the face that went with that hair and elegant physique; but the path curved, taking them out of sight.

The group that had come ashore had been disappointingly small – a private contingent, Ian McKinnon had said with his usual authority. It meant the tips would be meagre. If the women were to take their sheets in, there had to be good reason for it and two men alone could hardly reward everyone. The captain had been put up in her Uncle Hamish's cottage and the other two men would stay at the factor's house, for it was the largest on the isle. She didn't envy them having to endure Mathieson's hospitality.

'I'm just going to put this in the cool,' she said, lifting the churn onto her shoulder and walking out, Poppit trotting at her heels. She could see the visitors further down placing pennies into the palm of Mad Annie as she sat carding the wool and telling stories about broomstick marriages and snaring puffins. Unlike most of the village elders her English was good, but that didn't mean the others couldn't communicate, and Effie gave a small grin as she saw Ma Peg make a play of bustling and hiding from their camera, even though those days of shock at the new technologies were long past. More coins crossed palms.

She went round the back of the cottage and a short way up the slope that led to the plateau of An Lag, where they herded the sheep into stone fanks in bad weather. Beyond it, Connachair – the island's tallest mountain – rose majestically like a stepping stone to heaven. For some it was. Many had met their fate over the precipice, tricked into distraction by the summit's rounded hummock on the village side and caught unaware by the sheer cliffs – 1,400 feet high – that dropped suddenly and vertically to the sea, as if cleaved.

The lush grass was speckled with buttercups and thrift and felt springy underfoot as she moved past the countless identical stone cleits to the one where she and her father stored their butter and cream. She ducked down as she stepped inside and set down the churn. It was the very store her family had been using for this purpose for over three hundred years. There may have been over 1,400 of the hump-topped, stacked-stone huts on the island, but she could identify every single one that belonged to her family – this one below An Lag for the dairy; that one on Ruival for the bird feathers; that on Oiseval for the fulmar oil; that on Connachair for the salted carcasses, that for the peats . . . There were plenty that lay empty, too, but they also had their uses as emergency larders, rain and wind shelters, hiding places for courting lovers . . .

She came back down the slope again, jumping nimbly over the rocks nestled in the grass and seeing over the rooftops that everyone was beginning to gather on the beach, preparing for the visitors' exhibition.

'Are you joining them, Effie?' a voice called.

She looked over to find Lorna MacDonald coming out of the postmaster's hut, fixing her auburn hair. She worked there sometimes with the postmaster.

Effie skipped over, Poppit beating her by two lengths. 'Aye,' she grinned. 'You never know, there might be some pennies in it for me.'

'And more besides,' Lorna said with a wink.

'What do you mean?'

'He's a fine-looking fellow, the young one. A smile from him would be payment in itself,' Lorna laughed, her brown eyes twinkling with merriment.

Effie gave a bemused shrug. 'I only caught the back of him.'

'That's pretty enough too, I should guess.'

Effie chuckled. It was a wonder to her that Lorna was their resident old maid – all of thirty-three years old and still unmarried – for she was a terrible flirt. Alas, the visiting men never stayed for long and the St Kildan bachelor nearest in age to her was Donnie Ferguson, who had no interest in a wife seven years older than him, cleverer than him and almost through her child-bearing years.

'Who are they, anyway?'

'Rich,' Lorna shrugged. 'If that ship's anything to go by.'

Lorna knew about such things. She wasn't a St Kildan by birth but a registered nurse from Stornoway who had chosen to make her life here; she had seen another world to this one and what money bought.

'Good,' Effie sighed, catching sight of the men beginning to head up the hill with their ropes, the dogs running ahead in a pack. 'Well, then I'll still aim for some pennies from them and you can have the young gentleman's smile. What do you say?'

'Deal,' Lorna winked as Effie took off again and darted back into the cottage to grab their rope. It was thickly plaited from horsehair, supple and rough in her hand. Her father was sitting in his chair by the hearth now – he could never stand for long – tamping his black twist tobacco.

'Well, I'll be off then.'

He looked back at her. His eyes had a rheumy look, the whites yellowing with age, but they still revealed a strong man within an infirm body. He gave a nod. He wasn't one for sentimental farewells. 'Hold fast, lass.'

'Aye.' She nodded back, knowing those had been his last words to her brother too.

For a moment she thought he might say something else; the way he held himself, it was as if an energy for more words lay coiled within him. But the moment passed and she left again with just a nod.

Some of the men were already walking the slopes, ropes slung over their shoulders too. As she'd predicted, they were heading for the easterly cliffs. A small rock stack just out in the water provided enough of a break from the broadside waves for the dinghy to rope up in relative comfort whilst the show was put on.

She ran and caught them up, listening in as they chatted about the visitors and the news from 'abroad', meaning Skye.

'. . . friends of the landlord,' David MacQueen, Flora's eldest brother, was saying. 'So we're to make it good.'

'Shame the wind's up or we could have gone further round,' her cousin Euan said.

'There'll be no tips if they're sick as dogs,' Ian McKinnon replied.

'But the cliffs are lower here.'

'This will do them fine. It will all be high to the likes of them.'

She fell into step with Mhairi's older brothers, Angus and Finlay.

'What are *you* doing here?' Angus asked with his usual sneer.

'Same as you,' she shrugged, slightly breathless as their longer legs covered more ground than hers.

'We're not fowling. This is just for display.'

'Aye, so there'll be tips.'

'Then knit them some socks!'

'You know I'd get a fraction of what I can get up here and the agreement is whenever you're all on the rocks, I'm allowed to be too.'

'You're a pain in my side, Effie Gillies,' Finlay groaned.

'And you're a pain in mine,' she shot back.

They rolled their eyes but she didn't care. Her brother's friends, her friend's brothers, they had been teasing her all her life and she knew to give as good as she got. They had all grown up playing hide and seek in the cleits as children, learnt to read together in the schoolroom beside the kirk, and kicked each other during the minister's sermons.

But she couldn't ignore that things were changing. Or had already changed. A tension existed now, a low-level hum, that hadn't been there before. Her brother's death had profoundly affected them all and she was no longer John's little sister to them – or anyone but herself; sometimes she caught them looking at her in a new way that made her nervous. Finlay's eyes seemed to follow her wherever she went and Angus had tried to kiss her as she cut the peats one evening; he hadn't yet forgiven her for laughing.

For visitors wanting to take in the view – and they always did – this would be a forty-minute to hour-long walk, but she and the men did it in under thirty and were already spread across the top and looping out the coils of rope by the time the dinghy appeared around the cliffs. Birds whirled and screeched around them, feathers lilting on the updrafts. From this height, the boat looked no bigger than a bird either. Effie glanced down a few times, scanning the rock face for the line she wanted to take, then casting about for a rock with which to drive in her peg.

Looping the rope around the peg, she leant back, checking its firmness and tension. It vibrated with pleasing freshness and she wrapped it around her waist in the St Kildan style.

She looked down the drop once more. Cousin Euan had been right; it really wasn't so high here. Seven hundred feet? Half the height of Connachair. A single drop of the ropes would take them maybe a third of the way down. Still, they were merely going to be playing up here today. No bird hunting, no egg collecting, no saving stranded sheep. Just playing.

'You're looking peely-wally there, Eff,' Angus drawled. 'Sure you're up to it?'

She looked back at him with scorn. Angus prided himself on being the fastest climber on the island. He had won last year's Old Trial, a climbing race among the young men to prove they were worthy of providing for their families – and future wives. If he had wanted to prove anything to her, the point had been well and truly lost. Effie was certain she could have beaten him (and the rest) had she only been allowed to enter too. But as a girl . . . 'Actually, I was just wondering how quickly I could get down there.'

A smirk grew. 'You think you can do it *fast*?'

'Faster than you.' She pulled her fair hair back, tying it away from her face in a balled knot. The last thing she needed was a gust of wind blowing it about and blinding her on the route.

'Ha! You're all talk and no trousers, Effie Gillies.'

It was her turn to smirk. 'Well, yes, even I won't deny

there's not much in *my* trews.' Angus McKinnon might be the fastest man on the isle, but he wasn't the brightest. As if to make the point, she hitched up her breeches at the waist; they had been John's and were the only suitable attire for climbing, but she didn't wear them purely for reasons of practicality.

Finlay blushed furiously. 'Ignore her,' he said. 'You know she's only trying to rile you. Everyone knows you're the fastest, brother. Just give the rich people a show. This is an exhibition, not a race.'

Effie shrugged as if she couldn't care less either way, but they all knew the gauntlet had been thrown down. She – a girl! – was challenging Angus for his crown; the competition could happen here between the two of them. Why not? It was as good a chance as any. She watched him looking down the cliff as the islanders did final checks on their ropes and took their positions on the cliff edge.

Effie kept her eyes ahead, her hands already around the rope. Waiting. Hoping—

'H'away then!' Archie MacQueen cried. Flora's father, he had been an experienced cragger himself, but he left these shows to the younger ones these days; already lame in one leg, his grip wasn't what it used to be either. Besides, someone had to stay up top in case anyone needed hauling up.

It was the cue to go, to perform, to show off their derring-do and the skills that made the St Kildans famous around the world as they all but skipped and danced over the cliffs. Without hesitation, Effie leant back and stepped over. She felt the swoop of her stomach as her body angled into open space and the rope tightened. She pushed off, allowing the rope to swing on a pendulum, her bare feet already braced for contact with the rock face, ready to caper across it in a bold defiance of gravity. A visitor had once told them it was like watching spiders drop from the top of a wall. She herself loved the sound of the ropes under tension – a *huzzahing* – as she and the men scampered and sprang from side to side.

'First to the boat then?'

She looked across to find Angus on his rope, staring straight at her. She smiled at his tactic – finishing the race at the boat, not the bottom, when neither one of them could swim . . . 'Aye. But I'll wait for you, don't worry.'

Angus's eyes narrowed at her insult, but she was already off. Abandoning the acrobatics, her foot found a toehold and she brought her weight to bear on it as the other foot searched. The St Kildans never climbed in boots, always bare feet. The cliffs were too unyielding to give any more than a half inch to grab and there was nothing that compared to skin on rock. Shoes and boots – the hallmarks of civilization – had no place on a granite cliff.

She left the older men to the games, their powerful arms and legs flexed as they made a point of playing on the rock faces, bouncing off with their feet, reaching up for a fingerhold and pulling themselves up like lizards, before repeating again. Others scrambled sideways, scuttling like crabs over the rocks.

Effie just focused on going down. She could see the boat between her legs, far below her, as she descended on the rope, her arms braced as she lowered herself, hand over hand. She didn't have biceps the size of boulders to help her, but as she always said to her father, she didn't need them. She was wiry and light, skinny even, but that didn't mean she was weak. The less there was of her, the less she had to support. She wouldn't tire so quickly. She was more nimble, more flexible . . .

From her peripheral vision, she sensed she was already ahead of Angus, but only just. He had power, height and gravity on his side.

Soon enough she was out of rope. Balancing on a narrow ledge, she unwound the rope's end from her torso.

'What are you doing?' Ian McKinnon called sharply down to her as she began to free climb.

'Winning! Don't worry. It was Angus's idea.'

It always felt different scaling without the rope and she knew it was reckless, but there was something about the intensity it brought – her brain and eyes seemed to tune into hyper-focus, the adrenaline refreshed her muscles – that meant she could remember her mother's eyes and smile, hear again her brother's ready laugh. Somehow, by thinning the skein of life, it seemed she could almost reach the dead.

Down she went, agile and sharp until the horizon drew level, then hovered above her, and the crash of the waves began to intrude on her concentration. White splashes of cold sea were beginning to reach towards her, spraying her bare brown calves, but she didn't care about getting wet or cold. She just had to win. She had to know – and crucially, Angus had to know – that she was the fastest and the best.

She saw the dark sea, ominously close. She was less than thirty feet above the waves now, but the cliffs just sliced into the ocean depths, and as she scaled ever downwards, she realized that the only place where she could stand and pivot was a narrow ledge perhaps six feet above the surface, no wider than her hand's span.

For a moment, she felt a visceral spasm of fear. This was madness! If her father was to hear of the carelessness with which she was treating her life . . . Or maybe that was the point of it. Maybe she wanted him to hear of it. His heart had been broken by death too many times, and she was the only one left. He couldn't – or wouldn't – love her in case he lost her too. Was that it? If she was to slip, to go straight down, under the waves . . . would he weep? Would she be mourned like the others? On the other hand, if she won, would he be proud? Would he see that she could be enough?

There was no time to think. Everything was instinct. Her feet touched down and her arms splayed wide as she hugged the wall, gripping its surface with her fingertips, her cheek pressed to the cold, wet granite. Breath coming fast, she gave her muscles a moment to rest. They were burning, but she knew she wasn't there yet.

She glanced up. Angus was only a few feet above her. What he lacked in nimbleness, he made up for in power. In a few more seconds . . . She looked carefully back over her shoulder and saw the dinghy tied to a rock just a short distance away. Her Uncle Hamish, skippering, was frowning and watching her intently, the way Poppit had watched for the boat earlier. He saw her movement and seemed to understand she wanted in; that she was going to launch herself towards it, one way or another. If he was alarmed, he didn't hesitate nonetheless. Not in front of the guests. Quickly he pulled in on the rope, hauling the small dinghy as close as he dared to the cliff wall, knowing that if he went too far, the swell risked tossing them against the rocks.

A nervous flinch inside the boat betrayed someone's nerves as her intentions became commonly understood. Effie knew she would have to time the next wave and then leap. She hugged the wall as she watched and braced for the next break – just as Angus landed beside her.

A blast of white water broke upon them both, making them gasp with the shocking cold as they were soaked. She didn't care. As she felt the draft pull back, she twisted and leapt blind. Death or glory then!

For one stunning, protracted moment, she felt almost as if she could fly, like the very birds that soared and wheeled and sliced around her in this island sky. Then gravity took hold, and she landed – half in the dinghy, half in the water. She took a hard knock to her chest but her arms gripped the prow as the boat rocked wildly, water slopping over the sides. But it was flat-bottomed and made for heavy weather; it righted itself almost immediately, and she laughed victoriously as her uncle Hamish hastily got a hand to her waistband and dragged her aboard in one swift movement like a landed salmon.

'I didna' know you had decided to make it a race to the bottom,' Uncle Hamish said to her with a stern, disapproving look. It was the most he would reveal in front of the tourists, but she already knew he'd be telling her father about this. There would be trouble to come, most likely a hiding; but it was worth it. Effie's eyes were bright. She'd beaten Angus McKinnon! The fastest cragger on the isle. Not just that – he could make no further claims now of providing for her when she herself had beaten him.

'It was Angus's idea,' she panted, scrambling to her knees and looking back to find him still clinging to the ledge. With her leap to victory, he now stood frozen in place and was becoming more soaked with every breaking wave. He either had to jump too or climb back up, but he couldn't stay there.

With an angry sigh, he jerked his thumb upwards, indicating the latter. He had lost. What good was there in riding back with them now? She would only crow her victory at him.

Uncle Hamish nodded, understanding perfectly what had just happened between them. It was a man's look, the kind that cut her out, but what did she care? With a satisfied smile, Effie sat on the bench, pulling out her hair tie and wringing her long hair. Seawater puddled in the dinghy floor.

'Heavens above!' a voice said. 'It's a *girl*?'

She twisted back to face the visitors properly at last. In all her ambition to beat Angus, she'd forgotten who they were trying to impress in the first place. The three men seated towards the back were staring at her in wide-eyed amazement: Frank Mathieson, the factor, and the two men she'd glimpsed from behind earlier.

'Well, I can't climb in a skirt, sir,' she grinned, wringing out her tweed breeches as best she could.

'It wasn't just your clothes that fooled me. The speed! I've never seen a spectacle like it. You scaled that cliff like a squirrel down a tree!' It was the older man speaking. He was portly, with a dark moustache, lightly salted. Spectacles made it difficult to see his eyes past the reflection, but he appeared friendly as well as impressed. 'Do you mean to say females climb here, too?' he asked their skipper.

'Only this one,' Uncle Hamish said with a resigned tone, untying the rope from the mooring rock and beginning to row. 'This is my niece, Euphemia Gillies.'

'Effie is Robert Gillies's daughter. They live at number nine,' the factor added, as if that information was somehow enlightening. 'How are you, Effie?'

'Aye, well, sir, thank you for asking.'

'Becoming bolder, I see.'

'If by bolder you mean faster.'

He laughed. 'Allow me to present the Earl of Dumfries and his son, Lord Sholto,' he said. 'I'm sure you will be aware that they are great friends of Lord MacLeod.'

'Ah,' she said blandly, although she was aware of nothing of the sort. Who their landlord kept as friends was no business of hers, though it confirmed Lorna's observation that the visitors were rich.

'They were visiting his lordship at Dunvegan when they heard I was planning on making the voyage here—'

'It's been something of an ambition of mine to get over here,' the earl said brightly, interrupting. 'I'm a keen birder, you see, and Sir John very kindly agreed to my proposal that we might sail Mr Mathieson here ourselves. Two birds, one stone and all that.'

'Aye.' She could feel the younger man watching her keenly as she talked, but for as long as the others spoke, she had no such opportunity to cast her gaze openly over him. 'So will you be staying for long, then?'

The factor inhaled. 'Well, a lot will depend upon the wea—'

'Certainly a week,' Lord Sholto said suddenly, allowing a dazzling smile to enliven his features as she finally met his eyes.

'A week?' Effie smiled back at the blue-eyed, golden-haired man. Finally she could see his face at last. And she liked it.

'Miss Gillies.'

She turned to find the factor hurrying up the beach after her. Uncle Hamish was tying up the boat, the distinguished guests having been appropriated by the minister again the moment they'd set foot on shore.

'Mr Mathieson.' She tried not to show her impatience, but her tweed breeches were soaked from her half-swim and she wanted to get back and change. Their progress round the headland had been slow as they'd met the headwinds and she was shivering now.

He stopped in front of her, slightly downhill from where

she stood, so that she was aware of standing taller than him. He wasn't a tall man, stocky but not conspicuously short either, and the consequence of not standing out in any way seemed to work to his advantage; many times an islander had been caught saying things they shouldn't, not realizing he was within earshot. His relationship with the St Kildans was highly taut, for as the bringer of supplies every spring, and the collector of rents every autumn, he was both carrot and stick to the island community. He could smile and be charming when it suited him, but no one could ever quite forget that the power he wielded over them was almost absolute, and few – apart from Mad Annie – would clash with him. He wore finer suits than the village men and affected the manners of his employer, but reddened, pitted cheeks and the forearms of a wrestler betrayed him as a fighter first.

'Well, that was quite a display,' he said.

Effie wasn't sure this was intended as a compliment. 'That's the idea,' she replied vaguely. 'They always like it.' A sudden gust blew her long, wet hair forward and she had to use both hands to pin it back. The sky was growing ominously dark.

'Indeed.' He gave what she had come to learn over the years was his customary pause. It preceded a direct contradiction of what came after it. 'Although I'm not sure such daredevil antics require the added *novelty* factor.'

It took a moment to understand his meaning. 'Of a girl climbing, you mean?'

He shrugged. 'I understand your obligations to your father impel you to undertake men's work in a regular capacity, but when it comes to making a good impression on visitors . . . '

'But they seemed to like it.'

'Well, they're polite, of course, but things are quite different in the wider world. I know it's not your fault that you don't know any differently – why should you? – but decorum and good taste are held in high regard. Women scrambling over cliffs like monkeys . . . ' He pulled a face. 'No. It's important to think about the impression you make on these visitors and how you and your neighbours will be conveyed in their onward conversations. I'm sure you wouldn't want to embarrass Sir John, would you?'

She had never met Sir John. '. . . Of course not.'

'Very well, then. So we're agreed there'll be no more fits of vanity on the ropes. We must strive to make sure the guests are not made to feel uncomfortable by what they witness here. Best foot forward, yes?'

She stared back at him, shivering with cold and anger. '. . . Aye, sir.'

He looked over her shoulder, along the Street. 'How is your father, anyway? Still lame?'

Her eyes narrowed. 'And always will be.'

'Which only makes him all the luckier to have you,' he nodded, oblivious to her terse tone. 'But please tell him I shall need to find him later and discuss the rent arrears.'

'Arrears?' Alarm shot through the word.

'As I recall, you were short thirteen Scotch ells of tweed last year. Your uncle picked up some of the slack, but you were also down nine gallons of oil and seven sacks of black feathers.'

'It'll be fine this year,' she said quickly. 'We were only short because I twisted my ankle and couldn't walk for ten days. It was just bad luck that it happened when we were fowling.'

The factor looked unconvinced. 'I'll need to reappraise the quota with him. You will remember I extended a great kindness in not reducing the oatmeal bolls after your brother's accident and as a result you have enjoyed more than your share for nigh-on four years now—'

Effie looked at him with wild panic. What he said was true, but it still wasn't enough. The past few winters had been hard ones and their harvests had all but failed, save for a half-dozen potatoes and those oats that were only half blackened by frost.

'—I have been both generous and patient, but it's not fair to expect others to compensate for your shortfalls. Accidents will always happen, Miss Gillies. You cannot expect to be fit and well every day of the year.'

'But I do. And I will,' she said urgently. The factor didn't know it yet, but she and her father had lost four of their sheep over the top this year already, so they were already down on their wool yield. Her father had bartered 100 extra fulmars instead with Donald McKinnon and it had been a rare endorsement of Effie's climbing skills that both men believed she was capable of bagging the extra haul, on top of the usual harvest.

'Miss Gillies, you don't need me to remind you that you are a girl doing a man's job. The odds are already grossly stacked against you.'

'But I'm eighteen now, and I've grown this last year. I can do anything they can and I'll prove it to you. I'll show you, sir.'

The factor looked at her keenly. 'You receive more than you are due and you deliver less than you owe. You see my predicament? I must be fair, Miss Gillies. Why should I make – and keep making – exceptions for you? If the others were to know—'

'But they won't. I'll make sure we're square and level come this September.'

'So you're saying you want me to keep this a secret?'

'Secret . . . ?' Behind him, the reverend and the two gentlemen guests walked past on the path back to the village, the minister holding forth on the repairs made to the manse. Lord Sholto glanced across at them talking as he passed by and she found herself smiling back at him, as though he'd pulled it from her on a string.

'From your neighbours? And your father too?'

She looked back at the factor in confusion. He was watching her intently. '. . . No, please don't tell him. I don't want him to worry. I can make the quota this year, I know I can.'

He tutted. 'I don't know why I allow you to manipulate me, Miss Gillies—'

She frowned. *Did* she manipulate him?

'A "thank you" doesn't pay the fiddler, now, does it?' he sighed. 'Still, I have sympathy for your predicament and although I have a job to do, I believe in being a friend in the hour of need.'

Effie bit her lip – she had to – to keep from laughing out loud. What? There wasn't a person on the isle who would have considered the factor a friend. He bought their feathers at five shillings a stone and sold them at fifteen, and the supplies he brought over – oatmeal, flour, sugar, tea and tobacco – cost them three times what he paid. Was it any wonder the villagers tried to bypass him with money they earnt from the tourists and could spend directly themselves?

'Talking of which, I have brought you something, again.'

'For our studies?' She had finished her schooling four years ago, but he never seemed to remember this.

'I've left it in the usual spot. Just . . . be discreet, please. I can't oblige these sorts of favours for everyone.'

Favours? Secrets? 'But—'

'Good day, Miss Gillies,' he said briskly, assuming his usual manner as he noticed the three men now ahead of him on the path. 'I must get on. Our visitors will be requiring some refreshments after the afternoon's . . . excitement. Just remember what we discussed. We shall have to hope first impressions don't stick.'